SERIES COLLIDE

SERIES COLLIDE
VOLUME 2: DARK

KRISTINE KATHRYN RUSCH
AND DEAN WESLEY SMITH

Series Collide: Volume 2

Copyright © 2025 by Kristine Kathryn Rusch and Dean Wesley Smith

Published by WMG Publishing

Cover and layout copyright © 2025 by WMG Publishing

Cover design by WMG Publishing

Cover art copyright © grandfailure/Depositphotos

ISBN-13 (ebook): 978-1-56146-561-3

ISBN-13 (trade paperback): 978-1-56146-402-9

ISBN-13 (hardcover): 978-1-56146-434-0

Contents

INTRODUCTION: DARK
KRISTINE KATHRYN RUSCH

The second volume in our five-volume collection of stories, *Series Collide*, features stories we consider to be dark. They might have a happy ending, or they might not. But in most cases, the stories will take the reader from darkness into light.

Series Collide is part of a series itself—a group of short fiction collections that Dean Wesley Smith and I have compiled for the past five years. We were inspired to do this by Kickstarter, which includes a Make 100 promotion to boost January.

We have taken part for a while now, and initially, we did genres and subgenres. This year, Dean suggested collecting stories in our various series.

Turns out a lot of our series are, well, quite serious.

So in this volume, you will find a lot of murder and at least one kidnapped dog. There's magic of the good kind and of the scarier kind. Lawyers fill these pages, and for some reason, there's also a lot of rain.

But the stories are all powerful, and they are all worth reading. Or, at least, we think so.

We hope you agree.

—Kristine Kathryn Rusch

KRISTINE KATHRYN RUSCH SECTION

BLAMING THE ARSONIST
A PROTECTORS STORY

KRIS NELSCOTT

T
he first hint that an arsonist had infiltrated the tight community around Telegraph happened on the night of January 23, 1969, in the middle of the Third World Liberation protests.

Pammy had nothing to do with the protests. She had attended UC Berkeley ten years before and, like so many others, stayed in the city, working odd jobs and finally, used her business and physical education double majors to open her own gym.

At least, that was what she told anyone who asked. She never mentioned all the real reasons why she opened the gym. Like the night her friend Doris had died during a beating from her boyfriend. Or the afternoon some thug had attacked Pammy's friend Carol as he tried to steal her purse, slamming her head against a brick wall, rendering her speechless for months.

Even with Pammy's training help, neither woman would

probably have overpowered her attacker. But Pammy didn't just train women to fight back; she also trained them how to avoid a violent situation in the first place, using the skills her police officer father had taught her back in Philadelphia when he'd seen too many women hurt because they had no idea how to protect themselves.

The night of the fire she had closed up late. She'd been running a self-defense class that most of the attendees hadn't paid for. They were street people—hippies, flower children, little lost souls she'd been collecting since the doors to A Gym of Her Own had opened the summer before.

By the time she stepped outside the gym's front door, the night sky was strangely orange, and ash floated around her.

She looked up and down the street to make sure nothing was burning immediately next to her. Then she made herself lock the gym door, check the deadbolt, and pocket her keys. Calm, her father had told her all those years ago, solved more problems than panic ever would.

She slung her purse over one shoulder, the purse itself against her torso, and headed into the street. That was when she looked up. A fire towered over the neighborhood, a bright orange wall reaching toward the clear night sky.

Her breath caught.

The fire was *huge*, and farther away than she thought. It was north of her, but it couldn't have been north by much.

She ran to Telegraph Avenue, only to find everyone outside of their apartments. They were all looking toward campus.

The smoke was thicker here, the flames visible to her

right. She hurried toward Bancroft and the edge of UC Berkeley.

The campus was bathed in that weird orange glow. She couldn't hear sirens—not yet—and she thought that odd too. But she also didn't hear voices raised in a protest chant or bullhorns exhorting people to march forward—and she'd half expected it.

All month, the Third World Liberation Front, a coalition of minority student groups, had been agitating for an ethnic studies college as part of the university. The students weren't like the students in the Free Speech Movement four and a half years before; these students were militant, often wearing military gear, and provoking the campus police with small acts of violence.

As she walked up to Sather Gate, she expected to see a clash between protestors and police. But the students she saw on Sproul Plaza looked as confused as she felt. More poured into the area as each moment passed, and she finally heard sirens, getting closer and closer.

The fire was coming from her right—one of the buildings on South Drive. That thought galvanized her and she pushed her way through the growing crowd.

She ran uphill toward the Central Campus. The air was filled with smoke. Her eyes stung, and she had to blink hard to see through the haze.

Flames poured out of the roof on Wheeler Hall, one of the older buildings on campus. University security officers were dragging garden hoses up the flat white stairs into the open doors under the arches.

She needed to talk to security: there were hoses inside—

fire hoses along with fire axes, near the fire alarm. Didn't those security officers know that?

As she got close, though, someone grabbed her arm.

Professor Dwight Jones pulled her back. "You don't belong in there, Pammy."

He was right. She could feel the heat on her face. She knew about the hoses, but she didn't know how to fight a fire, especially one like this.

The blaze was big and bold, eating the top of the building. She wondered what it was using as fuel. Wheeler Hall was made of granite.

One of the city's fire trucks pulled in behind her.

She whirled, saw firefighters pouring out of the truck, giving instructions, surveying, already working the scene. One of them grabbed a bullhorn and yelled at the crowd to get back.

She backed off, moving to the edge of the crowd. Professor Jones still stood in front, clutching his old-fashioned book bag, the one he had used when she had taken his European Literature class almost a decade before.

"What were they thinking, Pammy?" he asked her.

It took her a moment to realize that Professor Jones believed this was arson.

"You think someone set this," she said.

"No one was using the auditorium," Professor Jones said. "And the flames just whooshed into life. We all heard it. Not quite an explosion, but something—like all the air got sucked out of the building. Yeah, I think someone set it. And not just anyone. Those damn protestors . . ."

"Did you see them?" she asked, ever her father's daughter.

"I was teaching a class, Pammy," Professor Jones said, as if she was being thick. Maybe she was. "Besides, how do I know who 'they' are? Half the campus is involved in this garbage, trying to tear down everything just because they didn't get all the toys as children. Selfish little bastards. Look what they've done."

His voice was thick, and she realized with surprise that he was close to tears. She looked at him—really looked at him—for the first time in a long time. He had spent his entire career here, and he had seemed old to her ten years ago. He was nearing retirement. The peaceful academic world he'd known had disappeared five years before, and he was clearly still baffled by the changes.

Another fire truck showed up, and then another. Campus security left the building, some still holding garden hoses. Several students gathered around, hands to their mouths.

Firefighters ran past Pammy, up the stone steps, and into the archway. Another truck—a ladder truck—parked on the grass between Wheeler and South Hall. A ladder rose, and with it, curtains of water began spraying the rising flames.

Ash fell thicker now, big globs of black, wet and thick, like ash-rain. Two security guards backed the crowd up, and a few firefighters threatened to set up some kind of rope. Another firefighter was in earnest discussion with one of the campus security officers.

Pammy put her hand against her mouth, her eyes stinging from the smoke, feeling helpless. The campus looked unbelievably bright from the fire and the lights of the fire trucks.

More students and faculty members had arrived, faces yellow and orange in the flames. Young faces, furrowed with concern. Older faces—professors, graduate students—stoic. One young woman was sobbing uncontrollably as she stood near the trees at the edge of the South Drive.

Sparks danced in the air. Smoke was thicker now. It seemed like the firefighters had started to get the flames under control.

Pammy whirled and walked back toward Sather Road. As she moved, she bumped into a group of students who didn't even seem to notice her. She tensed like she always did, hand securely on her purse. The students hurried toward the fire, and she looked up to see a man leaning against a tree.

He wore camouflage. She probably wouldn't have seen him at all if she hadn't been staring straight at him. His face was dirty, his hair long. He wasn't holding books, but that meant nothing. From the snippets of conversation she had heard, a lot of students and professors had left their belongings inside Wheeler as they escaped the flames.

She nodded at him. He half-smiled, as if he couldn't believe someone was greeting him. And then he slipped away in the direction of Strawberry Creek.

If he hadn't gone down the hillside, she wouldn't have thought the moment odd. But she did.

She crossed to the other side of Sather Road—always be practical, always err on the side of precaution—and then kept one eye out, glancing both ways to make sure she wasn't followed as she headed back to Telegraph. She needed to pick up her car.

She wanted to go home.

Pammy didn't learn anything about the fire until Friday.

She came in early that morning, and made some coffee in her private kitchen.

Once upon a time, the back of the gym had been two studio apartments. She had opened them up, using most of the space as the locker room. The two bathrooms came in particularly handy.

But she had separated off one of the kitchens as part of her office, so that she could make her own coffee and keep her own food in a refrigerator. The other small kitchen belonged to the locker room, and made it easier for the women who occasionally slept here to feed themselves and their children.

Pammy tried not to think about how many building codes she was violating. But she always felt like if the City of Berkeley cared about building code violations in this neighborhood, they would have gone door to door. Everyone down here was doing something wrong—and most of them were doing a lot more wrong than she ever could.

She reserved the main part of the building for the gym proper. She had one fighting space, two large mats, and four heavy bags hanging from the low ceiling. She had six smaller bags hanging off poles. Those bags were set about a foot lower than bags in any other gym she'd ever gone to, one of the many things she had changed for the women who came here.

On one wall, she had two racks of clothing—one a rack of T-shirts with the words "A Gym of Her Own" emblazoned across the front, and a matching rack filled with sweatshirts. On the other wall, she had arranged boxing gloves by size, the smaller the better. She also had a lot of tape and extra pairs of women's sneakers, since so many of the women who came here didn't even have the right shoes.

She loved the smells of chalk and sweat that permeated the space. Those smells signified home for her.

She needed that comfort on Fridays.

Her morning class was two hours long. It had no college students at all. The women who came to Friday's class didn't live in the neighborhood. Pammy had no idea how they found her, but they had. The group were housewives from the same part of town who got tired of having coffee together at each other's houses every morning, and decided to "have an adventure."

Initially, six women had come to the class. By Christmas, three remained.

Pammy hadn't really expected any of them to show up after the Wheeler Hall fire, but they did.

They slid in the front door as if they were doing something wrong. Stella D'Arbus was the only one who usually walked tall, but even on this day, she hurried through the door like someone who didn't want to be seen.

Marie Seabolt followed, clutching a bag that Pammy knew from experience contained all of their gym clothes.

They stored the clothing with Marie so that the other husbands didn't ask why their wives kept such horrid outfits anywhere near the house. Apparently, Marie's husband didn't care or didn't look in her bags.

LuAnn Amberson was the last person inside. She was so good at slinking that some Fridays Pammy never saw LuAnn enter at all. She had achieved a kind of ghostly invisibility that disturbed Pammy almost as much as the skeletal faces of some of the hippie women.

"I didn't think I'd see you today," Pammy said to them as the door closed behind them.

Stella waved her bejeweled right hand dismissively.

"We're not really here," she said as she stalked to the reception desk that Pammy had set up a few months ago because, she learned, women expected some place to check in.

"We're safe down here, aren't we?" Marie asked with a little too much concern in her voice.

"The protestors haven't left campus so far." Pammy realized she wasn't guaranteeing safety with that statement, but it was the best she could do.

She stepped behind the desk. She had a small cast iron safe on the floor. Stella had been the one who bought it.

I need some place to put my jewelry, she had said as she gave it to Pammy. *If I leave my regular jewelry at home, Roy is going to think that we're headed for divorce court.*

Pammy could never quite follow that logic, even though Marie had tried to explain it to her once. Stella's husband Roy liked seeing his wife sparkling with more jewels than the Queen of England.

It makes him feel important, Marie had said.

The thing was, in this state, Roy *was* important. He was one of the Board of Regents who ran the University of California system.

"But that fire was scary," Marie was saying now. "If those protestors can burn Wheeler Hall, they're going to burn the whole city."

"That fire was a one-time thing," Stella said, pulling off her rings. "Besides, Roy said it's got nothing to do with the protests."

Then her cheeks reddened. She had clearly spoken out of turn.

LuAnn spoke for all of them, albeit in a whisper. "But the chancellor spoke to the papers. He said it was the protestors."

"Papers schmapers." Stella took off her earrings, then reached behind her neck to unclasp a strand of pearls. "Roy says that they're pretty sure that the protestors didn't set the fire. The university thinks it's better though if everyone believes they did."

"They're not going to correct what the chancellor said?" Marie asked, sounding shocked.

"But, that means the real culprit goes free." LuAnn's voice got a little stronger as she stepped toward the desk. She was a slight woman with delicate features and bright intelligent eyes.

Stella looked trapped. She had to be political, even among her friends. Criticizing the chancellor was probably not the best idea.

Pammy set the jewelry, warm from Stella's skin, in the safe.

"The real culprit will get caught," Stella said without conviction. "I mean, they're looking for whoever it was. But they don't think it's those striker-protestor types. They think, from what they found, that it has something to with the movie nights there."

"Movie nights?" Pammy asked as she closed the safe and spun the combination lock.

Stella was still rubbing one of her earlobes. The other earlobe looked red. Her clip-ons must have hurt. "You know how they show old movies to raise money for various causes. One of the rule changes the university made was to say that student organizations that used Wheeler's auditorium couldn't use it to raise money for non-student organizations."

"So, no movies benefitting Meals on Wheels," Pammy said, realizing she was letting her bias slip through, because there probably had never been movies benefitting something like Meals on Wheels.

"Or movies donating money to the anti-war campaign," Stella said.

"Or movies raising funds to re-elect the Governor of California," Marie said with some heat.

Her two friends looked at her, surprised. Pammy wasn't sure what surprised them. She didn't know Marie's politics. Pammy couldn't tell if Marie was angry that no one could raise funds to re-elect the governor or if she was using that as an example to rile up Stella.

"Why would they think that it was the movie thing?" Pammy asked, trying to change the topic just a little.

"Because," Stella said, "Roy says fringe groups were using those movies to get a lot of money."

Pammy didn't see how. They didn't charge much to show the films, and the auditorium had seated less than a thousand people.

"So they're still blaming the protestors," LuAnn said softly.

Marie nodded. Those two had made the connection, even if Stella was oblivious to it.

"No, this is a different group," Stella said, ignoring the undercurrents as she so often did. "I don't think anyone in that movie club was raising money for the Third . . . Fourth . . . Liberating . . . Protestors—whatever they're called. No one is raising money for them."

Pammy's stomach clenched. She hated Stella's attitudes.

"What kind of proof do they have?" Pammy asked again. She realized that she had again broken her private vow to stay out of this, but she couldn't let it go. The images of those flames haunted her ever since she walked to Wheeler Hall.

"Oh, I don't know." Stella frowned at her. "I really didn't care enough to quiz Roy."

Implying that Pammy was quizzing her.

Stella shrugged. "I just asked enough so that I would know if we could come here today, and not enough to make him think I was actually interested."

And she clearly wasn't interested.

"Shall we change, ladies?" she asked her friends, and then marched toward the locker room.

LuAnn stayed behind for just a moment. She bit her lower lip, then frowned at Pammy.

Pammy had learned how to handle LuAnn these last few months. LuAnn was like a feral cat seeking affection. If Pammy waited long enough, then she might get LuAnn to trust her.

"You let people sleep here, right?" LuAnn asked softly. "I mean, that one morning we came early, there were some women leaving . . ."

Pammy waited. She wasn't sure what LuAnn was asking. Was LuAnn warning her that the women who slept here might try to harm the business?

LuAnn didn't say anything else, so Pammy finally spoke. "Yes, sometimes I let women sleep here, when they have nowhere else to go. It's not permanent, but it helps them."

LuAnn nodded. She opened her mouth to say something else, then Marie peered out of the locker room door.

"Hey, you going to change or what?" she asked.

LuAnn closed her mouth, swallowed, nodded at Pammy like a terrified rabbit, and hurried to the locker room.

Pammy frowned after her, wondering what that was about, and then shrugged. She might never know.

For days, Pammy kept turning over LuAnn's question in her mind, worrying about the protests and the arson, thinking about Marie's comment about burning the whole city.

Pammy knew that was a privileged paranoia speaking, but she also understood that edge Berkeley was walking on, the feeling that at any moment, the entire community could slip into out-and-out war.

The edge got even more slippery during the next week. The demonstrations on campus turned violent as sixty officers from police departments all over the area marched down Bancroft, slapping batons against their palms.

The protestors broke windows and disrupted classes, all the while trying to explain their position—their demands for an education that included everyone, not just the privileged white students.

When Pammy heard that someone threatened Wheeler Hall again—this time on the phone—saying it would burn all the way to the ground, she felt the beginning of fear. And felt no relief when the threat turned out to be a false alarm.

Then she learned about an actual arson attempt at Girton Hall. The flames got doused before they did any damage.

Girton Hall had been designed in 1911 by architect Julia Morgan as a place for the women on campus to go. Pammy loved Girton Hall. Designed by a woman for women, it was ahead of its time.

After she heard the news, Pammy walked over to Piedmont on one of her breaks, heading toward Girton Hall. She wanted to avoid the continuing protests, which mostly happened around Sather Gate and on Sproul Plaza. She figured she could avoid all the disruption if she went around that part of campus.

As she moved through the chill air, she heard faint chants of "Power to the People" even though there were no protestors up here. At the moment, this part of campus was empty.

But she kept seeing someone out of the corner of her eye, almost like she was being flanked. The hair rose on the back of her neck. She didn't want to whirl around because that would tell whoever it was that he had alarmed her. If indeed it was a "he." If indeed "he" was trying to alarm her.

She turned her head slightly to the right. She saw a young man wearing a white sweater over dark pants, carrying books at his side. He walked close to her, then veered off toward the Greek Theater.

Pammy made the same movement to look at her left side, and saw someone slip just behind her. Her heart pounded.

She was making this up; she had to be. No one was targeting her. She was simply upset by the fires, the police presence, and the demonstrators shouting near Sather Gate.

She hurried to Girton Hall. She let herself inside.

On this day, everything felt off. Despite the chill, there was no fire in the red brick fireplace. No smoke floated near the exposed redwood beams on the ceiling.

The interior of the building smelled like old coffee mixed with an undercurrent of something sharp and chemical. The chairs usually set up in the main hall had been placed against the wall. A cleaning crew of students scrubbed the floor with some kind of soapy substance.

No one greeted her, which was also unusual. Pammy

walked around the scrubbers and into the small kitchen. There she saw her old friend, Ada Templeton. Ada leaned against one of the counters, clutching coffee to her chest.

"Is it true?" Pammy asked without saying hello. "Did someone try to burn this building down?"

Ada turned. Her shoulder-length hair was black, and had always seemed a bit unrelenting. Now, the strands around her face were turning white, taming the darkness and adding gravity to her features.

"Seven gasoline-filled bottles with rags stuffed in them," she said tightly. "Someone had tried to light the rags, but the flames didn't catch. Or something like that. The fire department says we 'ladies' will all be fine."

She said that last with sarcasm. Obviously, Ada didn't feel fine at all.

Pammy put a hand on Ada's arm. Ada leaned into her, touched her forehead to Pammy's, and then stood upright again.

"I don't recognize this place anymore," Ada said softly.

Pammy nodded. She didn't either. It had been a very quiet campus when they were going to school.

"Were you here when it happened?"

Ada shook her head. "I came in after."

She glanced over her shoulder at the main hall, where the scrubbing continued.

"What did they do? Break a window and throw the bottles in here?" Pammy asked. Shattered bottles filled with gasoline would explain that tangy smell she caught underneath the scent of coffee.

16

"That's the weird part." Ada set her cup down on the counter. "The bottles were placed in here."

"Placed. As in upright?" Pammy asked. "In the *kitchen?*"

That could have been a terrible disaster. It was hard enough to see the kitchen floor on a good day. In the early morning, with the lights down, someone would have kicked the bottles, spreading gasoline everywhere, and probably dying in the process.

Ada shook her head. "In the main hall, near the fireplace. I've been trying to figure out that part. I mean, this building is old and made of wood. If you wanted to burn it down, the last place you'd put gasoline bombs was near the bricked-in fireplace. Maybe put them under the wooden deck, because the rest of this place would go up like a match. Especially with yesterday's wind."

She had a point. There were a dozen other places to ignite those gasoline bombs that would have completely destroyed Girton Hall before anyone could have stopped it.

"Do you think someone was leaving a message?" Pammy asked.

Ada shrugged her shoulders. "If so, I don't understand it. Do they hate us? Or hate the buildings that President Wheeler had had a hand in sixty years ago? After all, he approved Girton Hall, and Wheeler Hall was named after him. Because this really makes no sense."

"You don't think this has something to do with the protests?" Pammy asked.

"I don't see it," Ada said. "The protestors are fighting for minority rights here on campus, and a lot of them are talking about a women's studies program here too. So, if anything, the protestors would be supportive of places like this one, not try to burn us down."

Pammy tapped her thumb against her chin, as she thought about that. There had to be a reason Girton Hall, of all places, was targeted.

"There's a large group who hate the demonstrators," Pammy said. "Maybe they did it."

"If that's the case, then they should have gone after the Third World Liberation Front's headquarters. Or throw bombs at the demonstrators," Ada said. "Not come here. We've done nothing. We haven't even hosted their events. We've been pretty quiet through this whole thing."

Her voice wobbled, and tears filled her eyes.

Then she wiped at her eyes, as if her own tears had made her angry. "I don't get this. I really don't. What have we done to piss people off? We're not involved in any of the politics right now. None of it. What have we done?"

Pammy finally put her arm around her. Ada leaned into her, shaking slightly. She was still wiping at her eyes.

"Sorry," she said softly.

"Me too," Pammy said. She had no idea what else to say.

Ada took a deep breath and gave her a watery smile. "I feel like we should have some of your students stand guard or something."

She might have meant it as a joke, but Pammy wasn't certain. "I do think you'll need someone here around the clock for a while."

Ada nodded. "We already thought of that. The university frowns on it, but I don't care. We're setting up a buddy list of people who are going to stay here at night. We'll have at least two, maybe more."

"Make sure they can handle themselves if something goes wrong," Pammy said.

"We will. You can help if you want."

"I'd prefer not to," Pammy said. "I have my own business to watch over. But I'll fill in if you need me."

"I'll hold you to that." Ada hugged Pammy. "Thanks for coming."

"I wish it were under better circumstances," Pammy said, and slipped out of the kitchen.

She walked around the entire building, both inside and out, before she started back to the gym for the next round of classes.

Ada's comment about placing the bombs under the porch or near the eaves made Pammy go slow, as she checked to make sure all the bottles had been found. She saw some dry rot, and a lot of problems that the university needed to fix, but she didn't see any glass bottles filled with suspicious liquid.

Nor did she see footprints left by someone else walking around the building.

By the end of her tour, she was slightly chilled and more than a little discouraged. She walked out of the trees surrounding the hall to the main path. The protest chants had died down, but she could still hear angry voices floating up from the central campus core.

She rounded a corner, and a man stood in front of her, arms crossed. He looked vaguely familiar. His hair was cropped short and his eyes were narrowed.

"Find what you were looking for, bitch?" he asked.

She braced herself ever so slightly, making sure her weight was properly balanced so that if he reached for her, she could move out of his way and give him a swift kick at the same time.

"Looks like I just did," she said.

He raised his eyebrows. "You were looking for me?"

"If you're the one who tried to harm these women today."

He grinned. "You women think you're so important. Why would I care about you?"

She shrugged. "Why don't you tell me?"

His grin disappeared and he took a step toward her. "I can beat the crap out of you."

She smiled at him. "I'd like to see you try."

He leaned back, almost as if she swiped at him.

"So you can go whining to the police?" he asked after a moment.

"I don't whine," she said.

He glared at her. She watched his body language. He had moved off the balls of his feet, and he was leaning slightly sideways. He wasn't going to come at her, not from that position.

"You just wait," he said. "I'll get you."

And then he walked away, shoulders hunched. It wasn't until he quickly disappeared into the trees that she realized he was wearing camouflage.

He was the man she had seen the night of the Wheeler Hall fire. And now he had been lurking at Girton Hall.

She was going to have to talk to the police. She didn't want to, but she felt like she had no choice.

Even though she had gone back inside Girton Hall and had gotten the name of the detective investigating the arson from Ada, Pammy didn't call him. Instead, she went to the police department and filed an official complaint.

She ended up talking to the desk sergeant because he wouldn't send her back to any of the officers working cases. She made him write down the angry man's description, and she made the sergeant register the fact that she had seen this man at two different arson sites.

"Hours after the events," the sergeant said, trying to dismiss her just like she had known he would.

"*During* the event at Wheeler Hall," she said calmly. "And yes, hours after at Girton Hall. But he had no reason to speak to me like that."

"Lady, college boys got no reason to speak to anyone the way they been lately, but they are. Just because someone was rude to you—"

"Normally, I wouldn't tell you," she said. "But in this case, I think it's important. Someone threatened Girton Hall and burned Wheeler Hall's auditorium. Someone is actively using arson to make a point."

"Yeah, the point is that those students are little rich

babies who don't understand that they can't always get what they want," the desk sergeant said.

"That might well be the case," Pammy said. "But my father was a career officer with the Philadelphia Police Department, and he taught me to do things right, especially when crimes had been committed. I'm sure you feel the same way, sergeant."

The sergeant looked at her pointedly, then grabbed a complaint form.

"You're such a cop, you fill it out." He slid it and a pen toward her.

She took both and smiled sweetly. "Only if you promise you'll give it to the detective handling the case, and you'll make sure the complaint form ends up in the case file."

The sergeant's gaze narrowed. "Which file?"

"I'd say both," she said, "but if you have to choose one file, then I'd say the Wheeler Hall fire, since this man was there while the fire was still burning."

The sergeant made a disgusted noise.

"Just promise me this won't go in the garbage," she said, as she started to fill out the complaint.

"You don't think too highly of us, do you, missy?" he snapped.

She raised her head.

"Actually," she said using the same calm voice she had used with the man near Girton Hall. "I do think highly of you, or I wouldn't have brought the complaint to you. I know you can't act on these two encounters, but I want to make sure you can act if and when this man gets found."

"You're convinced he's setting the fires," the sergeant said.

"I'm not convinced of anything," Pammy said truthfully. "But I do find his behavior odd, and I think that's important in this circumstance."

"Everyone's behavior is odd these days." The sergeant grabbed a manila file folder and walked away from the desk.

She suspected he had done so to get away from her. She didn't care. She filled out the complaint form and waited until the sergeant returned. She handed it to him, resisted the urge to remind him of his promise, and left the precinct, with barely enough time to make it to her next class.

Pammy taught that class and the final class of the day, happy that afternoon's students were among her most experienced. She had two of the students playact an attack with her, and she had to be careful, because she knew she had a lot of aggression to work out.

After everyone left, she wrapped her hands before pulling on her favorite gloves. She pulled the ties tight with her teeth. She knew that she had to prep properly, because she was still so angry she might hurt herself if she wasn't careful.

Working out alone, she had learned, wasn't always the best idea. But she had no choice this evening.

Then someone knocked on the front door, rattling the glass above the knob.

She didn't jump, but her heart started to race. No one came to the gym after hours unless there was a problem.

She hugged her right hand to her chest and used her teeth to untie the glove. She slipped it off, letting it fall to the floor, revealing her wrapped hand. She had just enough flex in her fingers to open the door if she needed to.

She walked toward the door, ready to tell whoever was out there that the gym was closed for the night.

A woman had cupped her hands around her face and was peering inside. It took Pammy a moment to realize that woman was LuAnn.

Pammy managed to unlock the door. Then she used her wrapped hand to beckon LuAnn inside.

LuAnn grabbed the knob and pushed her way in, using that same almost invisible maneuver she used when she came with Stella and Marie.

"Sorry," LuAnn said as she looked at Pammy's hands. "I didn't mean to interrupt."

Pammy ignored the apology. "Are you alone?"

LuAnn nodded, then glanced over her shoulder. "Can we get away from the windows?"

"If you help me get this off," Pammy said, raising her left glove.

LuAnn nodded.

They walked past the main window, and stopped in the shadows. LuAnn's fingers were shaking as she untied the knots.

Then LuAnn tugged the glove off. Pammy unwrapped her hands quickly, and set everything on a nearby table.

Her fingers were red. She'd wrapped them too tightly.

She really had been angry. She wiped her sweaty palms on her pants, and nodded toward the office.

LuAnn swallowed, then headed in that direction. Pammy veered slightly off course to make certain the front door was locked and the closed sign blocked the window.

In the time it had taken Pammy to do that, LuAnn walked the length of the gym. She was favoring her right side, and limping slightly. Pammy hurried to catch up. She opened her office door, and LuAnn scurried inside.

"Are you all right?" Pammy asked as she closed the office door.

LuAnn scanned the room, clearly looking for windows. Then she wrapped her arms around her chest.

"LuAnn?" Pammy asked.

"No," LuAnn whispered. "I'm not all right."

She moved toward the back of the office, almost to the wall.

"What happened?" Pammy asked.

LuAnn's eyes met hers.

"I didn't kill him," she said. "I made sure he was breathing when I left. But I didn't call for help, either. I propped him up so he wouldn't choke, like you said people can do when they're unconscious and laying flat. I propped him up. But he was out. And bleeding. He was bleeding."

She swallowed hard, then bit her lower lip.

"I didn't kill him," she repeated.

Pammy let out a small sigh. She had been through this before, but never with a housewife. Usually with a college student or one of the hippie girls, and the scene of whatever had happened was often close by. In those cases, Pammy could see for herself what happened. In this case, she knew she couldn't.

Pammy had learned an order to these things. Take care of the woman first, then worry about the injured man. Figure out what happened, and how to report it. *If* there was any point in reporting it.

"Before we do anything," Pammy said, "tell me why you're limping."

"I'm not limping," LuAnn said.

"You limped in here." Pammy knew that sometimes people in the middle of extreme trauma were unaware of how they behaved. "I watched you. And you're not moving your right arm much."

LuAnn looked down at herself as if she were surprised. She clenched her right hand into a fist, then released it, moving each finger as if she were trying to see whether or not it was broken.

Her knuckles were skinned and bruises had started to form on them. Her thumb had a long bloody scratch that ran the length of it.

"Oh, God," she said, and her knees buckled.

Pammy caught her before she fell. LuAnn's shirt was damp, and she gasped as Pammy wrapped an arm around her.

Pammy helped LuAnn to a nearby chair.

LuAnn sank into it, moaning slightly. Then she took a shuddery breath, and her eyes filled with tears.

She looked up at Pammy. "I thought I was okay. I drove down here just fine."

Which led to the issue of where the car had been parked. Pammy didn't want to worry about that yet.

"Adrenaline," Pammy said. "Let's see what's really going on."

She didn't wait for LuAnn to answer. Instead, she grabbed LuAnn's shirt at the hem, and lifted. Pammy had learned to make that movement slowly. Six months ago, she had done the same thing with one of the street women, and got slapped in the face for her trouble.

LuAnn didn't slap her. Instead, she watched in surprise as the shirt stuck to her skin. LuAnn started to raise her arms like a child, then stopped in obvious pain.

"We'll cut it off if we have to," Pammy said. "Just stay still."

She looked at the mess before her. There was some drying blood, but not as much as Pammy had expected. There seemed to be more blood on the shirt than on LuAnn's skin.

But that skin was clearly bruised, and some of the bruises were so old they were yellow. Fresh bruises covered her stomach and her ribcage.

"I'm going to press softly," Pammy said, using a technique her first boxing coach had taught her. "I want to make sure your ribs are all right."

She touched gently, feeling the length of the ribs. With each movement, LuAnn sucked in air, as if she were holding back screams.

The ribs felt all right, but Pammy was no doctor. And she didn't like the look of the bruises on LuAnn's stomach.

The darkness of some of them made Pammy wonder if LuAnn had internal bleeding.

"You spit any blood?" Pammy asked, careful not to look up. Some questions were easier to answer when there was no eye contact.

"Not anymore," LuAnn said.

Pammy felt a slight frustration. "When did that stop?"

"Just after I left the house. I lost a tooth. I think it's in the shrubs." Then LuAnn let out an inappropriate giggle. "Fourth tooth this year. I'm going to look like Granny Clampett if he's not careful."

That joke sounded like something LuAnn had said before, and not to her friends. Maybe to the man she was referring to as "he." Pammy wasn't yet making any assumption about who that was.

"But you haven't spit blood since?" Pammy asked, keeping herself focused.

"No," LuAnn said.

"Are you peeing blood? Is there blood in your stool?"

"I don't know." LuAnn was bristling now. The questions had become personal. "I haven't peed since I left."

"Okay." Pammy wasn't going to push this anymore. She got up and went to her desk. "I'm going to cut your shirt off. We'll put one of those sweatshirts on you, okay?"

"I can pay," LuAnn said. "I brought cash."

But Pammy hadn't seen her purse. It was probably still in the car. Pammy hoped that LuAnn locked it, because otherwise that purse was long gone.

"You don't need to," Pammy said.

"You can't—"

"Let me do this," Pammy said, keeping her tone even. She cut the shirt in three places, then eased the pieces off LuAnn.

LuAnn's arms bore the mark of fingerprints. Her right arm hung a little crookedly.

Pammy had no idea how LuAnn had driven down here.

"I'm going to get that sweatshirt," Pammy said as she tossed the pieces of bloody shirt in an old grocery bag.

She picked up an ancient towel from the ragbag she kept near the door, and wiped off her hands. They were blood-stained from that shirt. She tossed the towel into the bag too, then rinsed her hands in her office's tiny kitchen sink.

LuAnn wasn't watching any of this. She was looking at her own hands as if she hadn't seen them before.

Pammy let herself out of the room, and hurried across the floor to the sweatshirts. She grabbed one of the larger shirts, and brought it back to the office.

A movement caught the corner of her eye. She stopped, and looked, thinking it might have come from the door.

She peered in that direction and saw nothing, except a blurred version of her own reflection.

She swallowed hard, then rushed back to her office. She set the shirt on her desk, grabbed another rag, wet it with warm water, and handed it to LuAnn.

"Let's get some of the sticky stuff off." Pammy didn't want to use the word "blood," because she wasn't sure what kind of reaction she would get from LuAnn if she did.

LuAnn took it with her right hand. Pammy frowned. She couldn't quite figure out what was wrong with the arm.

LuAnn tried to rub the rag over her skin with that hand,

couldn't, and switched the rag to her other hand. She washed gingerly, as if she were afraid to put any pressure on herself at all.

Pammy had never seen that many bruises on a woman. Pammy had seen a man look like that only once, years ago, when she wandered into the gym where her father worked out. A fighter had been beaten nearly to death by another fighter in an illegal match.

Pammy felt a wave of guilt. How often had she asked LuAnn to run or practice defensive moves when LuAnn looked like this under her clothing? What kind of pain had this woman been in?

"I'm going to drive you to the hospital," Pammy said. "We don't have to tell them what happened, but you need to have someone look at—"

"No." This time, LuAnn's voice was strong. Her gaze met Pammy's. "I'm not going to the hospital."

"LuAnn, I'm afraid you might have some injuries I can't see," Pammy said.

"He'll find me," LuAnn said. "And this time, he won't forgive me. I brought money, all my money, and my jewelry, and my bank book. I'm not going back."

"I don't see your purse," Pammy said, trying not to sound panicked. What a treasure trove LuAnn had brought for some of the street kids.

LuAnn unbuckled her pants, revealing a roll of tinfoil wrapped halfway around her hips, and secured with tape.

Pammy had no idea how LuAnn had done that as injured as she was.

"I promised myself," LuAnn said, "if he hit me again, I'd

leave. I was all packed up and ready. But I couldn't go upstairs for my suitcase. I kept this in the back of a kitchen drawer just in case. He never looks in kitchen drawers."

"We'll put that in the safe," Pammy said. "We'll take you to the hospital, and make sure you're all right, and then—"

"No," LuAnn said. "I came here because I thought you'd know what to do. I didn't kill him, Pammy."

"I know," Pammy said.

"But I hurt him. Real bad. And he'll never forgive me."

Pammy braced herself. An angry man—husband, probably—would descend on this gym at any point.

"If we take you to San Francisco General—"

"No," LuAnn said. "He'll look there. He'll look everywhere. You don't know him, Pammy."

Pammy didn't know him. She didn't even know his name. And she had learned the hard way to respect a woman who said her man wouldn't give up.

"I hit him like you taught me," LuAnn said. "Chop in the throat, and he choked. And he bent over, and that's when I hit him on the head with the lamp. He landed hard. He was still breathing. I heard it whistling."

"Where did the blood on your shirt come from?" Pammy asked.

LuAnn bit her lower lip. For a moment, Pammy thought LuAnn wouldn't tell her.

Then LuAnn said, "His head. I had to slide him upright. I wasn't strong enough to lift him. I had to sit down, yank him against my chest, and pull. It hurt."

It probably had, particularly given LuAnn's injuries.

Her description clearly wasn't all that had happened.

LuAnn hadn't gotten those bruises on her knuckles from hitting a man in the Adam's apple. Nor had she gotten that cut on her thumb that way either.

But Pammy wasn't going to worry about those details yet. She had too many other things to worry about.

Pammy had no idea how long it had taken LuAnn to get here, but Pammy did know that enough time had passed that a man who had suffered serious neck trauma might have his throat swell up completely.

And if he died, then LuAnn would be charged with murder—and Pammy as an accessory.

"I'm going to call a friend," Pammy said. "She has medical training. I want her to look at you. She'll come here, okay?"

"Okay," LuAnn said.

"Can you tell me one thing?" Pammy asked. "This man, will he come here looking for you?"

LuAnn let out that weird giggle again. "He doesn't know about this. I paid with coupon money. He doesn't know I did this."

Coupon money. Pammy had heard LuAnn talk with Marie about that. They had kept the money they saved from cutting coupons in a separate place from their weekly allowance, so they had extra spending money.

All the girls do it, Marie had said, when she had seen Pammy's surprised face. She had thought the housewives all had money. Stella had disabused her of that.

Our husbands *have money,* Stella had said bitterly. *We have allowances.*

Pammy let out a small sigh. At least the angry man—or

the angry man's friends—wouldn't show up here quickly. But they might after talking with Stella and Marie.

"This man," Pammy said, "the one who hit you. He's your husband, right?"

LuAnn looked at her with almost comical surprise. "I thought you knew that."

"Just wanted to make sure," Pammy said. "I just needed to make sure."

She left LuAnn alone in the office for a few minutes. Pammy didn't take the tinfoil-wrapped money because she was afraid to remove it from LuAnn's skin.

So Pammy decided to handle problems one at a time, as if they were on a list. And the first thing on that list was the phone.

Pammy grabbed the sign-in sheets she had developed when she realized that her potential students expected some kind of order and accountability. She hoped LuAnn signed her last name on at least one of the sheets, because Pammy had never asked for it.

LuAnn had signed in the week before as *L. Amberson.* Pammy let out a small sigh. Her job just got a bit easier.

She knew the women lived in the Berkeley Hills, so she used the Berkeley phone book she kept beneath the desk and looked up Amberson. She had a choice of five. So she looked up the address for Roy D'Arbus. Stella had said they were all neighbors.

Pammy found an Amberson on the same street. Her

heart was pounding again. What she was about to do was something her father would never have approved of, but it was the only thing she could do right now without revealing where LuAnn was.

Pammy called the Berkeley Police Department, and when a male voice answered, she swallowed, made herself sound panicked, and said, "I don't know what's going on, but there's a lot of screaming next door. The door's open, and I thought I saw some big men running in there. I think they're being robbed."

"Where's this, ma'am?" the male voice asked.

Pammy gave him the Amberson address and hung up. The police did not routinely trace calls—it took time and was expensive. She knew that call would fall into the "anonymous tip" category.

She also knew that her suggestion of a robbery and "big men" would lead the police in the wrong direction.

Her palms were sweating again. She rubbed them on her pants, then picked up the phone and dialed another number from memory.

When she heard a "Yeah?" she said, "I need you right now," and hung up.

She knew that the person on the other end of the phone would be here shortly. June Eagleton had never disappointed her.

Eagle, as everyone called her, had stopped in the gym shortly after Pammy had opened it the year before. She doubted that Pammy had the chops to run a gym, and once Pammy proved herself, Eagle said that Pammy needed a medic because if there were too many injuries coming out of this place—even minor ones—doctors would shut her down.

It would be the excuse they want, Eagle said. *Fighting women threaten men.*

She would know. It had taken Pammy months to discover that Eagle had spent years as a combat nurse in Vietnam. She had come home angry and bitter. Generally, she refused to talk about her experiences, but slowly, Pammy got bits of her story. She wasn't sure she would ever get all of it.

Pammy ducked back into the office to check on LuAnn. The bruise on LuAnn's jaw was getting darker.

"Where did you park?" Pammy asked.

"Down the block," LuAnn said. "Not very good either, I think. I don't know."

"Where's your purse?" Pammy asked.

LuAnn shrugged and then winced. "Home somewhere. Why?"

"Just checking," Pammy said. "My medic friend will be here in a minute."

"Okay." LuAnn sounded exhausted. Clearly, shock was setting in.

"I'm going to go wait for her," Pammy said. "It won't be long."

Then she let herself out of the office. She saw movement again near the large window, and hoped it was Eagle. Pammy was clearly on edge. She hated being put in this position, and yet, she knew, that just by opening the gym, she had put herself here.

Then a face appeared in the doorway. Eagle.

Pammy unlocked the door, and opened it.

Eagle stepped inside. She was thin and weathered, and she always looked tired. She was holding a medical bag just like Dr. Kildare did for his TV house calls. Pammy once teased her about that until Eagle froze her with a look. Pammy never made fun of the bag again.

"What happened?" Eagle asked. "I was expecting a class."

Pammy shook her head. "Husband. She won't go to the hospital, afraid he'll find her."

Eagle's mouth twisted. "She's probably right. I'll see what I can do. Office?"

"Yes," Pammy said.

Eagle nodded, and headed back there. This sort of thing had happened enough since the gym opened that they actually had a system in place. Pammy would keep the injured woman in the back, then Eagle would go in alone and introduce herself.

That prevented the woman from begging Pammy to have Eagle leave, and it also gave Eagle a minute to establish trust.

Pammy glanced at the door. She hadn't locked it behind them. She walked to it, and saw movement against the big glass window.

That bothered her enough to open the door and peer outside. The street was empty, but she heard voices on the breeze. More protests probably, or a rally, or something farther up Telegraph.

She also heard The Doors, filtering down from a nearby apartment.

The night was chilly, and smelled of rain—which was so much better than smelling of smoke.

Although she did get a hint of something sharp, and she immediately flashed back on the smell beneath the coffee odor at Girton Hall.

She looked to her left, where she had seen the movement, just as a dark shape tackled her sideways.

She thumped against the sidewalk, felt her elbow hit hard, but she managed to tuck her head so that it didn't slam into the side of the building. Then she brought her legs up and kneed her attacker in the groin. She hoped her attacker was male, and hoped against hope that she had hit her target.

He yelped, confirming she had.

She wrapped her arms around him, rolled him over so that she was on top, and then punched him repeatedly in the face as if he were a punching bag. She could hear his skull knocking on the sidewalk.

His hands came up, then fell to his side, and she leaned back.

He didn't move.

She waited another minute, thinking he might be playing possum, and then she realized that no man could lie this still after being kneed in the balls.

He was out.

She stood, dusted herself off, and was about to go back inside, when she saw three bottles gleaming in the thin light from the doorway of her gym.

She glanced at the man, realizing she hadn't seen him well because he was wearing camouflage and his face had been deliberately smudged.

"You son of a bitch," she muttered.

She hurried inside, grabbed two jump ropes, and brought them back out. She turned him slightly, tied his hands behind his back, then brought his feet up and tied them as well, anchoring them to his hands.

Then she grabbed him by the back of his jacket and, with one hand, dragged him inside.

In the full light, she saw his face.

It was the man who had confronted her at Girton Hall.

"Got you," she said.

Although she wasn't sure what to do with him—or with those bottles.

She had to get them away from her building. And then she needed to call the police.

Who wouldn't believe her.

But she had to try.

Bottles first. They were too dangerous to keep close to the building, but she couldn't easily dispose of them, particularly if she were going to contact the police.

She left the asshole just inside the door, put on some regular cold-weather gloves, and then went back out. She hurried into the alley and grabbed one of the metal garbage cans. She dumped it out, hoping her neighbors would forgive her for the mess, and carried the can to the curb.

She gingerly picked up each bottle and placed it inside the can. All of the bottles had rags in them, and the liquid was leaching out. She didn't know what to do about that, so she didn't do anything. She just hoped no one bent on destruction found the garbage can before the police arrived.

If they arrived.

She tried not to think about that. Sometimes she hated the fact that she was near campus.

She started to go inside when a Mercedes turned into the alley, and stopped.

Stella got out. Her hair, normally sprayed into submission, was windblown, and she wore a heavy coat that was too big for her.

"Do you know where LuAnn is?" she asked without saying hello.

"I've got other issues right now," Pammy said, not wanting to reveal LuAnn's location.

Pammy put the lid on the garbage can, and took a deep breath, hating the smell of gasoline that had just wafted over her. She had to use her training: pretending to be calm was often the same as being calm. Deep breaths kept the panic at bay.

Stella grabbed her arm, nearly knocking her off balance. "Pammy, where's LuAnn? She's missing and someone beat her husband to death."

So he had died. Pammy hadn't called soon enough, or maybe he had been dead when LuAnn dragged him across the floor.

"There's blood all over the house, and the police are saying there was a robbery. LuAnn is gone, and so is the car. Please, Pammy. Have you seen her?"

Pammy couldn't tell Stella about LuAnn now. That would get Stella involved after the fact.

"Sorry, Stella," Pammy said, and shook her off. She couldn't quite lie to her.

She pulled open the door, planning to close it before

Stella followed her, but Stella moved quicker than expected. She blocked the door and stepped in right behind Pammy.

Then stopped.

"What the hell?" Stella asked, looking down.

The arsonist was still trussed on the floor, still unconscious. All the color had drained from Stella's face.

"What have you done, Pammy?"

"What have I done?" Pammy asked. "What have *I* done? I've protected this place. This idiot was trying to burn it down. I just put three gasoline bombs into that garbage can and I was going to call the police. That's what I was doing when you got here."

The door to the office opened and Eagle leaned out. "Pammy, I—"

She stopped when she saw Stella. Stella's eyes narrowed. She had met Eagle before, and knew that Eagle helped with medical issues.

"When you're done, talk to me," Eagle said, and closed the door.

Stella wasn't ready to let Eagle go that easily. Instead, Stella stalked across the floor, heading toward the office. Pammy wasn't going to get rid of her no matter what.

Pammy sprinted after Stella and caught her just before she reached the door.

"You don't want to go in there," Pammy said.

Stella glared at her. "I sure as hell do."

Her use of profanity shocked Pammy almost as much as her glare. Stella had never behaved like this before.

"Look, you've already seen something you shouldn't. If

you open that door, you're involved, and believe me, you don't want to be."

Stella let out a small laugh. "What makes you think I'm not involved?"

"You don't know what's going on," Pammy said. "You have no idea—"

"LuAnn's in there, isn't she?" Stella said. "And she's in bad shape, isn't she?"

Pammy felt her face heat. She didn't want to answer.

Stella leaned in toward her. "He almost beat her to death in July. She came to my house, and he found her, and I chased the evil s.o.b. off with a baseball bat. But he convinced her to come home to him, don't ask me how, and told her to stay away from me. Thank God she didn't listen. Marie and I brought her here, hoping we'd give her some tools to defend herself. That's what she did, isn't it? She hit him back."

Pammy didn't answer.

Stella grabbed the doorknob.

"You open that door," Pammy said, "and you become party to a crime."

"You mean killing Bruce?" Stella asked. "She should have done it years ago. And it seems to me, Miss My-Father-Was-A-Police-Officer that anything LuAnn did tonight would have been in self-defense."

"Yes, it seems that way to you," Pammy said. "But it won't seem that way to any investigating officer. She fled the scene. Most women can't get away with—"

"I know," Stella said flatly. "But you covered that, didn't you? You called in a robbery in progress. Very smart. Now they're searching for the masked man, just like in *The Fugitive*. There's a blood trail, so the police will have an idea where he went. And when they find him, he'll be trussed up on your floor."

Pammy's breath caught. Stella meant to blame the arsonist for Bruce's death?

Pammy shook her head. "No."

"That's why you tied him up, isn't it?"

"I tied him up because he was trying to burn down my gym. Just like he tried to burn down Girton Hall. Just like he burned down Wheeler Hall. You're not going to be able to pin a murder on him."

Stella harrumphed and shoved the door open. Someone let out a small scream from inside.

Pammy pushed her way in.

Eagle looked at them both, her expression impassive. "I taped her ribs. I think they're just bruised. Her breathing sounds fine. Her right humerus is cracked, I think, but her ulna is definitely broken, one of those twisting injuries that you get when someone turns your arm the wrong way. She says she drove here. I have no idea how. I also have no idea how her fingers work. I think she'll need surgery. I want her to have X-rays, but she won't go to any hospital."

LuAnn's face was chalk white, her eyes sunken into her skin.

Stella glanced at Pammy, confused. Suddenly the situation wasn't so simple.

"You wanted to be involved," Pammy said.

Stella let out a breath. Eagle ignored her.

"I can take her to a friend," Eagle said.

"Where?" Stella asked.

Eagle glared at her. "I don't know you. Not really. And I have no idea why Pammy trusts you. So I'm not telling you a goddamn thing, except that this woman was beaten badly and she needs care and she refuses to get it in the Bay Area. I think I can get her out of the Bay Area with a minimum of consequences to her body and to the future use of that arm. And that's all you need to know."

That last was for Pammy. Eagle wanted Pammy to make a decision. She'd been in this situation with Eagle before. Eagle didn't leave an offer on the table for very long.

"All right," Pammy said. "Keep me informed."

"When I can," Eagle said.

Pammy nodded. They'd made that deal before too.

"You have to go out the back," Pammy said.

"I was planning to," Eagle said. She put an arm around LuAnn and helped her to her feet. They staggered out of the office door.

Pammy escorted them, making sure they were nowhere near the arsonist. He was awake now, because she heard him thumping against the floor. Fortunately, he wasn't shouting. He probably figured untying himself was more important than calling for help.

Stella looked in the direction of the sound, but Eagle didn't. She gently got LuAnn to the side exit.

"You need my car?" Pammy asked.

Eagle shook her head once. "No. I'll call you when I know something."

"Well, know this," Pammy said. "Stella tells me that things just got a lot worse."

LuAnn moved slightly. Eagle looked at Pammy and mouthed, *Did he die?*

Pammy nodded.

"Shit," Eagle said. "I'll make sure we'll deal with the information when the time is right. You gotta clean up here."

"I will," Pammy said.

Stella said, "LuAnn?"

LuAnn stopped and looked at her.

"I'm sorry. I should have gotten you out sooner. I—"

"Save it," Eagle said. "Feel guilty on your own time. I gotta get this girl some help."

And then she steered LuAnn out the exit and into the back of the alley.

Pammy shut the door behind them, and leaned on it for just a moment. Her heart was pounding. Her elbow hurt, and for a half second, she couldn't remember why.

"Is she going to be all right?" Stella asked.

"I have no idea," Pammy said. "But she's not going to come back here. And if Eagle has her way, LuAnn won't come back to Berkeley at all."

She didn't tell Stella that LuAnn had money and jewelry with her. If LuAnn wanted to stay away, she could.

It was out of Pammy's hands now.

Almost.

The thumping in the gym got worse. Pammy let out a breath. She knew he hadn't been able to hear or see what they were doing, but the fact that he'd been here for the last of this bothered her.

"What are you going to do with him?" Stella asked.

Pammy sighed. Her head was starting to ache too.

"Call the cops, and hope to Christ they come down here. I have the name of the detective in charge of the Girton Hall investigation. Maybe he'll think a problem near Telegraph is worth responding to."

"You're sure this is the guy who burned Wheeler Auditorium?" Stella asked.

Pammy nodded.

Stella's eyes narrowed. "Well, then," she said, sounding like the old Stella. "I feel like taking a few prisoners myself tonight. And since I can't work on the crisis I want to work on, I can help you."

"No, Stella, let me—"

"You're right, Pammy," Stella said. "The police won't listen to you. But they will listen to Mrs. Roy D'Arbus about something connected to the university. I will call the police. You will clean up your office."

"Let me check on him first," Pammy said, picking up some tape she usually used for people's hands.

She headed to the front of the gym. The man had rolled closer to the window and was trying to prop himself up so that he could attract attention.

She grabbed his shoulder and pulled him back, making him fall.

"You fucking bitch," he said. "You let me go before something happens. You have no right—"

She wrapped the tape around his mouth and pulled so tight his skin stretched. "My father used to say that all arsonists are sick cowards. He was right."

She pushed the man down, and checked the knots on

the ropes. Satisfied that they were tight, she walked back to the reception desk where Stella was on the phone with the police.

"What's the address here?" Stella asked.

Pammy gave it to her.

"Yes, he's inside," Stella said into the phone. "We surprised him, and were able to knock him out. He's tied up now. Please, come get him."

She sounded calm, calmer than Pammy felt. Pammy hoped Stella didn't say anything about LuAnn or anything else.

Stella hung up. "They'll be here shortly." She braced herself on the reception desk. "Now, what else can I do? Help you with the office?"

Pammy looked at her, trying to figure out Stella's motives. Which wasn't true. Stella had told Pammy the motive. Pammy just had to choose whether or not to believe her.

Pammy let out a breath. The reasons she didn't want to believe Stella were the pearls and the hairspray and the make-up. The powerful husband and the privileged life.

Judgment based on appearance.

"I'll take care of the office," Pammy said. "You sit some-where, but make sure you can see our prisoner."

Stella nodded. The word "prisoner" seemed to shock her a little.

Pammy looked inside the office. It wasn't as messy as she had expected. Just a bit of blood, and the bag on the floor with the remains of LuAnn's shirt.

Pammy couldn't put that in the garbage; the cops would find it and wonder what it was. Then she had an idea.

She leaned out the office door. "Do you know what kind of car LuAnn drives?"

Stella nodded. "It's a brand-new Buick. I saw it a block from here."

"That's how you knew she was here."

Stella shook her head. "I knew she was here when they said the car was gone. They figured the burglars stole it, but I knew she had come to you. She couldn't come to me after the last time. The time before that, she went to Marie, and Bruce had found her then too. So this time, she would go somewhere that he couldn't find her."

Pammy didn't want to think about what would have happened if LuAnn's husband had survived. Would she have gone back to him and let him beat her again and again until he killed her? Why did some relationships have to end like that, in blood and beatings and one or the other spouse dying? And why was it common enough that she had to ask that question?

"One block which direction?" she asked.

Stella pointed. Pammy nodded, then put on her gloves and grabbed the bag. She let herself out the same side exit that LuAnn and Eagle had used.

The alley was cold and dark. Pammy tried not to think about whether or not the arsonist had an accomplice. She doubted he did. The accomplice would have stepped in already.

She made herself hurry, picking her way across the gravel.

Once she got to the side street, she saw the new Buick parked haphazardly, not anywhere near the curb. The interior light was on, but the doors looked closed.

As she got closer, she realized that the driver's door wasn't shut all the way.

Pammy looked around. For once she was happy there were no working streetlights here. She looked up, saw closed curtains in the nearby apartments, and no one else on the street.

She pulled open the back passenger door, and dumped the pieces of the shirt on the floor. Then she crumpled the bag itself and threw it against the rear window.

The cops would find the blood, think it was LuAnn's and believe the worst.

Pammy almost left the driver's door alone, and then she thought about it.

Fingerprints. The police would take prints from steering wheel and the door handles. Either the police would find LuAnn and her husband's prints and no one else's or find the prints of someone innocent. And that would be as bad as blaming the arsonist.

Pammy rounded the car. She wiped off the driver's door handle inside and out, then wiped down anything LuAnn might've touched on the drive here.

The police would find the lack of fingerprints suspicious enough to continue the robbery story. They would think only criminals would wipe down a car. They would think—correctly—that a wife in the heat of the moment would never have the presence of mind to clean up after herself.

Pammy wiped the front passenger door as well. Then she

hurried back to the darkness of the sidewalk, and made herself walk back to the gym.

No cops yet.

She wanted to be there when they arrived. Because Stella would need all the help she could get.

It turned out that Stella didn't need any help at all. She saw the flashing red-and-blue lights as the police approached, and scurried out to her Mercedes. She stood beside it, arms crossed, as the police car pulled up.

As a uniformed officer got out—not the detective after all—Stella walked over to him.

"Thank heavens you're here," she said. "This man attacked my friend, and slipped. Fortunately, it knocked him out. I can't imagine what would have happened if he was able to finish the attack."

Pammy opened her mouth to object to the story, and then she saw the officer's face. He believed it.

The officer moved his head slightly, commanding his partner to join them. Stella showed them the gasoline bottles in the garbage can, and then led the officers to the gym, talking the entire time as if she had been terrified by the whole thing.

Pammy stayed back. She hated pretending to be a helpless female. But she also knew it worked.

And she admired Stella for the line she was walking. She was pretending to be a helpless female who also happened to be the wife of one of the most powerful men in the State of California.

The cops knew they had to treat her well.

They got the arsonist out of the building, and Stella told them she would follow so she could press charges. She stood near her Mercedes as the cops put the arsonist in the back seat of the squad car.

"Let's go," she said to Pammy.

Pammy almost refused. Then she realized just how sideways this could all go. The arsonist could call Pammy a crazy woman, and the earlier police report that she filed would make it seem like she targeted him.

Or Stella might accidentally mention LuAnn.

Pammy made sure the gym was locked, and then she climbed into the Mercedes. She had never been inside one before. It smelled of leather and money.

She leaned her head against the seat, suddenly realizing what a long night she had had.

"Thank you for the help," she said to Stella.

Stella let out that same small laugh. It seemed to be her default when something struck her as odd.

"It was nice to be able to help at least one woman tonight," she said.

Pammy smiled to herself. "Yes," she said softly. "Yes it was."

After Eagle's call the next day, Pammy never spoke about LuAnn again. Eagle had driven LuAnn to a hospital, and from the sound of it, they had gone to Sacramento to get help, although Pammy didn't know that for certain.

What she did know was that the Berkeley police believed some thugs had taken LuAnn and brutalized her, then killed her, dumping the body somewhere. The police had no suspects, no real leads. Even the car was a dead end.

Pammy also knew that LuAnn had defended herself, just like she said. Stella saw the evidence and talked to the police. All of Bruce Amberson's injuries were consistent with LuAnn's story, which Pammy found to be a relief.

The police couldn't tie the arsonist—whose name was Ryan Cosgrove—to the Wheeler Hall attack or the bottles left at Girton Hall, but they did charge him with assault on Pammy, and attempted arson at the gym.

There was no trial. He plead out, hoping to avoid being transferred downstate. The police had found other reports of fires, dating back more than a decade. Apparently, Cosgrove had used protests to cover his fires for the past two years.

The police said his choices were random, but Pammy didn't think so. The gym and Girton Hall were women-only. And it turned out, some of the major charities getting money from the movie nights in Wheeler Hall were some of the campus feminist groups.

Pammy couldn't prove it, of course. It wasn't her job to prove anything.

Her job was to train women to defend themselves in bad

situations. And as Stella talked up Pammy's capture of Cosgrove, women paid attention.

Even though Pammy felt like she had done very little. She had defended herself and her gym, but she had done it reflexively, while worried about LuAnn injured in her office.

LuAnn, who had come to the gym because her friends loved her enough to ask her to.

LuAnn, who had taken the classes seriously.

LuAnn, who had defended herself instead of dying at her husband's hands.

Pammy would have liked that outcome better if no one had died. Pammy would have liked it better if LuAnn had left that man before he nearly beat her to death.

But Pammy couldn't get everything she liked.

So she had to take the small victories—because she knew, at the moment, the world was too brutal for large ones.

War came to Berkeley months later with tear gas and students dying in the streets. And in the quiet afterward, Pammy's business thrived.

Everyone said it was because of the arsonist.

But Pammy knew that it wasn't. Stella told everyone about the arsonist because she couldn't tell them about LuAnn.

Not that it mattered.

Women came. They learned. And maybe, they'd figure out how to escape before someone died.

Like Pammy wished LuAnn had.

Family Affair
A Smokey Dalton & Protectors Story

KRIS NELSCOTT

I knew the day had gone bad when the white woman in the parking lot started to scream. I turned in the seat of my mud-green Ford Fairlane, and watched as Marvella Walker and Valentina Wilson tried to soothe the white woman. But the closer Marvella got to her, the faster the woman backed away, screaming at the top of her lungs.

We were in a diner parking lot in South Beloit, Illinois, just off the interstate. Valentina had driven the woman and her daughter from Madison, Wisconsin, that morning.

The woman was a small thing, with dirty blond hair and a cast on her right arm. Her clothing was frayed. Her little blond daughter—no more than six—circled the women like a wounded puppy. She occasionally looked at my car as if I was at fault.

Maybe I was.

I'm tall, muscular, and dark. The scar that runs from my

eye almost to my chin makes me look dangerous to everyone —not just to white people.

Usually I can calm people I've just met with my manner or by using a soft tone. But in this instance, I hadn't even gotten out of the car.

The plan was simple: We were supposed to meet Marvella's cousin, Valentina Wilson, who ran a rape hotline in Madison. The hotline ran along the new Washington D.C. model—women didn't just call; they got personal support and occasional legal advice if they asked for it.

This woman had been brutally raped and beaten by her husband. Even then, the woman didn't want to leave the bastard. Then he had gone after their daughter and the woman finally asked for help.

At least, that was what Valentina said.

Marvella waved her hands in a gesture of disgust and walked toward me. She was tall and majestic. With the brown and gold caftan that she wore over thin brown pants, her tight black Afro, and the hoops on her ears, she looked like one of those statues of African princesses she kept all over her house.

She rapped on the car window. "Val says she can make this work."

She said that with so much sarcasm that her own opinion was clear.

"If she doesn't make it work soon," I said, "we could have some kind of incident on our hands."

People in the nearby diner were peering through the grimy windows. Black and white faces were staring at us, which gave me some comfort, but not a whole lot since there was a gathering of men near the diner's silver door.

They were probably waiting for me to get out of the car and grab the woman. Then they'd come after me.

I could hold off maybe three of them, but I couldn't handle the half dozen or so that I could see. They looked like farmers, beefy white men with sun-reddened faces and arms like steel beams.

My heart pounded. I hated being outside of the city— any city. In the city, I could escape pretty much anything, but out here, near the open highway, where the land rose and fell in gentle undulations caused by the nearby Rock River, I felt exposed.

Valentina was gesturing. The white woman had stopped screaming. The little girl had grabbed her mother's right leg and hung on, not so much, it seemed, for comfort, but to hold her mother steady.

I watched Valentina. She looked nothing like the woman I had met three years ago, about to go to the Grand Nefertiti Ball, a big charity event in Chicago. She had worn a long white gown, just like Marvella and her sister Paulette had, but Valentina came from different stock.

Marvella had looked like I imagined Cleopatra had looked when Julius Caesar first saw her, and Paulette was just as stunning.

But Valentina, tiny and pretty with delicate features, had looked lost in that white dress. The snake bracelets curling up her arms made them look fat, even though they weren't.

They didn't look fat now. They were lean and muscular, like the rest of her. That delicate prettiness was gone. What replaced it was an athleticism that hollowed her cheeks and gave her small frame a wiry toughness that no one in his right mind would mess with.

I knew the reason for the change; she had been raped by a policeman who then continued to pursue her after his crime. Even after his murder by one of the city's largest gangs, she felt she couldn't stay in Chicago.

I understood that, just like I understood the toughness with which she armored herself. But I also missed the delicate woman in the oversized dress, the one who smiled easily and had a strong sense of the ridiculous.

"You know," Marvella said, leaning against the driver's side window, "as much of a fuss as that woman's putting up, I don't think we should take her out of here at all."

I agreed. We were supposed to take her to a charity a group of us had started on the South Side of Chicago. Called Helping Hands, the charity assisted families—mostly women and children—who had no money, no job skills, and no place to go. I found a lot of them squatting in houses that I inspected for Sturdy Investments. Rather than turning them out, I went to Sturdy's CEO and the daughter of its founder, Laura Hathaway—who, not by coincidence, had an on-again, off-again relationship with me.

Laura agreed that we couldn't throw children onto the street, so she put up the initial money and got her rich white society friends to put up even more. Without Laura's society connections, Helping Hands wouldn't exist.

It wasn't designed for people from Wisconsin. We had devised it only for Chicagoans, and mostly for those on the South Side. We had a few white families go through our doors over the years, but not many. We only had a few white volunteers. The white face that most of our clients saw—if they saw one at all—was Laura's, and then only because she liked to periodically drop in on the business and check up on everything herself.

"I mean," Marvella said, "what happens if she changes her mind again halfway between here and Chicago? If she starts screaming from the back seat of your car, the cops will pull us over in no time."

I winced. If the woman claimed she was being taken to Chicago against her will, then there were all kinds of laws we could be accused of breaking, not the least of which was kidnapping.

"Tell Valentina this isn't going to work," I said.

"Not going to tell her. She has her heart set on saving that little girl."

That little girl kept looking at me from the safety of her mother's thigh. I could see why Valentina wanted to save her. The little girl's eyes shone with intelligence, not to mention the fact that she was the only calm one in the trio.

Her mother was crying and shaking her head. Valentina was still talking, but it didn't look like she was going to get anywhere.

"You can't save someone who doesn't want to be saved," I said.

"You tell Val that," Marvella said.

"Bring her over here and I will," I said. "Because in no way am I getting near that woman with the diner crowd watching."

Marvella glanced up at them and frowned. I couldn't

quite tell, but it seemed like more bodies were pressed against the glass around the door. One huge white man was now standing beside his pick-up truck, twirling his key ring on his right index finger.

"Crap," Marvella said. "I'll see what I can do."

She walked back to the women. She put a hand on Valentina's shoulder and led her, not gently, away from the woman.

Marvella and Valentina talked for a few minutes. Marvella nodded toward the diner.

Valentina looked up for the first time. Her lips thinned. Then she nodded, just once.

She walked back to the woman and her daughter.

Marvella walked back to me and got in the passenger side.

"Let's go," she said.

"That's it?" I asked.

"Not really," Marvella said. "We need to call Helping Hands and tell them to put a white volunteer at the front desk, not that I think that's going to work."

"Why?" I asked.

"Because Val's convinced she can drive the woman to Chicago all by herself," Marvella said.

I looked at the three of them, still standing in the parking lot. The woman wiped her good hand over her eyes.

"Why would she go with Valentina and not with us?" I asked.

Marvella rolled her eyes. "Valentina has apparently reached honorary white person status. She nearly lost it when seen in the company of her Black cousin and the mean-looking Black driver. You should have heard the crap that woman spouted about niggers come to kidnap her daughter—"

"I don't need to hear it," I said, waving my hand.

"Me either," Marvella said. "I nearly told the bitch to shove it up her bony little ass, but Val wouldn't let me. She said she's just scared and out of her depth and had we forgotten that Madison is 90% white? I'm thinking maybe she forgot or she should have at least told us so we could've brought your society girlfriend along to make little miss holier-than-thou over there a lot more comfortable."

I let the dig at my society girlfriend go by. Marvella and Laura got along, now, after a lot of wrangling and harsh words over the years. This was just Marvella's way of letting her anger out without aiming it at the woman we had driven an hour and a half to help.

"So let's just go," Marvella said. "We'll pull over somewhere with a pay phone and call Helping Hands, and then our job here is done."

I hesitated for just a moment. The little girl was still watching us. Valentina turned slightly, waved her hand in a shoo motion, and I nodded.

I started the car, turned the wheel, and pulled out of the parking lot, glancing into my rear-view mirror to make sure no pick-up truck followed us.

None did.

After twenty minutes, I let out a breath.

After thirty, I knew we were in the clear.

After we had made the call to Helping Hands, I figured we were done with this job.

Of course, I was wrong.

Three months later, Marvella pounded on my apartment door. We lived just across the hall from each other.

"I have a phone call you need to take," she said.

I yelled to my fourteen-year-old son Jim that I would be right back, then crossed the hall. Even though it was December and the landlord had forgotten to turn on the heat in the hallway, Marvella was bare foot. She wore a towel around her hair, and a brown caftan that she clearly used as a robe.

"Since when am I getting calls at your place?" I asked.

"Since I can't talk sense into Val," she said.

I peered at her. I hadn't heard from Valentina since that day in September when she'd delivered the white woman to Helping Hands. After she had completed her mission, she had taken me, Marvella, and Marvella's sister Paulette to dinner. She told us about her life in Madison, which sounded a bit bleak to me, and then drove the three hours back so she wouldn't miss the university extension class that she taught the following morning.

Marvella's apartment had the same layout as mine, but was decorated much differently. Hers was filled with dark, contemporary furniture, and African art. The sculptures covered every surface, faces carved from mahogany and other dark woods. The sculptures were so life-like they seemed to be staring at me.

The phone hung on the wall in Marvella's half kitchen. The receiver rested next to the toaster.

"There she is. You tell her our policy." Marvella waved a hand at the phone. "I have to finish getting dressed."

She vanished down the hallway and slammed her bedroom door, as if I was the one who had made her angry instead of Valentina.

I picked up the receiver. "Valentina?"

"Smokey?" She was one of the few people who called me by my real name. Most people in Chicago knew me as Bill Grimshaw, a cousin to Franklin Grimshaw, one of the co-founders of Helping Hands. My real name is Smokey Dalton, and I'm from Memphis. A case four years ago put me on the run and brought me here, forcing both me and Jimmy to live under an assumed name.

On the night she almost died, Valentina overheard Laura call me Smokey, and she never forgot it. She once told me that Bill didn't suit me and Smokey did. Since Jimmy, Laura, and Franklin all called me Smokey, I never felt the need to correct Valentina.

"Marvella said I'm supposed to talk sense into you," I said, "only she won't tell me what this is about."

"Linda Krag disappeared," Valentina said.

The name didn't ring a bell with me. "Linda Krag?"

"The white woman I took to Helping Hands in September," Valentina said. "I'm sure you remember."

"I do now," I said, and then realizing that sounded a little too harsh, added, "She had that pretty little daughter."

"Yeah," Valentina said. "They've both been gone a week now."

"I thought they were in Chicago," I said.

"They were," she said.

"And you're still in Madison?" I asked.

"Yes," she said. "That's why I'm talking to you. No one told me she was missing until they sent my targeted donation back."

Valentina sent money every month to Helping Hands earmarked only for Linda Krag and her daughter. If the money couldn't be used for Linda Krag, then Helping Hands was duty-bound to return it. The policy was Laura's. She believed that everyone who donated money had a right to say how it would be used.

"So you called to find out what was up," I said.

"And discovered that she had left her apartment a week before. No one will tell me where she went."

"Did she take her daughter with her?" I asked.

"Of course," Valentina said. "She won't go anywhere without Annie."

I sighed. I knew the arguments Marvella had already made because they were the ones I had to make. Helping Hands followed its name exactly: It provided helping hands. If a client no longer wanted help, we couldn't force it on her.

Besides, we had rules. The client received her living expenses for the first month. We paid her rent and utilities and gave her a food budget. In return, we asked that she either apply for work or go to school.

If the client refused to do either, we stopped the support. If she couldn't hold a job, we got her more job training, but if she lost the job because of anger, discipline or a drug problem—and the client wouldn't get help curbing that problem—then we stopped providing assistance.

Linda Krag had been difficult from the start. She almost refused to go into Helping Hands, even though we had found a white volunteer to take her application. Chicago's South Side, filled with Black faces, terrified her. Eventually, Valentina talked her into the building. Once there, she agreed to all Helping Hands' terms and actually went to classes to get her GED.

But she hated the apartment that she was assigned. Not because it was bad or in a bad neighborhood, but because she and her daughter were the only whites on the block. She claimed to be terrified, and wanted an apartment in a "normal" neighborhood.

Since we knew of no programs to combat innate bigotry, we searched for—and found—her an apartment in a transitional neighborhood near the University of Chicago. She liked that. She had gotten her GED, applied for college, and found a part-time job, one that didn't tax her still-healing hand. Her daughter went to Head Start half the day.

Last I heard, everyone was happy.

But clients who started as roughly as Linda Krag often didn't make it through the program. They had too many other problems.

I said all of this, and more to Valentina, and as I spoke, she sighed heavily.

"Has anyone thought about her husband?" Valentina asked when I had finished.

I leaned against the wall. A wave of spicy perfume blew

toward me from the bedroom. Marvella was not just getting dressed. She was getting dressed up.

"What about her husband?" I asked.

"Maybe he found her."

"Or maybe," I said gently, "she just left."

"She wouldn't," Valentina said. "Her family is dead. She has no friends. That loser isolated her from everyone she knew when he took her to Madison. She wouldn't know how to start a new life."

"Actually," I said, making sure I kept the same tone, "Helping Hands was teaching her how to make a life for herself and her daughter."

"Exactly," Valentina said. "I got a postcard from her daughter Annie two weeks ago. She sounded happy. Linda added a sentence thanking me. She wouldn't just give up. Not now."

"You spoke to her about this?" I asked.

"No," Valentina said. "But leaving now just isn't logical."

Neither was staying with a man who nearly beat her to death, but I wasn't going to argue that point with Valentina.

"Val," I said, "a lot of women do things that aren't logical."

I winced as the words came out of my mouth. I should have said "people," but it was too late to correct myself.

"Women are not illogical creatures," Valentina snapped.

Marvella had come out of the bedroom. She was wearing an orange dress with a matching orange and red scarf tied around her hair. She had heard the last part of this conversation, and she was grinning now.

She knew the mistake I made.

"I didn't mean it that way," I said. "I just meant that people can be irrational."

"Linda's not irrational," Valentina said.

I was already tired of this fight. "You mean the woman who wouldn't get into the car with me and Marvella because she was afraid of Black people? That Linda?"

Valentina made a sound halfway between a sigh and a growl. "Smokey, look. You have to trust me on this. I got a real sense of her. It took her a lot of guts to run away from Duane. It took even more to go to Chicago. But she knew it was right for Annie. Linda wasn't going to go back to him. Not ever."

"I didn't say she would," I said. "Maybe she thought she could do better on her own."

"She knew she couldn't," Valentina said. "She was terrified of being on her own. That's why she didn't get into the car with you. She knew she couldn't defend herself and Annie, and you—I'm sorry, Smokey—but you look like every white person's nightmare. I don't think she'd ever spoken to a Black person until she spoke to me. Asking her to go with you and Marvella was one step too many for her. But she did go to Chicago, she did get her GED, she did start over."

"Yeah."

I must have sounded as skeptical as I felt because Valentina added, "You have no idea how hard all of that was for her. She wouldn't be the kind of woman who would do it all over again all on her own. Especially not with Annie."

I sighed. Marvella crossed her arms and raised her eyebrows, as if asking if I was going to finish soon.

"All right," I said. "Let's say I grant you that she wouldn't run off. What then, in your mind, could have happened?"

Marvella rolled her eyes.

"I think the husband found her," Valentina said. "I think she's in trouble, Smokey. Both her and Annie."

"And this is a gut sense," I said.

"Stop patronizing me!"

I almost denied that I was, but then I realized that I would have been lying.

"I need to know if you have facts to back up this assumption," I said.

Valentina didn't answer for nearly a minute. Finally, she said, "No."

"So," I said. "It begs the question. How could the husband have found her? Is he particularly bright?"

"I don't know," she said.

"Did you tell anyone where she went?"

"Not even the folks here at the hotline. Only one of the women knew what I was doing, and all she knew was that I was going to take Linda to some of my friends in Chicago."

"So," I said, then winced again. I was even sounding patronizing. "Would she have called this man for any reason?"

"I don't think so," Valentina said. "No."

"Then how could he have found her?"

"I don't know," Valentina said. "I just want you to check on her. You and Marvella have made it really, really clear that

Helping Hands doesn't track people who vanish. So how about this? How about I hire you to find her, Smokey? Does that work for you? I have a lot of money. I'll pay your standard rates plus expenses. I can put a check in the mail today."

I almost told her that it wasn't necessary, that I would do this one for free. But I was a little annoyed at her stubbornness, and besides, Jimmy was growing so fast that I couldn't keep him in shoes. My regular work for local Black insurance companies and for Sturdy paid the bills, but couldn't cover the added expenses of a growing teenage boy.

"All right," I said, and quoted her my rates. "I'm going to need a few things from you, too. I need some basic things. I need the husband's full name. I need to know where he lives and, if possible, where he works. I need to know where he lived with Linda and Annie."

"Okay," Valentina said.

"But—and this is very important—I don't want you investigating or talking to him. If you can't do the work by phone, using a fake name, I don't want you doing it. Is that clear?"

"I know how to investigate, Smokey," she said with some amusement in her voice.

"Good," I said. "Because the last thing I want is for this nutball to go after you."

"He won't," she said.

But I got the sense, as I hung up the phone, that Valentina Wilson—the new version, the muscular woman I'd seen three months ago—would welcome his attack. She'd welcome it, and happily put him out of commission.

"Well?" Marvella asked.

"Well," I said, "it looks like I have a missing persons case."

She rolled her eyes again. "And I thought you were a tough guy."

"Sometimes," I said, "it's just easier to do what the client wants than it is to convince them they're wrong."

"Is she wrong?" Marvella asked.

"Probably," I said with a sigh. "Probably."

Linda Krag's new apartment was in student housing near the University of Chicago. The neighborhood had once been filled with middle class professors' homes, but now those homes were divided up into apartments, with bicycles parked on the porch and beer cans lying on the lawn.

Those lawns were brown. Winter hadn't arrived yet, despite the chill.

In the early fall, when Linda Krag had seen this place, it had probably looked inviting. Now, with the naked trees stark against the gray skyline, the leaves piled in the street, the battered cars parked haphazardly against the curb, the block looked impoverished and just a little bit dangerous.

Or maybe I was projecting. Linda Krag, white and young, might have felt comfortable here, but I felt out of place, despite the University neighborhood's known color-blindness and vaunted liberalism.

I had the skeleton keys from Helping Hands. Linda's

stuff had not been removed from the apartment—she had until the end of the month before her belongings would become part of the charity's donation pile. I doubted anyone had visited this place once everyone realized she was gone.

The apartment was on the second floor. More bikes littered the hallway, and so did several more beer cans. The hall smelled of beer.

Linda's door was closed tightly. There were scrapes near the lock and the wood had been splintered about fist-high. I had no idea if that damage predated Linda's arrival. With student housing, it was almost impossible to tell.

I unlocked the deadbolt and had to shove hard to get the door to open. It had been stuck closed. As I stepped inside, I inspected the side of the door and noted that the wood was warped.

I pushed the door closed, but it bounced back open. The warped wood made it as hard to close as it was to open.

I had seen the apartment she had been given on the South Side. That had been a two bedroom with a full kitchen and stunning living room. I had put up another family there a year or so ago. They had worked their way through the Helping Hands program and had bought their own house last summer.

I couldn't believe she would have left that place for this one.

But people's prejudices made them do all kinds of crazy things.

The apartment smelled sour. A blanket was crumpled at the end of the couch, and a sweater hung off the back of a kitchen chair someone had moved near the window. The kitchen was to my right. The table, with two chairs pushed against it, was beneath a small window with a good view of the house next door.

A full ashtray sat on the tabletop, along with a coloring book and an open—and scattered—box of crayons. Dishes cluttered the sink, which gave off a rotted smell.

More cigarettes floated in the water, filling the bowls at the bottom of the sink. A hand towel rested on one of the burners. It was the only thing I moved, using the skeleton keys so that I wouldn't have to touch it.

Then I went through the kitchen into a narrow hallway. The second bedroom was back here. A bed was pushed against the wall. Clothing—pink and small—was scattered all over the floor. More clothes hung on the make-shift clothing rod by the door.

The clutter was everyday clutter, not slob-clutter. It looked like the kind of mess a person made when she left in a hurry, meaning to clean up later. It disturbed me that a woman who cared so much about her daughter—a poor woman—would leave most of her daughter's wardrobe behind.

The hair rose on the back of my neck. I didn't want Valentina to be right. If she were right, then we had lost more than a week in searching for this woman.

And a week, in a missing person's case, was a long, long time.

I made myself walk back through the kitchen and down another narrow hallway to the full bedroom. It wasn't much larger than the daughter's room. The full-sized bed left barely enough space between the wall and the side of the bed for me to walk around it.

The bed was unmade. Pillows sideways, blankets thrown back. But the bottom of the blankets—along with the sheets —was tucked in. The tucks were perfect military tucks, something that wouldn't last during weeks of restless sleep.

Linda Krag usually made her bed. She usually made it with great precision.

Her clothing hung in the small closet, separated by color. A pair of shoes was lined neatly against the wall.

The sour smell was stronger here. It didn't smell like dirty dishes, but something else, something that I should have recognized, but couldn't.

I pushed open the bathroom door, and the smell hit me, making my eyes water. Vomit. Old vomit. It lined the edge of the bathtub, the floor beneath the sink, and the toilet itself. It had crusted against the wall.

I made myself go into the room. Another cigarette butt floated in the sloppy toilet water. The bathroom mirror was cracked, and a small handprint—child-sized—marred a white towel still hanging on the rack.

I looked at the handprint, wondering if that delicate little girl had been the source of all this vomit.

But as I pushed against the towel, I realized the handprint was a different color.

The handprint was made of dried blood.

I couldn't find any more answers in Linda Krag's apartment, so I drove home.

I'm sure my neighbors wondered why I hurried out of my car that afternoon, and took the steps to my apartment two at a time.

Jimmy had a half an hour of school left before Franklin picked him and the Grimshaw children up and took them to an after-school program we had started three years ago. If I called Franklin now, I could probably arrange for Jimmy to stay the night.

I wasn't sure I would need all that time, but I figured I had best plan for it.

Linda Krag and her little daughter Annie had been missing for several days. Some would have argued that a few more hours would make no difference, but to me, they would have.

If the woman was in trouble, then every second wasted would be a second closer to her death. Because, if Valentina was right, and Linda Krag had been taken by her husband, that man wouldn't be interested in rebuilding their relationship.

He would punish her.

And he would do it one of several ways. If he was just a man filled with uncontrollable rage, he would beat her until he felt better. But if he was a sadist—and if what Valentina said was true, that Linda Krag's daughter was the most important thing in her life—then he would hurt the daughter to punish the mother.

People who got punched in the stomach hard or repeatedly often vomited, sometimes uncontrollably. I hoped that the amount of vomit in that small bathroom had come from an adult, but there was no way to tell.

I clenched my fists. Then I released the fingers slowly, making myself breathe. I picked up the phone, called Franklin, explained the case—since he was part of Helping Hands too—and asked him to take care of my son for at least the next twenty-four hours.

Then I hung up and set about finding Linda Krag.

Unlike the stuff you see on *Mannix* or *Hawaii 5-0*, detective work is seldom fisticuffs and confessions. Usually it's long and repetitive legwork. I was going to try to cram a week's worth of legwork into a single day.

So I went into my office and made calls.

My office was in the bedroom between mine and Jim's. I decorated it with used office furniture (bought at a bargain when I first moved here), filing cabinets that were nearly full, and a new-fangled answering machine that Laura had bought me. I hadn't taken the thing out of the box yet.

I pushed the box aside, picked up the phone, and called Valentina. She wasn't there, so I left a message, asking if she had found that information for me. I hoped she would call me back while I was still at home.

Then I started a series of calls to area hospitals and doctors' offices. I had found, over the years, that if I put on a slight East Coast accent and spoke a little quicker than I usually did, people gave me information without many questions.

Hospitals, trained to keep some information confidential, were a tougher nut to crack. But my years as an insurance company investigator helped there. If I called Billing and told them I had an unpaid bill from the hospital itself, I usually got full cooperation.

I did this now, saying that I had a bill for my client Linda Krag, without dates of her hospital stay or any listing of her procedure. I couldn't pay the bill unless I had that information.

Billing departments all over the city scrambled to help me. They hand-searched their records. I told them that we had received the bill today, which made us (or more accurately, them) believe that the procedure happened within the past month.

Each call took about fifteen minutes, because the billing person I spoke to did a thorough search. Each call also ended with the same discouraging phrase:

It seemed that Linda Krag had not shown up at any doctor's office or hospital in the Greater Chicago area in the past month. At least, not under that name.

The next thing I did was check the morgues and funeral homes. That was a little easier—with funeral homes, I asked when the Linda Krag funeral was scheduled, and with morgues, I just asked my question in a straightforward manner.

No one had heard of her.

When I finished, I realized I should have asked after her

daughter as well—Annie Krag. But the very idea of searching for death records for a child made my stomach twist.

I thumbed through the phone book, wondering if I could run the same hospital scam for the daughter on the same day, when my phone rang.

It was Valentina.

She gave me an address on the east side of Madison, the husband's full name—Duane G. Krag, age 35, and the make and model of his car, a white 1968 Olds with Missouri plates. Up until three weeks ago, he had worked at the Oscar Mayer plant not far from his home.

I didn't like that last detail at all. "Did he give notice or did he just disappear?"

"He finished his shift on Friday and failed to show up on Monday," she said.

"You got this information how?" I asked.

"A few well-placed phone calls," she said. "I know some people here now."

I didn't quite trust her tone. "You didn't go there, right?"

"No," she said. "I have no reason to. Do I?"

"None," I said.

"Besides," she said. "He's been using his phone."

I leaned back in my chair. "How do you know that?"

"One of my volunteers at the hotline also works for the phone company. It's amazing what they can find out about you."

I bet it was.

"Do you have information for me?" she asked.

"I've been to the apartment," I said. "So if she did leave on her own, she left a lot behind."

I wasn't going to tell her about the vomit or the blood. I had no idea what had happened, so I wasn't going to scare Valentina unnecessarily.

"She wouldn't do that, Smokey." That edge of worry had returned to Valentina's voice.

"I tend to agree with you. I'm about to go back to see if her neighbors saw anything unusual."

She was silent on the other end. I wondered if she could tell that I was withholding information from her.

"I hope you find her," she finally said.

"Me, too," I said. "Me, too."

I hadn't lied to Valentina about one thing: My next step was to return to the neighborhood and ask if anyone saw anything unusual. I didn't relish going back to this neighborhood, but I saw no other choice.

It was already dark when I drove back into the neighborhood, which made me even more uncomfortable. As I approached Linda's block, I debated whether or not I wanted to park there or on a nearby street.

I ended up with no choice. Every parking spot for blocks was taken. I finally found a parking place near a bookstore on 57th, and I walked to the apartment building.

I didn't have a date or an exact incident, but I did my best. I stopped student after student, asking if they had seen the woman with the little blond girl who lived just down the block. Most remembered her—there weren't a lot of children on this street—but none had talked to her.

And no one had seen her for at least a week.

By the time I got to her apartment building, I was feeling discouraged. I took the steps up the porch just as a young man came out of the front door wheeling his bicycle.

His red hair brushed the collar of his coat. He smelled faintly of incense and marijuana. His eyes were clear, however.

He started when he saw me.

"What do you want?" he asked.

"I'm here to see Linda," I said. "I'm a friend of hers from Madison."

He studied me for a minute, then he said, "Linda didn't have any friends in Madison."

Finally, someone who knew her.

"Who told you that?" I asked.

"She did," he said.

"Well, that's a little awkward," I said, trying to seem humble. "She lived next door to me and my wife and we talked all the time. We're in Chicago to see family and I was wondering if she and Annie could join everyone for lunch tomorrow. I guess I thought we were better friends than we were."

The boy shrugged. "Maybe I misunderstood her. We only talked a few times. My roommate knew her better."

"Knew her?" I asked, then realized the question sounded sharp, so I did my best to cover. "Did your roommate move?"

"No," the boy said. "Linda and her husband reconciled.

He said he was taking them back to Madison. I would've thought you knew that, since you lived next door."

I shook my head. "They haven't been back all month," I lied. "He moved out. I thought they were getting a divorce."

"Yeah, that's what I thought," the boy said. "But my roommate—he's Duane's brother—he said it was a love match and all it would take was some persuading."

I shivered, and it wasn't from the growing chill. Someone had clearly been persuaded, and not in a good way.

"I never thought it was a love match," I said, looking at the door, but deliberately not looking at the upstairs window, as if I didn't know which apartment she had lived in.

"I think the whole thing's kinda weird, myself," the boy said. "I was studying for my econ exam when he came to get her. It didn't sound like a love match to me."

"What do you mean?"

The boy shrugged again. "It's none of my business, really."

And he said it in a way that also meant it was none of mine.

"They fought?"

"Nothing like that. But that little girl sure cried hard. I'd never heard a peep from her before that."

"Was she all right?" I couldn't help the question.

The boy looked at me. He was frowning. "You know, I wondered. So I looked out the window. They all got into his car. He put suitcases into the back and Linda, she was holding her daughter. She saw me looking, and she waved at me. So I knew everything was all right."

I started in surprise. I hadn't expected Linda Krag to think of anyone except herself and her daughter. But she had protected her neighbor. By pretending everything was okay, she made sure he didn't intervene.

"When was this?" I asked.

"A week ago Wednesday. I know because the exam was on Thursday." He grinned. "And of course, I aced it."

"Good for you," I said, and hoped it didn't sound patronizing. Then I thanked him, and went back down the stairs.

There was no point in asking anyone else questions.

Duane's brother had clearly alerted him to Linda's presence, probably on the weekend between the time Duane last punched in for work and the Monday when he hadn't shown up. Duane had come here, tried to talk to her, hit her so hard she threw up or hurt the little girl somehow.

Then, when he realized Linda actually knew people here, he took her and Annie out of the apartment. He drove them somewhere.

But the question was where.

I didn't have the capability to track someone like him, even with his white car and Missouri license plates. Ten days was a long time.

And he could have taken her anywhere.

Except, Valentina told me that he had been using his telephone.

He was in Madison, in his old stomping grounds, and if we were lucky, Linda and Annie were still alive.

I didn't break any speed limits heading to Madison, but I wanted to. I wanted to get there as quickly as I could.

Had he kept her in Chicago, I would have had options. I knew people in the police department, I had friends who worked alongside me and could act as back-up. I even knew people who could have discretely checked on the apartment and let me know he was inside.

The only person I knew in Madison was Valentina. And I didn't want to involve her. But I was beginning to think I wasn't going to have a choice.

Because I couldn't see any good way for this to play out.

Madison was a white town. I couldn't just barge into a white man's apartment and demand that he hand over his wife. I couldn't call the police with my suspicions—and they couldn't do anything anyway. A man was entitled to treat his family anyway he liked. Only when things got "out of hand," and the definition of that phrase varied from police department to police department, could the police step in at all.

So as I drove, I tried to formulate a plan, but I couldn't come up with a good one.

I only hoped that Valentina's friends included someone other than the lady who worked for the phone company.

Because otherwise, I was about to make a difficult situation worse.

Valentina's hotline was housed in an old church near Lake Mendota, not far from either the state capitol building or the University of Wisconsin.

I knew better than to show up unannounced at a hotline run primarily by women who dealt daily with rape. The last thing they needed to see was a muscular, scarred Black man pounding on the church door. So I called ahead, leaving Valentina worried, but willing to open the hotline's doors for me.

Three cars were in the parking lot when I showed up around ten. The church looked like it had once been a monstrosity of the Protestant type—some stained windows, but not a lot of iconography. A tasteful cross carved into the brick chimney, but little else besides the building's shape to even suggest it had once been a church.

Valentina was waiting outside, wrapped in a parka that looked two sizes too big for her. She waved as I pulled up, then shifted from foot to foot while I got out of the car.

The minute I stepped outside, I knew why she was dressed so heavily. It was a lot colder here than it was in Chicago. There was also a dusting of snow on the ground, visible under the church's dome light.

Valentina didn't say hello.

"The fact that you're here means something bad is going on, doesn't it, Smokey?"

"Yeah," I said, since there was no reason to lie. "Where can we go to talk about this?"

She led me inside and up a flight of stairs into the former sanctuary. It smelled of freshly cut wood. She flicked a light switch and a dozen overhead lights came on.

Instead of revealing church pews, a choir loft, and an altar, the lights revealed piles of wood, several saws, and some half-built walls.

She waved a hand at it. "We need room for women to stay overnight, and after what most of them have been through, we can't ask them to share a room like some kind of church shelter."

"Overnight?" I asked as I stepped over a pile of 2x4s.

"So many won't go home after they've been raped. They won't go to the hospital, and they won't see a friend, particularly if they've been battered. Most don't have money for a hotel room either." She ran a hand through her short hair. "Actually, it was Linda who gave me this idea. She was so afraid of Duane."

She let the words hang. We stopped near stairs that had clearly once led to the altar. Someone had pulled the carpet off them, and one of the stairs to my left had already been dismantled. But we sat on the top step, surveying the work in progress.

"I take it the hotline itself is somewhere else," I said.

"In the basement," she said. "I figured it was best if my volunteers didn't know what was going on."

I nodded. As carefully as I could, I told her what I had learned. I also told her that I had come to find Linda.

"You can't go to that neighborhood at night," Valentina said.

"I can't go period," I said. "No one can walk up to the door of that apartment and ask Duane Krag what he did with his wife and daughter."

Valentina rested her elbows on her knees. To her credit, she didn't say I told you so nor did she reprimand Helping Hands for not searching for Linda sooner.

"What can we do?" she asked.

"We can't do anything," I said. "But I need some information from you. Tell me about those apartments."

She frowned for a moment. Then she said, "They're single-story, low-income housing."

"Government built?"

"Yes, with Model Cities money," she said, citing one of the many Johnson era programs that Nixon had dismantled in his first term. "They were built to look like row houses, so that each family could feel like they had privacy."

"But they're attached?"

"Yes," she said.

"They're government buildings. They should have fire alarms. Do they?"

She frowned. "It's not something I normally notice, and I was there three months ago, not really paying attention. But the city is pretty anal about making sure every building follows code. This place isn't like Chicago at all. No one can buy off a building inspector."

I nodded, hoping that was the case. "Then the buildings have to have fire alarms. The trick is where."

"I have an idea," she said. "I'll tell you mine, if you tell me yours."

"Done," I said, and then told her what I was planning.

Of course, she wouldn't let me go alone. I should have known that when I arrived outside the hotline building. I had forgotten how stubborn Valentina could be.

"You have to do exactly what I tell you," I said as we drove to the apartment complex.

Madison at night was pretty deserted. On the wide swatch of East Washington Avenue, I had only seen two other cars. I drove underneath well-tended streetlight after well-tended streetlight, past warehouses and buildings from the turn of the century.

No one could break into one of those buildings without drawing some kind of attention, even though the streets were empty.

"I will do exactly what you say, Smokey," Valentina said with some bemusement. "You don't have to keep repeating that."

"I just don't want you hurt," I said. "If the cops show up, you have to get out. Is that clear?"

"I know a cop to call," she said. "We'll be all right."

I glanced at her. She was staring straight ahead, the light playing across her face. The occasional shadows hid the hollows in her cheeks and she looked a lot more like the woman I had met four years ago.

"Is he one of your contacts?" I asked.

"I have to know everyone from police officers to the best criminal attorneys," she said. "I'm getting quite a list."

I nodded. "Well, they're not going to like what we're about to do."

"Don't like it," she said. "I just don't see any other choice."

Neither did I.

She gave me good directions to the apartment complex. I drove past it once, to see it for myself.

It was already starting to look worn. The hope that the city had placed in its low-income housing had faded with the Johnson Administration. But there were still things that made this place unusual.

It had functioning lights over every front door. Each apartment number was clearly marked. The sidewalks in front of each apartment had been shoveled. None of the windows were boarded up, and none had security bars either.

The lights were on in the Krags' living room. Someone had pulled the curtains against the outside, but I could see the flickering shadows of a television set.

Someone was inside.

Which made me sigh with relief.

Just like driving past the building's side, and seeing a giant fire alarm built onto the outside wall.

"Looks like you were right," I said to Valentina.

"It was the only logical place," she said. "I'm going to have to run to pull two alarms."

"It's necessary," I said. "I don't want him to think that we've targeted his building."

"Okay," she said. "Drop me off here. The parking lot is—"

"I'm going to park in front of his apartment," I said.

"He'll see you."

"It's all right," I said. "I know what I'm doing."

Unfortunately, I had snuck into neighborhoods before. I knew how to do it, and do it well.

I dropped Valentina on the corner, then went around

the block. She was supposed to wait five minutes before she went anywhere near that first alarm.

I hoped she listened.

As I got ready to turn back onto the Krag's street, I turned off the car's lights and took my foot off the gas. I coasted to a stop in front of his sidewalk, and shut off the ignition.

Then I unscrewed the dome light. I opened the driver's door as quietly as I could, and slipped out, careful not to close the door too tightly.

Staying on the street, I walked around the corner. There was no alarm on this side, but I didn't expect one. The alarm was on the other end of the building, hidden in that alcove between two buildings.

I waited at the front corner of the building, in the shadows so that I could see the street but no one could see me.

Then an alarm clanged. It sounded very far away.

Another followed. The second one was deafening.

Valentina had been right; Madison's low-income housing was up to code.

Now we'd see how long it took the fire department to respond to a major fire.

I hoped it was a long time.

People started shouting and screaming. Families came out the front doors, wearing bathrobes and pajamas, barefoot against the cold.

I silently apologized to them.

No one came out of Duane's apartment.

Families, carrying children, holding blankets, turned and

looked at their homes. Voices rose in confusion at the lack of smoke and flames.

Valentina ran to my side. No one seemed to notice her in all the chaos.

"Where are they?" she asked.

"No one came out," I said.

"What are we going to do?"

I was about to tell her that I would break in the back, when the door banged open. The little girl came out wearing footie pajamas. Her hair was a rat's nest and she was sobbing.

"Help me! Help me!" she yelled. "My mommy won't come. My mommy won't come."

"Get her to the car," I said as I sprinted for the main door. I didn't want anyone else to answer her summons.

So far, no one had noticed her. They were still talking and yelling and looking in the opposite direction.

Valentina ran at my side. We reached the little girl at the same time.

"Annie," Valentina said, crouching in front of her and putting her hands on the girl's shoulders. "We're going to get your mom out."

"*Get her to the car,*" I repeated, then pushed the door open.

The apartment was a jumbled mess—overturned chairs, a ripped couch. The television was on, but no one was watching it.

That sour smell was here too, and it turned my stomach.

I hurried down the corridors, checking the kitchen, then the bathroom, and finally one of the bedrooms. The interior smelled of old blood.

I flicked on the light.

A body was leaning against the wall, a spray of blood behind it, and a pool of blood below. It took me a second to realize that the body did not belong to Linda Krag.

It was a man's body. It had to be Duane.

Sirens started in the distance, very faint, but growing.

I cursed.

A gun was on the bed.

I left it there and checked the other bedroom.

Linda Krag was huddled in her daughter's bed, eyes wide. "Leave me," she said, but I didn't know if she was talking to me or just repeating what she had been saying to her daughter.

I wasn't even sure she had seen me.

I scooped her in my arms. She moaned when I picked her up. I carried her down that hallway. I could feel dried blood against her skin, but I didn't know if it was hers or his. She hadn't showered in days. The stench of her made my eyes water.

The sirens were getting closer.

I hurried out of the building. People were wandering around, searching for the fire. In the distance, I could see flashing red lights.

Valentina was standing beside my car, leaning on the passenger door. Annie was inside the car, in the back seat.

"Open up," I said.

She didn't have to be told twice. She opened the door to the back seat. Annie leaned forward and Valentina shooed her away.

I put Linda inside. She toppled toward her daughter, but I didn't care.

We had to get out of there.

"Get inside," I said to Valentina as I pushed the door closed.

She did. I got in the driver's side, and started the car all in the same move. Then I backed around the corner, so that no one could see my plates. I backed the entire block, then turned right, away from the apartment buildings, heading toward East Washington Avenue.

"Screw in the dome light," I said to Valentina.

She gave me a funny look, visible in the streetlights, then did as she was told.

"What are we doing?" she asked.

"I'm dropping you off, then we're going to Chicago."

She leaned over the back seat. "Linda needs medical attention."

"She's not getting it here," I said.

"Smokey," Valentina said.

"You didn't ask me where Duane was," I said.

She looked at me. "Where's Duane?"

"Daddy's dead," Annie said in a very small voice.

"Jesus," Valentina said, looking at me. "What happened?"

"Don't know," I said. "Don't want to know. And this is the last we're going to say about it. Right, Annie?"

"Smokey," Valentina said, reprimanding me for my tone.

"Right, Annie?" I repeated.

"Okay," Annie said.

The capitol dome loomed in the distance. We were only a few miles from the hotline.

"Where are you taking them?" Valentina asked.

"Back to Helping Hands. We'll find them a new apartment," I said. "Can you get into the back seat, and see if Linda will make it all the way to Chicago?"

"I'll make it." Linda whispered the words. "I'm just fine. Thank you."

I was relieved to hear her respond directly to me. But I knew she wasn't just fine. She wasn't protesting my presence like she had the first time I tried to take her to Chicago.

"I'm going with you," Valentina said to me.

"No," I said.

"You need me," she said.

I turned toward her, trying to keep at least part of my gaze on the road. "Maybe you don't understand. I am about to commit a felony. I don't want you involved."

"Don't," Linda said from the back. "We'll be all right."

"If I take you to a Madison hospital," I said to Linda, "they'll arrest you and take Annie. Do you want that?"

"Nooo." The reply was soft, and I wasn't sure if it came from Linda or Annie herself.

"Jesus," Valentina said.

"So," I said to Valentina, "I'm taking you home."

"No," Valentina said. "You need me. They need me. We'll work this out. I'll take a bus home tomorrow."

The truth was, I did need her. I needed her to monitor Linda's condition. I needed her to keep Annie calm.

I needed her to keep an eye out, to make sure we weren't being followed.

"All right," I said. "Let's get the hell out of here."

Three hours and one furtive gas stop later put us in Chicago at four in the morning. I drove immediately to the hospital nearest my house.

Valentina blanched as we pulled into the parking lot. I had driven her there once, saving her life and changing it forever.

Linda had passed out sometime along the drive, but she was breathing evenly. I had Valentina bring Annie inside. I carried Linda.

The emergency staff took her from me, placing her on a cart. In the florescent hospital lights, it became clear that she was bruised everywhere. The cast on her arm from her previous injury was cracked and ruined. And there was dried blood around her mouth and nose.

"What happened?" The emergency room nurse asked me. She was glaring.

"Her husband happened," I said, deciding not to lie about that at least. I lied about the rest, though. "She lives next door to us. I couldn't just leave her there."

"Good thing you didn't," the nurse said, and wheeled her away.

I stayed and filled out the paperwork, using my own apartment building as Linda's address, and making up a last name for her. I figured the hospital would never check, and Helping Hands would cover the bills.

Valentina took Annie to the waiting room while I worked. When I finished, I followed them there.

They were alone in the room. Newspapers were scattered around them. Valentina had used one to cover Annie. Valentina had fallen asleep in the chair by the door, Annie on the couch near her.

I sat down, my heart pounding.

Now I would have to deal with my split-second decision. Obviously Linda couldn't take the beatings any longer, and she had shot Duane in the face. Then she collapsed. Annie hadn't known what to do or maybe was too frightened to move, until the fire alarm forced her out of the building.

They might have been alone with that corpse for a week or more, until the neighbors reported something. Then the police would have come, charged Linda with murder, put Annie in foster care, and no one would have heard of them again.

No one would have cared that Linda had been repeatedly beaten within an inch of her life. Her only hope would have been an insanity plea, which probably would not have worked—especially since the prosecutor would have said that she had run away from Duane before, and she clearly did not want to be with him.

I was giving Helping Hands a hell of a burden—the damaged mother, the terrified child—but I figured we could deal with it. And if someone determined that Linda was no longer fit to care for her child, we would find Annie a good home, a sympathetic home, one that would help her grow and overcome these last few years.

I'd seen that work. It had worked with my son Jimmy.

Annie sighed and twitched in her sleep. The newspaper fell off her, and I picked it up, gently putting it back over her.

Then I looked at her, really looked at her, for the first time since we picked her up.

She had an ugly bruise on her forehead. It was black and purple and it had seeped down to her nose. Something had hit her hard there.

I felt a quick anger at Duane, and then I froze. I looked at her hand, dangling down toward the floor.

Her thumb was bruised too. And there was a pinch mark on her index finger—the kind you got when you didn't know how to properly hold a gun.

My breath caught. The bruises lined up. If she had held the gun on her father, and the gun had gone off, the recoil would have sent her hands backwards, hitting her forehead with enough force to make that bruise.

Daddy's dead, she had said.

And her mother was in Annie's room, not the adults' bedroom.

Hiding?

Letting her daughter defend her?

I shivered just a little. I didn't want to know, and I wasn't going to ask. I had already broken enough laws for these two. I would let the experts from Helping Hands work with them—and I would never mention my suspicions.

I had brought them here—risked at least two felony charges—so that they could stay together.

I wasn't going to be the one to get in the way of that.

Valentina stirred. "How's Linda?" she asked sleepily.

"Badly beaten," I said. "But they think she'll be all right."

"Good." Valentina looked at Annie. "Bastard beat her too. I had someone look at the bruise. She doesn't have a concussion."

"That's a relief," I said.

Valentina was still looking at the sleeping child. "Think they'll be all right?"

"At least now they have a chance," I said.

And no one could ask for more than that.

SWEET YOUNG THINGS
A SWEET YOUNG THINGS STORY

KRISTINE KATHRYN RUSCH

P awnshops were all the same. Crowded with junk, reeking of cigarette smoke, they always had one guy who hadn't bathed in a week sitting behind a glass counter. The counter was the only thing that had been cleaned in twenty years.

Fala rested her palms against the countertop, feeling the warmth of the glass beneath her skin. Old lights illuminated the jewelry inside. Some of it glistened. Much of it was as worthless as the junk on the walls—old class rings, Masonic pins, cheap rosaries—but some of it had possibilities. A garnet ring with emeralds on the side, clearly 1950s. A Tiffany pin, all gold, shiny and complete. A grandmother ring, ostentatious with its twenty different jewels, half a dozen of them small rubies.

Estate jewelry. Desperation jewelry. The last of a large lot.

"Sixty-five dollars," the scrawny guy said, taking the

jeweler's eye from his own. His fingernails were black, and his hair was matted against his skull.

She reserved her shiver of distaste for later. The ring he held was worth four thousand, minimum. The diamond was an emerald cut from the 1920s, rare these days, and the setting was pure white gold.

"A hundred and fifty," she said.

"Lady—"

"C'mon," she said, trying to sound whiney. "It was my grandmother's. I doubt I'm coming back for it. At least give me something."

"A hundred." The ring clinked as he set it on the countertop.

"I need a hundred and fifty."

He wouldn't get a deal like that anywhere else, but then again, he wouldn't turn it around that quickly either. She knew how it worked, maybe better than he did.

"You're lucky I'm a soft touch." He reached the shelf behind the counter, tapped the old-fashioned cash register, and it opened with the ring of a bell. She hadn't heard that sound since she'd been in college.

He handed her six twenties and a ten, all crumpled, all feeling slightly greasy. She counted them, forcing her hands to shake as if she couldn't believe her good fortune.

Actually, she was making sure each bill was legit. The last time she'd done this, in Detroit, she'd gotten two counterfeit twenties, all the "unduplicatable" kind. But the bills she held in her hand this time came from the last century: none of that phony color Monopoly money stuff.

She shoved them in her right-hand pocket as he filled out

the brown ticket with her fake name and address. He slid the top half back to her. She put that in her left pocket, knowing she'd lose that little stub within a day.

Not that she cared. The ring hadn't been her grandmother's and she wasn't here for the money.

She'd come to check out the place before she made the owner an offer he couldn't refuse.

Division Street in Gresham, Oregon, still wore its 1950s roots with pride. Once the main drag in a city that had once been more than a suburb, Division had decaying supper clubs with faulty neon lights, taverns with one single greasy window up front, and more pawnshops than any other stretch in the Portland metropolitan area.

If you drove with your eyes half-closed, you could see how classy this place had been: an overgrown golf course hugged the bend in the road, and motels that advertised color television led into a development of 1950's houses twice the size of an ordinary ranch.

There'd been money here once—not a lot, but enough to give its residents a sense of power and pride. But sometime in the '70s, the highway bypassed Division, taking the important business traffic with it, and nearly killed the street. The moneyed elite either moved to Portland proper or watched sickness and old age eat away their tiny pot of gold.

The houses got shabbier, the businesses rattier, and the neighborhood filled with outsiders who had too many babies and bought their clothing at Wal-Mart.

Fala had known it was the perfect place the moment she'd driven past the newly opened discount cigarette store, right next to the boarded-up bank. It was only a matter of time before Preston Lidner—or someone like him—would show.

She bought the Fast Cash Pawn Shop for two-hundred-thousand-dollars cash, about a hundred-and-fifty thousand more than it was worth. The business might've been a going concern twenty years ago, when it'd been the only pawnshop on Division, but now it had rivals on every block, most of them computer savvy and willing to take the absolute junk for much higher prices.

Behold the great god eBay.

In the back, beneath a decade's worth of newspapers, she found a four-foot high cast-iron safe with a combination lock. She called a locksmith from Portland, had him reconfigure the lock, and, the moment he left, placed the estate jewelry inside. She set up her computer, added a DSL line, and established more firewalls than she really needed.

Then she spent the next two days combing through the junk, looking for the buried valuables, and placed them in the back as well. When she got a chance, she'd take the larger items to a storage unit she had just rented. The storage unit was at the edge of Lake Oswego, another once-independent city that had become one of Portland's high-end neighborhoods.

Her new home, though, was a trashy apartment at the

edge of Division, in a concrete cinderblock building that had never seen better days. Every morning when she went to work, she tucked her long hair under a Seattle Mariners baseball cap and put a fresh pack of Pall Malls in her purse, next to the scratched vintage lighter she'd found in Topeka.

She kept her nails short, but painted them ruby red, wore matching lipstick, a little too much blush, and fake eyelashes that brushed against her upper cheeks every time she blinked. She made sure all her denim shirts were one size too small. She tied them at the waist, left them unbuttoned, and wore a bustier beneath them instead of a bra. Her stonewashed jeans, all of them ripped at the knees, were too tight. Every day, she matched the color of her high heels to the color of her bustier, and she'd disappear into the shop, determined to impress no one.

The first week, not a single customer pushed open the grimy glass door. She spent her days watching the black-and-white 12-inch television the greasy-haired former employee had left her.

The second week, she had a couple of customers, and they were elderly, just like she expected, looking to sell rather than buy. She gave the old man a fair price for his 1950s Timex and lied to him when he tried to sell her his grandfather's pocket watch, telling him she had too many pocket watches right now.

The elderly lady's eyes teared up when she tried to pawn a gold brooch that looked like a peacock's tail. It only took a little prodding to get her to admit that her husband had given it to her on their twentieth anniversary oh-so-long ago.

Fala pushed the brooch back across the countertop, but

paid nearly two hundred dollars for the Bakelite bangle bracelets the old lady wore on her right arm. The bracelets weren't even worth one-tenth that.

The old woman had clutched the brooch to her heart as she left, eyes still filled with unshed tears.

Damn Preston or whatever the hell he was calling himself these days. Damn him forever for bringing her here, and forcing her to make choices she never would have considered ten years before.

T en years before, she'd been twenty-five, newly divorced, and naïve as hell. She'd been pretty too, in a wholesome all-American girl way, with her rounded cheeks and bright blue eyes and not-quite-blonde hair. Anyone looking at her had to trust her, because she wore every emotion she'd ever had all over her unlined face.

Preston had been five years into his business then, and thinking of making a change. Only she hadn't known that. All she'd known were two things: he'd hired her despite her lack of experience, and he was the most dynamic man she'd ever met.

Dynamic: that was a word she hadn't understood until Preston. He wasn't conventionally handsome—his nose was too wide, his eyes too small—and he wasn't very tall. But he had a beautiful head of shiny black hair, so thick every woman longed to run her hands through it. His mouth was generous, and his smile was endearingly crooked—just like he turned out to be.

She'd been lonely, she'd been hurt, and she'd been broke, all three of which made her the perfect shill for H.T. Corrent Investments, the company that Preston supposedly owned.

He'd been brilliant, even then. He'd rented office space in a brand-new building, bought furniture at a tax liquidation, and set up all three rooms as if he'd just moved in. Boxes sat in the corners, all of them labeled with a date and a letter of the alphabet, all of them taped shut so thoroughly that only a lot of work with a knife or a straight razor would get them open.

Dusty filing cabinets filled the smallest room, along with an early '80s microwave and a half-sized refrigerator. Preston's office had the large desk and an oversize leather chair, along with some photos which, Fala later learned, he'd bought at an estate sale.

Out front, a middle-aged woman sat behind a smaller desk, working the phones. She kept a pencil in her sprayed hair, and wore a sweater against the chill of the air-conditioner. Other women, all under the age of thirty, sat in chairs along the wall, waiting for their turn to be interviewed.

They'd gone inside one-by-one, and Preston had smiled at the group each time he closed the door, as if he expected to get lucky with each and every one of them.

He'd gotten lucky with Fala and her favorite pair of black shoes, which fell apart—literally—as she walked through his office door. She'd tripped, leaving the sole of her right shoe on the threshold. Preston had picked it up, ever so gallantly, and that crooked smile of his had turned into the widest grin she'd ever seen.

"Now that you've established how badly you need the job," he'd said, "how about answering a few questions?"

She'd been so mortified that her cheeks felt like they would burn off. She'd pressed her hands against them, trying to cool them, and refused to look in his eyes as he went through her one-paragraph resume.

When he gave her the job two days later, he'd told her it was because of the shoe.

That was probably the only time in their entire relationship that Preston hadn't lied.

The signs went up a month after she bought the pawnshop. This time, they'd been professionally printed, with the word "cash" in such large letters that a driver could see it from the street.

When she arrived at work that morning, she saw one on the telephone pole half a block away, and her stomach gave a little lurch. Other people stapled signs to telephone poles and headed those signs with the word "cash" in gigantic black letters. But she knew, even before she walked those last few yards, that someone in Preston's employ had stayed up all night, walking the streets and stapling.

CASH!!
Planning to sell your home?
We'll give you cash on the dollar this week!

Fala memorized the phone number at the bottom of the

list, and then walked away as if the notice meant nothing to her. Still, she opened her purse, grabbed the unopened Pall Malls, and pulled them out, her blunt-edged fingernails finding the edge of the cellophane wrapper. She opened the package like a chain smoker missing her fix, tapped out the first cigarette and stuffed it in her mouth before she realized what she was doing.

By that point, she was at the shop's front door. She left the cigarette in her mouth as she unlocked the door.

Only when she got inside did she toss the cigarette in the nearest wastebasket. Her hands shook. She shoved her purse under the counter, placing one foot on top of the open leather top, before she was sure she wouldn't grab another cigarette.

Then she reached for the phone, dialed a number she hadn't used in nearly two months, and counted the rings. At ten, someone picked up.

"He's here," Fala said, and broke the connection.

The hell of it was, the only job she had ever loved was her job at H.T. Corrent. Every day, she'd drive to the office, get a list of prospects from Reggie, the office manager, then head to the first appointment. Fala always arrived two minutes late, per Preston's instruction. Get the clients looking around, get them interested, get them antsy.

She'd thought it smart then. Only later did she realize that the manipulation occurred long before she arrived on the scene.

Most of the people she met were young marrieds or professors about to take their first assignment. She never thought it strange that none of them were locals. She'd never worked as a rental agent before; she didn't realize that in most rental agencies, especially in a college town, 95 percent of the clients already lived here and were simply looking to upgrade.

She was happy to show these wonderful people the small rental homes, walking them through the empty rooms, describing how the place would look with a couch over there and a bed over there and the perfect table just below that window.

People loved her and they trusted her. Most of them never came back to the office, instead filling out an application right then and there, writing a check for the security deposit to get the process started. Preston had been so very smart—his rental houses were cheaper than the rest, easier to get into. He didn't add first and last month's rent to the security deposit. He demanded just enough to seem legitimate.

We have to trust them from the start, he'd said to Fala, and that was what she said to the clients. *We trust you. We're going to be in this together for the long haul.*

She was better than Preston expected. She'd rented all 200 units that he had scattered throughout the city in less than two weeks. She was a natural-born saleswoman with a true interest in people, and she worked as hard as she could to place the right renters with the right house.

When she'd finished, she asked Preston what the next

stage was, and he'd smiled at her. That crooked, crocked smile.

Now we manage, he said.

That last week, she'd stayed in the office, filing all those fulfilled applications in the new drawer, first by client's name, then by property address. All the other filing drawers were locked, but because she was so new, she thought nothing of that either.

That last morning, she'd been the first one in the office, just like usual. She'd put on the coffee, tuned the radio to NPR, and started answering the phones while she waited for Reggie. The first call was strange: a hysterical woman wanting to make sure she had the right address.

Fala had been warned not to give information over the phone—that was Reggie's job—so she promised to have Reggie call back.

But Reggie didn't show, and neither did Preston, and by noon, every call had an angry person on the other end, demanding addresses, demanding keys, demanding money back. Finally, Fala turned off all the phones, let the service handle the crisis, and headed to the nearest address.

It was also her favorite, a tiny one-bedroom on the edge of campus, with a view of the nearby lake. A small U-Haul van was parked against the curb, the passenger door open, and a woman sitting forlornly on the front steps. When Fala got out of her car, the woman ran to her.

"You gave me the wrong address," the woman said.

But Fala hadn't given her the wrong address. Fala remembered her; this woman had rented this house, and was supposed to move in on this day. But the house had furniture inside now, and an upset man who claimed he owned the place.

Fala tried to reason with him, but he screamed at her. So she drove to the nearest pay phone and called the police.

She returned to the house to discover that the police had already arrived.

The phone number Fala took off the sign belonged to a landline that rang in an office several blocks away. The office, in a new complex near the MAX train line, fit Preston's M.O. perfectly: rent in a new space, buy old furniture and pack several boxes with newspapers, seal them, and make it look like you're still moving in. The smell of new paint always convinced, as did all the empty office suites still for rent down the hall.

Once she found the landline, her job got easier. She decided to go old-fashioned instead of high tech, splicing into the line late one night. She could record off-site, just like the feds used to do in all their investigations. No one looked for low-tech anymore; they had firewalls and virus protection and spyware, but no one expected a simple bug in the line, established at the routers in the basement, routers that wouldn't get checked in a building so new, not even if there was some kind of outage.

She was amazed at the skills she'd learned in the last few years: how to enter an empty office building without anyone getting suspicious, waiting in the dark in an unrented office suite until everyone had gone home, working the basement lines with a flashlight between her teeth.

Technically, she hadn't done any breaking and entering. She hadn't broken at all, and she'd entered during normal business hours. She hadn't stolen anything, nor had she left any fingerprints down on the lines.

And if she played this right, no one would get hurt.

No one, except Preston, of course.

The police arrested her for two hundred counts of fraud. Preston and Reggie were long gone, leaving the office, filled with her fingerprints only, and empty file cabinets—except, of course, the one drawer that was unlocked, the drawer with four hundred files, two hundred by client name, two hundred by address, all the information in Fala's handwriting, and all the forms touched only by Fala's hand.

By Fala's reckoning, Preston had skipped town with more than one-hundred-and-fifty thousand dollars for three weeks work. For that same amount of time, Fala had received $810 gross pay, three nights in jail, and a legal nightmare that would extend for the next three years.

It'd been a brilliant plan. Preston had scouted real estate records, found empty houses that had just sold, called the real estate agents, identified himself as a welcome wagon volunteer, and asked for the closing dates. Most of the time, he got them.

He only picked vacant houses whose closing dates were

at least a month out. In a college town, such places proliferated in the summer. He waited until the lockboxes came off, then broke in, and changed locks only on the doorknob itself. The deadbolts remained the same. He carefully left the deadbolts unlocked and locked only the doorknobs, giving himself—and Fala—access throughout the entire month.

Once the place rented to some poor unsuspecting sap from out of town, Preston returned to the house, unlocked the doorknob and locked the deadbolt from the inside, leaving by a side window.

It was a variation on an old scam, renting the same apartment to a dozen unsuspecting people, all of whom showed up on move-in day, and duked it out among themselves. Preston's version was more sophisticated, and probably wouldn't have caused an immediate crisis, if one man hadn't received permission to move in one week before his closing was finalized.

None of the stiffed renters had ever seen Preston or done more than speak to Reggie on the phone. For all they knew, Reggie could have been Fala disguising her voice. Fala's first break came her third day in jail when the attorney she hired with the hundred dollars she'd managed to scrounge from her ailing bank account found the owner of the office building. Preston had been cautious; he'd rented the office sight unseen, over the phone.

But the owner, conscientious and a bit paranoid, had dropped in unexpectedly that first week to make sure his new clients liked their brand-new office space. He saw Reggie and Preston and the entire set-up. Then a few of the other applicants came forward, remembering that series of interviews. A few of them even remembered Fala.

Still, she remained under suspicion, and every so often, the police would drag her to the station for no apparent reason. The stiffed renters all sued her and she found herself on the evening news, running from cameras, her purse raised high to hide her face.

She couldn't get work, she couldn't get help, and she couldn't leave town.

She had no money.

Her lawyer quit because she couldn't pay him, and she got evicted. She slept in her car for two weeks before she finally gave up and called her ex-husband.

He loaned her enough money to start her revenge.

Half a dozen calls had already come through the landline before Fala decided to make her own. She was sitting in the back of the pawnshop, staring at another unlit cigarette, as she listened to that day's recording.

"Herbert, Steinmen, and Wilkes. May I help you?"

To Fala's relief, the woman's voice sounded nothing like Reggie's. Either Reggie wasn't a part of this scheme or she had moved upstairs, delegating the receptionist role to someone else.

Most of the callers were elderly, inquiring about the flyer. One caller sounded like a real estate agent: he was told to call back in a week.

That gave Fala a double confirmation of her timeline:

the flyer had said *this week*, and the real estate agent, whom Preston wouldn't deal with, had to call back next week. Preston expected to be done in just a few days.

It made sense. When Fala had found his flyers in Detroit, the phone number had already been routed to a calling service. She'd traced him to Topeka and managed to speak to someone on the phone, but no one occupied the office when she arrived.

He'd always been one step ahead of her, and she was getting tired of it. Years of research, fundraising, and planning; extra points for anticipating. It helped that Preston had gone more or less legitimate.

It also helped that he liked patterns.

So did she.

Patterns had saved her the first time. The new lawyer, the one she hired with her ex-husband's money, said she'd get off the hook if she could prove Preston had done this over and over again, always leaving some sweet young thing to hold the bag.

Of course, the emphasis was on her proving it; no one else was going to do the work, not even the new lawyer and the detectives employed by his fancy firm.

Her scam had been his biggest. Later, she learned it was his last hurrah. He'd been in real estate long enough now to realize there were legitimate ways to make a fortune by doing very little work; all it took was the same kind of planning he'd been doing, and this time, no one could touch him.

But that was in the future. In the past, he'd left a trail of broken promises, empty office suites, and people sobbing in their U-Haul trucks. When Fala looked deeper, she also found one other thing he left behind: a gaggle of sweet young things, all impoverished, who had ended up with the blame.

Fala could guess which homeowners Preston had approached; she certainly knew which neighborhood they were in. But she didn't want to go door-to-door. That would make her suspicious, and she'd worked hard this last month avoiding suspicion.

Unfortunately, she hadn't made many inroads anywhere else either. Her pawnshop had almost no clientele. The bar next door was filled with elderly male vets who had no room for a middle-aged female, no matter how slutty she dressed, and the supper clubs were nearly empty, on the verge of closing.

She had made a few nodding acquaintances, but no one who would confide in her. No one who would help. If anything, she was as suspicious as someone who knocked on doors and offered cash; she hadn't realized that Oregonians —especially those in the old neighborhoods that had once been real cities—didn't trust any newcomer. Either you'd lived in the state most of your life, or you were an outsider, pure and simple.

So she had to do it the risky way, which, she acknowledged late at night, was the way she preferred. She'd set up for it from the beginning, but that was overplanning. The only way the operation could work was if she covered all contingencies.

She called Preston's new office which sounded like a law firm, but could just as easily be a brokerage firm or a mortgage broker or a group of certified public accountants. She noticed that no one ever put a designation after the names, and there wasn't one on the door. Just Herbert, Steinmen, and Wilkes. Three very solid, three very trustworthy names.

When the new receptionist answered, Fala made herself sound hesitant. "I'm calling about your signs?"

"Yes?" The receptionist was all business. "How can we help you?"

"It's not me exactly," Fala said. "It's my grandma. She wanted me to call for her."

Then she put her hand over the phone, and mumbled. She deepened her voice, as if someone were responding, and kept twisting her hand, so that the receptionist heard only voices and that scratchy clutchy sound of flesh against plastic.

"Sorry," Fala said when she got back to the phone. "Is your sign really right? Do you mean cash this week?"

"Yes, ma'am. We'll buy your house from you, and pay you immediately. There'll be a lot of paperwork to sign. Does your grandmother own her home outright?"

And so it went. The receptionist alternated between explaining the very familiar procedure of a home sale done without the intervention of a real estate agent or a standard lender, and adding little queries of her own: how much was the home worth? Where was it located? What kind of condition was it in?

"Of course, we'll have to inspect, but only after you talk to us. We prefer to see you in person, just to make certain everything is on the up and up," the receptionist said.

Fala wondered how she could make that statement and still sound sincere. Or perhaps the receptionist was the person in the Fala position: the young, naïve, nearly broke good girl who would do anything her boss asked.

There were so many young women like that in so many towns; it was one of the many reasons Preston had had the success that he'd had.

Fala had found three sweet young things in her own state, four more two states over, and five scattered throughout the Midwest. It hadn't been easy; she'd spent weeks in the university library, reading the local sections of various newspapers, hoping for an article about the people who had moved to a town believing they had rented an apartment when they actually hadn't.

She wrote down the names, the towns, and the dates, and realized just how patterned Preston had been. First, he picked college towns, with definite move-in, move-out times. He targeted professors, young marrieds, and families because they usually didn't have rich parents who would chase him to the ends of the earth. They would swallow the loss, and move on, although not happily, and certainly not well.

She found two suicides that she could attribute to

Preston's actions: men who were on their last legs, hoping to make a go of it in one more town, only to discover that someone had stolen their very last dime. She'd found several more divorces—those young marrieds couldn't handle the strain, and split up—and an even larger number of children who lived in poverty, because their parents lost the opportunity that had brought them to the big, bad city and sent them spiraling back to the welfare office.

But, with the exception of the suicides, they weren't the worst off. The worst off were the girls, the young ladies, the innocents who had happily taken a job with a rental agency, only to find themselves holding the bag for fraud.

The lawyer used them to get a judge to dismiss all the cases against Fala. He also used them to make the police leave her alone, and to interest the FBI in Preston Lidner, who happened to be running scams across state lines.

But Fala used those girls—women now—for a different purpose.

She used them for revenge.

Fala sat at her kitchen table, her feet crossed at the ankles, her red high heels resting on the back of her ratty couch. The apartment smelled of old grease and newly fried bacon. An untouched BLT rested on the Formica tabletop, half a foot away from Fala's tapping index finger.

"No," she said into her disposable cell phone, "I don't have proof it's him, but I know it's him. And besides, if it's not, it's someone just like him who has to be stopped."

Tess, the woman on the other end of the phone, sighed heavily. She'd heard the argument before; Fala knew that because she'd made it. Twice she'd been right—Topeka and Detroit; three times, she'd been wrong. But in those three cases, the Club, as they called their organization, had still managed to salvage something from the mess.

"Just send the team," Fala said, "and hurry. He expects to be done by Monday."

Then she hung up, her finger still tapping. She reached for her purse, which sat on the counter near the landline she'd gotten for her pawnshop owner persona, a phone that had only rung five times in the month-plus that she'd lived here. She had her hand on the purse's leather strap before she realized what she was going for: those Pall Malls, now open, luring her with an ever-so-tantalizing memory of their taste.

Fala dropped the purse strap and closed her eyes. Smoking was one of her many legacies from Preston. Smoking and fingernail biting and the inability to trust.

She thought she'd been hurt by her divorce, but it turned out her only mistake had been marrying much too young. Her ex-husband had been more of a support than she had expected during the long years of her post-Preston recovery. Her ex hadn't been interested in rekindling the romance, but he had taught her the meaning of friendship, and it had been a valuable lesson.

It enabled her to work with the Club now, to make choices that benefited everyone, and to interact on an equal level.

She hadn't been able to do that at any other job. After

Preston, she never believed her employer would stick around; she always asked why she had to sign a particular paper or how come she was the only one assigned to a certain task.

Like all those others touched by the hand of Preston Lidner, she ended up damaged in ways she couldn't completely comprehend.

At first, the Club had no idea how to proceed. At first, they weren't even a club. They didn't have a name or an organization or a meeting room. They didn't even live in the same town.

Fala put them together. She figured a group of women, ten strong, could do anything they wanted to. The first thing they did, before they even met, was find more women. In little more than five years, at a minimum of four scams a year, Preston had ruined the lives of more than twenty sweet young things.

Fala wasn't sure what they could do. She had envisioned all the sweet young things finding Preston and making him pay, a kind of all-women's detective agency. But it was Tess who figured out what their mission had to be.

Under Preston's guidance, they had hurt hundreds of families. It became the mission of the Club to help those families heal.

Soon, though, they realized they couldn't help the actual families heal. Some of the hurt was years in the past; people had disappeared, lives had ended. Instead, Tess said, they had to help others in need, figure out a way to provide transitional housing, cheap mortgages, and easy credit.

The Club couldn't do any of that while its own members were having trouble, and so the first focus became reassembling their own lives. Fala came up with a way to do that. The women switched apartments with each other—all of them subletting in different cities, places where they weren't known, where their faces hadn't been plastered all over the nightly news.

They got jobs, then they got education—the real kind, not Preston's kind—and then they went to work.

And it would have stayed like that if it weren't for one thing.

While on a business trip to Las Vegas, Tess and Fala ran into Preston Lidner.

Fala made her appointment with Herbert, Steinmen, and Wilkes for nine a.m. She stopped at the pawnshop on her way in, placing a sign on the door, delaying her opening hour until eleven. Not that anyone would stop, but just in case.

She wanted everything to look legit.

Because she was trying to stay in character as she dressed up, she wore a black leather mini, her red bustier, and a man's white dress shirt tied at her waist. She wore black high heel sandals, and painted her toenails red. She pressed-on two tattoos—a butterfly on the back of her left knee, and an elaborate spider's web just above her right breast, the edge of the web partially visible above the bustier.

On the way inside the brand-new office building, she actually lit a Pall Mall with her vintage lighter, and watched in satisfaction as the smoke wove its way down the hall. This time, she didn't have to force her hands to shake; they did so all on their own as she took her first drag in nearly six months.

Of course, the receptionist made her tamp the cigarette out the moment she stepped inside the office suite. The receptionist, another middle-aged woman who didn't look nearly as old as Reggie had, pursed her lips when she saw Fala's outfit, but said nothing. Instead she took Fala's name, and directed her to the fifth floor, where their "experts" would take her information.

Fala climbed the stairs, still catching the faint hint of her now-lost cigarette in the recycled air. Her legs hurt—she wasn't used to walking this far in heels this high—and she had to be careful not to let that leather mini ride up any more than it already had.

When she reached the fifth floor, she wasn't surprised to see a large conference room set up with desk after desk after desk, rather like a Charles Addams cartoon. Behind each desk sat serious young people in suits. In front of each desk, an elderly person sat, clutching a purse or a pile of papers.

Fala was assigned Desk 14. Behind it sat a young woman wearing a black business suit, a white blouse, and a tiny gold Phi Beta Kappa key on her right lapel. She gave Fala a perfunctory smile as she bade Fala to sit down.

The young woman, who called herself Kayla, was clearly not a sweet young thing.

"Where's your grandmother?" she asked, almost without preliminaries.

"She's bedridden," Fala said. "I explained that to your receptionist when I made the appointment. I have to do all the stuff, and bring it to her to sign."

"We have to work with her," Kayla said. "We can't do anything with you unless you own the house."

"I have her—what is it?—attorney power? I got that," Fala said.

And Kayla softened, just like Fala knew she would. Kayla explained rules and regulations, all of them legal, pressed a sheaf of paper forward, and went through it bit by bit.

Fala had no real house to sell, but she had given Kayla factual information taken from the title of a house just outside the neighborhood, enough on the fringe that she figured they hadn't checked it out. She had; a young married couple had just bought it from their grandmother, and the title was in the process of being transferred.

For the moment, and only for the moment, all of the information (excepting phone numbers) that Fala gave Kayla was correct.

The information was a lot less important than the procedure. Kayla worked on a relatively new Dell. The other desks had the same equipment. It appeared that they were networked. All the better for Fala.

As Kayla spoke, Fala tilted her chair sideways just enough so that she could see the screen. Kayla used standard real estate software. The toolbar showed a continued

Internet and e-mail connection, probably to check court-house records. And the desktop system itself looked like standard Microsoft.

Fala finished the meeting by exasperating poor Kayla. "My grandmother wants to see the documents before we sign."

"But you have power of attorney. If you deem this sufficient—"

"I still let her make the decisions," Fala said. "It's polite, and all. I'll bring them all back tomorrow, signed by us both."

"You realize that we won't be able to get you the money by Friday if you don't sign today," Kayla said. "We need your signature before we do a title search, which can take three days or more."

"Title search?" Fala asked, pretending ignorance.

"To make sure there are no irregularities with the home's ownership. Once we've cleared that, we will have all the documents for you to sign. When we finalize the deal, we will cut you a check."

"You can't do this stuff, like, you know, based on a good search?" Fala asked, trying to avoid jargon.

"You mean can we have you sign on the contingency that the search won't turn up anything?"

Fala nodded.

"We can, but you'll still have to come in to finalize the documents. We don't hand out checks until everything is complete."

Fala bit the polish off her right thumb. "Gram has some bills we gotta pay. Isn't there, like, an advance you could give us or something, a loan, just 'til everything comes through?"

"I'm sorry." Kayla was clearly a pro at this. "We've found that it's better to dot our 'i's and cross our 't's before we hand out any money."

Protecting the company against some old person stealing a few thousand dollars. How rich.

"And no way to hurry this stuff up, right?"

"I'm afraid not," Kayla said.

Fala sighed. "It's hard to come back. I got my business, you know."

The pawnshop gave her legitimacy. If Herbert, Steinmen, and Wilkes asked around, they would know that she had owned the shop for more than a month, which made sense for someone who had just moved to Gresham to take care of her grandmother.

"I can't change our policy. We'll give you cash faster than anyone else can." Kayla gave her an insincere smile. "But you will have to show up during business hours then, too."

Fala nodded. She gathered the papers, having no intention of signing anything, and rolled them before sticking them under her arm.

"Thanks," she said, trying to sound as humble as she could. "You people are real life savers."

That last lie nearly tore her up inside. They weren't lifesavers, although she would have wagered some of the younger people behind those desks in that upstairs room thought they were. Those young ones, like Kayla, weren't involved in the other side of the operation: the conversations with the various developers, getting them to outbid each other for a hunk of valuable land now owned by one company.

Gresham was in the process of rebuilding. Six blocks from her pawnshop, a brand-new Safeway store paved the way for a new upscale neighborhood. That neighborhood would backtrack from the Safeway, through the run-down houses and Division Avenue, all the way to this new office development complex near the Max train line.

Eventually, five or ten years from now, no one would know that this part of Division had once looked like its better days were behind it. And instead of the homeowners who tended these places for fifty years getting the profit, they got little more than they originally paid for the houses, not even what the bare land was worth. They were old; they were tired; they were ill. They didn't have the time to research, probably didn't even know enough to look up the tax-appraised value.

Instead, they got what sounded like a small fortune to them in exchange for signing some documents, moving into the assisted living development the kids had been begging them to join, and maybe never discovering that they could have gotten ten, twenty, thirty times more if they'd just sold their house through a reputable agent.

Fala had until Friday. Friday seemed like a harsh deadline, but she knew the Club could make it work.

F ala had only one more task, and she had to wait until after five before she could even start.

She had to get the list of people who had considered selling their homes to Herbert, Steinmen, and Wilkes.

She knew it wouldn't be tough. The network looked standard, the computers were standard, and that meant the firewalls were standard too. She figured it would take her two hours maximum to hack into the system, find the information she needed, and e-mail it directly to the money group, holed up in Portland's Hilton downtown.

It took her a lot less time than she had figured. More than one little wage slave had left a computer on, with the Internet connection running. Fala hacked in, tapped a few buttons, looked through the files, and found all the information she needed.

She paused long enough to delete every mention of her fake name, and the name of her pretend grandmother. She even went into the receptionist's log, and took out the record of her phone call.

And then, because she could, she went through all the personal and confidential office files, searching for a mention, any mention, of Preston's name.

She found a Preston L. Steinmen, President and CEO of Herbert, Steinmen, and Wilkes. The picture on the company's only ad brochure sure looked a lot like an aging Preston Lidner.

"We're going to get you where it hurts, buddy," she whispered.

That fantasy of getting Preston Lidner first surfaced in Las Vegas at 3 a.m. Fala had just turned down a pickup from one of the best-looking men she'd seen in a long time. It'd been years since she trusted a man enough to spend more than a night with him and, as Tess had reminded her, Fala didn't have a night.

She had a rigorous exam in three days. She wasn't at a conference; she was at an advance training course in real estate law, and she needed the certification.

The last person she expected to see was Preston. He sat down at a craps table not fifty feet from her. He didn't look any different. His hair was slicked back in a more modern style, but his jaw was still square, his smile crooked. He had several stacks of one-hundred-dollar chips in front of him, and he was playing with a single-mindedness of a man who had money to burn.

"Look," Fala whispered.

Tess did, and got noticeably pale. Even then, Tess had a solidity that made her seem more powerful than she was. Her legacy from Preston, besides the legal fees and jail time, was an additional 100 pounds on her 5'2" frame. Tess made it work, though. She dressed like she was worth a fortune, designer dresses in a size 18, and expensive shoes for her tiny feet.

That night, she looked like the CEO of a major corporation, and Fala, in her baggy jeans and University of Chicago sweatshirt, looked like her ratty kid sister.

"Can you believe it?" Fala whispered. "I'm gonna call the cops."

Tess grabbed her arm. "It won't do any good."

Fala frowned. "You know what he did. We all have proof."

"Old proof," Tess said. "I don't know what the statute of limitations is on fraud, but I think it's pretty short. He might not even be wanted anymore."

"Fat chance," Fala said. "He hasn't gone straight. Look at all that money."

"Tell you what," Tess said, her voice barely audible over the ping-ping of nearby slot machines. "Let's find out what he's been doing these last few years, and then call the cops."

"Maybe round up some evidence?" Fala asked.

Tess nodded.

"Think he'll recognize us?"

Tess let out a loud snort. "Definitely not me. And probably not you, either. How many people has he seen over the years, anyway?"

"Still," Fala said.

"If he does, we haven't lost anything," Tess said. "Let's give it a shot."

And a fantasy rose up, just for half a second, not the fantasy of conning Preston, but the fantasy of giving him a different kind of shot—one he wouldn't live through.

Then Fala nodded. "All right," she said. "I got fifty bucks. Wanna play some craps?"

Thirty people had filled out enough information to let Herbert, Steinmen, and Wilkes run title searches on their property. Another forty had taken information and promised they'd be back. But the list contained twenty more names, none of whom seemed to have come to the Herbert, Steinmen, and Wilkes' offices.

It took Fala a while to figure out why.

In one of the computers, someone had found a neighborhood map. The property of each person who had filled out information was marked in blue. The property of each person who promised to come back was yellow. Any properties that adjoined either of those other two kinds was marked in red for "urgent." For Preston's plan to work, he needed entire swatches of land. Any property owner who refused to sell or hadn't approached him at all, and got in the way of a swatch, had an urgent tag.

Fala downloaded the map as well. She wondered what kind of tactics Preston had used in other cities to get the urgents to sell. She doubted the tactic was illegal—Preston didn't want any charges of fraud to get in the way of this new kind of profit—but she also had a hunch he skirted the very edges of legality when he approached these folks.

In the end, it wasn't her problem. She was the advance man and researcher, the person who put it all together. Now the rest of her scheme relied on teams of women who would visit these elderly sellers, and explain their rights, offering to intercede with them at banks and other institutions.

When the Club had run this operation three times in the past (the three times that weren't Preston), most of the elderly took out reverse mortgages after learning how much their homes were worth. A lot of older people didn't know that the bank would pay them to stay in their homes, often at a sum that many older folks called "princely."

If some company wanted to buy them all out to build a shopping mall or supermarket, then the Club would intercede on the part of the homeowners, making sure they got more than market value for their home.

The last time Fala had worked this was Dallas, where it turned out the scumbag trying to screw the older folk using the letter of the law hadn't been Preston at all, but some local Preston-clone, who'd gotten the nasty idea all by his little self.

The Club hadn't put him out of business, but they had made certain that he didn't get his pennies on the dollar initial sales. He also got several write-ups in the papers, and on local TV stations, talking about his unethical but totally legal business practices.

The difficult part of this was that the Club often made money in these transactions. Whenever the Club interceded, it did so for a percentage: people, particularly older people, mistrusted things they got for free. The Club always made money on the resale of the property purchased for the advance man, like the pawnshop Fala bought. The Club would wait until the neighborhood started its transition, then sell the property for more than the Club initially paid for it.

Club members paid themselves salaries, and plowed the money back into the organization, but still felt uncomfortable making profits. Money, to every member of the Club, was the root of all things Preston—another legacy he had bequeathed them.

Fala leaned back in her chair. In three days, Preston would know his house of cards was collapsing when no one showed up to sign the final paperwork and pick up checks.

With luck, he'd learn nothing until then. The teams would help the older folks stay silent—saying that Herbert, Steinmen, and Wilkes wasn't exactly on the up-and-up, adding credence by bringing local banks in on the Club's side, and working quickly to make people a lot of money instead of screw them.

But there was always the possibility that someone would talk.

Fala's only job these next three days was to monitor the phone lines and the computer systems, to make sure nothing leaked. Or if it did, that it seemed like an isolated incident, one that Herbert, Steinmen, and Wilkes could handle.

At the craps table, Preston had been slightly drunk. He had switched from beer to Coke just before the women arrived, but he still swayed slightly as he pushed his chips onto the come line.

Fala and Tess pretended they knew nothing about craps. They let him explain the game, and they followed his lead, squealing like schoolgirls whenever they won.

He didn't recognize them, of course. Sometime during the night, his hand migrated down Fala's back to her ass. She moved away, but he always managed to touch her, to squeeze, brush, and fondle.

Once she sent a help-me look to Tess, who glared at her, as

if reminding her to keep at it. Fala could barely hide her revulsion. She kept finding reasons to move away from Preston, but somehow he always ended up beside her, groping and rubbing as if he had the rights to everything, including her soul.

The game finally ended at 5 a.m. when he declared himself hungry. Fala was up $500 and Tess had made even more. ("Just not enough to pay me back for all the court costs," Tess later said, bitterly.) They accompanied him to one of the nearby restaurants, and ordered breakfast.

He insisted on sitting next to Fala. When she managed to slip to the other side of the table, his foot found her leg. She twisted away. They played this game during the entire meal. Tess was the one who spoke to him, telling him lies about their pasts, pretending they were here for some kind of teacher's conference, which only made Fala think of her upcoming exam, and the fact she'd had no sleep at all.

Finally, when he finished his bacon and eggs, Preston told them a little about his life. "I sell property."

"Oh," Tess said in this fakey little girl voice she'd managed to find inside herself. "You're a real estate agent."

"Better than that," he said. "I work big deals. I find communities on the verge of turning themselves around, and purchase a lot of property at bargain prices. Then I find a big business to go on them."

He made it sound like he was helping the communities. Fala's stomach turned, and she pushed away her half-eaten pancakes.

"How do you find communities?" she asked.

He looked at her as if she had suddenly, and surprisingly,

grown a brain. Tess caught the look too and elbowed her, encouraging her to shut up.

"It takes a little urban planning knowledge. First you go to a state with high unemployment or a backwards economy. Then you find a community that has, for some reason, started to grow. You look at the surrounding communities, and find the one that hasn't changed in thirty, forty years. That's the one that'll rebuild because the land is cheap. And you buy up what you can."

"There's money in that?" Tess asked before Fala could ask anything else.

"If you sit on the property for the right amount of time." Preston made it sound like he sat on the property for weeks, months, maybe years. And that was what had screwed the Club up in its early pursuit of him. They looked for someone who acted on the long-term rather than the short.

He didn't reveal anything else that night, not even the name of his company, although he did give Fala his room number. He made her promise to come upstairs with him. She shot a trapped glance at Tess who shrugged, offering no help at all.

Fala's breakfast threatened to make a reappearance. She forced herself to smile at Preston. "I'll be right up," she said, and hurried to the ladies' room, hiding there until her nausea passed.

It took nearly half an hour. By then, Preston had gone upstairs, and Tess had lost $50 in a nearby slot machine.

"You should've gone," Tess said. "Imagine what you could've learned."

"He would have died," Fala said which was one of her

favorite phrases, an attempt to sound tougher than she was. But she wondered, as she pried her friend away from the slot machine, if there wasn't more truth in that statement than she wanted to acknowledge.

Deep down, she wanted her pound of flesh from Preston. Tess liked to think that pound would come as actual money, repayment for all they had suffered. At first, they thought he was working Vegas. It was only later they discovered that he was just passing through.

Still, Fala and Tess worked out the beginnings of a plan that morning, a plan that the Club would implement all over the country, in an attempt to destroy Preston's life the way he had destroyed theirs.

But Fala wondered if poverty, jail time, and humiliation were enough to satisfy her. She wanted to hurt Preston, hurt him so badly he had no sense of self left.

Preston had already climbed out of poverty with his schemes, and he didn't seem to have an understanding of humiliation. He was the kind of man who might talk his way out of jail time.

She kept falling back on the primitive solution. She wanted to bash his head in, to strangle him, to take a knife and chop him into 5,000 pieces.

Fala wanted Preston's complete and utter destruction, and she wasn't sure how to get it.

Three days after Fala had given the list to the Portland team, the guards positioned outside Herbert, Steinmen, and Wilkes's building reported only two elderly folks who had come for their checks. Both were intercepted, both reminded of the benefits they could have if they sold their property through a real bank or used a reverse mortgage.

Both left before going inside.

By Monday, Preston's scam had utterly collapsed. The suits inside were calling prospectives, asking them to come in and discovering that they had already made other arrangements, all through a variety of institutions. The receptionist cold-called the remaining homeowners to learn that no one was interested, and Preston called the office manager, who was obviously in cahoots with him on the entire scheme, and demanded to know what exactly had gone wrong.

The panic and fear in Preston's voice as it came through Fala's bug into the pawnshop was almost enough to satisfy her. At least he had a small taste of her life, of the way she had felt when she discovered that he and Reggie had disappeared on her, leaving her with two hundred renters, all of whom had been cheated of their money and their home.

Almost enough to satisfy: later she played the tape for the teams, and they toasted each other with champagne that Fala had brought to the hotel suites that cost the Club more money than some of them had earned in those early rebuilding years.

Almost enough: the frustration and the fear and the growing understanding from the entire staff at Herbert, Steinmen, and Wilkes that someone had gotten to their marks just in the nick of time, and that Preston and his

froze in place. No one looked out the window to see what the noise had been. No one had even noticed her.

She had dressed in Oregon casual: a pretty knee-length skirt and a t-shirt, along with a pair of Birkenstocks. She had parked two blocks away, and walked toward Preston's rental house as if she belonged in the neighborhood.

Except for the sprinkler moment, everything had gone well.

Now she was damp and uncomfortable, and more than a little frightened. She really didn't have a plan. She just felt she had to confront Preston for the first and final time.

The back door was open. Only the screen stood between her and the kitchen. In a faraway room, she heard an electronic voice—whether it was television or radio, she couldn't tell. She pushed on the screen door. It wasn't locked. Quietly, she stepped inside.

The inside of the house still retained the day's heat. The kitchen smelled of coffee and brandy. An empty tumbler sat beside the sink, along with the remains of a Subway sandwich.

Fala pulled the gun out of her purse, and carefully walked down the hall toward the electronic noise. Light spilled across the hallway. She was heading toward a den. She kept her back to the wall, and the barrel of the gun pointed upwards.

Her breathing was coming in short, sharp bursts.

When she reached the den, she saw a large-screen TV turned to CNN. Preston lay on his couch, his face fleshier than she remembered, jowls hanging off his chin like whiskers. His thick dark hair had thinned and gone mostly gray. He had a pot belly, and his hands, once things of beauty, seemed pudgy and small.

He was sound asleep, snoring slightly, coffee on the table beside him. The room smelled faintly of booze.

It would be so easy to wake him, so easy to scare him and make him squeal in fear. It would be just as easy to shoot him, to carry out all those fantasies that she'd had for years now, to make sure he never hurt anyone again.

He snorted, then turned slightly. The anchor on CNN talked of car bombings and combined deaths and fires. The crawl at the bottom of the screen mentioned fifteen soldiers who died in an ambush.

She was about to ambush Preston. He had ambushed her all those years ago, taken her innocence and ruined it forever. The other sweet young things had recovered, thanks in part to her. They had real jobs, most of them had families, they had lives.

She didn't. In fact, he had left her with the taint of crime, and she continued it, breaking into office buildings, hacking into computers, carrying guns into someone else's unlocked house.

She could take that criminal behavior to its logical conclusion. She could murder a man, take the very last thing he had to give, and do it simply for her own pleasure.

Not that he was even a criminal anymore. Sure, he bilked old people out of their homes, but like all good con artists, he made sure the old folks left happy. His behavior wasn't ethical, but it was legal—and her revenge, until now, had been both ethical *and* legal—except for the breaking and entering, the hacking, the bugs on the phones. She did all that. Everyone else, her friends, the Club, they didn't break a single law.

She wouldn't let them.

She sat down on a nearby armchair, slipped the gun beside her, and kept her right hand on the barrel. She made sure the gun was out of sight.

Then she coughed loudly.

He snorted again, wiped his mouth, and sat up, looking very confused. The confused look grew as he realized where he was, then focused on her.

He clearly didn't remember her.

"What the hell's going on?" he asked.

"Do you care about the lives you've ruined?" she asked.

"What?" He ran a hand over his face.

"I just wonder. You've ruined, by my count, at least three hundred lives. I wonder how you sleep at night, if you think about the people you've hurt, if you even care."

"Who are you?" There was fear in his voice.

"I suppose you probably don't think about them," she said. "I suppose you figure people get what's coming to them. I suppose you believe what happens has nothing to do with you."

"What are you talking about?"

"You," she said, "and all your cons."

He stared at her for a long moment, as if he was trying— and failing—to figure out who she was. "What do you want?"

She paused.

The answer suddenly became clear. She wanted the past to go away. She wanted to be someone else, someone who had a perfect life, someone who never made a mistake, who never allowed herself to be hurt by a con man, never allowed herself to help him destroy countless lives.

"I want you to know," she said quietly, "that you won't succeed again. I want you to know that every time you try to take something from someone who can't match wits with you, I will be there to prevent it. I want you to know that my goal in life is to make sure you ruin no one else's life—except your own."

"You're the one," he said, blinking with surprise. "You're the one who stopped all those people from working with me."

She inclined her head just a little, like a queen acknowledging a subject.

"Why?" he said. "I wasn't cheating them. They helped determine the price. I haven't broken any laws."

"These days," Fala said.

He frowned. His eyes were red, either from sleep or drink. "Do I know you?"

She almost answered yes. Then she stood up, the gun clutched in her right hand. He looked at it, and went so pale that she thought he might pass out.

"I just want you to remember my face," she said. "Every time you try a new scheme, realize I'll be watching you, and I'll be there to make sure you fail."

"Why?" he whispered. "What have I done to you?"

She almost laughed. It had been so personal to her for so long, and he didn't even recognize her, didn't even remember her, didn't even realize how he had hurt her.

"Remember what I told you," she said, and backed out

of the room. Once she realized he wasn't following her, she ran down the hall and out the back door.

She would leave prints from the sprinkler-soaked grass. She hurried through a small copse of trees, across other yards, taking a shorter path to her car, so she could get away before the police arrived.

What had he done to her?

He had given her something to push against.

He had given her a determination she hadn't realized she had.

He had made her stronger.

She reached the car, unlocked it, set the gun on the seat, and started the car. Then she sped off, hurrying to the freeways, taking a long and circuitous route back to her makeshift home.

What had he done to her?

He had taught her how to hate, and she had become very, very good at it. Better at it than he was.

Better than most people.

The ironic thing, the sad thing, was that she wouldn't be here without him. She wouldn't have changed all those lives, helped all those people, without him.

She didn't want to give him any credit. She couldn't. He hadn't meant for her to become a better person.

He'd meant to ruin her, and he hadn't.

He never would.

When she reached the apartment building, she parked the car in the lot across the street, then hurried upstairs. She let herself in, took off the suburban clothes, and wrapped herself in a terrycloth robe.

Then she sat on the couch, picked up her cell phone and called Tess.

"We're going to have a party when you get back," Tess said. "We miss you here. We're celebrating already."

"Save some champagne for me," Fala said. "I'll be back in a week or two."

"That long?" Tess asked.

"I have to shut things down here. And I have one other thing to do."

"What's that?" Tess sounded suspicious.

Fala didn't want to say that she was going to make good on her promise to Preston. She had his new name, his license plate number, his company's business records. She was going to watch him, electronically, personally, digitally.

She was going to track his every movement, and she was going to make certain he never hurt anyone again.

"It's nothing much," Fala lied. "I just have to take care of an old friend."

Two days later, she pulled the jewelry out of the safe. Item by item, she checked the names and the addresses, setting aside the pieces whose owners she couldn't entirely identify. If she couldn't figure out who the pieces really belonged to, she would take them to the police.

Then she picked up the phone, and called the number on the tag hanging off a necklace.

"Mrs. Spaight? This is Fast Cash Pawn Shop. I have your ruby necklace here. We've had it for more than a month, and we haven't been able to move it. I'd like to give it back to you. Would you mind picking it up in the next few days...?"

"I can't afford to repay you," the quavering voice on the other end said.

"I know." Fala kept her own voice gentle. "I'm giving it back to you. We're changing our focus here."

"But you gave me money. It was a loan—"

"I know, ma'am. I had the piece for more than a month. Let's just call it even."

Silence. Fala held her breath.

Then the woman on the other end let out a short laugh. "Bless you, child. Bless you."

Fala smiled. She liked her work. She liked doing it for the right reasons—not for hatred and revenge, but because she wanted to.

Because she could.

She finished the call, and started another, slowly working her way through the pile, giving back treasures, and restoring other people's dreams.

CHRISTMAS EVE AT THE EXIT
A SWEET YOUNG THINGS STORY

KRISTINE KATHRYN RUSCH

"Will Santa know how to find us?" Anne-Marie asked as she hopped out of the van.

"Of course he does, honey," Rachel said, just like she'd said every time they'd stopped.

Anne-Marie didn't answer. She slammed the door hard enough to shake the entire vehicle, and hurried across the empty ice-covered parking lot. Somehow she kept her balance and didn't fall, despite the pink tennis shoes she wore. Her red mittens hung off a string threaded through her pink coat. She'd lost three pairs so far, which Rachel figured had to be some kind of quiet rebellion.

Eight hundred, maybe nine hundred, miles to go, she thought to herself. She hadn't been willing to check the GPS. She wasn't sure if it transmitted the van's location.

Even though she had never even seen the van before she removed it from a storage unit in Winnemucca, Nevada. Even though the van, its license plates, and that storage unit weren't in her name. Even though she had taken a taxi to the units from that weird hotel and casino.

She'd left a trail. It was impossible not to. If someone had followed her, they would have figured it out. She had to leave Anne-Marie with the casino-provided babysitting service, which frightened Rachel more than anything. Then the taxi driver kept talking about how unusual it was to have a woman take a cab to a storage unit. He pressed his card into her hand, told her to call him if her ride didn't show up.

I know you're in trouble, little lady, he'd said through teeth broken so long ago the cracks had turned yellow from the cigars he smoked. *So you just call me and I'll make sure you get back to the hotel, no problem.*

She'd thanked him, trying not to cry. She hadn't wanted him to notice her. She hadn't wanted anyone to notice her. She wanted to be invisible, even though she didn't look like she belonged.

She belonged in Boise, with her trendy blue ski parka and $500 athletic shoes, not in small-town Nevada where she was so obviously a tourist that everyone asked her if she needed directions.

In the end, she hadn't needed the cab driver. She used the key she'd been mailed to open the storage unit, then followed the instructions pasted to the van. Three different identities inside, all with three different credit cards, an entire wad of cash, birth certificates for her and Anne-Marie, and directions to their new place.

Plus seven different pre-programmed cell phones, one for each state. They were numbered. Every time Rachel crossed a state border, she was supposed to toss out the phone she had been using, and take the next one. She'd thrown the first away near the Bonneville Salt Flats, heart pounding, and somehow that—not the abandonment of her own car, the use of a new identity, the loss of all her possessions—had finally convinced her there was no turning back.

She still had the feeling she was being followed. She liked to attribute that to the fact that all modern cars looked alike, so the dark blue SUV she saw in Salt Lake might have had nothing to do with the dark blue SUV that cut her off in Rock Springs. Or the beige sedan that seemed to dog her trip from North Platte to Kearney.

She ran a hand through her wedge-cut dark hair. She'd bought and paid for that wedge cut, as per instructions, at a beauty shop in Cheyenne, where the kind sad-eyed woman there also gave her a pencil for her eyebrows—to thicken and darken them—and taught her how to alter the shape of her face with blush, foundation, and the right kind of lipstick.

The wind blew hard here in Omaha, carrying with it a chill she hadn't felt in a decade. Her brand-new ski parka felt too thin despite its state-of-the-art promises. Of course, the radio had been telling her that she was driving into a holiday "polar vortex" that filled the air with cold that could kill in less than an hour.

She was glad for the van, glad for the clothes she wore, glad for the interstate with its protective traffic, but she hoped to be off the road soon. She was afraid for Anne-Marie and afraid for herself, and the weather didn't help matters.

She pulled on her gloves, and carefully followed her daughter inside. The ice was so thick that it added another layer to the parking lot. The lot had been well-tended; the snow from a massive storm two days ago—one that had been ahead of her all the way—was piled alongside the edges of the lot, taking up at least one row of spaces.

Anne-Marie watched her from inside. Her blond hair wisped out of her blue-and-pink cap, her round cheeks were bright red with cold, and her blue eyes twinkled in the Christmas lights framing the glass door. She looked like a child waiting for Santa Claus instead of a little girl who had no idea how much her life had already changed.

Rachel pushed the door open, heard the bing-bong of electronic notification, and saw a twenty-something dark-skinned man behind the desk. His appearance momentarily startled her. She'd lived in Idaho so long that she had forgotten how diverse the rest of the country was.

He looked at her and grinned. The expression softened his face, and made the red-and-green silk scarf around his neck seem appropriate. "I assume this little one belongs to you?"

"She does," Rachel said with a smile that she had to force. She put her hand on Anne-Marie's shoulder and guided her daughter toward the tall front desk, festooned in garlands.

A real Christmas tree took over a corner of the lobby, filling the air with the scent of pine.

"She and I have been discussing Santa," the young man said. His nametag identified him as Luke.

"She and I have as well," Rachel said. "She thinks he won't find her because we're very far from home. I told her that Santa is magic, and can find everyone."

"Yes, he can," Luke said, leaning over a little so that he could see Anne-Marie on the other side of the desk. "And people like me, we help Santa when he needs it."

Rachel's stomach clenched. She tried not to look frightened by that admission, but it was hard. She wanted to ask Luke who else he would help if need be, but she didn't.

She wanted to seem as normal as she could for a woman who brought her daughter to a chain hotel off I-80 on Christmas Eve.

"What's the largest room you have?" She really couldn't afford it, but it was Christmas, and she wanted the room to be festive somehow.

"We have a choice of everything," Luke said. "We're empty at the moment, although I expect the usual travelers and truckers after ten."

She smiled. His good mood, surprising for a man working on the holiday, was infectious. He smiled back and tapped at the computer keyboard. As he did so, the Christmas lights woven into the garland above him winked off the tiny sparkly red-and-white candy canes in his pierced ears.

"When do you get to go home and celebrate?" she asked as she pulled out her wallet. She was pleased that her hands weren't shaking.

"I'm here all night, ma'am," Luke said, sounding distracted. He was still staring at the screen in front of him.

"Will Santa find you?" Anne-Marie asked, her voice a little shaky.

Rachel braced herself for him to say something disparaging like, *Santa hasn't found me for years, honey.*

Instead, Luke reached to one side of the computer and grabbed a real candy cane. He kept it under the lip of the desk, then looked up at Rachel, a question on his face. She nodded her approval.

His smile became real then and he leaned over the desk again, offering the candy cane to Anne-Marie. Anne-Marie took it like it was the most precious thing she'd ever received.

"Santa doesn't have to find me," he said. "I'm one of Santa's helpers."

Anne-Marie clutched it to her pink coat. "Really?" she asked breathlessly.

"Really," he said.

She backed away a little. "Can I put this on the tree?" she asked Rachel softly.

But Luke heard. "It's okay, hon," he said as he tapped the keyboard some more. "The tree has enough candy canes on it. That one's for you."

Anne-Marie frowned. Rachel smiled at her, encouragingly. The last thing she wanted was for her daughter to be this wary. Had she taught Anne-Marie that? Or had Anne-Marie learned it through observation?

"You can put it on our tree when we get upstairs if you want," Rachel said.

Anne-Marie nodded seriously, and clutched the candy cane to her chest. Luke was looking at Rachel over the computer.

His questioning gaze startled her.

"We've been setting up a small tree at nights in the hotel rooms," she said, feeling as if she were giving him the secrets of her soul.

He grinned. "That's wonderful," he said. "Great thinking."

She braced herself again for more questions, like she'd had at the other hotels. *When will you get to your destination? Are you spending Christmas with your family? Where's your husband, sweet thing?*

But he didn't ask them, and she didn't volunteer. Her heart was beating hard, the wallet in her hand feeling like an accusation. She had to remember which identification she was using. It was hard, because she looked at them all every night.

The instructions told her to change identification only if she felt she needed to, and she wasn't sure what that meant, especially since she felt like she needed to change identification every minute of every day.

"We have a suite," Luke said. "No one's booked it. I think it's late enough that I can give it to you at a lower rate."

The price he quoted to her made her heart pound harder but, she reasoned, she'd planned to pay that much anyway, the moment she walked in the door.

All she could feel was the money going out. She wondered how much of it she would owe later.

But she couldn't think about that. Not yet.

"Credit card?" he asked, extending one hand while the other still tapped on the keyboard in front of him.

Her fingers twitched, and she swallowed hard. Then she pulled out the card on top, checked the name, made sure it matched the driver's license in the front of this wallet, and set the card in Luke's hand. He shifted the card so that it fell between his thumb and index finger—clearly a maneuver of long-standing—and then slid it through the card reader.

He had to be able to hear her heart. Everyone had to. Even Anne-Marie who had moved to the Christmas tree like it held the secrets of the world.

She hadn't asked after her father. She hadn't even asked where they were going.

That wasn't natural, was it?

Rachel didn't know. She'd never done anything like this before.

All Anne-Marie had asked was about Santa Claus, over and over again. That, Rachel believed, *was* normal.

"Your card," Luke said, still without looking up. He was holding it out.

Rachel's breath caught. She expected him to finish that sentence: *Your card ... didn't run. Do you have another?*

But he didn't. He was just handing it back to her. He hadn't even asked to see ID.

"Your key," Luke said, holding a little folder with a black credit-card sized square and a room number hand-written inside. "You're on the third floor. Just take the elevator up. Would you like help with your luggage?"

Rachel didn't see anyone who could help, besides Luke himself. She was about to say no when she glanced at Anne-Marie, still staring at the tree.

"Yes," Rachel said. "Yes, please."

The van had a compartment in the back built for the spare tire and for some repair equipment. When Rachel found the vehicle inside the storage unit, she had taken the tire out, and placed it flat on the van's carpet, then added the repair equipment on top of it. Later, at the hotel, she had taken out the bag of Santa presents she had bought before leaving Boise, and placed them inside that little compartment.

Then she'd added the suitcases she'd bought just that afternoon at the local Walmart, plus the new overnight bags. And stepped back to look at her handiwork.

So much new stuff, such a lack of familiarity. Only Anne-Marie's favorite toys remained, mostly because Rachel hadn't had the heart to toss them out.

She'd bought a little tree, too, with the lights already attached.

Even though the two of them were running away, she had vowed that her daughter would have Christmas.

Luke had come out with her, leaving a woman Rachel hadn't seen when she checked in to watch the front desk. And Anne-Marie. The woman was watching Anne-Marie, too. The woman looked tired and stressed, and something in her disheveled blouse and wrinkled skirt screamed shift's end, a fact confirmed by Luke just before he left the lobby.

"It's just a minute, Sherrie," he had said to the woman. "I promise. Then you can go home."

"Always just one more minute," Sherrie had said. "I gotta get to the stores before they close."

"Kmart's open until ten," Luke had said, and in his voice

was just a bit of contempt. Because he thought Sherrie should shop at Kmart or because she *did* shop at Kmart?

Rachel couldn't tell, and truly didn't care. She just didn't want the woman to see her—at least not much.

Luke, well, Rachel was taking a chance with him. This was the first time since she left Winnemucca that anyone other than herself and Anne-Marie had seen inside the van.

Anne-Marie was still inside the lobby, holding the candy-cane and staring at the tree. She wouldn't even sit down. She had asked Sherrie if she believed Santa would find them.

"You'd be surprised what Santa can find," Sherrie had said.

Rachel pulled the Santa bag out of the hidden compartment. "Is there any way to put this behind the desk for a few minutes without Anne-Marie seeing it?"

Luke grinned at her. "No wonder you weren't worried about St. Nick. He's already been here. Anything good in there?"

"If you're seven, like pink, and have always longed for at least one more Barbie," Rachel said, rather surprised she could banter. She had thought the ability to banter had left her years ago.

He smiled at her. "She'll remember this trip forever," he said as if that were a good thing.

"Yes," Rachel said. "I suppose she will."

She grabbed the overnight bags and slung them over her shoulders. Then she double-checked to make sure she had the key fob. She grabbed the small tabletop tree before slamming the lift gate shut.

"I'll be down for the bag after my daughter falls asleep. You'll still be here?"

"Of course," Luke said. "You've already had dinner?"

For a moment, she thought he was asking if he could join her. Her stomach clenched. Then she remembered that he had said he was working all night. He was just asking for information.

"No, we haven't yet." Her breath fogged the air as she spoke. "I suppose no one's doing delivery tonight."

"Not tonight." Luke sounded apologetic, as if it were his fault that no one else was working. "But most of the restaurants around here are staying open. And there's a church about three blocks away if you're so inclined."

"I think we're too tired," she said. She *hoped*. She didn't want to leave the room after they'd eaten something. It was just too cold.

As if hearing her thoughts, Luke shivered. "I'm taking this in the back, then I'll meet you."

Without waiting for her to answer, he picked his way across the parking lot, slipping more than she liked.

The wind seemed even colder. Cars still whizzed by on the interstate behind her. The lights from the chain hotels and the chain restaurants that hugged this exit should have seemed festive, but they didn't. They seemed like beacons of a past life.

She didn't look at them, instead making certain she got across the slippery parking lot with her burden.

Luke went in a side door, then came back outside without the bag. He truly was Santa's helper. He grinned, took the tree from her, and opened the main lobby doors.

Anne-Marie turned, eyes wide, as if she were expecting someone else, someone she didn't want to see.

Rachel hated how jumpy her daughter had become.

"You brought the tree!" Anne-Marie said to Luke.

"I did indeed," he said, then looked at Rachel. "Will you need help setting it up?"

Rachel was tempted, but she couldn't quite face having a stranger take her to her room.

"Do you have a bellman's cart?" she asked. "That's all we need."

He nodded as if he understood, then disappeared in the back, tree in hand. Anne-Marie watched it go as if he were never going to bring it back.

"Tough traveling on Christmas, isn't it?" Sherrie said to Rachel.

"People are friendlier," Rachel said, and it was true. People *were* friendlier, particularly when they saw her daughter. They assumed that Rachel was on her way to see relatives, that maybe she got behind or needed an extra bit of help.

She never dissuaded them.

"That friendly will end tonight," Sherrie said. "The folks who show up after nine are generally upset because they can't get to Grandma's house or because they got no one to celebrate with."

Rachel gave her a hard look, hoping she'd quit being negative.

Sherrie didn't seem to notice. "Thank the good Lord for Luke, though. Ever since he came here, I haven't had to work a Christmas Day. He calls it his gift to all of us."

"He doesn't have family?" Rachel asked, despite herself.

This time, Sherrie did look at Anne-Marie. Anne-Marie was leaning toward one of the ornaments, as if she'd never seen anything like it.

Sherrie shook her head. Anne-Marie turned around, as if she expected to hear Sherrie's answer. So Sherrie put on a bright smile.

"He loves New Year's. He takes the days around New Year's off. One year, he flew to New York to watch the ball drop. Said he damn near froze his ball—"

"Crudeness on Christmas is not allowed," Luke said, interrupting her. He was dragging a gold bellman's cart, with the tree set on one side of it.

"Where *are* you going this year?" Sherrie asked, as if she couldn't be dissuaded from anything.

"Miami," Luke said. "Party central. And it's *warm*."

At that word, Rachel shivered. She would give anything to live somewhere warm now, but that wasn't in the cards. She had made her choices, and they were good ones.

Or they would be. Once she got to Detroit.

She set the overnight bags on the cart, careful not to knock the tree off it. Her shoulders ached from carrying the bags, and from the stress of driving.

Hours to go, she reminded herself, hearing her fourth grade teacher intone Robert Frost's most famous poem, just like she always did when she realized she couldn't sleep no matter how exhausted she was.

"There's an in-room Jacuzzi," Luke said softly, loud enough that only she could hear him. "Perfect after a long day. Merry Christmas."

"Thank you," Rachel said. She had done nothing to deserve this man's kindness, and yet he had given it to her.

The one thing she did not regret about traveling at Christmas was exactly what she had said to Sherrie: people *were* friendlier. It was as if a bit of the season had infected them, and gave them just a little bit of joy.

"Come on, Anne-Marie," she said, and Anne-Marie scurried to follow her.

Rachel wheeled the cart to the elevators behind the stairs. Anne-Marie didn't even ask if she could ride it. She had in Cheyenne.

"Is Santa really going to find us?" Anne-Marie asked.

"If you fall asleep," Rachel said as the elevator doors opened. "Just like last year."

She regretted the words the moment she spoke them. Anne-Marie had a look of horror on her face.

Without Daddy, Rachel wanted to add. *You don't have to worry about Daddy.*

But she didn't. She'd mentioned last year, and she couldn't take it back.

"I don't like Christmas," Anne-Marie said as she stepped inside, head down.

Rachel's heart twisted. Little kids weren't supposed to say that. Little kids were supposed to plan all year for Christmas, do special things to get in good with Santa, and be so excited that they couldn't sleep the night before.

They weren't supposed to turn off the Christmas specials, and keep their faces averted during the commercials. Christmas wasn't supposed to make them *sad*.

That emotion was for grownups, especially the ones for whom nostalgia was not enough.

Rachel put her hand on her daughter's fuzzy little cap, and didn't say a single word.

R achel put the little tree on the round table in the suite's kitchenette. The suite was bigger than anything they had stayed in so far. It seemed like luxury, even though they hadn't been traveling very long. Part of her had already forgotten the wealth in her past life.

She took small presents out of the overnight bag and scattered them under the tree, the first time she had done that. It made Anne-Marie frown.

"I don't got nothing for you, Mommy," she said.

"It's okay, baby," Rachel said. "This trip is for me."

Anne-Marie's lower lip trembled, and Rachel wanted to curse Gil. He'd thrown a fit last year when he realized he hadn't gotten as many presents as Rachel had. Anne-Marie had thought he was blaming her, when he wasn't blaming anyone. He was just being an asshole, his specialty.

"I didn't buy the trip," Anne-Marie said softly.

"I know, sweetie," Rachel said, making sure she sounded cheerful. "But you came with me."

Anne-Marie let out a little sigh, then went to her toy bag, and pulled out the stuffed dog that had become her lifeline. She set it on the bed nearest the kitchen, claiming that bed for her own.

"You hungry?" Rachel asked.

Anne-Marie nodded.

"Then bundle back up," Rachel said. "We have to go outside again."

They couldn't really walk to the nearby restaurants, as much as Rachel wanted to. They had to drive, just because of the severe cold. They waved at Luke on the way out and got into the chilly van.

He had been right; most of the chain restaurants were open. Normally, Rachel would have stopped at a super-large truck stop with six restaurants inside of it, as well as shops and showers. No one noticed the people who came and went from those places.

But she decided not to because Anne-Marie had mentioned gifts. Rachel didn't want her daughter to attempt to buy something for her.

Instead, they stopped at the closest family restaurant chain. They all had a disagreeable sameness to her. They smelled of coffee and grease, even in the evenings. They served pancakes at all hours, and usually had pies that looked a little tired in a glass case near the cash register.

This restaurant had an open floor plan, a busboy wearing an elf hat, a manager wearing a tie covered with reindeer, and a waitress whose brown uniform had no holiday decoration at all.

She waved them to a table, then brought waters and menus before Rachel and Anne-Marie could even get settled. They ordered, got halfway decent food, and some free cookies courtesy of the manager.

Rachel was trying to decide whether she wanted to pay with cash or a credit card when she heard Anne-Marie gasp.

Anne-Marie's face had gone a kind of white that Rachel hadn't seen since they left Boise. A look that usually meant Anne-Marie had been doing something she thought her father would disapprove of.

Rachel followed Anne-Marie's gaze, and saw a Santa accepting a menu from the waitress. He wasn't wearing any padding under the suit, so it hung loosely, and his beard hung around his chin, as if he'd loosened it. He looked as tired as Rachel felt.

His appearance must have shocked Anne-Marie, who had only seen fat Santas so far. There had been a lot of them. She'd seen Santas everywhere, from the men manning the Salvation Army buckets by every public building to the men standing outside malls, smoking before they went back to work.

"What's wrong, honey?" she asked Anne-Marie.

Anne-Marie shook her head and then scrunched down, as if she didn't want Santa to see her.

Someday, when Rachel got back on her feet, she'd get her revenge on Gil. She wasn't sure what that revenge would be, but her husband had put the fear of God into their child.

And into her.

Or she wouldn't be running now.

The food she had eaten rolled over in her stomach. It had taken a village to get her out of Boise. Her husband was so rich that she'd never thought she could escape him. But a forbidden phone call to her sister had changed her mind.

Helen had begged her to find a pay phone and call back. Helen had asked that before, and Rachel had refused. But this time, she would listen to anything. Helen had hated Gil from the beginning and warned Rachel not to marry him. Rachel had resented that once. Later, she wondered what Helen had seen.

Still, Helen's pushing had made her uncomfortable. It had also embarrassed Rachel. She felt so stupid. But that day, she had gone past her embarrassment, past her inferiority. She was nearly dead inside. And Anne-Marie's eyes were dying too.

So Rachel had found a pay phone near the ladies room in the back of a very large, very old grocery store. Rachel had felt naked making that call, standing to one side, and watching the employees go by, hoping no one recognized her. She had barely been able to concentrate on her sister's words.

Helen had told her that she knew a group of women who could help her and Anne-Marie, if she only followed instructions.

Rachel needed the help. A shelter couldn't take her in, and she had no money of her own. Plus Gil had more resources than any women's organization.

But Helen had reassured her: The organization—SYT— had an incredible amount of money, and Rachel was exactly the kind of woman they could help.

The cost to Rachel? One year's work at the organization, helping women just like her escape from whatever bad circumstance they were in. It would mean donating time and energy to a rehab project in Detroit, using old design skills that had led Rachel astray in the first place.

Once upon a time in a land faraway, she had been the best interior designer in Idaho. She had helped with projects from Boise to Sun Valley, and that was when she had met the multi-millionaire charmer who would become her husband.

She should have known what a control freak he was right from the beginning. He'd had his fingers in every part of her work on that project. But she had agreed with him—his suggestions were good ones—and she hadn't thought anything was amiss until six months after Anne-Marie's birth, when he'd grabbed Rachel's arm so hard during a disagreement that she'd had bruises for weeks.

She'd always thought women who stayed with men like him were doormats, so she tried to escape on her own. That's when she discovered he had his own private army. He called them security, but they tracked every move she made and everything she did.

They had even asked her why she had used that pay phone on the way to the ladies room, and she had told them it was pretty simple: her cell had died.

They hadn't double-checked. Nor did they check her purchases the next time she went shopping. She'd bought what her sister called a "burner phone" every time she shopped, and she hid them in the purses she had stacked in her closet like extra shoes.

"Mommy, can we go?" Anne-Marie asked.

Rachel nodded. She decided to stop waiting for the waitress to come back with their bill. Instead, she went to the cash register and paid with cash.

The Santa was the only other person in the restaurant. He looked out the window. Then his gaze met hers through the glass. Rachel gave him an uncertain smile, mostly for Anne-Marie's sake, and he nodded at her.

Anne-Marie grabbed her hand, and held tightly.

"Let's make sure you're buttoned up," Rachel said. She hated this kind of cold. It required preparation just to walk from a restaurant to the van.

But she had to get used to it. At least a year in Detroit, rehabbing, and getting her credentials back—under one of her new names.

They stepped outside and she sighed. The cold air burned her lungs. Anne-Marie nearly pulled her to the van, making her slide on the ice.

Everyone was nice here. Maybe she would stay one extra day. She wasn't looking forward to a drive on Christmas. Most places were closed, and this arctic blast made travel so treacherous.

She would call Helen after Anne-Marie fell asleep.

They got into the van and drove the short distance back to the hotel. Luke was still at the front desk. He was watching some religious ceremony on television; it took Rachel a minute to realize it was the service from the Vatican.

She waved at him and mouthed, "I'll be back soon," as she and Anne-Marie headed toward the elevator.

They barely made it to the room, before Anne-Marie decided she needed to get some sleep.

Rachel wished she could sleep. Ever since she'd fled Boise, she'd dozed, but never slept deeply. Every time a hotel room heater clicked on, she bolted awake thinking the sound was someone racking a shotgun.

Gil had threatened to kill her if she ever took Anne-Marie away from him, and she hadn't doubted he could make good on the threat.

But Helen was convinced they could build her a new identity, and that no one would ever find her, if she did the right things. Helen had always worked with women's groups, and this one, SYT (short for Sweet Young Things), seemed more organized and wealthier than anything Rachel had ever imagined.

They had had quite a plan for her, and she'd executed 99.9% of it. The hardest was leaving her Lexus SUV in the parking lot of that hotel-casino in Winnemucca, and pretending that she actually had a drinking problem.

She had hidden whiskey all over her house before she left, disguised to look like tea or juice or a whole variety of things, as if she had been a secret drunk all along.

Helen had promised her that someone would take the SUV, and leave it in the snow on a spur road between Winnemucca and Boise. Tracks would lead away from the SUV, and rescuers would believe that she and Anne-Marie had walked away from the car. There would be a high-profile search, and then nothing, until spring, when someone might find a bit of their clothing and Rachel's purse out in the wilderness.

Rachel thought it all a long-shot, but she'd lived in the west long enough to know that families went missing there all the time. They took the wrong road, got stranded, and had no cell service. Rather than wait for rescue, like they were supposed to, they'd try to hike out, and generally die of exposure.

Everyone would believe the story, particularly after all that alcohol got found in the house.

Everyone, she suspected, except Gil.

But Rachel had to trust Helen. It was her only shot. Anne-Marie's only shot. Because Gil terrorized his daughter. Mostly, he wasn't home, but when he was, just a twitch of his lips could make her turn that horrid shade of white that Rachel had seen in the restaurant.

Anne-Marie was terrified of him. As far as Rachel could tell, only because Rachel was frightened of him. To Rachel's knowledge, he hadn't physically hurt their daughter . . . yet.

But Rachel had known it was only a matter of time.

She sat near the television, turned so low she could barely hear it, and wished she smoked. Or actually did drink. Just to give herself something to do, something that would relax her.

She was on her own until she got to Detroit. Well, sort of on her own. The woman who had cut her hair in Cheyenne told her it got better. When Rachel asked if she was trading services, the woman had gotten very serious and nodded, finger to her lips.

There are women like us everywhere, she'd said. *We're setting up a network. I know it's hard to trust, but you'll be okay, if you just do what they told you.*

And she had. Everything except the toys. And those, she had searched over and over. She'd even stopped in a spy shop in Laramie, and asked if they had one of those electronic bug-finders.

They did, and she asked if she could see how it worked. She brought in the bag of toys and the man demonstrated, finding nothing. He showed her that it did work with some demo they had, and told her that the toys were tracking free.

She believed him. And she had seen him before Cheyenne, before her hair and appearance changed, before she dumped yet another coat, before she had done anything to make herself look like someone new.

Helen hadn't said she had to avoid stores and things. Just warned her to be careful, and to leave her old life behind. No friends, no phone calls, no gloating e-mails to Gil.

Not that Rachel would have done any of that. She had no real friends, not ones she had contacted since her marriage, and she wasn't about to contact her husband. Her cell was gone, left in the Lexus with her purse and her old identification.

Since she got on the road, she was a different woman, although she still felt the same inside.

A knock on the door made her jump out of her skin. She glanced at Anne-Marie, to see if her daughter had heard it.

She hadn't.

Rachel got up and almost went to the door, thinking it was probably Luke from the desk. Then she wondered if he would just come up with the Santa bag. Wouldn't he wait for her call?

She swallowed hard, heart pounding.

If something feels wrong, Helen had told her, *then it probably is wrong. Your subconscious sees something you don't. Get out of that situation.*

Only there was no way out of here. Except the window,

which was probably blocked against opening, not to mention the jump from the third floor, into the damn polar express or whatever the hell that cold was called.

Rachel got up and moved silently away from the kitchen area, finding the house phone. She hit "0" and Luke answered.

"You ready for the presents now?" he asked cheerfully.

"You didn't just knock on my door?" she asked very quietly, and even though she tried to control it, she could hear the fear in her voice.

"No, ma'am—damn. I didn't see him go up there. There's a Santa on security camera. He's outside your door. You expecting someone?"

"No," she said.

"Didn't hire a Santa?"

"No." And now she was chilled. She glanced at her daughter. What had Anne-Marie been trying to tell her?

"Okay." Luke no longer sounded cheerful. He sounded businesslike. "He doesn't belong here. I'll kick him out."

"No," Rachel said. "He might be dangerous."

"A *Santa*?"

"How did he get past you?" she asked. "And how did he know we were here, in this room?"

Luke cursed. "Good point. We don't have security tonight either. I'm going to have to call the cops. You hang tight and don't open that door."

And he hung up before she could tell him no cops. The last thing she wanted was cops.

She reached into the purse she was carrying tonight and took out the stun gun that SYT had left in the van with mace and a few other protective things. Her hand was shaking terribly.

"Open the door, Rachel," said a male voice she didn't recognize. "I'm sure we can find a way to convince your husband that this was all a misunderstanding."

Tears threatened. They'd found her. Gil's army, just like she knew they would.

She didn't go near the door. She turned up the television a little more, so that Anne-Marie wouldn't hear, then crept toward the bathroom, keeping the bathroom wall between her and the little corridor that led to the door.

"I'm thinking we fly back to somewhere near Winnemucca, and I bring you and the little one out of the wilderness, saving your lives. It might mean you need to lick your fingers and stand outside in this cold for fifteen minutes because frostbite would really help the story, but if we do that, Gil won't know a damn thing."

Rachel wanted to ask why he would do that, this mystery Santa, but she didn't. She knew better than to engage. If she engaged, she had already lost.

She held the stun gun like it was a real gun. Helen had told her not to get a real gun, not with Anne-Marie in the van. Because Rachel didn't know how to use it, and Helen said, too many bad things happened around children and guns.

"You're not saying anything," the man continued. "I know you want to."

She peered around the wall. The safety chain was on, and she'd dead-bolted the door, plus pushed in that so-called security lock. The only way in was for him to knock the door down, right? Or she had to let him in.

That's why he was talking. He wanted her to let him in.

"Mommy?" Anne-Marie asked.

Rachel put a finger to her lips and then she covered her ears, so that Anne-Marie would too. They used to do that when Gil got home from a long day, angry, and wanting someone to take it out on. Rachel would mime instructions to her daughter: remain quiet and don't listen.

"Is Daddy here?" Anne-Marie whispered, and Rachel heard the fear in her voice.

Rachel shook her head. She then indicated that Anne-Marie should join her, because there was protection against this wall, particularly if the man outside wanted to shoot them.

She didn't know if he did. She wasn't sure what the point of that was. But she knew that sometimes Gil could be irrational, and she had no idea who worked for him, or why they felt it necessary to carry so many weapons.

"We can make this work," the man outside the room said.

Anne-Marie grabbed her dog and her slippers, then tucked in behind her mother. Her daughter's warmth made Rachel feel stronger.

"I bet you're wondering why I'm willing to help you," he said. "I've been thinking about it for the last three days as I watched you drive. It's pretty simple, really: you have a big allowance from that husband of yours. You just give me part of it, under the table, and you'll be free and clear. Back in the arms of your family, safe and sound. You don't want to be on the road like this forever, do you?"

She closed her eyes. Maybe, a few years ago, she would have done that. Maybe. But she'd seen Gil get mad at Anne-Marie too many times. She'd seen him clench his fists and unclench them like he meant to hit her.

And Anne-Marie cringed a lot, even now.

"Open the door, Rachel," the man outside the door said.

God, what would he tell the police? That she had faked her death in Nevada? There were no restraining orders against her husband, no calls to 911, nothing to prove her claims of abuse. There was nothing that would prevent him from flying out here and getting her and Anne-Marie.

Rachel was back where she started, no matter what.

She stood slowly, putting her finger to her lips. She wasn't sure she could shut him up, but she had to try. The stun gun, as Helen had told her, could knock down a man five times her size. And then she could—what? Stab him with a butter knife? Use his gun if he carried one?

This hotel clearly had security video, and if she killed him, it would be recorded.

She shouldn't have listened to Helen. Rachel should have known that this plan would all go to hell.

She was never going to escape Gil, never, no matter who made the promises or how big the network was or how much money they threw at the problem.

It had been a dream all along, and she had let herself believe it.

"Honey," Rachel said to Anne-Marie, knowing that she would be damning her daughter too. "I'm going to—"

Sirens. They got louder and then they cut off. But red-and-blue lights reflected in the windows.

At least the police arrived before she could do something stupid. Before she even tried to hurt this unknown man. Not that it would have helped.

Now he was going to the police station, and he'd give them her identity, and—

"I thought you said someone was in the hall," a new male voice said outside her room.

"I did." That voice belonged to Luke. "I'll show you on the security feed. Send your guys out looking. He couldn't have gone far. Some weirdo in a Santa suit. He was menacing my guests."

And then they walked off, still talking.

Rachel's heart kept pounding. Slowly she sank back down, keeping a death grip on the stun gun. After a few more minutes of silence, she put her fingers to her lips again, then quietly, in a crouch, made her way to her purse.

She took out Nebraska's phone, and hit the pre-programmed number.

"Hi," she said breathlessly. "I'm Rachel—"

"I know who you are," said an unfamiliar female voice on the other end of the line. "What's happened?"

Rachel told her, in a low voice, then turned away, adding, "He's seen the van. He knows who we are. He knows where we are. I just wanted to say thanks, but I'm going to have to go home now. Because there's nothing anyone can do—"

"You stay put," the woman said. "I'll have someone meet

you in fifteen minutes. We'll have a new vehicle for you and a safe place to stay."

"But how can you get here so fast?"

"Omaha, right?" the woman asked. "Thank God you listened and didn't stop in a small town. Then it might've taken hours for us to reach you. But you're okay there. It might take twenty minutes, seeing it's Christmas Eve, but no more than that. You stay on the line with me while you wait, okay?"

"Okay," Rachel said.

She heard the tapping of a keyboard, some voices, and someone say, "We got it."

Then she glanced at Anne-Marie.

"It was Santa," Anne-Marie said like an accusation.

Not *like* an accusation. It was an accusation.

Rachel nodded.

"He was *everywhere*," Anne-Marie said.

Rachel closed her eyes for just a minute. Like that stupid song. *He sees you...*

And she had seen him. In truck stops and cafes, smoking outside a gas station in Rawlins. She'd thought him a different Santa every time.

Santa was everywhere this season.

It was the perfect disguise.

The house phone rang and she almost tossed the stun gun into the air. She made herself set it down.

"What's that?" the woman on the other end of the burner cell asked.

"The hotel phone," Rachel said.

It stopped ringing.

"Have you talked to anyone?" the woman asked.

"I called the guy at the desk," Rachel said. "When someone knocked on my door. I wanted to see if it was housekeeping or something."

"Then call the desk," the woman said. "Tell him you're all right. You are all right, aren't you?"

If she didn't think about her elevated blood pressure, then maybe she was. "Yes," Rachel said.

She picked up the hotel phone, and hit "0" again. "Sorry, I—"

"It's all right," Luke said. "The police scared him off. I'm the one who should apologize. They couldn't find him, but at least he's not outside the door. They'll talk to you if you want."

"No," she said. "It's okay."

He hadn't been caught. She didn't know if that was good news or bad.

"Tell him that Candy Mills is coming for you," the woman's voice said on the burner cell. "Tell him it's okay to let Candy come see you."

Rachel told Luke that, even though it felt odd.

"I think I see her pulling in," he said. "I'll send her right up."

Then he hung up.

"I don't know anyone named Candy Mills," Rachel said, and she would remember. The name was weird.

"I'm texting a photo and the passphrase now," the woman said. "She'll give you the passphrase. You'll recognize her from the photo."

"Okay," Rachel said.

"And I'll be on the phone to hear everything."

The cell vibrated in her hand. Rachel looked at it. A middle-aged woman with a weathered face smiled tentatively at the camera.

There was a knock on the door. "Rachel?"

This time, it was a woman's voice.

She said, "There's an awful lot of Sweet Young Things on the road."

The passphrase.

And the moment of truth.

Rachel walked to the door, then peered through the peephole. A woman wearing a heavy jacket let down the hood, revealing a version of that weathered face from the photo.

Rachel crossed her fingers, regretting the fact that she'd left the stun gun behind. She opened the door slowly, keeping the security chain on.

"Candy Mills," the woman said.

"Rachel," Rachel said because she for the life of her couldn't remember her fake name. "And this is Anne-Marie."

She turned to point out her daughter, and her breath caught.

Anne-Marie was standing behind them, pointing the stun gun at the woman. She looked fierce. Her hands didn't tremble at all.

But Rachel's did. She nearly dropped the cell. The woman on the line was asking what was going on.

"Give me the gun, Anne-Marie," Rachel said quietly.

"We don't know her," Anne-Marie said.

"I know, honey, but it's okay," Rachel said.

"Do you know Santa?" Anne-Marie asked the woman.

The woman looked confused. She glanced at Rachel, who drew in her breath slowly. She couldn't help. She didn't dare help. But she tried to convey that the usual answer was the wrong answer.

"I've never met him," the woman said after a moment.

Anne-Marie considered that. Then she set the gun down. Rachel hurried toward it.

The woman closed the door. Rachel picked up the stun gun and put it in her purse. Then she wrapped her arms around Anne-Marie. Anne-Marie clung to her.

"We're going to get you out of here," the woman said. "You'll spend the holiday at my house. It's not much, but it'll do. Christmas put a kink in our plans. But by the 26th, we should have a new van for you, and new stuff. You'll have to leave everything behind."

"Except Anne-Marie's toys," Rachel said. "I checked them. They don't have a tracker."

She thought about the Santa bag at the front desk. Maybe they could pick those up on the way out, and she could thank Luke.

The woman—Candy Mills, if that was her real name—frowned. "I'll double-check. I have some equipment."

She didn't seem too concerned.

"Will he find us again?" Rachel figured it was okay to ask. Anne-Marie had been asking for the entire trip.

"No," Candy Mills said. "We think if there was a tracker, it was on the van. We'll know for sure tomorrow. You said he followed from Winnemucca, right?"

"He had a whole plan," Rachel said.

"Well, we'll take care of that now. He shouldn't be hard to find." She glanced at the tree, gave it a once-over that looked a bit sad.

"You sure you can protect us?" Rachel asked.

Candy Mills smiled, which made her seem younger and friendlier. "Yes," she said. "We've helped a lot of women escape situations worse than yours."

"What if he called Gil and told him where we were?"

"That's why we're going somewhere else. He had no idea where you were headed, right? You never told anyone, right?" Candy Mills sounded a bit intense, as if she wanted to make sure.

"I never said a word," Rachel said. Not even to Anne-Marie.

"I'm signing off now," said the voice on the cell. "You're in good hands."

And before Rachel could say thank you, the woman on the other end of the line hung up.

Rachel swallowed. She didn't want to admit it, but she was happy to have help, even for a day or two.

She felt less alone.

Candy Mills looked at Anne-Marie. "Get your stuff. We're going to go."

Anne-Marie hugged her dog to her chest. She didn't move. "Will Santa know how to find us?"

Candy Mills looked at Rachel, smart enough to realize these questions weren't what they seemed.

"No, honey," Rachel said. "Santa will never find us again."

The sentence made her heart hurt. Somehow, she was going to have to give her daughter Christmas magic again. But not this year.

This year, she was giving her daughter freedom. A real life. A life away from Gil.

"Good," Anne-Marie said, and reached for her clothes. "I hope I never see him again."

"Oh, honey," Rachel said, knowing that wish was impossible. "I hope so too."

THE DISAPPEARANCE OF WICKED

A SEAVY COUNTY STORY

KRISTINE KATHRYN RUSCH

F irst, let me preface my story by telling you that none of us liked Wicked. He was an obnoxious little yappy dog, with long curly white hair that needed trimming and a propensity for peeing on anything vaguely food-like, from a bag of groceries in the open trunk of a car to the kibble set out for the neighborhood cats. He barked most of the time he was awake. When he wasn't barking, he was yipping, a sad little high-pitched sound that was twice as annoying as any bark could be.

Even Isabel, the dog he lived with, an elderly female mix about the size of a Lab, hated him. Isabel, who faithfully guarded our neighborhood hilltop for the past thirteen years, would slink away whenever Wicked was outside, as if to say, *Don't look at me. I have nothing to do with that smelly, undisciplined little thing.*

None of us had much to do with Wicked, not even his so-called owner, Ike Maize. Ike had inherited the dog from his daughter, Roxy, who was going through a messy divorce. Ike and his wife Stella promised to care for Wicked while Roxy went back to California to move her things to Oregon.

I had assumed Roxy would get an apartment when she got to Oregon. Instead, she showed up with the furniture and a six-month-old no one had told me about. The divorce wiped her out financially, so she moved in with her parents.

And that meant Wicked stayed too.

I work at home and am usually immune to the neighborhood noise pollution. I'm not the kind of man who investigates each blaring radio or early morning chain saw. Normally, I play my own stereo so loud that I don't hear much during the day.

But I could hear Wicked. Nonstop. Barking, barking, yipping, and barking.

By the end of the first day, I wanted to strangle the little thing. By the end of the third day, I spent more time glaring at Wicked than I did working. By the end of the week, I was actively plotting the dog's death.

I'm an inventive plotter. The critics say that's one of my (only) strengths as a novelist. In fact, they claim I've been on the bestseller list for the past ten years because I can plot better than anyone else in the business.

Outwardly, my home does not reflect the wealth that my plotting skills have brought me. I kept the same footprint— as my realtor likes to say—and built up to make three full stories. It's quite a redesign, but it fits into the neighborhood —or it pretends to.

And that's all that matters to me.

Because I don't want to leave the Crest Hill Subdivision.

This house was the first house I ever bought—and I vowed not to sell it. Back then, it was a simple split-level, built in 1972, and not remodeled in twenty years. I pulled the orange and green shag carpeting, remodeled the kitchen by myself, and turned the free-standing garage into my writing office, which I still use without many modifications.

In fact, the free-standing garage/office is the problem. The walls are thin because here on the temperate Oregon Coast, houses don't need insulation. I haven't replaced the cheap windows I put in during my first redesign, which is why I can hear that early morning chainsaw and the blaring truck radio.

Normally, I don't mind.

But that was before Wicked.

It was all before Wicked who, oddly enough, changed my view of the neighborhood forever.

The Crest Hill Subdivision was built on a sandy ridgeline, 700 feet above sea level, several blocks east of the Pacific Ocean. The story of the subdivision is a story of neighbors—common in most places around the country, but extremely uncommon here on the Oregon Coast. In Seavy Village, three out of four houses are vacation rentals or second homes. These houses are full every Fourth of July. Two-thirds are full on Thanksgiving. A third are full during spring break.

Seavy Village has housing for forty thousand people, and hotel rooms for twice that many, but its year-round population is 7,000. Most neighborhoods are entirely empty most of the time or have only one year-round family residing on those quiet streets.

Crest Hill Subdivision has always been different. We are a small enclave in a sea of empty houses. All twenty houses in Crest Hill are owner-occupied.

For the most part, we get along. We have an annual barbeque at Dave the Plumber's. When we see each other during the rest of the year, we always wave. If we have time, we stop on the street and chat.

Not a week goes by without a group of us gathered in front of the mailboxes, exchanging the village gossip, and catching up on each other's lives. We watch out for each other as best we can, and sometimes we even babysit each other's children or feed the pets during the occasional long weekend.

When my money started pouring it—and it did pour: one minute I was scrambling to make my mortgage, the next I was talking to my broker about various places to store excess cash—I could have built a true mansion on a cliff face overlooking the ocean. But every bare piece of property I looked at, every tumbledown house that could be replaced for something better, existed in that sea of empty houses.

I didn't like that much isolation, so I stayed in Crest Hill, along with Ike and Stella next door, the Sandersons one house up, Old Mrs. Gailton across the street, and Annalita Carmica on the corner. We formed the foundation of the neighborhood and over time, we acquired even more full-timers. Dave the Plumber and his wife (whose name I always forget), Joyce the Hollywood Producer who retired to her dream house, and the McMillians who bought, for a song, a McMansion that lost its view to the six-plex.

We're a pretty quiet bunch who lived in very safe place— or so I thought, in those days before Wicked moved in.

The morning Wicked disappeared seemed like any other. I had trudged through the rain from my back door to my freestanding office, a hot mug of coffee in one hand, and an offering to the Goddess in the other.

The Goddess was the elderly cat who lived alone in my office. She bit the hand that fed her each and every day. I was inordinately fond of her, enough that I put up with her nasty temper and her inability to get along with anyone, including me.

She spent that morning in the library window, watching Wicked, as she often did. She hated the barking more than I did. Once, she had seen him peeing on one of her dishes that I had set down outside. She had pushed the screen out of the window, then attacked him, beating him so badly that I had to go over to Ike and Stella's and offer to pay for Wicked's trip to the vet.

That's when I learned how much Ike hated Wicked.

"Let the damn dog suffer," he said. "He's got to learn that the world isn't his toilet."

During Wicked's stay on the hilltop, the Goddess glared out the library window—the only room in my office that had a good view of Wicked's yard—and occasionally made little growling noises. Mostly, she seemed to believe if she stared hard enough, Wicked would feel her anger and shut up.

It spoke to my desperation that daily I wished she did have magical powers. I wanted something to shut that damn dog up.

About 11 o'clock that morning, I got my wish. Wicked let out one of his sad yips, followed by the strangest bark I'd ever heard. It was high pitched and sharp, almost sounding startled. Then he let out a long half-bark, half-yowl that seemed more like a human scream than a noise any dog was trained to make.

That sound didn't end. It got cut off. I leaned back in my office chair and listened, waiting for the barking to begin again.

It didn't.

Instead, I heard the squeal of truck tires against gravel. Rocks pelted my newly built fence (good fences make good neighbors; they also keep out little peeing yappy dogs).

Then silence.

After a moment, the Goddess sprinted across my desk. She landed in my lap, meowed in my face, and pawed at my hands. I hadn't seen her that agitated since a yellow tom sprayed one of the rose bushes outside the office's sliding glass doors. So I followed her into the library.

She jumped onto the window ledge and pressed her face against the glass.

I peered out. From this one window, I could see over the fence and into the Maize's yard. No truck sat in the drive-way, even though I had heard one. Isabel, the elderly dog, was sitting on the walkway to the back door, head tilted to one side.

I didn't see Wicked.

The Goddess was murping, a sound she made when something in her universe was out of order. I frowned, my stomach knotting in a little ball.

I realized I recognized that sequence of sounds.

I hadn't heard it in years, not since the Maize's daughter was little and Ike drove up the driveway too fast one afternoon, running over one of their cats.

He scooped the bleeding, broken creature into his arms, placed it on the floor of the truck, and then backed out of the driveway, peeling away as fast as his old Ford one-ton could go.

He made it to the vet's in record time, but it was still too late. He'd crushed his daughter's favorite cat beneath the wheels of his truck and it took months for her to forgive him.

Now, I figured the same thing had happened. Right in the middle of her messy divorce, one that threatened to spill into a long custody battle over her own daughter, her father runs over the dog she has loved since she moved away from home.

Ike had to be devastated.

I really didn't want to be there for him—there were some things that were beyond neighborly, even in Crest Hill Subdivision—but I knew I had to investigate, just in case my writerly imagination had leaped to the wrong conclusion.

I let myself out of the office. The morning rain had

turned into a light drizzle, the kind that looks harmless but actually can soak you within five minutes.

Red and gold leaves littered my driveway. Sometime during the night, a raccoon had clearly pulled part of a white plastic trash bag through the slight hole in my garbage can's lid, scattering plastic food containers and paper plates across the yard.

I ignored the mess and walked to the fence. It was a picket fence, painted brown, with the pickets rising over six feet, so that few people could see over the top of them. I pulled open the gate in the center and stepped into the Maize's unpaved driveway.

The rainstorm had left the ground so wet that the retreating truck had torn up deep grooves in the muck. I walked to the edge of them, expecting to see some pieces of white curly hair ground into the dirt or maybe a bit of blood on the already wet rocks. Maybe even a smashed collar or the impression of a small dog's body in the dirt.

To my disappointment, I saw none of that. I didn't even see Ike's footprints in the muddy gravel, although mine were clearly visible.

I frowned and looked up. Isabel, who was used to me, stared at me, a matching frown on her large doggy face. I couldn't tell if she was perplexed to see me standing on her driveway or if the truck's quick retreat had surprised her.

I clasped my hands behind my back and walked farther up the driveway, so that I could peer inside the garage. No injured Wicked lying on his side on the concrete. No impish brown eyes peering at me through the small window beside the garage door.

Nothing barked, nothing yipped.

The silence was profound.

Isabel sighed, seemingly in relief, and put her head between her paws. Again, I couldn't understand the reason for her emotion. Relief that a human was on the case? Or relief that Wicked had finally shut up?

Or both?

I felt no relief. The depth of my Wicked hatred surprised me. Part of me really wanted to see that dog dead. I had never actively wished anything dead before, not even the raccoons who constantly defeated each garbage can I bought.

I had hoped to find evidence of that dog's demise.

Finding none disappointed me.

But at least, something had forced Wicked to become quiet. As I peered into my neighbor's garage, I realized I should accept the gift.

I hurried back to my office—after stopping briefly to clean up after the raccoons—and had the most productive day I'd had in the month and a half since Wicked had moved in.

The silence didn't last.

As I microwaved the take-out I picked up for dinner, someone knocked on my door. Even though our neighborhood was close, very few people knocked. The UPS guy knocked every morning, and the newspaper delivery boy knocked once a month, but almost no one else came to the door.

I pressed *stop* on the microwave and walked to the door. The door was solid core, with no peephole, something I'd meant to remedy. So opening it always contained, for me, a small bit of adventure.

Someday, my vivid thriller writer's imagination told me, the person on the other side of that knock would be a serial killer, coming to attack me. My logical mind told me that serial killers didn't knock, but my vivid imagination would counter with the fact that thieves often did, just to see if someone was home.

Fortunately, the person waiting on my stoop wasn't a serial killer or a thief.

It was Ike.

He was a big man with long, graying hair that showed his hippy roots. He slouched on a good day, but this evening, he was nearly bent in half.

He gave me a sheepish half smile. "I don't suppose I can ask you a question."

"Sure," I said. "Come on in."

I stepped back and he walked in, careful to stay on the throw rug I put over the hardwood at the start of every rainy season. Even though we had been neighbors for more than fifteen years, we hardly went inside each other's homes. I couldn't remember the last time he had been in mine.

He looked at his mud-covered shoes as he said, "My daughter sent me over here. Seems Wicked is missing."

His voice had the right combination of sincerity and loss, but he wasn't meeting my gaze.

"Wicked stopped barking about 11 this morning," I said.

Ike looked up, frowning at me much the way his elderly dog had when I stood in their driveway.

I told Ike the entire story, such as it was, leaving out, of course, the Goddess's odd attack and her murping sounds, as well as my desire to see Wicked's blood seeping into the muddy tire prints.

"A truck?" Ike repeated.

"I thought maybe it was you," I said. "You know, that whole incident with the cat."

He winced. "No one lets me forget that. I didn't mean to hit the damn thing."

"No one ever does," I said, then realized I wasn't being neighborly. "You want a beer?"

"I want an entire keg," he said tiredly. Then he smiled at me. "But a bottle will do."

I got him a Rogue Brewery Pale Ale from the fridge, then kicked out one of the dining room chairs. "Sit for a minute."

"I'll track all over," he said.

"Who cares?" I said, catching myself before I added, *I have a housekeeper who worries about such things.* I had a lot more money than my neighbors—hell, these days, I had more money than the entire town—but I didn't try to call attention to that.

Although it was hard not to notice in my maple and cherry kitchen, with the matching formal dining table, the brand new appliances, and every cooking gadget known to man lining the kitchen counters. Not that they saw those.

What they usually saw was my one and only toy. My late-model Jag, which I replaced each and every year.

He sat down and took a sip from the longneck bottle.

"That goddamn dog," he said. "If my karma determined that I had to run over only one animal with my truck, why did it have to be Roxy's kitten? Why the hell couldn't it have been Wicked?"

"If the neighborhood had known you were looking for volunteers . . ." I said, letting my words trail off.

He looked up at me, startled. Then he realized I was joking. He leaned against the table, resting his elbow against the tablecloth my housekeeper insisted on changing every Tuesday.

"There were times I might've looked," he said. "The Bastard—" That was his nickname for his daughter's soon-to-be ex "—trained the little fucker, or didn't train it, as the case may be. Wicked loves my daughter and that baby, and will guard them with his little doggy life, but other than that, he isn't a dog at all. He's a goddamn menace. He doesn't shut up, he pees all over everything, he tears up the furniture."

"He's still a puppy," I said, not exactly sure why I was making excuses for a dog I hated.

"A puppy?" Ike said, sitting upright. "Are you kidding? Wicked is three years old. I've been trying to train him all month. It's not working."

Obviously, I nearly said, but didn't. No sense in causing my neighbor more pain.

"I haven't heard Wicked since that truck," I said. "You'd

think if he got injured or snuck into the woods, we'd hear him."

"You'd think the entire town would hear him," Ike said. "I'm hoping the little bastard ran off."

The little bastard, trained by the Bastard. I had never put Ike's language together before. He hated Wicked not just because he was an uncontrollable dog, but also because the dog represented an uncontrollable soon-to-be ex-son-in-law.

"If Wicked did run off," I said, "he did so chasing that truck. Silently."

"That dog isn't quiet about anything," Ike said. Then he paused for a moment before adding, "You thought I was driving that truck?"

I nodded.

His frown grew deeper. "Not many trucks sound like mine. Did you see it?"

"Nope," I said, taking another sip of my ale. "I heard it. It sounded big and heavy, like yours does when it comes up the driveway. But you usually don't peel out. In fact, the only time I ever heard you peel away down the driveway was—"

"The cat incident," he said tiredly. "I know."

He started to take a sip from his beer, and stopped.

"The Bastard," he said.

"Hmmm?" I asked. I wasn't sure if he was talking about the soon-to-be ex or the little dog.

"The Bastard," Ike said to me, slowly, like he was having a realization. "He used to peel."

I sipped. Thought. Remembered.

He did peel. It was one of the noises I had gotten used to. Roxy had started dating the Bastard in high school. It became one of those neighborhood dramas, something everyone in Crest Hill Subdivision talked about, since the Bastard came from a family of do-nothings on the wrong side of town.

In a town of 7,000, the wrong side is pretty low-key. We don't have murderers, thieves or knife-wielding maniacs. Our do-nothings are well named. They're freeloaders who try to live on county money without doing any work. If they do get a job, from an unsuspecting out-of-towner, they lose that job within the month.

The Bastard's family was pretty notorious. Entire generations lived in a small trailer on an expensive lot near the ocean. They wouldn't move, no matter how much developers offered them, and they wouldn't work either. Mostly, they sat outside—rain or shine—and drank, throwing their empties into an ever-growing pile in a part of the yard that had once housed a driveway.

The Bastard had that bad-boy charm. At least, that was what fifteen-year-old Roxy had thought. She had been a straight-A student, and remained so, graduating at the top of her class, earning several partial scholarships—enough so that the Maizes could send her to the school of her choice in California.

The Bastard followed. By this point, he had dropped out of high school, lost three jobs, and had his first DUI. Yet for her, the charm remained.

For Ike, who complained about him every moment he got, the Bastard was a gigantic version of Wicked, peeing all over the neighborhood, then barking and yipping when anyone else got in his mangy little way.

When the Bastard followed Roxy to California, I stopped thinking about him.

"I thought he was still in California," I said. That was what Stella had told me one morning when we met at the mailboxes, both of us picking up our rain-soaked copies of the *Oregonian*.

"He went to live with his mother in Vegas," Ike said.

"Oh, jeez." I didn't even have to ask how that was working out. When you took do-nothings and gave them the opportunity to get rich quick for very little effort, they spent every dime they hadn't earned on penny slots and the upcoming big win.

"Yeah," Ike said. "Good riddance, I thought. But he threatened to come back and get his things. I told Roxy to get a restraining order, but she thinks he doesn't have the balls to drive all the way up here."

"But you think he does," I said, trying to keep the surprise from my voice. I agreed with Roxy on this one. A third generation do-nothing wasn't going to drive across three states just to retrieve his things. That would take too much effort.

"Yeah, I do," Ike said. "He's a mean, weasely little bastard who thinks my daughter is something he owns."

He took the final sip of his beer and sighed.

"I'm not the smartest man in the world," he said, "but I've seen guys like him before. When they think they're losing the only things they own, they get dangerous."

I hadn't thought of that. Ike was right; sometimes do-nothings became violent and possessive. I hadn't seen that in the Bastard, but then I hadn't done much more than exchange a few sentences with him in a little more than five years.

"Why would he take Wicked?" I asked.

Ike gave me a chilling glance. "Because my daughter loves that horrid little dog. Although for the life of me, I have no idea why."

In the next few days, the Wicked saga became the focus of neighborhood gossip. From Dave the Plumber, I heard that Ike had the cops searching for the Bastard's truck. From Old Mrs. Gailton, I heard that Roxy had been getting threatening phone calls. From Stella, I heard that Roxy had finally hired an attorney to finalize the divorce and to get that all-important restraining order.

The whole family believed that the Bastard had stolen Wicked, although the chief of police, Dan Reilly, thought the little dog had finally run away.

"Good riddance," he said. "The nasty thing peed on my leg one afternoon."

We had run into each other at the local A&P. We stood in the fresh fish aisle, which smelled of both fish and cocktail sauce. Twice during our conversation, the butcher snuck us bits of a steak he was cooking up in the back.

"We're looking for the Bastard, of course," Reilly said. He was a big man with gym rat muscles. They made him look formidable in his gray-green uniform.

As he spoke, I smiled to myself. Ike had everyone in town calling his daughter's soon-to-be ex the Bastard. "But I doubt we'll find him. He knows better than to come back here."

"Why's that?" I asked.

"He's got a bench warrant," Reilly said. "You didn't know that?"

"No," I said. "Does Ike?"

"Now he does."

"What did the Bastard do?" Even I had picked up the phrase.

"Robbed the Cruise Inn one Friday night using his father's .45. Got away with about one hundred dollars, but the crime's pretty serious. See, it's—"

"Armed robbery," I said. "A felony."

Reilly's eyes twinkled. "Forgot you write about this stuff."

Usually I write about bigger things. Stockbrokers taking down entire corporations and having hit men after them; the President surviving assassination attempts; and, of course, my biggest seller, the serial killer truck driver working the Pacific Northwest who finally gets caught by the plucky female cop from the Oregon Coast.

"How come I never heard about this robbery?" I asked.

Reilly shrugged. "The Cruise Inn doesn't want anyone to know how easy they are to rob. Or how often they do get robbed."

"How often do they get robbed?" I asked.

"At least once a month. We leave it out of the police report as per their request."

I shook my head, this time letting my amusement show. These things happen in small towns. In fact, when I moved to Seavy Village, Ike Maize told me that the best way to get your news was to talk to the locals. The paper didn't cover most of the interesting stories, since we were a tourist town and we didn't want our tiny crime waves to scare the tourists away.

"How long has he had that warrant?" I asked.

"Since before he went to California," Reilly said.

At least a year then. "Why didn't you tell Ike? He knew where the Bastard was."

Reilly sighed. "I thought about it. But Ike and Roxy fought about the Bastard enough. Ike almost lost his daughter because of it. So I never said anything to Ike, although I did find out where the Bastard and Roxy lived. I tried to get someone down there to act on the warrant, but they wouldn't. Seems a $100 theft, even if the thief used a .45, is small potatoes to them."

I wondered how much anguish it would have solved for the Maizes to have the Bastard arrested in California. But that would have been before the marriage went south, and Roxy might've gotten stuck, like so many women did, waiting for her man to get out of prison.

"What if he *has* come back to town?" I asked.

"I would've heard about it," Reilly said. "Everyone's looking out for him."

"Now they are," I said. "But a week ago? I had no idea this was going on. Neither did anyone else in Crest Hill. And we were the ones most likely to see him."

"He's not in town," Reilly said. "You can take that to the bank."

If I took it to the bank, I wouldn't be able to deposit it. Much as I liked Dan Reilly, he was a placeholder chief of police, one of the local boys made good until the out-of-town replacement showed up like she was supposed to do sometime in the following spring.

Reilly, for all his certainty, really didn't know much about police work. He knew Seavy Village, and nothing else. Usually, in this town, that was enough. But bench warrants, armed robbery, and hints of violence took the Bastard out of the local small-time range and into something much more dangerous.

Something I really didn't want on the other side of my fence, not even for a short, dog-stealing visit.

Still, I didn't hear any more trucks except Ike's reliable one-ton. Occasionally Isabel barked, but those were welcome-home barks for her family or her standard warning to the UPS guy not to get too close.

The Goddess and I worked every day. I progressed on the latest book. She growled at the raccoons. We both had a productive week.

Until we heard a truck zoom its way up the Maize's driveway. The Goddess murped at me as she ran from the double glass doors to the library window.

I didn't go to the library window at all. I hurried out of the office, grabbing my cell phone along the way.

The truck I heard was bigger than Ike's. It was one of those with the double-long bed. I had no idea what kind it was—trucks aren't my specialty—but I called this kind, which stood higher, wider, and longer than most trucks, penis shrinkers. I figured any guy who wanted one of these was overcompensating for something, and the overcompensation was worse if he actually found the dough to buy one of these monsters.

I had already dialed 911 as I approached the fence. Through the slats, I could see the Bastard. He had stepped out of the truck's cab, leaving the door open. The truck was running, and even over the roar of the diesel engine, I could hear the dinging of the warning bell, reminding us all that the keys were in the ignition.

The Bastard ignored the sound. He was one of those guys who changed from a thin, somewhat good-looking teenager to a muscular, menacing twentysomething.

As I reached for the gate's handle, I saw Roxy step out of the garage. Isabel was barking, a strange, frightened bark I hadn't ever heard from her. She blocked Roxy's path, but Roxy went around her.

Roxy, still carrying baby weight around her hips and stomach. Roxy, carrying the baby—now a cute blond toddler—tightly in her arms.

"You're not supposed to be here," she said in a frightened voice as the 911 dispatch answered on my cell.

I stopped, softly gave my address, and said, "We need police up here immediately. We have a felon with a bench warrant against him in my neighbor's yard, threatening everyone he sees."

Then I pulled the phone away from my ear, opened the gate, and stepped onto the Maize's driveway.

The Bastard whirled toward me. He had something

white and bloody in his arms, and I realized that was Wicked. I couldn't tell if the dog was alive or dead.

"Go away," the Bastard snarled at me. "This is a family matter."

"It's a neighborhood matter," I said loudly, hoping the 911 dispatch could still hear me. "You're not supposed to be on Ike Maize's property. There's a restraining order against you."

I said all of that for the 911 dispatch, not for the Bastard. Still, he glared at me with so much anger that my pulse started to race.

"Is that Wicked?" Roxy asked, her voice shaking.

"Stay back," I said.

But her question had turned the Bastard back to her.

"Yeah." He tossed the dog onto the driveway. The dog bounced on the gravel and then, appallingly, whimpered.

Time and time again, I had imagined horrible, hideous ways to kill that dog, but now that I saw it in front of me, I ashamed for myself and terrified for the dog.

So was Roxy. She ran to the dog, and as she did, the Bastard ran toward her.

"Roxy, don't!" I yelled, and I ran toward both of them.

But I was too far back. The Bastard grabbed his daughter from Roxy's arms and raced for the truck. He cradled the toddler against his chest as he jumped into the cab, pulling the door closed.

"Noooo!" Roxy screamed, running for the truck. I ran for it too. She got there ahead of me, grabbing the door handle.

The Bastard shoved the truck into reverse and sped up,

sending gravel in my direction. It hit me like sharp needles, but I kept going.

Roxy lost her grip, falling backward.

For one horrible moment, I thought he was going to back over her, but he didn't. He put the truck into drive, and sped off down the driveway.

I reached her side a moment later. Her knees and hands were scraped and she sat there, defeated, staring at the truck down on the road.

"Here," I said, thrusting the cell phone at her. "I've already called 911. Give them the license plate and the make of the truck. I'm going after the Bastard."

I didn't give her time to argue. As I ran back through the gate, I realized I should have told her to call her dad as well. I hoped she was smart enough to figure that out.

I ducked inside my house, grabbed my car keys and sprinted for my one indulgence. That Jag could outperform any other car in Seavy Village. And it could outperform a penis shrinker too.

I slid into the driver's seat and started the car in the same motion. It purred into life, the engine ready to go at whatever speed I wanted.

I peeled down my driveway—something I had always wanted to do, but never dared to, not in this quiet subdivision. I turned right at the bottom of the driveway, thanking whatever developer had designed this place for the long twisty road that took us out of the subdivision to the highway.

I could just see the truck at the intersection. He didn't

come to a full stop—he was kidnapping his daughter after all —but the stupid Bastard had his signal on.

He was turning left. To the straightaway that would take him out of Seavy Village and down Highway 101, away from the police and into a kind of legal no-man's land.

He pulled out and for the first time, I cursed the fact that I had given Roxy my phone. I wanted to tell the dispatch what direction he was going in.

Of course, in this tiny town, he only had two choices— north or south. The smart direction was south. Anyone with a brain would think of that straightaway and legal no-man's land.

There, in the miles between Seavy Village and Whale Rock, the Seavy Village Police Department lost its jurisdiction. For ten miles, only the state police could arrest anyone. Then the Whale Rock police took over.

The state police, underfunded and undermanned, never patrolled that section of the highway. If they had to come in to make an arrest, they often had to come from another part of the county—sometimes from another part of the state.

When I reached the intersection, I didn't stop either. I turned left, sliding behind a black Subaru and in front of a bright blue Smart Car. The Smart Car slammed on its brakes, but I was already in the other lane, heading south at 80 miles an hour, double the speed limit.

There weren't a lot of cars on the road, but there were enough that I had to weave and dodge around them, moving from the southbound lane to the passing lane to the shoulder in the areas where I could see far enough ahead to make sure there were no cyclists on the road.

The hotels and convenience stores, the kitschy restaurants and antique stores sped by me in a blur. My engine roared as I shifted into the final gear, cranking the speed up to 100 miles per hour.

I had never driven these roads this fast. Part of me hoped someone would report me to the police—I could lead them on a goose chase to the Bastard, and then, since they were already on the scene, they could arrest him for the state police.

Part of me prayed that I wouldn't hit anything or anyone. If I hit someone going this fast, I'd kill them. My Jag was so well built that I'd probably survive, but I wasn't sure I could live with myself.

Then I thought of that little girl. I had only gotten a glimpse of her, even though she lived right next door for the past few weeks. Tiny, blond, quiet for someone that age, on this afternoon, she had been wearing a pink dress that showed her chubby legs.

Those legs were probably coated with Wicked's blood, rubbed off from the Bastard's hands.

I shuddered, gripped the steering wheel tighter, and pressed hard on the accelerator. I continued to weave, continued to pray, and finally, as the road narrowed and curved up the mountain between Seavy Village and Whale Rock, I saw the truck.

It was hard to miss with that extended back end. A lot of young men in Seavy Village loved those trucks, but most couldn't afford them.

It had to be the Bastard.

I drove even faster.

The truck moved closer at a rapid pace.

Now if I swerved, I would hit the guardrail, maybe bounce over it and fall wheels over roof all the way to the ocean. Or if I crossed into the northbound lane, I would hit the mountainside.

I wouldn't survive either of those.

My breath caught. I had to make myself exhale and think. I couldn't force the Bastard off the road because he had the toddler with him.

But there was a wide area in the road about eight miles from this point, where another road—coming from the east —intersected it. I could force him down that road, away from the ocean.

That road dead-ended into a large parking lot that led to a state park.

I zoomed up to him, then around him, hoping that he was smart enough to stop or turn when he came across an obstacle. He knew these roads better than I did, and I hoped that would influence his driving as well.

When I reached the road that formed a T with the high-way, I glanced east. The road was as wide as I remembered. Someone driving fast could make a quick turn—even if that someone was in an extra long truck.

I stopped only a few yards away, turned on my flashers, and blocked both lanes. I kept watching both lanes, hoping that the first vehicle to approach—on either side—was the Bastard's truck.

Of course, it wasn't. A minivan heading north pulled up and stopped. A middle-aged man with a paunch and graying hair got out. He walked around to the driver's side and knocked on the window.

"You okay?"

"No," I said. "Move away from my car."

"You can't block the road."

In the distance, I saw the truck. I pointed at it.

"You see that truck? The man in there is wanted for armed robbery. He kidnapped the baby in the car with him. I'm trying to force him to stop. You got a cell phone?"

The man was looking at the truck, squinting. "Yeah."

"Call the police. Tell them that you've seen the gray long-bed truck that everyone's looking for. Tell them he's gone into Whale Cove State Park. Can you do that?"

"Um—"

"Because I'm going after him and I need backup."

The truck had nearly reached the T. He was at the point where he would see the car blocking the highway. At that moment, I realized it was good to have the middle-aged man alongside my Jag. The Bastard wouldn't know I was waiting for him.

He turned east, just like I expected him to. His truck was too big to make a U-turn. The drive to the parking lot and back would allow him to drive north again.

"Move!" I said to the middle-aged man.

Smart guy, he ran behind my car, so that I could zoom after the Bastard.

My initial plan had been to follow the Bastard down to the parking lot, but as I drove the few yards, I realized that was stupid. The best thing I could do was park in front of the T. He'd have nowhere to go.

I parked over both lanes of the state park road, blocking it, my Jag facing north.

Then I shut off the ignition, set the parking brake, and got out.

I was only a few feet away when the Bastard crashed into my car. The sound was tremendous, overpowering everything, the scream of metal on metal.

His truck shoved my car toward me. I had to dive into the ditch between the highway and the mountainside to get out of the way. My car rolled and then hit the guardrail.

The Bastard turned north and drove away as if nothing happened.

I lay in the ditch. I had landed in cold brackish muddy water. I made myself climb out slowly, my heart pounding, my breath coming in short gasps.

I never expected him to hit my car, not with the toddler in his truck. I thought he'd get out, scream at me, and stay busy until the police showed up.

Maybe I'm not as good a plotter as the reviewers say I am.

I pulled myself up by my hands, then got onto the state park road and walked to the highway. I stood beside the highway, looking north, probably as forlornly as Roxy had looked as the Bastard drove off with her baby girl.

In the distance, I heard sirens.

I turned, slowly, and saw the middle-aged guy with the van. He was walking toward me, clutching a cell phone.

I refused to look at my Jag.

"That was like a monster truck rally," he said. "I kept expecting him to drive over your car."

He sounded almost excited. His cheeks were flushed. As he got closer, I realized he was probably younger than I was. All I had seen before was the gray hair and paunch. I'd missed the roundness to his cheeks, the brightness of his eyes.

Or maybe that came from the adrenaline brought on by witnessing an accident.

"He did enough to my car," I said without looking at it. I didn't want to know exactly what happened to it. I knew the moment it hit the guardrail that he had totaled it.

Because of my vivid imagination, I did not want to know what the driver's side looked like. I didn't want to have nightmares about what might have happened to me had I been inside.

The middle-aged guy waved the cell phone at me. "They said that they already had reports on the guy and they were heading this way. They said that they'd catch him now that he turned around. You forced him back to Seavy Village, you know?"

I knew. That hadn't quite been my plan—I didn't have a plan past blocking the road and waiting for the police—but it would have to do.

I would rather have the police take down the Bastard with the baby in the truck than have me do it.

"How'd you know what was going on with the guy?" the middle-aged man asked.

"I was there when he took the baby." I suddenly felt very tired. My whole body hurt.

I wanted to go home. It meant I would leave the scene of

an accident, which was a crime, but not a major one if no one got injured.

I had a hunch I could talk my way out of that one.

And even if I couldn't, I could pay the damn fine.

"Can you give me a lift?" I asked the middle-aged guy. "I want to go home."

The middle-aged man grinned. "I'd be happy to," he said. "Just don't ask me if you can drive."

The middle-aged man, whose name was Tom Yates, chattered all the way to Crest Hill. I figured it was a nervous reaction and let him talk. I had him let me out at the bottom of Maize's driveway—for some reason I didn't want him to see my house—and then I waved as he drove away.

He had told me he was going to the police station to make a report. What a good citizen he was. I figured they could come to me if they wanted to talk.

As I reached the top of the driveway, I was stunned to see Ike's truck, two police cars, and an ambulance. One of the paramedics was working hard on something on the ground.

It took me a moment to realize he was bandaging up Wicked.

Ike wasn't around. Neither was Roxy.

But a uniformed police officer—a man I recognized but didn't know by name—walked over to me.

"You the famous writer neighbor?"

"Yeah," I said tiredly.

"I didn't expect you here, sir," he said. "I thought you'd be by Whale Cove State Park."

"I was. But the other guy at the scene offered to drive me home."

The policeman stuck out his hand. I stared at it a moment before taking it. He shook hard, then let go.

"You're a real hero, sir. They have the baby. She's fine. The Maizes have gone down to the station to get her."

"So they caught the Bastard," I said.

"They did. He's going away for a long, long time."

I hoped so. I hoped that the legal system worked the way it was supposed to. I would testify against him, that was for certain.

But I didn't say that. I just nodded at the police officer and walked over to the paramedic.

"Didn't know you guys worked on dogs," I said.

"That girl," he said, "she was hysterical. Dispatch thought she had been injured and sent me up here. She asked me to work on the dog. How could I say no?"

I looked down at the stretcher. Wicked's eyes were glassy and he was panting. The paramedic had bandaged his back legs.

"That guy who took the dog—he cut its tendons in its back legs. Knew what he was doing too, because he stayed away from major arteries. This poor thing'll probably never walk right again."

Wicked's gaze met mine. He was clearly in pain. He whimpered.

Lifting his leg was probably impossible now. He

wouldn't pee on my groceries again. He probably wouldn't ever run again.

I never thought I could feel sorry for that dog, but I did.

"I've got him stabilized," the paramedic was saying. "Can you let Ike know I'm taking the dog to Seavy Village Animal Clinic? They'll know what to do with him."

"Think they'll have to put him down?" the officer said from behind me.

"No," the paramedic said. "He's not a horse. You don't have to shoot him just because he's injured his leg. Right, buddy?"

To my surprise, he put his hand gently on Wicked's side and Wicked didn't even try to bite him. The dog closed his eyes. His tail thumped.

"I'll tell Ike," I said. I wasn't sure he'd be happy. But he would have a different dog than the one he hated. Wicked would never be the same.

Neither would Roxy. I only hoped her daughter wouldn't have lasting scars.

Knowing the Maizes, they would do everything they could to make that little girl feel loved and wanted, not the product of some felon who had seduced their only daughter.

The paramedic wheeled the stretcher into the back of the ambulance, got in beside it, and pulled the double doors closed. The ambulance backed up in the very tracks left by the Bastard's truck, then eased carefully down the driveway as if its cargo were as precious as an injured human being.

The officer watched from beside me. Then he looked at me and frowned. "You okay?"

"Tired," I said.

"No kidding. You did a great thing."

I hadn't done anything great. If anything, I'd been reckless and stupid, letting my vivid imagination get away with me, making me think I could be as heroic as the people I wrote about.

"What do we do about my car?" I asked. "It's crumpled on the side of the road by Whale Cove State Park."

"I'll take care of it," the officer said. "And we'll need you to make a statement whenever you're ready."

"I'm ready now." I wanted this incident behind me.

I didn't want to think about Wicked or the Bastard or Ike's helpless hatred of both. I wanted to go back to my office and use my vivid imagination to create stories.

I thought it would be easy to go back. But I found I couldn't shake the memories. Which is why I'm writing this.

Wicked is home. He'll limp badly, and he'll be a mostly indoor dog. The incident changed his temperament—or, as Ike says, being helpless has. Wicked lost all the aggression that made him the nasty little piece of work that he was.

Roxy's divorce went through. The Bastard pled out to the minimum on both kidnapping and the armed robbery. He'll be gone for years.

And the neighborhood has gone back to normal. Except that people ask me for advice now, as if my impulsive moment has given me some kind of wisdom.

Actually, Old Mrs. Gailton says they don't see me as wise so much as the neighborhood leader. The mayor of Crest Hill Subdivision.

Apparently, it's an appointed position. It's certainly not one I want.

I blame Wicked. If it hadn't been for the little bastard, I'd still be the mostly invisible weird writer who lives next to the Maizes, not the thriller writer who channels James Bond in his off-time.

So I hide in my office with the Goddess. She hunts raccoons again, having no interest in Wicked now that he's not barking incessantly.

I have a little more interest. Sometimes I wonder what he went through in his last days with the Bastard. Sometimes I wonder if Wicked realized he meant nothing to the man who had trained him. And I wonder if the little dog had wanted to die when the Bastard tossed him onto the driveway.

I'll never know, and Wicked will never tell.

He's quiet these days. Isabel actually stands guard over him, as if she understands the changes too.

Sometimes in the middle of the afternoon, when no one's around, I go to the Maize's yard and pet him.

I have the sense that, ever since the incident, Wicked needs comfort.

And I know that I do too.

Jury Duty
A Seavy County Story

KRISTINE KATHRYN RUSCH

Pamela sat in the center of the courtroom, not too close to the front because she didn't want to call attention to herself, and not in the back because she didn't want people to think she was hiding. She had done everything she could to blend in: she wore no make-up, and her clothes were Northwest business casual—a pair of brown slacks with an off-white sweater. With her left hand, she fingered her juror number—267—thoughtfully provided on a little wooden keychain so that she wouldn't lose it.

The court clerk pulled numbers out of a box and handed them to the judge. He was balding, and the top of his head shone in the fluorescent lights. His nasal voice boomed through the courtroom without the aid of a microphone, "Five-hundred-and-eighty-one. Five, eight, one."

As the unlucky man rose from his seat on the left side of

the courtroom, the remaining members of the jury pool swiveled to watch him walk toward the jury box. Six people sat there already, hands folded, heads down, waiting.

The judge had said they would pick twenty-seven, enough for two juries and three extras. Both juries would listen to the case, although one jury would be designated as "alternate." The remaining three people were alternates also, added protection for a death penalty case that could last over a month.

Pamela had been called up two weeks ago, along with 1,000 others out of this county of 50,000, and she had stood in her kitchen, clutching the letter, feeling an uncomfortable sense of irony.

When she had come to Rickets Rock, a town so small that it seldom showed up on any map, she had decided that she would live as quietly as she could. She didn't want to draw attention to herself, good or bad. That meant getting a driver's license, registering to vote, being a good citizen. It meant concocting a history, and trying to smile at the locals. It meant lying, each and every day.

The jury summons had caught her in the lie: she couldn't back out because she had used a false name on her voter registration form. She had to go along with the fiction that she was Pamela Jackson, and hope that something about Pamela would keep her off the largest and most notorious jury the county had seen in decades.

"Juror thirty-four," the judge said. "Three-four."

A woman two seats from Pamela stood, and nearly tripped as she tried to get out of the row. Pamela kept turning her number over and over, the hard wood edges catching on her fingertips.

She had decided, when she had gone to orientation and received the outrageously long questionnaire, that she wouldn't lie if at all possible: she knew that trying to remember too many lies had tripped up more than one person.

So she had placed her personal views on the pages, thinking that they would disqualify her. Particularly the carefully worded questions on pages 10 through 13, the ones about law, the death penalty, and murder.

Question 33: Do you believe that some acts are so heinous that they can only be punished by death?

To which she had replied: *Yes.*

Question 50: Have you known or are you related to anyone who was murdered?

To which she had replied: *Yes.*

And *Question 117: Do you believe Raymond Northrup is guilty of the crimes of which he has been accused?*

To which she had replied: *I could care less.*

She had felt certain that the defense attorney, going through the questionnaires, would demand she be taken out of the jury pool, especially when she had had to explain her answer to question 50 on a later questionnaire. (*How was the deceased related to you?* Husband; *Explain the circumstances of the death:* He was a jackass. Of course, she didn't write that. Instead, she made up a lie about a beloved uncle who died in a convenience store robbery.)

"Two-sixty-seven," the judge said. "Two, six, seven."

Pamela's hand clenched around the number. She touched her round juror button, pinned to her sweater, and cursed silently. Her luck had abandoned her.

Now her goal was to be dismissed in the voir dire.

She grabbed her book—Patricia Cornwell's treatise on forensics and Jack the Ripper—and slung her purse over her shoulder.

Then Pamela eased out of the row, past the loggers and the truck drivers and the waitresses, and walked, head down, shoulders slumped forward, to the jury box.

Her heart was pounding. She had often pictured herself in a courtroom, but not here, not among the jury.

Instead, she expected to be at the tables, an attorney beside her, defending what was left of her miserable little life.

Another half hour went by before the rest of the twenty-seven victims were chosen. Then the questioning began, starting with the first juror picked, a dapper man who was the only person in the room, besides the attorneys, to wear a suit. Fifteen minutes into his voir dire, he was dismissed for claiming he did not have a strong stomach.

As he stepped down, the clerk drew a new number from the box, and another prospective juror took the first juror's place.

Pamela noted the excuse, and apparently so had the second juror. He made the same claim, which caused the judge to issue a gusty sigh.

"If we dismiss everyone with a weak stomach, we'll have

no one left." He faced the defense attorney, who had posed the question. "If you believe these crimes are too graphic, we'll make sure there'll be no crime scene photos after lunch and we'll provide sickness bags, just like the airlines. Now, move on."

Pamela was the first up after the luncheon break. She returned to the courtroom logy from the personal pan she'd had at the nearby Pizza Hut, and exhausted by a morning of listening to other people's lives.

During lunch she had toyed with changing her strategy, possibly saying that she did not approve of the death penalty or that she did not believe a person was innocent until proven guilty. But all of those answers would have contradicted her juror's questionnaire, a questionnaire that had informed her on the top of every page that her answers had the force of answers given under oath.

A new answer would call attention to her. If she was lucky, she would escape without much attention being paid to her at all.

Finally, the attorneys reached her. She had to repeat her name and her address.

"You own a bookstore, Ms. Jackson?" The prosecutor, Daphne Sullivan, stood in front of the jury box. She was a middle-aged woman who wore a stylish black suit that seemed out of place in this small county.

"Yes." Main Street Books, the new-and-used bookstore she had opened in what passed for Rickets Rock's downtown. When she had first received her jury letter, she had hoped that being a small business owner would disqualify her, but the clerk of courts had quizzed her, found out that she had a part-time assistant, and that the store sometimes closed when Pamela planned a day off, and decided that the store could afford to lose Pamela for a few weeks with little or no hardship.

"Do you enjoy reading?" Sullivan asked.

"Yes."

"Do you often read books like that one?" Sullivan nodded at the Cornwell.

"Yes." That was a deliberate lie, one concocted to get Pamela off the jury.

"Would you hold the book up so that everyone can see it?"

Pamela did. Her copy, a hardcover with a shiny dust, looked black and official.

"We won't have to worry about a weak stomach with this one," the judge muttered, even his soft words echoing throughout the courtroom.

"Do you watch *CSI*?" Sullivan asked.

"Sometimes," Pamela said.

"*Cold Case Files*? The forensics programs on The Learning Channel?"

"Sometimes," Pamela said.

"So you feel you have a grasp on the forensic side of police procedure?" Sullivan asked.

Pamela shrugged.

The judge said, "We'll need a verbal response for the record, Ms. Jackson."

"When you say 'a grasp,' I don't know what that means," Pamela said.

"Do you understand it?" Sullivan said.

"It's just science," Pamela said.

"And you understand science?"

Of course, you fool. I have more advanced degrees in biology and chemistry than you can dream up.

Pamela had to bite back the response. She wasn't a scientist now. She owned a bookstore. She was a mousy woman with mousy clothes who tried to disappear when people looked at her.

"I try to understand it," she said, which was as close to the truth as she could come.

"I have no problem with this juror," the prosecutor said, and turned toward the defense attorney, Jake Chivara.

He was too slick for this part of Oregon. His suit had the shine of silk, and his hands were manicured. His black hair had a layered cut that cost more than Pamela's entire outfit, but his eyes shone with an intelligence that she recognized as a match for her own.

He adjusted his suit coat as he walked toward the rail. "Do you consider murder your hobby?"

Her fingers clutched the book, its hard edges biting into her palm. "My *hobby*?"

He nodded toward the book she held. "You read about it. You watch television programs about it. You obviously think about it a lot."

True enough. She didn't like how perceptive he was. "I watch television programs about politics and biography and history, too, but I don't consider them my hobbies. I live alone. I run a bookstore. I read almost everything that comes through the door."

"But you brought that book for a reason, didn't you?" Chivara asked.

"To read while I waited," she said.

"You could have brought a romance novel," he said.

She shrugged. "I would have finished it in the time allowed. I wanted something that would last me all day."

"Be honest, Ms. Jackson. You brought that book so that we'd assume you know police procedure. You wanted to force us to kick you off the jury."

She looked at him in surprise and knew, at that moment, she had been caught. She had never been caught before, at least, not in her manipulations. It was a strange sensation.

Chivara smiled at her. "I don't like being manipulated, Ms. Jackson."

Pamela's hands slid on the book's cover. She was sweating.

"Your questionnaire says you believe that some crimes should be punished by death," Chivara said.

"Yes." She swallowed hard. This was the first time, in all of the questioning, that someone had mentioned the questionnaire.

"Does that mean you believe in the death penalty?" he asked.

"I haven't given it any thought." At least not in that way. The law was the law and she had nothing to do with it. She didn't plan it nor could she change it. Human laws weren't immutable like scientific ones, but they existed and nowadays she did her best to live within them.

"Do you have a problem sending a man to his death?" he asked.

"Not in the right circumstances." Her answer had too much of an edge to it. She wished she could take the words back the moment she uttered them.

Chivara smiled again. "What sorts of circumstances, Ms. Jackson?"

Her mouth was dry. "I thought we were talking about the death penalty."

"We are. What circumstances? *These* circumstances?"

"If he did it," she said.

"Do you think he did it?" Chivara asked.

"I could care less," she said, repeating her answer from the questionnaire.

"Really? You don't care one way or another?"

She didn't like this attorney. He was irritating her. "Unless you put me on this jury, this crime has no impact on my life. I don't really care what that man did. I don't really care what the President does either, and he has a lot larger impact on my life than some petty murderer."

"Petty murderer," Chivara repeated softly. "You're quite interesting, Ms. Jackson. You know science and read about the law, but you say this case doesn't concern you. If we put you on the jury, would you care then?"

"Not really," she said. "I'd just be doing this because you're making me."

Chivara's smile became broad. "At least you're honest."

He walked back to his table, examined his notes, and then leaned over the railing, clearly speaking to his jury consultant.

Pamela's heart pounded hard. She tried to keep an impassive expression on her face, but she found it difficult.

For the first time since she'd shown up in this courtroom, she was frightened.

After a moment, Chivara looked up.

"Ms. Jackson, do you know my client?" Chivara swept his arm toward the defendant. Until this moment, Pamela had refrained from looking at him.

She had seen his photograph on the county newspapers and once on the front page of the *Oregonian*, but she hadn't really looked at him. Nor had she looked at him the one or two times he waited on her.

"We've never formally met," she said.

"But you have met," the attorney said.

"He waited on me once at the Sneaker Wave," she said. "And at the Italian Noodle."

"Did you have a conversation?"

She shrugged, then added for the record, "Probably not."

"Probably not?" Chivara repeated.

"I go out alone with a book," she said. "I usually don't have conversations."

Truthful again.

Chivara's eyes narrowed, and she had the sense that he thought she was holding something back.

Chivara turned away, and she hoped he would dismiss her for cause. Instead, he said, "I have no problems with this juror."

The judge turned to her. "Is there any reason you believe you should not sit on this jury?"

Dozens. She had dozens of reasons, but none she could admit to. Neither attorney had given her a way out.

"I don't know if I can be impartial," she said, "given that I've met him."

The judge let out another of his gusty sighs. "The interactions you've had with the defendant are no different than sitting across a courtroom from him day in and day out. So give it a try, Ms. Jackson."

"Your honor," Chivara said, "this is why we wanted the trial moved."

"You made that motion and I dismissed it," the judge said. "If you want to try this case for the court of appeals and not for the jury, go ahead, Mr. Chivara. Otherwise, get over the loss and move on."

Pamela's cheeks were warm. Her ploy hadn't worked, might even have backfired.

"Juror two-six-seven," the judge said, "you'll be sitting on this case."

Since it was the off-season, the cut-rate hotel that the court used to sequester juries was happy to have them. The jurors even got to have their own rooms, a luxury for which Pamela was grateful. She didn't like company in the best of circumstances, and this certainly was not the best of circumstances.

Those first two days in the courtroom were difficult, especially for the other jurors. The prosecution laid out its case, and the defense gave its own theory of the crime. Most of the jurors were already familiar with the crime, but the details made them squeamish.

Pamela didn't mind the details, but she had trouble wrapping her mind around the crime at all.

Apparently, the defendant, Raymond Northrup, arrived home one afternoon in a rage. He shot his wife, his two daughters, and his infant son, supposedly planning to kill himself as well. In the end, he chickened out (or "came to his senses," as Prosecutor Sullivan said), and called 9-1-1 instead. The paramedics arrived to find a house filled with blood, and Ray Northrup sitting on the couch, watching reruns of *The Simpsons* as if nothing was wrong.

The prosecution promised pictures and the tape of the 9-1-1 call; the defense promised experts showing how the police botched the investigation, figuring that they already had the killer when, of course, the defense claimed, they had not.

Pamela listened with—she thought—clinical detachment, picturing both versions of the crime: a man pushed to his limits by bills, sick children and a nagging wife, hauling the shotgun out of the front closet and turning it on all of them; and the same man pushed to his limits, who arrived home after a hard day's work as a waiter (he could get nothing else in this small town) to find his entire family slaughtered.

But the clinical detachment didn't take, or perhaps it was a façade, designed to fool even herself. For that night, and two nights thereafter, Pamela had the nightmare, the one she had fled when she had come to Oregon.

The images were jumbled: Jason stumbling backwards, his hand up; Jason on the floor, his face gone; Jason's blood staining the wall beside their stove. She started to grab things

—her ring, his watch, their checkbook, and then she set them down.

She knew better—even her dreamself knew better—and instead, she took the cash from the drawer, and the bike leaning against the old Billingsly house next door.

More images from before: the water from the shower draining pink; her clothing in the wash machine, the smell of bleach in the air; the half-eaten ham sandwich that had started it all.

She had been clutching it, trying to force it down, when he had walked in. *You can't do anything right,* she had said to him. *I wanted hot mustard, not sweet. Don't you ever listen?*

His voice, meek and soft, infuriated her, and at that moment, she woke up, covered in sweat, shaking, uncertain where she was, figuring at first it was some anonymous hotel on the trip west, then remembering how she had gotten herself into this new predicament years after the fact.

The hotel looked the same as the others: a double-bed barely bigger than the single she'd had in her first apartment; end-tables so cheap that if she leaned on them, they'd crack; a television set bolted to the dresser, and a double-size window with a single pane of glass so thin that it could shatter with the pressure of a determined fist.

Pamela got up and paced, her feet cold against the worn carpet. She was glad she was alone—who knew what she had cried out, what she had actually said?

That first night, she didn't go back to the bed, sleeping instead on the scratchy sofa, an equally scratchy blanket pulled over her scrunched-up form. She didn't sleep much and when she did, she dreamed of being uncomfortable, not of the past.

And she returned to that couch after every day of difficult testimony, after every photograph and replaying of the 9-1-1 call, until the clinical detachment she thought she had achieved that first day became an actual reality.

She could listen, store facts, theories, and opinions in one side of her brain, and kept them separate from the other side.

The emotion side.

The side that had always given her too much trouble.

Three-plus weeks of testimony, arguments, breaks and confusion. Three-plus weeks of "retiring" to the jury room to wait while the lawyers and the judge worked something out. Three-plus weeks of small talk with people who probably never would have entered her store, people who probably hadn't voluntarily picked up a book in their lives, people who—with the exception of the transplanted Californian—had never lived anywhere but here.

Small minds with nothing but television and the trial to occupy them. Talk of the trial was off-limits until the testimony was over, so the Small Minds discussed the previous night's *Frasier* or the *Buffy* rerun or the late-night movie they were given on tape so they wouldn't watch the local news and talk shows.

She didn't watch any of it. She didn't discuss any of it either, preferring to read. The guards—at least they felt like guards—let her assistant deliver books, sometimes four and five a day, and Pamela read rather than socialized. So long as her mind was busy, her body remained calm.

The guards would paw through the bags, of course, verifying that everything Pamela's assistant brought were books, verifying that her assistant hadn't hid a newspaper article about the trial as a bookmark, verifying that there was no note advising her how to vote at the end of the trial.

But no one looked at the titles either. She finished the Cornwell, moved onto a history of the fingerprint, then followed that with a history of the corpse. A few tomes on forensics, a study of ballistics, and of course, dozens and dozens of novels—all shapes and sizes.

She read and thought and listened, and wished she had known all of this years ago, before she had come west. She would have done things oh so very differently. How easy it would have been to make it seem like *he* had gotten angry over the sandwich, *he* had hit her repeatedly, *he* had grabbed the gun.

But she hadn't known any of it. She had done the best she could with the little bits of knowledge she had, and she had managed to escape.

She lived here now, a new life she mostly enjoyed, and saw no use re-evaluating every second of the past.

Then, finally, the moment arrived. The closing arguments ended, the jury instructions were repeated *ad nauseum*, the defendant staring at jurors as if he were trying to fathom what each and every one of them were thinking.

This time, when they went into the jury room, there was a palpable sense of relief. The restrictions were off: they could discuss anything now, and the Small Minds all started to talk at once, offering opinions, offering advice, discussing what an ordeal they'd been through, how they couldn't stand the pictures.

Pamela couldn't stand the voices. Middle-class, grating, most of them with that slightly dulled speech she'd learned to recognize from locals. She sat in one of the upholstered chairs nearest the door, and wondered how she would get through this.

The jury room itself was small with two exits—one leading back into the courtroom, the other into the hallway. The room had no windows. Whoever had designed this room had certainly visited and obviously enjoyed the ambiance of hell's anteroom, because even the temperature was correct: hot enough to make the already small space seem unbearably stuffy.

"Right, Ms. Jackson?"

She heard her name and looked up. The transplanted Californian was looking at her. He was a wiry blond with a scraggly mustache whose rope-thin body and denim shirt made him look like a man who belonged outdoors, not trapped in a room furnished with modular office chairs and a cheap fake-wood conference table.

"I'm sorry," she said, peering at his name badge. Z. Wilson. She should have learned his name in the past few weeks. She should have learned all of their names, but of course, she hadn't.

"I said. I think we should get around to electing a foreman first, then talk about the case. What do you think?" His blue eyes studied her with an openness she didn't like. Obviously he expected her to be on his side.

"Looks like you're already doing a fine job," she said. "We don't need a vote."

"We'll vote." His voice had that irritated edge Jason used to get when she didn't give him the answer he liked.

She leaned back in her chair, deciding to give Z. Wilson some distance.

The woman who wore the giant silver cross on the front of her blouse each and every day reached to the center of the table and took twelve little pieces of paper from a notepad. Then she grabbed pencils and handed them out as if she were a school teacher.

She gave Pamela her paper and pencil last, smiling at her. Pamela did not smile back.

"Perhaps," said the Silver Cross, "perhaps we should say a small prayer so that God will guide our work."

"A small prayer?" Pamela asked, unable to keep silent in the face of this new irritation. "What kind of guidance do you want? Dearest God, please let us know if you want this killer to go free or if you want the state to fry him. Amen."

"Ms. Jackson," said the Californian. "That's enough."

She shrugged and pressed her lips together, but she had made her point. Two of the Small Minds who hadn't said anything yet—the first man chosen, and one of the other women—glared at Pamela as if she had killed the three children and the namby-pamby wife.

The wife, quite frankly, sounded like she deserved it, but the kids, well, Pamela didn't believe in killing kids. Kids couldn't be blamed for the situations they found themselves in. Only the parents were responsible for that.

"Write down the name of the person you think most suited for jury foreman," the Californian said. "Then put your paper in this little bowl next to the notepad. Don't sign your name."

"Why don't we just have a real election?" Pamela asked, clutching her pencil. "You and whoever else is enough of a control freak to want this idiot job?"

"You mean you?" another Small Mind asked.

"I don't want it," Pamela said.

"Vote for whomever you'd like," the Californian said.

Pamela sighed and shook her head. Then she wrote down *Z. Wilson: Because I believe in validating power grabs*, folded the paper into tiny squares and set it in the bowl.

Hers was the sixth. One Small Mind—a twenty-something man who was already going bald—chewed his pencil and looked from person to person before writing on his paper. He was the eleventh to put his vote in the bowl. The Silver Cross lady was the last, and she looked spooked.

"Mr. Acenan," the Californian said to yet another Small Mind, "would you mind reading the results? Mrs. Dunbar will tally them."

The Dunbar woman took another sheet of paper from the stack and held her pencil poised. The man dug inside the bowl, removed a piece of paper and read the results aloud.

Pamela wished she could take the book out of her purse. Who would've thought that average citizens would take this job so very seriously?

The Small Mind reading the papers had finally gotten to Pamela's. He glanced at her, his face flushed, and only read the name, not the commentary.

"You know," Pamela said mildly, "censorship is against the law."

"And you're a disgrace," the Small Mind said, still clutching her paper. "Can't you be serious about this?"

She thought of answering him honestly, but she knew the word "no" would piss him off. So she said, "I just want to get down to business. I've already lost a month of my life to this mess. I don't want to lose another one because you people dither."

"An election isn't dithering, Ms. Jackson," the Californian said.

"You've already taken over," Pamela said. "Why do we have to bother with the election?"

"Because," the Californian said, "it's part of the instructions. See? Item four. Elect a jury foreperson."

"You said foreman before. Can I change my vote?" Pamela asked. "I didn't consider any women."

Someone made a sound of disgust. Mrs. Dunbar said loudly, "We already have a majority for Mr. Wilson. So he is our fore*person*, unless there's an objection."

Pamela almost objected, just out of spite. She had to entertain herself somehow. But she was beginning to realize that her own antics might prolong this already painful situation, so she said nothing.

She crossed her arms and listened to Mr. California-Wilson read the jury instructions that the judge had already read to them, then ask if there were any questions that needed discussion or clarification before they got down to the "nitty-gritty."

Everyone said no, except Pamela, of course, who really didn't like the grade-school way this deliberation session was turning out. But she had decided to be quiet, and so she would be. She listened, or pretended to, while the jury discussed the rules, then reviewed the rules, and then discussed them even more.

Finally, at four o'clock, Mr. California-Wilson suggested that they take a preliminary vote—gosh! Just like the instructions suggested!—to see how far apart they all were. The vote would be anonymous, of course, and all the little pieces of paper would go into that damn bowl again.

She put her little piece of paper on top of her book, a novel called *A Certain Justice* which Pamela had chosen more out of irony than interest, and then paused.

She really hadn't given the fate of Mr. Raymond Northrup much thought, although she had done her part. She had listened, without prejudice and with that hard-won clinical detachment, to days and days of repetitive testimony, to argumentative lawyers and bad judicial rulings, to witnesses who hadn't known a damn thing and to witnesses who believed they had.

She had listened, she had absorbed, and she had come to no conclusion.

Yet they were asking her for one now. And if she was going to be the good citizen she was pretending to be, she had to give a real opinion. She supposed finding him guilty would get her out of here the quickest. After all, that was what the Small Minds seemed to believe, if their post-trial conversation was any indication.

But she couldn't write *guilty* on her piece of paper. Her hand froze over the page every single time. She was stunned to discover that the decision really did matter to her.

After all, she could have been the person sitting next to Chivara. She could have been pacing some jail cell right now, wondering if 12 disparate people would sentence her to a lifetime of imprisonment. She owed Northrup as much consideration as she had, mostly because she hoped someone would give her the same consideration if (when?) her time came.

She bit her lower lip, then glanced up at the bowl. It looked full. A number of the Small Minds were staring at her again.

Her hand shook over the paper. She gripped the pencil tightly and wrote *Not*, leaving off the guilty. She didn't want Mr. California-Wilson to misconstrue her intent.

She folded her piece of paper in half this time, just like everyone else had, and then she shoved it into the bowl. The Silver Cross woman grabbed it and handed it to California-Wilson as if he weren't capable of grabbing it himself.

He nodded toward the Dunbar woman and she got cut yet another piece of paper so that she could tally the results.

Pamela expected more than one not-guilty vote. After all, it was pretty obvious that Northrup didn't have the balls to kill his entire family, no matter how angry and frustrated he got.

But she was the only not-guilty. California-Wilson tried not to ask for names, but she knew they'd find out, so she admitted it.

And that was when the clerk of the courts arrived, and told them to break for the night.

The next morning, the Small Minds had game plan ready. They were going to review the evidence to convince her.

"Don't you want to know why I think he didn't do it?" Pamela asked.

"It doesn't matter what you think," Silver Cross said. "You obviously didn't care enough to listen."

"I listened," Pamela said. "I even made notes every evening. Did you people bother doing that?"

No one answered her. No one even looked at her.

"Look," she said. "I could change my vote so that we could get the hell out of here. Lord knows, I don't ever want to see you people again. But I don't think this guy did it, and I'm not going to send him to jail just because I want to sleep in my own bed tonight."

She was rather proud of herself. She sounded like a Real Citizen, like someone who cared about her fellow man.

"So," Mr. California-Wilson said with a notable lack of interest, "why do you think he didn't do it?"

"Because," Pamela said, careful to keep her tone respectful and polite, "he didn't run."

"Most people know better than to run," Wilson said.

"Most people know better than to kill their families," one of the Small Minds muttered.

"What?" Mrs. Dunbar asked.

The man shrugged. "I'm just saying if you're going to apply that kind of logic, then the whole case all falls apart."

The Small Minds argued among themselves for a long time, apparently forgetting that Pamela was the one they had to convince to change her mind. For a while, she thought she had convinced a few of them, but no.

They simply liked arguing.

And another day went by without any progress at all.

The week blurred into a series of questions and answers, followed by arguments.

"Ms. Jackson," someone asked at one point, "how can you think he didn't do it? He was covered in blood."

"So was the house," she said. "Didn't you look at the pictures? He sat on the couch, by his own admission. It was soaked in blood. Maybe he even hugged one of the kids like the defense attorney said. What would you do if you came home to your entire family dead?"

Of course, during the ensuing argument, she didn't say that she wouldn't have hugged a dead kid. But the arguments were never really about her, anyway.

"Ms. Jackson," one of the Small Minds said long about day three, "he told everybody at work that he was on edge, that he felt like he was going to explode. It's pretty clear that he did."

"Hell," she snapped. "I'm on edge. Does that mean I'm going to go on a rampage and kill you all to calm myself?"

It sounded tempting, but she knew better. She hadn't hurt anyone—deliberately—since she washed her husband's blood off her skin five years ago.

"Ms. Jackson," the Silver Cross idiot said to her on day five, "who else could have killed that family? Nothing was stolen and no one else even knew them, so no one else had a reason to kill them."

"You mean someone has a reason to kill an infant?" Pamela snapped. She ignored the wife. The wife bothered her. Pamela would have killed the wife given half a chance. Just because the woman hadn't been happy with her reproductive choices and her husband's inability to earn a living didn't give her the right to whine all the damn time.

Like these people were doing. The room really had to be bigger, much bigger, so that Pamela could pace.

She was alone and remained alone on this not-guilty thing. Even when she convinced the entire jury to go back into the courtroom and listen to the read-back of some testimony about the way that Northrup was found. His voice on the 9-1-1 tape, filled with emotion (she knew from personal experience that after killing someone, the emotion drained away), and the way he sat on that couch—as one cop put it —like he had nothing left to live for.

Ten days. Ten days they argued and fought and screamed at each other. (She didn't scream. She hated raised voices.) And they couldn't make her change her mind.

Ten days and 3 hours. The lunch break was when Mr. California-Wilson, whom she'd taken to calling the remaining Beach Boy to his face because he irritated her, knocked on the court-side door, and told the clerk that the jury was hung.

Fascinating word, hung. Past tense of "hang," an active but unhappy word which meant to suspend or to die by hanging or to deadlock. All of those meanings had a little murder in them.

Just a little.

She had committed a killing after all.

And like the one she had committed before, she hadn't given it much thought until she actually completed the act. By then, the deed was done and she had to deal with it. It simply felt wrong to change her mind, as if she had lost a principle or something.

So when the judge polled the jurors—all of them, including her—and asked if there was any way to resolve the deadlock, she had spoken a forceful no.

The judge had no choice but to release the jury from its duty. The case was over, and the prosecutor had lost by one vote. The defense didn't cheer, although Northrup had looked for someone—anyone—to hug and got no volunteers.

Pamela filed back into the jury room with the Small Minds, happy she would never see them again, collected her things, and left the courthouse.

She had to go to the hotel to pack, and then she would be able to go home. Packing took longer than she expected—

she had lived in this dive for nearly two months—and when it was over, she found that she would actually miss the place.

She'd learned to sleep in the bed, finally feeling like the ghost of Jason and his hideous death were behind her. The nightmare, completely gone.

It was almost as if she had been on trial and had forgiven herself.

The drive from the hotel to Rickets Rock took her past the courthouse. The cameras and crowds were gone. The place looked almost deserted. She was nearly past it when she realized that she had left her book inside.

She almost thought of donating it, then changed her mind.

She had donated enough to this stupid cause already.

She parked in the lot, just like she had on that very first day, and went inside by the front door. The anteroom was empty except for one of the court employees, sitting behind a counter.

The employee looked up, and clearly didn't recognize her. Pamela had taken off her juror button the moment they had been excused.

"May I help you?"

"I was on the Northrup jury," Pamela said, "and I left a book in the jury room."

The employee swiveled her chair, looked behind her, and reached down, lifting *A Certain Justice*. "This it?"

It was. Pamela had never summoned enough energy to read it. She thanked the woman, took the book, and turned.

"Ms. Jackson?"

The familiar voice sent a shiver through her. She looked

over her shoulder. "Mr. Chivara. I thought you'd be off cele-brating with your client."

Chivara smiled. It wasn't that predatory smile he used in court, but a rather wistful one. "I had a few things to get out of the courtroom. I see you did too."

She nodded, tucked the book under her arm, and started to leave. He kept pace with her.

"I understand you're the one who hung my jury," he said.

"So?" she asked.

"So," he said as he pushed open the door leading outside, "it surprised me."

"I'm sure it didn't, counselor," she said. "You picked me for some reason and it wasn't my good looks."

He laughed. The sound echoed across the empty street. "That's true. I thought you'd help my client, but not in this part of the case."

She stopped. "What does that mean?"

"It means, Ms. Jackson, we found that you lied on your jury questionnaire."

She felt cold. She knew better than to say anything. If she confirmed or denied, she would play right into his little game, whatever it was.

"And since we found that out, we figured we could use you as the basis for our appeal."

"You planned an appeal?" she asked.

"Every good defense attorney keeps one eye on the current case, and one eye on appeal. You were my ace-in-the-hole."

"I was your ace-in-the-hole when you picked me?"

"Now that wouldn't be quite right, now would it?" This time he gave her the predatory smile. "Of course, no one can prove when we learned that you didn't have a murdered uncle. Nor can they prove when we discovered that Pamela Jackson isn't your real name."

Her chill increased.

"Lying on a jury questionnaire is perjury, Ms. Jackson," Chivara said, "and I'm an officer of the court. Technically, I can't let you get away with that."

She forced herself to breathe. Then she turned around. "I can't say anything to you. You're accusing me and doing it in a do-you-beat-your-wife fashion."

"Am I?" he asked, his arms crossed.

"Besides," she said because she had to, because she couldn't keep silent, "if I did lie, and you discovered it, are you going to serve your client by reporting it? After all, I did hang your jury."

Chivara studied her for a long moment. "If I were still prosecuting, I'd already have you for identity fraud, and perjury. If I keep digging, what else would I find?"

A trail of temper, which had ceased. She had found her own kind of peace here in Seavy County.

"I like fiction, Mr. Chivara," she said. "We established that on the day of jury selection."

"You like crime dramas, Ms. Jackson," he said. "We never established that you liked only fiction."

She remembered the feeling she'd had that first day in the courtroom—that he was the only worthy adversary she had ever found. He was as smart as she was, which was a problem.

"We never established what lengths you'll go to in order to win a case," she said softly. "Looks like we'll learn that one today."

Then she turned around and headed down the steps to her car, feeling his gaze on her back. She half-expected to hear his footsteps following her, to feel his hand grab her arm, to pull her back and take her into that courtroom.

She'd be the one going to jail, and then she'd be the one going to trial, defended by someone like Chivara. Just like she'd imagined.

Just like she'd feared for the past five years.

But Chivara didn't follow her down the stairs. In fact, when she got into her car, and looked out the window, he was still watching her.

He had to choose between letting the client he had clearly thought guilty (after all, why else scheme for the appeal?) go free or letting a woman who had changed her identity and committed at least two small crimes that he knew of go free.

Poor Mr. Chivara. Such choices he had.

Such choices she had. Did she stay and pretend like nothing happened, trust the bastard to do what was in his best interest? Or did she run, again, losing all the money she'd put into her store and her home?

She clutched the key to her car. People who ran were guilty: she had argued that in the jury room, and her argument would come back to him. He'd know she'd done something.

But if she stayed, he'd have only his own conscience to wrestle with.

As a good defense attorney, he did that each and every day.

She put the key in the ignition and started the car. Chivara was still watching her.

She waved at him as she drove out of the parking lot.

Away from the courtroom and juries and the law.

Screw Chivara and his suspicions. She was going back to her store, her home and her life, her solitary life as a model citizen, a woman who did her duty and nothing more, just like everybody else.

OVERWORKED

A SEAVY COUNTY STORY

KRISTINE KATHRYN RUSCH

Mick Hanrahan had forgotten how much he hated the Oregon Coast. The reminders had come slowly—getting stuck in the no-passing lane behind some dumb tourist who didn't know how to drive mountain roads, the overpowering smell of fish after twilight, and the clammy dampness of his hotel room.

Early the morning after he arrived, the rainy season hit with a vengeance. His subpoena stated he had to be at the courthouse by 8:45 a.m., not that he needed a damn subpoena. He hadn't left law enforcement; he had just left law enforcement in this podunk county, and he'd been happy to slap the sand off his boots as he drove to his new job in Portland.

Sometimes, that Portland job wasn't any better than his job here had been. Sometimes, Portland was worse, particularly when the city erupted into politically correct and pointless protests over something that had happened far away.

He'd been in Portland two years now, and he'd come to recognize the same 100 protestors, folks who really and truly needed a life.

Of course, he didn't say that to anyone. He never said much of anything. He was suspect because he was a cop— automatically on the wrong side of Proper Portland Opinion, even though he was (most of the time) more liberal than half the people who judged him by his non-existent uniform.

He had worked his way up to detective relatively quickly, and he liked it. He loved digging in files and interviewing witnesses. He loved solving crimes.

He'd found home.

And it wasn't Whale Rock, Oregon. All he had from here were bad memories and the enemies he'd made during the world's worst divorce.

Which wasn't entirely fair. He had friends here. He'd had dinner with five of them the night before, and would see them again before he drove back to the Willamette Valley, where his life could resume.

After this little visit to his unpalatable past ended.

The horizontal rain and fifty-mile-per-hour wind that greeted him in the morning didn't change his attitude. He drove the six blocks from the hotel to the courthouse, and pulled up to his favorite parking spot in the back, only to realize that some idiot had replaced the parking spot with a gigantic Dumpster. Apparently, someone thought no one used that parking spot (which, if Hanrahan were honest, was partly true: it was one reason he had managed to find it over and over again back when he lived here).

After failing to get his usual spot, Hanrahan drove

around the courthouse lot three times before giving up. He went to the Cop Lot next door, saw the signs that said unauthorized vehicles would be towed, and realized that these days, his vehicle was unauthorized.

He had to park an entire block away, which meant that by the time he entered the courthouse's front door, his rain gear was soaked. He stamped and shook like a wet dog, only to find himself confronting something else brand new: TSA-level security, complete with X-ray machine and one of those beeping metal detectors.

Portland's courthouse didn't have anything this nice. Obviously, someone in Seavy County knew how to work federal grants in the county's favor.

A young cop, in shape, eager, and a little out of his element, beckoned Hanrahan forward. Hanrahan had left his gun and Taser in the car. He'd always believed that fewer weapons in the courthouse was a good thing, especially when some disgruntled criminal decided to jump a bailiff as a prelude to jumping bail, something Hanrahan had seen too many times to count.

Still, Hanrahan had his badge, and the young cop's eyebrows went up as Hanrahan placed it, along with the contents of his pants pockets, in the security tray.

"Portland," the kid said. "Wow. You on a joint case?"

Someone should've told the kid that the reasons people came to the courthouse were none of his damn business. Hanrahan was feeling wet and grumpy, but not wet enough or grumpy enough to educate someone else.

"Something like that," Hanrahan said as he walked through the metal detector, and down the hall.

Finally, he hit a part of the courthouse that hadn't changed. Half the staff in the main floor office hadn't arrived yet. Through the window where the good citizenry paid their parking tickets and their small-potatoes traffic fines, Hanrahan could see movement, but no one would fling that window open until 9 a.m. sharp.

He took the nearby stairs two at a time until he reached the third floor where the courtrooms were. Then he stopped, heaving a sigh.

At least thirty people had formed a line in the hallway, all of them looking sodden and annoyed. Another dozen sat on benches, bright blue JUROR buttons attached to their shirts.

He had forgotten one of the joys of this courthouse: the jurors had to remain in the hallway until called into their various courtrooms. The early morning witnesses had to remain in the hallway too, because they weren't allowed in court until they testified.

He hated mingling with the civilians, particularly pissed-off civilians who had been tossed out of their daily routines to sit in judgment on someone else. All of the people in this hallway wanted to be somewhere else; all of them wanted to know when they could leave.

Hanrahan pushed his way through the throng to the side corridor that led to the main entrances into the five tiny courtrooms. The Seavy County Courthouse initially had three large courtrooms, but they got carved up in a remodel when Hanrahan had been in his first year with the sheriff's department. The remodel installed cameras and surveillance equipment, audio equipment, and safer ways to bring prisoners into the courthouse itself.

Hanrahan scanned the faces of the folks sitting on the benches, looking for someone familiar. He didn't know the deputy district attorney who was handling this case. Already Hanrahan thought very little of him—one Jesse Riordan, who only bothered to communicate with Hanrahan by email, and who had decided not to prep him for the trial at all.

Hanrahan hated going in cold.

Jesse Riordan's last e-mail had been blithe: *We'll touch base at the courthouse.*

It's your show, Hanrahan had written back, *but it's been my experience that cases always go better when the witnesses have gone through prep.*

And by that, he had meant when the *lawyers* had gone through prep. Because witnesses—himself included—could pop off with any damn thing that might tank a carefully constructed case.

Although, to be fair, he had no idea how carefully constructed this case had to be. It was typical Seavy County: a mixture of alcohol, vehicles, and not enough road.

He'd been unlucky enough to witness the entire incident. He'd been trying to pull over the driver, one Charles Delany Cowell, known as "Seedy" ostensibly for his first two initials. Seedy Cowell's vehicle, an ancient dark green Saab, had been weaving all over the road.

The moment Hanrahan turned on his squad's flashing lights, Seedy sped up. Then Hanrahan turned on the sirens, and Seedy floored that crappy Saab.

Seedy had no hope of outrunning Hanrahan. Hanrahan used the radio and notified the local police in Seavy Village that Seedy was heading their way. Hanrahan had been extremely confident that Seedy wouldn't turn off the highway onto another road. There were almost no roads off the highway, and all of them were to Seedy's left, heading east into the valley. West put him in the ocean.

If Seedy had tried to turn, Hanrahan would have gained on him, catching him in no time. Besides, Seedy would have to know the roads to pull off, and most people who sped through Seavy County were idiot tourists who had no idea there were other through roads.

Seedy wasn't a tourist, but he wasn't a rocket scientist either—at least when he was drunk. He pegged that ancient Saab at 130 miles per hour until he came to the corner near Hoover Bay. He lost control on the sharp turn and slammed into the stone guardrail, flipping the car over and landing it upside down in the Dee River.

Hanrahan arrived seconds later, irritated that he had to rescue an idiot, worried that the idiot was dead, and bracing for surprises. The thing Hanrahan hated the most about working for the Seavy County Sheriff's Department was that he worked alone. No partner, no backup within miles. Just him and whatever he encountered at the literal edge of nowhere.

What he encountered that night was pretty simple: a car that landed mostly on the passenger side; a lucky drunk who was crawling out of the broken driver's window; and two unlucky passengers, one dead at the scene, the other so badly injured that Hanrahan wasn't sure she'd survive until an ambulance arrived.

Hanrahan had done what he could for the lone survivor, Veronica Newmark. He had carefully held her head in place so she wouldn't drown, deciding that saving her life was more important than handcuffing Seedy. Seedy, who was slogging through two feet of river water when Hanrahan's backup arrived. Seedy, who refused to give up his keys at the bar across town. Seedy, who swore to the bartender that *no sir, I'm not driving anywhere, sir, my girlfriend has an apartment near here.* Maybe his "girlfriend" had had an apartment nearby, but neither of the women in the car lived in Seavy County, although both of them had died there.

Hanrahan had thought this case would resolve easily. He hadn't given it much thought when he left the sheriff's department. He expected Seedy to take a plea, and that would be the end of it.

But Seedy had fought the charges, and the court case got rescheduled more times than Hanrahan wanted to consider. Initially, the rescheduling had been on the part of the District Attorney's office. Veronica Newmark spent almost a year in a vegetative state before finally ceasing to breathe on her own late one night. The DA's office amended the charges to two cases of Aggravated Vehicular Homicide.

Hanrahan sighed. He should have checked in at the DA's office on the second floor, although he'd been instructed to come to the courtrooms. A sign above each courtroom listed the day's business just like an arrivals/departure sign at an airport.

Seedy's trial was scheduled for Courtroom 305.

Hanrahan made his way through a pack of jurors to the courtroom door, looking to see if Jesse Riordan was waiting for him up here. Hanrahan suspected that, even though he had no idea what Riordan looked like, he could find the DDA just by the look of his clothing.

Most of the jurors sitting on the benches were wearing coast normal, which didn't even rise to the level of business casual. Very few jobs here required business attire. Most jobs required a uniform, provided by the employer. In fact, the worst dressers in Seavy County Court were the folks Hanrahan did recognize, all of whom owned their own small businesses, and none of whom wore anything nicer than a pair of ragged blue jeans.

So Hanrahan scanned for someone in actual business clothing. Standing near the entrance to Courtroom 305, he saw a woman with wedge-cut black hair. She wore a black business suit, a white silk blouse, and enough makeup to enhance her thin lips and dark eyes. She also wore fragile high heels that seemed completely undamaged by the rain.

She was talking softly with two local attorneys, both men, both in their sixties, wearing suits they should have retired twenty years before, their grayish hair wild and in need of a trim. No one acknowledged him.

He peered into a nearby courtroom, saw a plea finishing up, and jumped when someone touched his back. The little woman who had been taking names and handing out JUROR badges stood behind him.

"Do you need to sign in, Mister—?"

"Detective," he said. "I'm here to . . ."

She took his arm and moved him away from the klatch

of jurors. "They don't need to hear why you're here," she said.

He nodded. She was right, not that he cared. He wanted this experience to end soon.

"I'm here in the Cowell matter," he said.

"For the prosecution?" she asked, even though she probably didn't need to.

He nodded. "I was supposed to meet Jesse Riordan, but I don't see him."

"Her," the woman said. "And last I saw her, she was in front of the door for Courtroom 305. Black hair, black suit. You can't miss her."

Something in the woman's tone added *Riordan's not from around here*. But that wasn't possible, since she was a DDA. She had to live here now.

The woman with the wedge-cut hair was still standing in front of the doorway to Courtroom 305. She was speaking urgently to one of the local attorneys, something about meeting in her office to deal with Child Protective Services later in the week.

"DDA Riordan?" Hanrahan asked, not quite using his street voice. Still, he got the attention of everyone with a JUROR badge sitting nearby.

The wedge-cut woman glared at him. "What?" she snapped in a tone that instantly put him at ease. They didn't teach that tone in law school. Lawyers had to learn it as their confidence grew.

"Mick Hanrahan. I was to show up—"

"Yes, Detective." She held up an index finger. Her nails had been painted a red that matched her lipstick. She wore no rings, but the tennis bracelet on her wrist was worth at least one month of Hanrahan's pay.

"Call my office," she said to the lawyer. "We need to set this up sooner rather than later. That child needs a permanent home, and it's not my office's job to get that for her."

"Such a bleeding heart," the lawyer said with obvious sarcasm.

Riordan grinned at him, then stepped around him. She was the most put-together person in the hallway. She looked like she belonged in a Portland courtroom arguing for some major corporation, not in Seavy County's tiny courthouse.

"Come with me," she said to Hanrahan.

He followed her through another door, one he'd never been in before. He knew it was where lawyers sometimes met with their clients during trial.

The room was small, with an old wooden table that seated six max, and a portrait of the Chief Justice of the Oregon Supreme Court hanging crookedly on the far wall.

"I need to brief you on a few things," she said. "I'm hoping you won't have to testify at all, at least today. I'm trying to get another continuance—"

"Another?" he asked.

"It's better for you if I do," she said.

"Frankly, Ms. Riordan, it's not better for me. I don't want to come back here any more than I have to. I'm not happy to learn that I might not be testifying today—"

"Detective," she said. "Somehow Mr. Cowell ended up with Sam Ashton, an excellent attorney with Rodriguez Roest, one of the largest firms on the West Coast. Ashton's young, trying to make his bones with major cases outside of his firm's home base, which is Los Angeles. There's money here, and I'm not sure exactly where it comes from."

Hanrahan frowned. "Why are you telling me this?"

"Because if you do testify today, you're going to have to be careful. We don't want your statements on the record. That's why I haven't brought you over here until now."

He let out a small snort. "I'm your primary witness."

"In this case, yes," she said.

He waited. There was another shoe. He could almost hear the cartoon whistle as it dropped toward the floor.

"Ashton has initiated several suits, including one against the sheriff's department, claiming false arrest. They—"

"False arrest? The bastard was drunk. He killed two people."

"That's not what they're claiming," she said. "They're claiming that you forced him to drive too fast and it was your recklessness that forced him off that bridge. There is nowhere else to go. He was stuck on Highway 101—"

"He could have pulled over," Hanrahan stated.

"Yes, he could have, but they have something about a pathological fear of arrest—"

"Which isn't my issue," Hanrahan said. "He was driving, Monica Knowles died, and Veronica Newmark was so badly injured that she eventually died too. He has no case—"

"In the case of Knowles, that's probably true. No local jury is going to give him the benefit of the doubt. But he wants money, and Ashton wants practice. The plan is, as far as I can tell, to get your statement on the record, particularly the bit about you holding Newmark's head. Her spinal cord was badly damaged that night, and they're going to argue you did it, and that her death was caused by you, not by their client."

"Oh, for crissake," Hanrahan snapped. "What was I supposed to do, let her drown in that muddy water he'd driven her into?"

"And that's the kind of response they want on record, Detective," Riordan said.

He made himself take a deep breath. "That still doesn't absolve Cowell in the death of Knowles."

"I know," Riordan said. "After they lay the foundation for your responsibility on the death of Newmark, they plan to meet with the judge, get the charges against Cowell dismissed on Newmark in return for a plea on Knowles."

"They could have done that earlier," Hanrahan said.

"They didn't have your testimony," she said. "We wouldn't take anything less than prison time on both deaths."

Hanrahan let out a large breath. Lawyers. Courtrooms. This case should have been straightforward, and they were making it difficult.

"How do you know all of this?" he asked. Usually prosecutors weren't privy to defense strategy.

She smiled slightly. "Our boy's big mistake is that he hired a local secretary. Small towns have their advantages."

And those advantages included untoward gossip.

"I didn't want you anywhere near this place," she said. "That's why I've been so unresponsive in email."

"Then you shouldn't have sent a witness subpoena," he said.

She glared at him. "There is a chance the trial will happen. You know that."

He shrugged. "You need to tell the judge about this, especially about the plan to waste the court's time."

"What makes you think I didn't, Detective?" she asked in that annoying way lawyers had when they didn't want to discuss something.

"The fact that I'm standing here, Ms. Riordan."

She let out a small laugh. "I met with Judge Goodrich. She asked me for proof. I told her that we should bring in Mr. Cowell's attorney and ask him, and the judge said that she wasn't going to let me troll for the other side's strategy in her courtroom. Then I told her that we could bring in the gossip who had told me everything, and the judge asked if the source of the gossip worked for the attorney in question."

Hanrahan braced his hands on the tabletop. He had a hunch he knew the answer.

"And of course, the source doesn't," Riordan said with disgust. "He's married to the secretary's cousin, of all things. You know how small towns work. As the judge said somewhat patronizingly, trials are different here, and that's the bitch of it. Trials *are* different here. It's the first place I've ever practiced where the judge identifies the attorneys, the court reporter, the witnesses, and the defendant to the *entire* jury pool, and asks them to search their memories *before* being called up for voir dire, because everyone knows everyone. I've had clients of the defense attorney sitting on a jury because the client didn't have any pressing business at the time. I've had the county dispatch sitting on a jury because she had no personal business with the defendant. I've had—"

"I know, Ms. Riordan," Hanrahan said quietly. "I lived here for ten years."

The tangle of lives and business had always been a problem in Seavy County. The county was spread out over 2,000 square miles, but much of it was uninhabitable. The bulk of the county's 40,000 residents were crammed into the 101 corridor that went north-south along the Pacific Coast, in and out of a dozen villages, but only two tiny cities, where everyone shopped and went to school and hired lawyers.

If a judge excluded everyone in a jury pool who knew someone involved in a case, there wouldn't be enough people from which to choose a jury.

"A big city judge would disallow all of this," Riordan said bitterly.

That was true, but not relevant.

"Why are you in Seavy County, if you don't like it?" Hanrahan asked.

The lawyer pose fell from Riordan's face for just a moment, and he saw her—a woman heading into middle-age who couldn't believe that her life had come to this.

"My husband's father is dying by inches, and my husband feels he needs to care for his father here. His father's never lived anywhere else, so we moved here because my husband puts family first."

"No other siblings, no mother—"

The lawyer of the withering glances returned. "We've already gone through all the options, Detective."

"And you became a prosecutor rather than join one of the local firms?"

Riordan barked out a laugh. "Have you *been* to the local firms?"

"And to the DA's office, plenty of times," he said.

"Then you know," she said. "There are two kinds of small-town attorneys. Those who excel at everything the law throws at them, and those who excel at nothing."

He paused for just a second, then asked, "Which are you, Ms. Riordan?"

Her gaze met his. "I'm a big city attorney locked in purgatory because I made the mistake of falling in love with a decent man."

Someone knocked on the door. An eager-looking young woman peered in through the window and nodded at Riordan.

Riordan cursed. "Looks like I'm up. You get to wait in the hall."

"With the jurors," he said.

She shrugged, as if to say, *I didn't design this stupid system.* "And half of them are for my case. If I don't get the continuance, I'm going to stretch out jury selection. You and I will have lunch in my office. Unless you get called back to Portland."

She gave him a meaningful look and let herself out of the room. He stood there for a long moment, his hatred of this place mixing with his knowledge of all the goodhearted people who did their very best to make sure that this tiny courthouse worked the way it should.

The county was understaffed and underfunded. He'd

left in part because the territory he was supposed to cover every night as a sheriff's deputy was about to triple. It meant he wouldn't be able to respond in any meaningful amount of time, and unsolved crimes would probably quadruple.

Now, he was going to get blamed for behaving by the book. A big law firm was involved, so that meant there would be some kind of play for money, and a probable lawsuit against the county for mistaken prosecution or whatever the hell that was called because some drunken jackass who had killed two people had enough cash to hire a good lawyer.

And whether she liked it or not, that DDA was in over her head. The attorneys with the big law firm could have been playing her. They could have planted that information with the secretary or made sure her cousin overheard it all, with the hope that word got back to Riordan.

Ashton, the defendant's lawyer, had nothing to lose. If Riordan hadn't heard the gossip, nothing would change. But if she had, then she would present a weakened version of her case, and she would defeat herself.

That was how Hanrahan would have played it. But then, he was a small-town boy who had two years' experience with the cut-throat attorneys who came out of real cities.

A middle-aged attorney in a bad suit threw open the door, saw Hanrahan, and asked, "Who're you waiting for?"

"No one," he said. "I'm just leaving."

Hanrahan walked out of the open door as a group of jurors were filing into Courtroom 305. Hanrahan peered through the door as he passed it. Jurors were threading their way into the seats behind the counsel tables. No one would need him for at least an hour. And if they did need him immediately, then Riordan would get her wish: he would be momentarily unavailable.

He slipped on his rain gear and headed outside. The horizontal rain had become a horizontal downpour. The wind gusted so hard he had trouble holding his hood in place.

When he reached his car, he grabbed the waterproof bag he used for his case files, his computer, and his tablet. He tucked it all underneath his raincoat, slammed the car door shut, locked it all, and ran back to the courthouse.

He slogged inside, went back through security, and hurried upstairs. By the time he arrived in the hallway, all of the jurors had gone into their respective courtrooms.

A woman wearing a green cardigan sweater and pilled black pants sat near one of the courtroom doors, her hands threaded together, fingers tapping her skin nervously. Another woman sat across from her, looking down. Near the table where the juror registration had been set up, a too-skinny man sat on the floor, twitching and staring at the stairs as if he was wondering if he could make a run for it.

Hanrahan sat as far away from all of them as he could. He took off his coat, shook it, and hung it on the edge of the bench. Then he moved a little sideways so he wouldn't put any of his materials in a rain puddle of his own making.

He had reviewed the case files the night before. The county had sent him printed copies, even though he had asked for a log-in to review online. He was no longer an officer with the sheriff's department, so they didn't want him to have access to current information about anything.

Instead, they sent him the files "as a courtesy," his old boss had said, as if there were anything courteous about it.

Hanrahan was losing two days of his own time testifying for them. He wasn't getting paid for this, and only an argument with his own superior at the Portland Police Department got him paid time off to come over here.

He let out a small breath, realizing just how annoyed he was.

He made himself focus on the files. He knew what was in them backward and forward. The problem was that they weren't complete—not for a standard homicide investigation. For a vehicular homicide actually witnessed by a sheriff's deputy, they were perfect. Textbook. About as good as it got.

So what was the defense's angle here? Riordan's reaction was typical for an overworked prosecutor—she thought it was all about cases and events.

But that made no sense, particularly for big city attorneys. They had to see that there was no money to get out of Seavy County. Even the county's insurance for this sort of thing was miniscule compared to anything they'd see in California.

Riordan hadn't told Hanrahan how Seedy Cowell had managed to hire an expensive law firm, which meant she had investigated and hadn't found the answer suspicious.

But she clearly hadn't asked the question that was bothering Hanrahan. Why *was* that big-city firm handling the case by itself? Why hadn't it partnered with a local attorney and made him handle the grunt work?

The tactics Riordan described didn't need a slick high-priced attorney to carry them out. If the little local attorney failed, it didn't matter. Seedy was still looking at a plea deal or a conviction. It wasn't a slam-dunk for the defense, and it really wasn't something a major attorney would want on his record.

But the firm had sent their own people because they didn't want some local hack to screw this up.

And that bothered Riordan. This firm was investing a lot of money into a case that had, at best, a million-dollar payout—and that was if they won against the county, six months to a year down the road.

The percentage the lawyers would get wouldn't even pay for their shoes. And Hanrahan couldn't see the court authorizing the kinds of fees and expenses that these assholes would ring up, even if the county ended up paying court costs.

The first rule of investigation: follow the money.

And right now, there was none.

But there had to be. He just had to find it.

The first thing he did was investigate Seedy Cowell. Hanrahan didn't look at the files he had because they were two years old. Instead, he used the 4G on his tablet and logged into the Portland PD database with his current I.D. He didn't want to fight for access to the Seavy County's system, and lose the next few hours to some kind of weird jurisdictional fight.

Two kinds of families bestowed ostentatious names like

Charles Delany Cowell upon their kids—families with a lot of money and families without. The wealthy ones needed to acknowledge some distant but "important" relative; the poor ones needed to give the kid a boost of confidence right from the get-go.

Seedy Cowell himself had no money, but at the time of the accident he was driving an ancient Saab, which was not the go-to used car of choice for most impoverished losers. Either someone gave him that car or he had inherited it from a family member.

Hanrahan knew the car was registered in Seedy's real name, the name that matched his driver's license and his fingerprints. When Seedy was arrested two Januarys ago, he had just been evicted from his own apartment above one of the stores lining 101, not for non-payment, but for excessive and dangerous partying. Too many noise complaints, too many fights in the hallway.

Seedy had been sleeping at his so-called girlfriend's place for a week while he searched for a new place to live. He had a job at a local restaurant waiting tables, a job he'd held for nearly a year.

Hanrahan had investigated all of that as a matter of course, searching for patterns, drug usage, any prior DUII, anything that might escalate the charges to something with a little more teeth. He'd found one DUII, and that had pleased him.

It didn't take much more digging to determine that, indeed, Seedy came from money—Old Philadelphia money. But he hadn't been disowned. Instead, he had publicly disavowed his own family and their "bourgeoisie expectations."

Hanrahan rolled his eyes at that. Mom and Dad wanted Seedy to amount to something. Seedy didn't want the pressure of their expectations. It explained the car, at least a little. But it didn't explain the law firm, especially when Hanrahan cross-checked the case file with his memory.

A major Philadelphia law firm had initially defended Seedy, using one of the local defense attorneys as its mouthpiece. Or, at least, the firm had handled the case until Seedy found out where the support had come from, and severed the relationship with that attorney.

No wonder Riordan hadn't looked much deeper into Rodriguez Roest. Seedy had already had prestigious—and expensive—representation, if only for a short time. Another expensive firm wouldn't have seemed suspect to her.

But it did to Hanrahan. If Seedy wasn't using Mom and Dad's money, where had he gotten the cash to hire Rodriguez Roest?

Hanrahan couldn't find that tidbit. So he dug for more on Seedy.

The kid was trying to turn his life around. While out on bail, he had been attending Oregon Coast Community College, and it seemed that he was sincerely trying to clean up his life. There were hints of AA meetings and several volunteer shifts at a local food bank that Hanrahan did not think had occurred on lawyerly advice.

Old Seedy was feeling guilty, as he should be. And Hanrahan wondered what he'd find out if he pulled Seedy aside. Did Seedy even know his lawyers' plans to get him to take a plea in the middle of this case? If so, why wasn't Seedy taking that plea now?

Two people walked past Hanrahan. They pulled JUROR badges off their shirts, and dumped them in a little basket on the table. Jury selection was not just under way in one of the trials going on behind him, it was proceeding apace.

Hanrahan shook his head slightly. What he knew of the judges here was this: they hated it when cases came to trial. They saw those cases as failures from the get-go. So the judges were slightly surly as a case went into jury selection. Because the courtrooms were so small, the judges also felt a ticking clock. They needed to get the trials completed so that the courtroom was open for all the pleas, hearings, and other routine business of the court.

Hanrahan had to work a little faster. He could spend all day digging into Seedy and finding nothing. So, for the first time in the history of this case, Hanrahan decided to look at the victims.

After the accident, Hanrahan did get to know the victims somewhat. He had watched Monica Knowles die as the car flipped, and he had held Veronica Newmark, hoping she survived until help came. He even visited her a few times in the hospital, until he realized she would never come out of her coma. Sometimes he felt vaguely guilty about her—not that he blamed himself for her injuries, but that if he had been just a bit slower to get to her side, or maybe a little less diligent, she wouldn't have ended up in a twilight of existence, dying by millimeters.

He knew better than to say any of that in court. He

couldn't make any claim of guilt even if it was how he felt. Hanrahan knew the blame fell squarely on Seedy. He had made reckless choices, and those reckless choices had ultimately cost two lives.

Hanrahan decided to scan their obituaries to see if he found anything before moving onto the girlfriend and other associates of Seedy, to see if the money for the lawyer had come from them.

A group of jurors threaded out, all dumping their JUROR buttons in the basket as they headed to the stairs. He waited for a moment to see if anyone else followed, but no one did.

He looked down at his tablet. The obit that came up first in a Google search was Newmark's.

And that was when he found some answers.

Veronica Newmark had come to Seavy County on vacation with her friend Monica Knowles. They had been driving up Highway 101, planning to head to Seattle, then drive home on Interstate 5, visiting friends in major cities along the way. They stayed an extra day, met Seedy in a bar, and ended up in that Saab on the fatal night. Newmark's obituary didn't mention Seedy's name or why Newmark ended up in the Saab, only that she had died from injuries sustained in the accident.

But—and this was the important part—Veronica Newmark was the daughter of a major Los Angeles real estate developer, a woman with a lot of contacts all over the city, who had built some of the most important buildings in the last five years. Newmark's father was the CEO of the second-largest grocery chain on the West Coast.

Hanrahan did a Google search for the law firm that represented either company and hit a jackpot. Ashton's firm, Rodriguez Roest, handled both the real estate firm and the grocery chain. Rodriguez Roest also had an entire division dedicated to liability.

Hanrahan felt cold. Liability, which was what they would go after the county for. This wasn't just a money case; it was a keep-your-client happy case, and the client wasn't Seedy. It was the Newmark family, whose grief was fresh enough to demand as much blood as possible.

Another juror dumped a button into the basket before she headed toward the stairs.

"Excuse me," Hanrahan said to her.

She turned, looking alarmed.

"What courtroom did you come from?" he asked.

"300," she said. "Why?"

"Just wondering how jury selection was going in 305, but you wouldn't know that."

"Thank God," she said. "I'm going home."

And then she bounded down the stairs as if she had been let out of prison herself.

He frowned. A gaggle of jurors had gone by earlier, and there had been no stragglers in quite a while.

He glanced at his watch. It was only 10. But it looked like juries had been chosen in both cases.

He hoped both sides in the Cowell case had long opening statements. Otherwise, Hanrahan would be on the stand before lunch.

And he wouldn't have a chance to tell Riordan what she was really up against.

At 11:30, Riordan found him.

"We have two hours," she said. "I'm buying lunch, but we're eating in my office."

She waited for him to gather his things. He let her guide him to the second floor where the DA's office complex sprawled.

She opened the door, and asked the clerk at the window to have take-out delivered from the usual place. Since Hanrahan wasn't fussy, he didn't care where the usual place was. It probably would be something he was familiar with and hadn't missed.

Her office was toward the back, reflecting her relatively new status as a deputy district attorney. She had a small desk which was amazingly organized. Files were stacked neatly. In the normal spot for a big computer, a laptop stood open.

She set down her satchel, beckoned him toward a leather chair on the side of the room, and said, "We're under way. I'm going to need you this afternoon, unfortunately. I figure we get you on and off the stand—"

"You need some information first," he said, and then told her what he'd found about Rodriguez Roest.

Riordan sank into the chair behind her desk midway through his recitation. "You'd think I would have found that on my own," she muttered more to herself than him.

"It was counterintuitive," he said. "You were concerned about Seedy, not about the victims."

She closed the laptop and frowned. "They're playing all sides against each other. Get Seedy to take a plea on what he thinks is a lesser charge while establishing his liability and Seavy County's. They can go after his family's money as well as the county, and maybe even the hospital if they do it right. Who's paying for his defense?"

Hanrahan shrugged. "Not his parents. Most likely Newmark's parents or maybe they convinced the firm to take the case pro bono."

"Damn." Riordan clenched her fist and almost pounded the desk, but stopped herself just before her skin hit the wood.

"That's why they sent a new lawyer to play this out. He's one of their young defense attorneys. He has no idea what Liability is up to," Hanrahan said.

"And we have nothing but supposition for the judge," she said, "unless we can prove that Newmark's parents were involved. And that won't even matter until the liability case gets filed. *If* it gets filed."

Hanrahan took a deep breath. "I want you to put me up first, and let me talk."

She shook her head. "We really need to work this out. Because one wrong word—"

"I know," he said. "But you have no idea what I'm going to say. You need to hear me out. No one knows what I did that night."

Her eyes narrowed. "You said you won't lie for this case."

"I won't," he said. "I don't have to. You can win without it."

She gave him a sideways look, as if she didn't believe him. "I don't have to accept the plea. I need to tell my boss about this."

"The judge won't be happy if you refuse the offer you tried to give Seedy in the beginning," Hanrahan said.

"Duh," she said. "That's why I need to talk to my boss. Because—"

"Go talk to your boss. But make sure we have time to go over my testimony," Hanrahan said. "You need to be prepared."

"And so do you," she snapped, and left the room.

When the bailiff finally brought Hanrahan into the courtroom a little after two, he was surprisingly nervous. He hadn't been nervous about testifying in years.

It hadn't been Riordan's demeanor that made him nervous either, but her earlier admonition: Hanrahan really did have to watch every single word.

The courtroom felt even tinier than he remembered. It had a 1970s look, even after the recent remodel. The swivel chairs in the jury box had blue cushions, and the wood was a blond maple. Even the witness chair had soft padding.

Judge Goodrich's bench was astonishingly close to the witness chair. The judge had just been elected when Hanrahan left. She was younger than he remembered, but her eyes had a pinched, tired look. She nodded at him.

He nodded back as he settled in. He took his oath, and watched as Riordan glanced at her notes before walking toward him. She was doing that for effect. She knew exactly what she was going to ask him.

Cowell watched everything with a vaguely terrified air.

He was too thin, and his skin was pallid. He had deep circles under his eyes. He looked decades older than the man in the mug shot that Hanrahan had been staring at for the past week. Hanrahan almost felt compassion for him.

Almost.

Cowell's attorney, Sam Ashton, had a yellow legal pad before him, and kept a pen in his hand. He wore a black suit that looked as natural on him as jeans and a T-shirt did on most men. His eyes were dark and filled with a sharp intelligence. This was not a man to underestimate.

Riordan had her back to Ashton. She was turned slightly, so that she faced the jury, the judge, and Hanrahan.

First Riordan established who Hanrahan was, what he was doing now, and what his job had been two years before. Then she moved on, without asking him why he left the coast. It was a breadcrumb for Ashton. Whether or not Ashton followed it would be another matter.

She and Hanrahan had decided to leave Ashton a number of breadcrumbs, hoping he would pick up a few. Hanrahan was beginning to respect Riordan. In their short meeting, she had come up with as many breadcrumbs as he had.

Riordan led Hanrahan through his evening, starting with the radio call about a driver weaving all over the road to the car chase. She lingered on response times.

"We were lucky," Hanrahan said. "I was nearby when the call came in. I was able to find the car in question within five minutes."

Another breadcrumb. They both knew that Ashton wanted the county's response times on the record, and they were leaving that thread dangling, so that he would pick it up and think he had a case.

"What happened when you turned on your flashing lights?" Riordan asked.

"The car I was pursuing sped up," Hanrahan said.

"Is that unusual?" she asked.

"Not with drunks," Hanrahan said.

"Objection," Ashton said without getting up. "It assumes—"

"Oh, for God's sake," said Judge Goodrich. "If you want statistics, Counselor, I'm sure that the sheriff's department can provide them for you. Hell, I can. Every day, we deal with a speeding drunk in my courtroom who thinks he can somehow outrun law enforcement on Highway 101. Objection overruled."

Ashton looked shocked.

Welcome to the coast, Hanrahan thought, and struggled not to look smug. Trials really were different here—and that was why most firms partnered up with a local attorney. To prevent reprimands just like that, coming from the judge.

Somehow, Riordan's expression had not changed, even though Hanrahan felt her amusement. Or maybe he was channeling his on her. A few members of the jury who, until this moment, had looked deadly serious, were smiling at the judge.

"When the car sped up," Riordan asked Hanrahan, "what did you do?"

"I radioed for backup," he said.

"To the sheriff's department?"

"No," he said. "I contacted all local law enforcement.

Frankly, I thought the car would make it to Seavy Village and the police there would slow him down."

"But you gave chase," she said, as if he had done something wrong.

They had practiced this. She thought it crucial. He didn't. He trusted the locals on the jury.

Still, he gave the answer he and Riordan had settled on, in a voice that had no sarcasm or anger or even surprise.

"It was my job, ma'am," he said.

"You were required to chase the car?" she asked.

"Yes, ma'am," he said. "As long as the car was speeding, it was a danger to the entire community. The car needed to pull over."

"Is that the other reason you called for backup?" she asked.

"Yes, ma'am," he said. "Just six months before, a Lincoln County police officer was shot and nearly killed in a routine traffic stop not fifty miles from here. After that, we were all instructed to use extreme caution, particularly when dealing with an unusual traffic situation."

"You just stated that a drunk speeding up is not unusual," Riordan said. "Then why call for extra backup?"

"A citizen who speeds up when law enforcement asks him to pull over is unusual, ma'am," Hanrahan said. "At that moment, I did not know if the driver was drunk or had contraband in his car or had some other reason to flee."

"I see." Riordan paused on that for a long moment. Then she walked him through the accident itself. She had pictures of that corner Seedy had missed, which she had blown up for the jury. There was a few moments' tussle with

Ashton over the photographs, but that tussle was clearly for the record, not because Ashton believed the judge would disallow them.

By then, Hanrahan had been on the stand for almost an hour. He glanced at Seedy. Seedy met his gaze, then flushed, and looked down at his hands. He probably didn't want to relive those few hours any more than Hanrahan did.

What an awful night.

Riordan finally came back to Hanrahan. "When the car hit the guardrail, what did you do?" she asked.

"I contacted dispatch as I was pulling over and asked for an ambulance. Then I said I needed backup immediately."

"Did she tell you how far out backup was?" Riordan asked.

"She told me that backup would be there shortly," Hanrahan said.

"And you took that to mean?"

"Within five minutes," he said. "Otherwise she would have told me it would be there as soon as possible."

"Are these technical terms within the sheriff's department?" Riordan asked.

"I don't know if they are now," Hanrahan said. "But that was how it worked two years ago."

Riordan nodded. She asked a few more establishing questions, and then got to the moment she and Hanrahan had spent the most time on. She got him to the car, upside down in a foot of water.

"The Dee is a tidal river, is it not?" she asked Hanrahan.

"Judge," Ashton said. "We will stipulate to that."

He clearly didn't want the jury to think about what "tidal river" meant.

"I would like the definition on the record, Your Honor," Riordan said.

The judge glanced at the jury. At least two jurors looked confused, although Hanrahan couldn't tell if they were confused by the interchange or the phrase "tidal river."

"A tidal river," Judge Goodrich said to the jury, "is one that is affected by the tides. The Dee is a tidal river. Now," she said to Riordan, "continue."

"Thank you, Your Honor," Riordan said. She looked at Hanrahan. "Did you know roughly where the tide was at that point?"

"I always checked the tide tables at the start of my shift, because that makes a difference in my routes," Hanrahan said. "So, yes, I knew where the tide was at that point. It was coming in."

"What did you do?" she asked.

"I surveyed the situation," he said. "I was alone, and I had three choices. I could go after Mr. Cowell, who was running away. I could pull the women from the car, or I could help them survive until backup arrived."

"You chose to help them survive, did you not?" Riordan asked.

"Yes," he said. "I wasn't sure what I'd find inside the car. The car had landed on the passenger side, and was slightly tilted. I could only look in the driver's window. When I shone my flashlight into the interior, it was clear to me that Monica Knowles had died on impact, but Veronica Newmark was still alive."

"Was she conscious?" Another important question.

"No," he said, "and at that moment, her head was leaning against the back of the seat, with her nose elevated."

"What did you do?" Riordan asked.

"I shut off the ignition, then opened the driver's side rear door and climbed inside the car. As I did, I realized I did not dare move Ms. Newmark. The EMTs had to do that."

"But you are an EMT, aren't you?" Riordan asked.

"Objection," Ashton said. "Not in evidence."

"We're putting it into evidence now, Judge," Riordan said.

"Go ahead," the judge said to Hanrahan. She was clearly getting annoyed at Ashton.

"I'm not an EMT," Hanrahan said. "I do have the same training that EMTs go through. Seavy County made EMT training a requirement for all sheriff's deputies as our budget got slashed, when it became clear that we might be the only ones on an accident scene for around an hour as we waited for assistance."

Riordan let that comment hang. She had been pleased to learn that fact over lunch. Even though she had worked in the county for nearly a year, no one had told her about the EMT training before.

Ashton sputtered.

"So, in a nutshell," Riordan said after her pause, "the difference between you and other EMTs is?"

"I don't have the equipment they do. I didn't have anything more than a first aid kit in my squad that night, not that it would have helped."

"And your opinion is based on . . . ?" Riordan asked.

"The thing EMT training gives us is the ability to size up a situation in a few seconds and do the correct thing for the correct moment."

"What was the correct thing?" Riordan asked.

"The correct thing was to have an ambulance get Ms. Newmark out of there immediately."

"Objection—"

"Don't even try, Counselor," Judge Goodrich said before nodding at Hanrahan to continue.

"The thing I could do was protect her. The tide was coming in fast, and I knew the car would shift as the water lifted it. I braced my arms, wrists, and hands, and held her head in the position I found it in. I decided I would keep her stable as long as I could, hoping that the ambulance would arrive quickly."

"What was your greatest fear?" Riordan asked.

"My greatest fear at that moment was that she would drown as the tide came up," he said. "I was particularly worried that her head would fall to one side and she would be face-first and unconscious in water."

"So you weren't protecting her head against movement, were you?" Riordan asked.

"Of course I was," Hanrahan said. "That's EMT 101. I had no idea what damage had been done to her body. I needed to keep her as stable as possible."

"How long did you hold her?"

"It seemed like forever, but they tell me it was about four minutes."

"And did she move in that time?" Riordan asked.

"No," he said.

"Did you move her?" Riordan asked.

"No," he said.

"Did the water move her?"

"No," he said.

"What did you do when the EMTs arrived?" Riordan asked.

"I helped them with Ms. Newmark."

"And what happened to Mr. Cowell?"

"Officers from Seavy Village showed up while we were trying to save Ms. Newmark, and they arrested Mr. Cowell. I don't know the timeline. You'd have to ask them. I was busy. But I do know that Mr. Cowell hadn't made it out of the river yet."

Riordan nodded to him, clearly sensing that a smile was not appropriate. She asked a few other questions before turning Hanrahan over to Ashton.

Hanrahan's stomach actually clenched.

Ashton stood, adjusted his suit coat, and as he stepped forward, said, "Officer Hanrahan—"

"It's detective, actually," Hanrahan said. Ashton had known about Hanrahan's job in Portland. Like anything a lawyer said in court, Ashton had called Hanrahan by his old title to make a point.

"Oh, yes, Detective. Sorry. You're with the big city police department now." Sarcasm. So there would be no gloves.

Hanrahan threaded his fingers together. He felt calmer now that this had started.

"Why *did* you leave Seavy County?" Ashton asked, as if leaving were a horrible thing.

Hanrahan paused for just a second. The phrasing of the

question caught him. Why had he left? He had loved it here once.

Then he made himself focus.

"I left for a variety of reasons, some personal, which I can discuss if you like," Hanrahan said, making himself sound easy-going. "On the work level, I got discouraged by the continual budget cuts. Knowing that I would have to patrol alone over a territory double the size I had already been policing deeply upset me. It already took a long time to get backup. I foresaw that time doubling, and more lives being lost."

"Yes, time," Ashton said, thinking Hanrahan had just played into his hand. "Are you certain about the response times you mentioned?"

"As certain as I can be without the logs in front of me," Hanrahan said. "I reviewed everything before getting on the stand."

"Four minutes," Ashton said. "That's a very long time to have your hands in one position. Are you certain you didn't move them?"

"Yes," Hanrahan said.

Irritation flashed across Ashton's face. "How can you be certain of that, Officer—I mean, *Detective*. After all, we make involuntary movements all the time—"

"It was part of my EMT training," Hanrahan said, "and a part I used often. There are tricks to keeping yourself steady."

"Even when a car is shifting?"

"It hadn't started to shift yet," Hanrahan said.

"Not even when you climbed in?"

"Not even then," Hanrahan said.

Ashton was getting frustrated. He expected an easier cross. "So you left this county because you thought there weren't going to be enough officers on the road, thereby ensuring that there wouldn't be enough officers on the road. Had you thought that through?"

Now the questions were getting tougher. But Hanrahan did not smile. Ashton really should have hired a local attorney to help him.

"The department was going to have to lay off at least one deputy with the cuts. My decision to leave not only saved the jobs of the other deputies but gave the county more money." Hanrahan nodded slightly at the jury, a few of whom were smiling. "At the time, I was the highest paid deputy in the department."

Ashton's eyes narrowed. Hanrahan wanted to say, *Did you learn Rule Number One of cross examination? Never ask a question you don't already know the answer to.*

"Are you sure you just didn't want to be put in the position where you'd kill another person ever again?"

Hanrahan felt a thread of anger. He was being accused of killing Newmark in open court.

"Again?" he asked, working to keep his voice level. "I've never killed anyone, Counselor."

"So, you don't understand that you ultimately caused Newmark's death?" Ashton asked.

"The accident caused the injuries that led to her death," Hanrahan said in that same tone.

"But you moved her head around," Ashton said.

"No, sir, I kept it stable. Veronica Newmark's injuries

were a direct result of your client's decision to get behind the wheel of his car while drunk."

"But not her death," Ashton said. "Her death was caused—"

"That's enough, Counselor," the judge said. "I know what you're trying to do, although I'm not sure why you're trying to do it. The jury will decide your client's responsibility in both deaths. Am I clear?"

"Your honor, it matters—"

"No, Mr. Ashton, it doesn't." The judge pivoted her chair toward the jury. "I want you to disregard the last few statements Mr. Ashton has made. He was out of line. Detective Hanrahan acted sensibly in his handling of Miss Newmark. And the autopsy results, which Ms. Riordan will put into evidence—"

At that, the judge looked at Riordan. Riordan looked startled, but nodded.

"—clearly state that Ms. Newmark's death was a direct result of injuries sustained in the car accident. Your determination this afternoon will be the cause of that accident, not what happened after the car went off the road. Is that clear?"

The jurors nodded. They looked startled as well.

"Good." The judge turned back to the attorneys.

"Sidebar, Your Honor?" Ashton asked.

The judge's lips thinned, but she nodded. Both attorneys walked up to the bench. Ashton was clearly angry.

Hanrahan leaned back. He would be able to hear everything.

"Your Honor," Ashton said softly, "we have to establish cause of death in cases like this. It's rudimentary—"

"Are you saying I don't know the law, Counselor?" Judge Goodrich asked just as quietly. There were no microphones in this courtroom.

"I'm saying a few things today have been irregular, yes. Your Honor," Ashton said.

"Maybe for big city courtrooms," Judge Goodrich said. "Here, we try to get through the day as fairly as possible."

"But you've been unfair to my client," Ashton said.

"Tell me how I have been unfair, Mr. Ashton," the judge said. "Your client is facing homicide charges in the case of Monica Knowles and Veronica Newmark. If you had wanted to try Ms. Newmark's case separately, the time to do so has long passed. If you want to appeal this case, go ahead, but at the moment, it looks like the error in the conduct of this case is yours."

Ashton flushed.

"Let me give you one piece of advice," Judge Goodrich said. "Next time you step into a courtroom in a community you're not familiar with, young man, hire a native guide. Step back."

Ashton looked like he'd been slapped. The entire courtroom was silent.

"I do believe you're in the middle of cross-examination, Counselor," the judge said with something like amusement.

Ashton nodded. The jury watched avidly. They clearly wanted to know what had happened a moment ago, but they couldn't.

Ashton cleared his throat. "Detective Hanrahan, when you forced Mr. Cowell to speed—"

"Don't go there, Mr. Ashton," the judge said.

Ashton took a deep breath. "When you and Mr. Cowell sped—"

"Mr. Ashton, find another line of questioning," the judge said.

Ashton gave Hanrahan an angry glance as if it were Hanrahan's fault that Ashton was screwing up cross.

"Nothing further at the moment, Your Honor," Ashton said, "although I reserve the right to cross this witness later if need be."

"Fine," the judge said. "Redirect, Ms. Riordan?"

"Not at this time, Your Honor," Riordan said from her spot behind the table.

"You're excused," the judge said to Hanrahan. "But you will remain in case Mr. Ashton thinks of a question that you can actually answer."

Hanrahan did not smile, and he thought that a victory. "Thank you, Your Honor," he said, and stepped out of the witness stand.

He made his way out of the courtroom, feeling everyone staring at him as he went. A laugh was bubbling inside of him. It had been a long time since he'd seen an attorney melt down like that, and Hanrahan partially knew the cause.

Ashton had had a mission from his firm, which was why he had taken the case. With his cross, he had just failed at that mission.

Just like he had failed at his job as a defense attorney. He should have put his client's interests before his firm's interests.

He hadn't, and it might have cost him his high-powered career.

But, by the time Hanrahan sat down on the cold bench outside the courtroom, that bubble of a laugh had disappeared.

That feeling he'd had after Ashton's first question, that queasy sense of something unseen, had returned.

Why did you leave Seavy County?

The answers all seemed easy and obvious, the same thing he'd been saying for years, the answer he had given in court.

But the follow-up question had stung: *Are you sure you just didn't want to be put in the position where you'd kill another person ever again?*

The accusation had made him angry, and it wasn't like Hanrahan to get angry in court. He knew that a trial was an adversarial process, and he knew he would get grilled because of it.

But there was a tiny bit of insight inside that question.

The question had had the wrong thrust. Hanrahan never felt like he had killed anyone that night. He knew he had no responsibility in that accident.

But he had witnessed the accident alone, he had handled the crucial parts of that case alone, and he had known he was probably watching a woman die as he cupped her jaw carefully between his large hands.

He had hoped, of course, that she would survive. But a part of him had seen something the rest of him hadn't. He had known her survival would be a long shot, and that knowledge became more certain as the weeks passed and she never came out of her coma.

He always blamed his leaving on the changes in the budget. His entire career in Seavy County had become about making do.

From the beginning when newcomers to the department had to take mandatory lower salaries than the previous newcomers to that last year when service got cut in half, he had watched the effectiveness of the sheriff's department diminish as well.

And the accident had brought it all home for him. Because that night hadn't been the end of his career. It had been a vision of his future in Seavy County, braced inside a car, hands stationary as rocks, a woman growing paler with each passing moment, her breathing shallow, her eyes closed.

He had known Veronica Newmark wouldn't be the last person he would have to deal with on a Seavy County road. But she had been the image of things to come.

And he hadn't been able to face that.

He had been right on the scene. He had handled everything by the book. If he'd had a partner, they could have caught Seedy, as well as dealt with the injured.

If there had been a patrol car nearby—truly nearby, not a village away—then maybe they could have headed off Seedy before he missed that corner.

But half the roads were cliff sides in this county, and another quarter ran along the ocean. There was only one highway and it was mostly two-lane. Accidents happened all the time, usually in the remote parts, and usually late at night.

Hanrahan hadn't wanted to stumble on a dying family and be unable to help them. He'd rather face off a mugger on Portland's streets, settle an unruly mob of demonstrators, and investigate one of Portland's thirty or so annual homicides. He didn't want to watch anyone die because some politician decided that cutting law enforcement was better than raising—or maintaining—taxes.

He just didn't.

He leaned his head back and closed his eyes.

He hadn't hated Seavy County or the coast. He had just hated the choices his job had forced him into.

"Detective?" Riordan stood over him. He hadn't heard her emerge from the courtroom.

A few other people entered the hallway.

"You done?" he asked.

She nodded. "The jury's deliberating. May I buy you a beer?"

She seemed almost jubilant.

"Ashton didn't ask for a plea," Hanrahan said.

"You took the wind out of him, and the judge wouldn't let him take a break because she knew that he wanted to call his law firm. The judge gave me a look after the jury left that told me she knew I had been right about his motives all along." Then Riordan grinned. "Actually, you were the one who had been right, and I never told the judge about that. But she understood Ashton was being fishy, and she kept a tight rein on him."

"You think the jury will convict Cowell?"

"Oh, yeah," Riordan said. "The question is of what. If Ashton had actually presented a case, Cowell might have ended up with something like Failure to Perform the Duties of a Driver."

"You asked for that?" Hanrahan was surprised. Failure to Perform was a felony with five years attached if someone died, but still, that seemed pretty minor, all things considered.

"We asked for Failure to Perform as well as Aggravated Vehicular Homicide, Criminally Negligent Homicide, and straight-out Criminal Homicide. The jury has a cornucopia of charges to choose from. I think they'll find something," she said.

"You want him off the street," Hanrahan said.

"I want a conviction. Two people died," she said.

He nodded.

"So," she said. "A beer?"

They had a while to wait, just based on the charges. Things that were familiar to law enforcement and attorneys were strange new territory to jurors. If the jurors wanted to convict Cowell, they had to agree on a charge. It would take time.

"Yeah," Hanrahan said, "a beer would be good."

He stood and gathered his things. Riordan watched. As he slipped on his coat, she said, "You know, Detective, you're mighty good at your job."

"Which job?" he asked, thinking she had never seen him work in Portland.

"The detecting part," she said. "I owe you. If you hadn't done that research, I might have gone light on some of the details."

She had almost let another attorney get into her head. Hanrahan had prevented it.

He wanted to say it was nothing. But it hadn't been nothing, and they both knew it.

She had missed the connection within Rodriguez Roest

because she was overworked. Judge Goodrich had sped the case along because *she* was overworked. And Hanrahan had done some research because, for a brief moment on a rainy morning, he hadn't been overworked.

Sometimes the pressure of the sheer volume of stuff worked in their favor. Sometimes it cost lives.

Hanrahan followed Riordan to her office so she could get her coat.

They both had done the best they could with the time and information they had been given.

And, much as he hated it, that was all anyone could ever ask.

SHADOW SIDE
A SEAVY COUNTY STORY

KRISTINE KATHRYN RUSCH

alfway up the mountain, Dan Retsler regretted returning to Oregon. He had a perfectly good job in Montana. The small town at the base of the Bitterroots had its own charm, and everyone now knew his name. He'd investigated his share of crime too—real crime, from shoplifting to domestic abuse allegations to more than the usual (to his mind anyway) number of shootings.

Yet, when he'd seen the advertisement for a police chief to handle a small town around the Oregon Caves, he'd jumped at the chance.

The Oregon Caves, he told himself, weren't the Oregon Coast. He wouldn't find selkies or ghosts or ugly mermaids or any other kind of fantastic creature that he failed to understand.

Instead, he'd be in the mountains, far from the ocean. Tourists would flock here, sure, but he had grown up in a tourist town. He understood how tourists fit into the local economy, and he knew how Oregon worked.

But as he turned west and south out of Grant's Pass, heading into the Coastal Mountain Range where the spectacular Oregon Caves threaded for miles, his stomach flipped, his shoulders tightened, and he nearly turned around.

He forced himself to continue by reminding himself that the committee expected him. He'd headed these hiring committees. He knew how much of a problem it caused when an applicant didn't show, particularly one good enough to warrant an interview.

He owed them that much. Besides, he was nearly there.

The committee set the morning meeting at the Marble Chalet, a place he'd never been to. He'd been to the Lodge at the Oregon Caves dozens of times. The Lodge was part of the National Park Service, and had actually been featured on PBS. His family loved to vacation there when he was a kid.

But everyone ignored the equally historic Marble Chalet. It had been in ruins for decades. In the flush 1990s, an enterprising private company restored it, and applied for a permit from the National Park Service to have a second public opening into the miles-long Oregon Caves complex, the opening easily accessible from the Chalet's parking area.

The Park Service decided a second opening was a bad idea. Retsler never found out why, but it made the Chalet a second-tier hotel by default.

If he took this job, he wouldn't work at the Chalet. He'd work in Marble Village, which the enterprising private company had originally built to house its workers, but which had grown like crazy. In the flush years before the century turned, a lot of Californians bought land and built homes here, so the village had more amenities than it deserved—from cell phone towers to high-speed Internet. It had also lost a lot of amenities to the Great Recession, like the three-plex movie theater, although the faux vaudeville theater, which played old movies and second (or third)-run films, did enough business to stay alive.

Retsler had found out some of this from a quick Internet search. He remembered parts of it from his years living in Oregon, and the rest the town fathers had told him as they tried to entice him up here for the job.

They wanted an Oregonian; they made that clear. They were even happier that he was a native Oregonian, since such creatures were rare. They also wanted someone with experience in tourist areas.

He fit that bill.

He just wasn't sure about the rest of it.

The road forked outside of Marble Village, with the steeper, more difficult part heading toward the Marble Chalet. The initial signs heading to the Chalet were modern, with lettering that would reflect a car's headlights. But the closer he got, the signs changed, becoming rustic. Eventually, he realized these were the original signs, built in the 1930s, as the hotel itself got built as a WPA project.

For the first time, he actually felt a thread of excitement at seeing the Chalet.

He parked near the entrance to the lodge. A wide sidewalk led him around the rocks. He stopped, his breath gone.

Flower baskets hung from cut and polished Old Growth

logs, harvested before anyone realized the old trees had to be protected. The logs formed the brace for a gigantic canopy that covered the walkway leading into the lodge itself. The rock way, made of cut marble, had to have come out of the Caves—again, before anyone knew this stuff had to be preserved.

The front of the lodge looked Swiss as interpreted by a group of provincial West Coasters who'd never really seen anything outside of the United States. The brown-and-white slats, along with the decorated shutters, seemed authentic enough, but the big logs that formed the foundation of the gigantic building ruined any tiny Swiss intimacy.

The word "Chalet" was wrong too. This wasn't a tiny house with a steep roof; this was a large resort with hundreds of rooms, surprising in its audacity. He wondered if there had ever been a time when all of these rooms had been occupied.

He doubted it.

The big wooden doors stood open, and he stepped into a large lobby. It took a moment for his eyes to adjust to the dimness. More flowers stood on tabletops and along both edges of the reception desk. A single dark-haired woman stood behind it. She smiled when she saw him.

He introduced himself so that he could check in. She handed him an old-fashioned metal key with a beautifully carved wooden fob attached. The fob declared his room number in large font.

He had no idea that ancient keys like this still existed in working hotels.

"They're waiting for you in the River Room," she said.

He pocketed the key when her sentence registered.

"River?" he repeated, not liking the word. He knew there had to be water up here, but he had come to associate water with trouble—at least in Oregon.

"Well," she said, her smile widening, "we couldn't very well call it the River Styx Room, now could we?"

His heart rate sped up. Why the hell would anyone name a room after the river that in Greek mythology divided the living world from the world of the dead?

He hoped it was some interior designer's twisted imagination.

"Up the stairs and to your right," she said, as if she believed he hesitated because he was lost, not because his stomach had knotted to the point he felt queasy.

He gave her an insincere smile, then went up the flat wooden stairs and turned left. The hallway opened into a maze of rooms, but he could see the River Room at the very end, not because of the large sign above the door (he had initially missed that) but because people milled inside.

He probably should have ducked into his room first, brushed his hair, and checked his shirt for lint. But he had decided somewhere between River and River Styx that this job wasn't for him. So it didn't matter how he looked.

As he walked in the door, six people turned in his direction, including four women. Not the town fathers then, but the town parents. A woman walked over to him. She had her magnificent blonde hair gathered on top of her head in some kind of elaborate coiffure that he hadn't seen outside of a photo spread in a magazine.

"Chief Retsler," she said. "I'm Ron Bronly. Welcome to Marble Village."

Okay. He tried not to let his surprise show. One of the drawbacks of e-mail, apparently, were the assumptions. Retsler had imagined Ron Bronly as a comfortable middle-aged, middle-income man with a slightly round belly and a lack of hair.

He hadn't expected a woman as attractive as this one. In addition to her careful hairstyle, she wore just enough makeup to jazz up her Oregon-casual outfit of tan slacks and tailored blouse. The hand she extended to him was manicured.

He took her hand, shook, and repeated that insincere smile. Everyone else looked more like what he expected. Three somewhat tired-looking women in jeans and jackets, two middle-aged men whom he would have taken for Ron Bronly if Ron Bronly hadn't introduced herself.

"Thank you for coming all this way," Bronly said. Her voice was smooth, buttery, but it had a bit of an accent. Bryn Mawr, unless he missed his guess. Very Katharine Hepburn.

"I was curious," he said. "I hadn't been to the Chalet before. I've only been here a few minutes, but it looks like the restore was lovingly done."

He could afford to be nice. It didn't hurt that, in this case, nice was also honest.

"We're proud of it," she said. "It's the jewel of our little community."

"Have you had a chance to drive around?" one of the men asked. He wore one of those stick-on name badges that read "Martin." Everyone else had a name badge as well, including Bronly. Hers read "Rhonda."

No one offered Retsler a name badge. Of course, he was the only stranger here. Apparently, they were trying to make him feel at home.

The spread on the back table also should have made him feel at home. Pastries, coffee, all kinds of non-alcoholic beverages. He glanced at them, saw that the group had already partaken of some of it. He wasn't really hungry, more tired. And he wanted to get this over with.

"I came directly here," Retsler said.

"Pity," Martin said. "You'd be surprised at Marble Village. Most Oregonians expect some place like Sisters, when really, it's a lot more like Monterey, California."

"Without the ocean," said the other man whose nametag read "Stanley."

Retsler trotted out his insincere smile for the third time. "I've done my stint around oceans."

"Yes," said one of the women. Her name tag read "Anna," which somehow suited her serious mien. "We spoke to the folks at Whale Rock. They would love you back."

"I'm sure the new chief is doing just fine," he said.

"Why did you leave?" Bronly asked.

He looked at her. Direct. To the point. Usually, he liked that in a person. Here, though, it made him uncomfortable. How could he explain that the world he thought existed didn't? Whale Rock wasn't so much a place he disliked as a place that confused him and made him question everything about himself.

"I was ready to move on," he said, and it sounded true. It

was true on some level, but not quite true in the way he wanted it to be.

She nodded, as if the answer didn't satisfy her. "And what's wrong with Montana?"

He smiled—and this time the smile was real. "Nothing really. In fact, as I drove up here, I realized I was probably wasting your time—"

"Excuse me." The woman from the front desk peered into the room. Her eyes were wide, and her tone seemed a bit panicked. "I'm sorry, but it's back."

"Dammit," Martin said and took off at a run. The others followed, leaving Retsler behind.

He hadn't thought such conservative people could run like that, especially Bronly, who wore heels too high for anyone but an actress to move quickly in. Yet she had managed.

With just a few words, the entire group seemed to have forgotten him, and just as he was getting to the important stuff. Maybe he shouldn't feel so guilty.

But he couldn't help it. Nor could he help himself. He had to know what "it" was.

He walked quickly into the hallway, half expecting someone to stop him. But no one did. One of the side doors stood wide open, and he heard loud, panicked voices coming from that direction.

He looked in, saw a flight of stairs that had probably been designed for employees but now modern regulations made it a mandatory exit from this floor.

He took the steps down—wooden also, and not as well reinforced as those in the lobby—and found himself on the ground level on the far side, with a door that opened toward the Caves (or so the hand-lettered sign said).

It felt like he had entered the 1930s. More Old Growth wood, expertly carved and polished to a sheen, and through an interior door made of a single pane of glass, a diner the likes of which he hadn't seen since he was a kid.

No one manned the counters made of that same Old Growth wood, but voices echoed from the back. Voices he recognized on such short acquaintance.

". . . should do."

". . . not like it sees us."

". . . the mess, though."

He followed the sound to a swinging door, and pushed it open.

The six town parents, a man in a chef's uniform, and two waitresses stood in front of a back door. Beside them, steel tables had fallen on their sides, and the floor was covered in flour.

They all peered out the back door, and it wasn't until Retsler got close that he saw why. Prints from a pair of bare feet led down the path toward a rock outcropping.

"Problem?" he asked.

Everyone jumped. Everyone. He'd never seen that before.

Bronly turned around, and it was her turn to give him an insincere smile. "Nothing we can't handle," she said.

"Tourists? Vandals? Is this the kind of crime I'd be handling if I came here?" he asked. Not that he was planning to come here, but he hated it when people deliberately hid information from him. Perhaps that was one of the reasons he became a cop.

"It's not really a crime," Martin started to say as the chef said, "It's my fault. If I hadn't moved the table . . ."

"But you like the table there," one of the waitresses said. "It makes for a more efficient kitchen."

"A more efficient kitchen is one you can cook in," the chef said, and sighed. He was older—that indeterminate age some men got, where it was impossible to say if they were 35 or 75. If Retsler had to guess, he'd say the chef was closer to the upper limit than the lower one, but only because of the man's calm. "I just shouldn't mess with it."

"We're going to have to mess with it," Stanley said. "That grill has to come out. We can't keep repairing it. And then what'll happen? Will the new one get trashed?"

"Someone want to tell me what's going on?" Retsler asked.

"Nothing important," Martin said, giving him an insincere smile.

"It was important enough to interrupt our meeting at a run," Retsler said.

They all looked uncomfortable, the kind of uncomfortable that people often got with outsiders whom they felt would not understand. Retsler's heart sank. He didn't like the feeling he had, but he was a cop and a damned good one, and it looked like they needed something, so he pushed, even though his instincts warned him against it.

"Let me take a look," he said, and before anyone could argue, he followed the flour footprints out of the kitchen. They padded beside the newly installed stone path, which he thought odd, considering the owner of those feet had been barefoot. The stone should have felt better against naked skin than the sandy rocks beside the path.

"Chief Retsler, please."

He could hear Bronly behind him, but he also knew that she wouldn't be able to keep up with him, not in those heels on this incline.

The path wound into the trees and away from the parking lot, toward the mountain itself.

The footprints remained visible, even though the flour should have dispersed after a few yards. He felt a tingling he hadn't experienced since his last years on the Coast.

He wasn't going to like this. He really should have heeded their advice and turned around.

A six-foot-high mesh fence covered the path and disappeared behind boulders that had clearly fallen off the mountainside. Behind the mesh fence, grass grew summer tall, nearly up to Retsler's chest. The grass blocked part of a well-worn dirt path that led to a boarded off opening into the mountainside.

That denied entrance into the Oregon Caves. The Park Service had actually boarded it all off.

There was no easy access through the mesh fence either. A large sign posted to the right stated that the entrance to the Oregon Caves was a half mile away, with a map provided in case the wanderer forgot about all the signs he'd seen coming up to the Chalet.

The footprints continued on the other side of the mesh. They followed the path all the way to the boarded opening of the Caves. From this distance, it looked like the footprints went into the Caves itself.

Retsler swallowed hard, that knot in his stomach so twisted that he felt vaguely ill. He forced himself to look at the ground underneath the mesh fence.

Sure enough, one of the footprints went under the mesh, half inside the fence and half out, as if the fence wasn't even there.

He closed his eyes for half a minute. What he saw was impossible. He knew it was impossible, he hated that it was impossible, and yet it was there in front of him, which meant that what he saw was very possible indeed. Retsler just had to figure out what actually happened.

He opened his eyes. The footprint remained. Dammit. He grabbed the fence with his right hand. The mesh was cool against his palm. He shook the metal and it rattled, but it didn't give. He'd hoped that it was rusted, broken off somewhere that he couldn't quite see, and easy to move and replace. But of course, the simplest and most logical explanation wasn't the one that faced him at the moment.

"Chief Retsler, really." Ron's voice came from behind him, a bit breathless and a little exasperated. "You don't need to investigate this."

He turned without letting go of the fence.

Her perfectly coiffed hair had slipped its bun, half of it trailing down the side of her now-red face. Beads of sweat had formed on her collarbone, and sweat stained the area around her armpits. Brambles and leaves clung to the hem of her pants. She no longer looked like a society matron, but like a woman who would have been a lot more comfortable in sweats and blue jeans, a glass of water in her left hand.

"I don't have to investigate," he said, "because you know what this is."

Her mouth thinned. "I told you. It's nothing, really. Not what we wanted to talk with you about."

"Nothing?" he asked. "Something did about one-hundred dollars damage to that kitchen, maybe more considering the cleanup time. Then there's the problem of the grill and the fact that your chef doesn't feel like he can put anything in his kitchen the way he wants it. Now, unless I miss my guess, the Chalet is already operating at a loss. You want to tell me that you can write off an expense, even a small one, that seems to occur on a regular basis?"

"I didn't say this had happened before," she said.

"No, your receptionist did when she came into our meeting room," Retsler said. "She said that she was sorry but that 'it' was back."

Ron's eyes widened. She glanced over her shoulders, but the remaining town parents hadn't followed her, or if they had, they were moving at an incredibly glacial pace.

Since she clearly wasn't going to say anything else, Retsler continued. "It's also notable that your receptionist didn't give the vandal a gender. I thought maybe an animal when I saw the overturned table, before I saw the footprints. After all, we don't call other people 'it' very often, now do we?"

Bronly brought a hand to her destroyed bun, realized that it was falling apart, and pulled out the pins. She shook her head, letting her hair fall. The hair wasn't blond like he'd thought, but silver. With her hair at shoulder length, she looked younger than she had a moment ago.

She still didn't seem willing to answer him.

"Why don't you be upfront with me?" he said, trying to keep his tone even. "When you set up this job, you didn't want an Oregonian. You didn't even want an average chief of police. You could have done just fine with some local hire, maybe a disgruntled park service worker or someone who had retired up here and just needed the extra money for a few hours of his time every day. That is, that would be all you needed if things were normal around Marble Village, which they're not, right, *Ron*?"

He couldn't help himself: he had to emphasize her odd misleading nickname, maybe to keep the other anger in check, the one that rose whenever he felt both embarrassed and betrayed.

She held up a hand, as if her palm could block his words. "We were doing a legitimate hire."

Were. He wondered if she even knew she had used the past tense.

"No one could understand why we needed someone full-time. And most people, they don't like how remote it is up here," she said. "You're perfect. You've been chief of police in two remote towns, one here in Oregon. That's all we're looking at."

Yet her gaze didn't meet his.

"Uh-huh," he said in the back of his throat, that Oregon acknowledgement that was both dismissive and somewhat rude, something he hadn't done since he moved to Montana. "You've had Hamilton Denne up here, haven't you?"

Retsler had worked with Denne in Whale Rock.

Denne was the Seavy County Coroner, and a local who first introduced Retsler to the idea of the supernatural. That discovery had strained their friendship. Retsler's move might have broken it entirely. He hadn't tried to find out.

Bronly blinked, then took a deep breath. "We had a mysterious death a few months ago. The Oregon Crime Lab recommended Doctor Denne."

Retsler hadn't heard Hamilton called Doctor, maybe ever. "A mysterious death. What did Hamilton tell you that you had? A fairy? A troll? Maybe some kind of orc?"

She shook her head. "No, no, the victim was human."

"Really?" Retsler asked. "Then why was Hamilton here? He likes things that resemble space aliens."

That wasn't exactly fair. Denne had saved Retsler's butt those last few years in Whale Rock, and had somehow kept him sane. But Denne did like the stranger things in the world. He found them fascinating.

Retsler just wanted them to go away.

"We had a desiccated corpse," she said softly.

"Which, given the dry conditions, the caves, and the heat in the summer, shouldn't be that unusual up here," Retsler said.

"Except that he was fine a few hours before. Alive, laughing, and fat as a man can be and still be considered strong and tough."

She had known the corpse, and Retsler had been rude. He felt a flush build around his ears. He willed it away.

"I'm sorry," he said in his formal voice. "I didn't realize you had known the deceased."

She shrugged, blinked again, and he realized she was fighting tears.

"We lost a few others like that," she said, deliberately ignoring his sympathy. "Tourists, it turned out. Hikers, two of them. When we found those bodies, we thought like you just did, that they had mummified because of the heat and the dry conditions, and the alkaline nature of some of the stone up here—God, we had a thousand explanations."

"And none of them right," Retsler said, making it a statement instead of a question. Statements kept people talking; questions made them stop.

"It was a *thing*." She shuddered. Apparently, she'd seen that *thing*, whatever it was. She held up her hands. "Long story. Not appropriate at the moment."

"But Hamilton helped you identify that thing," Retsler said.

"Oh, yes, after Chief Davis's death," she said.

Retsler's fingers tightened on the mesh. The metal cut into his skin but he didn't let go. "The chief was the desiccated corpse?"

She nodded. "He was heading up Mount Elijah to investigate a cougar sighting last we heard. Just two hours before someone found him on the road. Like that."

Tears welled again. The chief had meant something to her.

Retsler shook his head. This was going to be one of those stories he didn't want to hear. Something supernatural, something no one would believe until they saw the thing kill something else, and even then they'd find it hard.

"I take it you all solved whatever it was causing the

deaths," he said in the most clinical voice he had. If Denne had been up here, he would have known just how angry and trapped Retsler felt. He was back in Oregon, and he was back in hell.

"Yes," she said in a somewhat strangled tone. "Yes, we figured it out."

She straightened her shoulders, ran a hand through her hair, then gave him a watery smile.

"I'm sorry I didn't tell you that the previous chief had died suspiciously," she said.

He shrugged. "We barely got through the introductions."

She glanced at his hand, still wrapped around that mesh. "I feel like I'm not being fair to you. Doctor Denne told me a lot about you, about the strange things that happened in Whale Rock, and then I Googled you. We did do an open hire, we did. It was just—Marble Village isn't a normal place. People want normal, they go to Cave Junction. Or Medford. Not here. And all of the applicants, they were either too old or too practical or too expensive. And so, I was complaining to Doctor Denne over the phone, and he told me about you. That's when I e-mailed you. That's when I hoped you would come home."

This isn't home, he almost said, but didn't. Oregon was closer to home than Montana, that much was true. But this part of Oregon was very different from the coast, different enough to have its own weather, its own customs, and, apparently, its own monsters.

He didn't want to know. Better to return to Montana, where the monsters were humans prone to domestic quarrels fueled by too much alcohol and an easy access to firearms.

Still, he couldn't just walk away. Not with his fingers wrapped around this mesh fence, and that footprint below. He'd always wonder.

He saw that as both a personal failing and as a curse.

"All right," he said. "Time to tell me what's going on here."

She swallowed, blinked, sighed, clearly steeling herself. Then her gaze met his.

"This one really isn't important. We weren't going to mention it. No one's been hurt, nothing has gone wrong—"

"Except the damage," he said.

"Which we can limit if we don't move anything in the kitchen," she said. "The problem is that the new chef—and it's really not fair to call him new, since he's been here five years—he wants to make the kitchen more efficient. And the grill is dying. We can't keep repairing it. It's from the 1930s. They don't even make parts anymore and we can't find any others."

Retsler was still focusing on how she started. "What do you mean you can limit it if you don't move anything in the kitchen?"

She gave him a small smile. "I feel so stupid discussing this."

"Believe me," he said with more feeling than he had intended. "I understand."

Her smile widened just a little. "We thought we had a little girl. It's not. It's something else—"

"A poltergeist?" He'd read up on the supernatural after

he moved away from Whale Rock. And as he did, that always made him speculate if he had let go after all.

"Yeah, that's what someone called it," she said. "But that's not really true. We didn't have a little girl ghost. It's a thin young woman, I think, or a feminine boyish man, someone to whom that kitchen meant a lot. When things are running smoothly, in fact, when the hotel is full and so is the restaurant, you can see her—him—it—sitting near the door, a smile on his—her—its face as if it liked the bustle. Sometimes, it would even help one of the morning cooks. Our previous cook—a matronly woman whom everyone loved—would occasionally let it help her pick ingredients. She wrote the recipes down; they're spectacular."

"A cooking ghost that lives in the Caves?"

Her smile disappeared as if it had never been. Her dark eyes flashed, and her chin set. "Go ahead. Make fun."

Retsler had used the same tone with her that he used to use with Denne. It was a reflex, a way of pushing back at information he really didn't want to hear.

"Sorry," Retsler said. "I didn't mean to make fun."

She took a deep breath. Clearly she had to overcome his tone so that she could continue. She expected him to make fun of her, and it almost shut her down.

He wondered who else had made fun, and what had changed.

"Whatever it is," she said with a little less enthusiasm, "it loves the kitchen just the way it's always been. We got new dishware and fortunately, it wasn't china, because the whatever it is tossed the dishware around the kitchen for weeks, trying to get rid of it. A few pieces chipped, finally, but we replaced them."

"When did that stop?" he asked.

"After a few months. But we can't wait this one out. We don't want it to trash a new grill, and you saw what it did with the flour."

"Yes," he said, and looked down. The footprint was fading. Had there been a wind? He hadn't noticed. "Did you know that this creature lives in the Caves?"

"I'm still not sure it does," she said. "But whenever it gets angry, it leaves footprints, coming to this site. We've actually sent people into the Caves to follow the prints, but they disappear just inside the opening."

"So this isn't flour." Retsler let go of the fence and crouched down. He touched the print. It was ice cold.

"Are you sure you should do that?" she asked.

"I'm not sure about anything," he said. He checked his fingertip just to make sure the white whatever it was didn't transfer onto his skin. So far as he could tell, it hadn't. "Has anyone else tried to figure out what these prints are made of?"

"By the time we get experts here, the footprints have faded," she said. "You can understand why we're reluctant to call folks in."

He nodded, then stood. "You have worse problems than this ghost?"

She bit her lower lip. "Apparently—and we didn't know this during the boom of the 1990s—but Marble Village was built on the site of one of the first settlements ever on Mount Elijah. There's water near here—"

"Don't tell me," he said. "The River Styx."

She smiled. "No. Well, yes. But no. The River Styx runs through the Caves, and that really is its name. Outside of the Caves, it's called Cave Creek. There are tributaries all over the mountainside. One of the largest is here, although it does dry up during summers like this one."

"And floods in spring," he said.

She nodded. "See why we want an Oregonian?"

"Anyone who lives around mountains knows how winter runoff works," he said. He still wasn't convinced about the Oregonian part. "But you were telling me about the water."

"The initial settlers thought they had a great water supply," she said, "so they built here instead of at Cave Junction. Then they abandoned the town."

"That's not unusual in the West," he said. "There's a million ghost towns just like it, places that people tried, figured wouldn't work, and moved on."

"Yeah." She glanced around him at the Caves, as if she saw something. He hoped she would trust him enough to tell him if she did. "But they didn't leave because the creek dried up or because of a wildfire or anything. They just disappeared one night. Half the town fled and the other half was never heard from again."

"I don't remember reading that," he said. Then he smiled at her. "You're not the only one who knows how to use Google."

"Tourist town," she said. "Resorts. We didn't put some of the old history on any website, and fortunately, the initial stories of Marble Village, which was called Limestone Creek back then, weren't published in any guidebooks."

"You think this history is important," he said.

"I didn't at the time," she said, "but I do now."

He brushed off his hands and stood. The footprints were nearly gone now, but he saw where they disappeared and made a mental note of it.

"Why do you think so now?" he asked.

"Because we're under assault, Chief Retsler," she said. "That's why we want you. Someone we don't have to convince that this is important, that it could be an emergency. Someone who *knows*."

He sighed. Back in Oregon, having the same old discussions. "Didn't Hamilton tell you? I left Whale Rock because of the supernatural."

"He did," she said. "He also said he didn't think you'd take the job, but he said I should push."

Retsler nodded, sighed. "So, you've done your duty. You've pushed."

The wind toyed with her hair. She grabbed some loose strands and tucked them behind her ears. "You're going to say no, aren't you?"

"Yeah," he said, and almost added, *I ran away from all this*. But he didn't.

"Well." Businesslike again. She stuck out her hand. "I'm sorry we wasted your time."

He glanced over his shoulder. "Let's make sure it's not wasted completely, all right?"

Then, without waiting for an answer, he shook the fence. It rattled, warning whatever was behind it that he was coming. He wasn't sure if he had done that deliberately. He liked to think he hadn't.

"How do I get through this?"

"You don't need to," she said.

"I'd like to," he said.

She hesitated, then pointed to an overgrown blackberry bush near one of the boulders. "Through that."

He'd tried to go through blackberry bushes before. They were stubborn, and sometimes hid things with thorns.

"I guess I'll climb," he said, and gripped the mesh. The diamonds were big enough for the toes of his somewhat dressy shoes. He hauled himself up, and carefully eased over, landing in the dirt on the other side.

At least she wouldn't follow him here.

"I'll get someone to open the gate," she said.

He nodded absently, not caring if she did or not. "I'd rather have an expert on the hotel's history, preferably not a scholarly type, but someone who's been around for a few generations."

"Um, but—"

He didn't listen to her answer. Instead, he followed the fading footprints down the incline to the mouth of the Caves.

The prints stopped just outside the opening. He touched them again. Cold, but damp, as if they were made of ice and the ice had started to melt. Water, again. Dammit.

He sniffed his fingers, wondering if the dampness had an odor. It didn't, or at least, it wasn't an odor that he could smell over the pines and the dirt and the fresh Oregon air.

He stood. The boards over the cave entrance were old

and rotted. They hadn't been replaced in years. Some had broken along the sides. He touched them, and two boards fell down, leaving a space just large enough for a young adult woman or a slender young man who hadn't reached his full growth to slide through.

Retsler peered inside. No lights, but a chill against his skin. The Caves had an ambient temperature of 41 degrees, a fact he remembered from his childhood. As a boy, he had wondered why the settlers hadn't built their homes inside the Caves—they would stay relatively warm in the frigid mountain winters and remain cool in the summer. He had mentioned it to his father, who had laughed.

Boy, forty-one is too cold for comfortable living, no matter what the season.

It was also too warm to keep ice frozen, so the water inside the Caves—that damned River Styx—would continue to flow.

Retsler wondered if he should break the wood and go inside. Then he decided against it. He didn't have the equipment for one thing. Just his cell phone, which could double as a flashlight, but wouldn't have service deep inside. And this was a part of the Caves that the Park Service had deliberately blocked off, so finding him wouldn't be easy if he got lost or turned around.

Or attacked.

He picked up the wood. He would wait until he had permission, or even knew if he had to go inside.

Voices echoed along the path. He decided not to wait for someone to cut the brambles away from the gate opening so he could get out. He climbed the mesh for a second time, his fingers complaining as the metal dug into his skin.

He landed on the path just as Bronly returned with one of the town parents. The curled name badge reminded Retsler that the man was named Stanley. Stanley didn't look as winded by the walk as Bronly did. Despite the extra weight he carried around his middle, Stanley was surprisingly fit.

He held up hedge trimmers. "Was gonna help you get out."

"Thank you," Retsler said.

"Guess you didn't need it."

"I figured climbing was easier."

Stanley looked at him through narrowed eyes. Then he said, "Bronly here says you want to know about our ghost."

He sounded calm about it, calmer than Bronly had. She glanced at him, then at Retsler.

"I did," Retsler said, matching Stanley's calm tone, "but I would rather have heard from someone who maybe lived here in the 1930s."

"Ain't got many of those folks left and what we do are down to the Village. I could give you some names of folks in a home in Medford." Stanley wasn't looking at Retsler. He was peering over Retsler's shoulder at the Caves.

"See something?" Retsler asked.

"Naw," Stanley said. "Just like to be watchful, is all. This ain't the best side of the mountain to be on."

"Why not?"

"Creepies, crawlies, things that go bump in the night. They like the shadow side best."

"And this is the shadow side?"

Stanley nodded. His gaze moved from the Caves to Retsler's face. "Let's go to the diner," he said. "I bet you could use you some pie."

"You don't have to ask me twice," Retsler said He glanced over his shoulder at the Caves behind him. The white footprints were gone, but his remained. His and Ron's and Stanley's, tromping all over each other, showing their confusion and indecision. The only odd thing he noted was that on the other side of the fence, no footprints showed at all, not even where he had jumped.

Retsler frowned. That felt important, but he wasn't sure why.

Or, at least, he wasn't sure why—yet.

Half a dozen patrons sat in the W-shaped counters lining the diner. None of the patrons were the town parents, many of whom nursed coffee near the kitchen door.

Bronly led Retsler to the farthest side of the W, facing the windows that overlooked the small manmade pond and beyond it, the Siskiyou National Forest.

This part of Oregon was pretty, he had to admit that, and pretty in a different way from Montana. Maybe it was the color of the dirt, or the narrowness of the sky or maybe it was just the smell in the outdoor air, which he shouldn't have been able to smell in here.

That faint scent of fried hamburgers grew stronger now, particularly since one of those burgers on that grill was his.

The waitress, wearing a blue-and-white checkered uniform and a little protective hat that made her look like something out of the 1930s, had already given him ketchup and mustard in red and yellow plastic squirt containers, without any labels. Nothing had labels, trying to maintain the illusion of history. He wondered what he would get if he asked for artificial sugar to go with his iced tea, then decided not to ask.

He didn't want to spoil the illusion either.

Bronly also ordered a burger, which surprised him. He would have thought that a woman like her would order a salad. Although he hadn't seen any salads prominently displayed on the old-fashioned menu.

Stanley had ordered a piece of apple pie à la mode, and the waitress had already given it to him, along with a cup of diner coffee—nothing fancy at all, no half-caf lattes or sprinkles allowed.

"We're talking over here," Stanley said as he turned his plate so that the point of the wedge-shaped piece of pie faced him, "because the others think this's all crazy, that some kids're doing pranks."

"You don't?" Retsler asked. His stomach growled again. That piece of pie looked like something out of a magazine, perfect crust, glistening apples covered in a lovely brown sauce.

Then Stanley ruined the perfection by slicing off the tip. "You seen it. You want to tell me how them footprints got where they are? And icy to boot."

"You've touched the prints, then," Retsler said.

"First time I saw them. Windy day, but the prints stayed

the same. Ice shocked me. It was strange, and back then, I didn't like strange." Stanley shoveled the pie into his mouth.

"You do now?" Retsler asked.

"Let's just say I'm used to it," Stanley said around the pie in his mouth.

Bronly glanced at the town parents, still talking near the kitchen door. Her glance seemed almost furtive, as if she didn't want them to overhear—which they couldn't, given how far away the door was.

"So this has been going on for a long time," Retsler said.

"This, that, and the other thing. The killings, though, those were new." Stanley cut another piece of pie, shoving the side of his fork so hard into the surface that the plate moved.

"And Hamilton Denne helped you with those," Retsler said, wanting to make sure.

"Theoretically. He said, though, things're changing He was seeing more weird things, and he blamed all kinds of nutty stuff—global warming, some kind of creature rebellion, pollution, you know. All that liberal conspiracy crap."

Bronly leaned back just enough to catch Retsler's eye behind Stanley's back. She shook her head just a little, warning him off this part of the topic.

Retsler already knew to move away. He'd met this Oregon type before. They were prevalent in the mountains, guys who had their own beliefs about the world and who believed that anyone who disagreed with them was crazy or nutty or worse. Retsler had always thought of them as the precursors to the survivalists who had moved up here in the 1980s. When he was in Montana, which had a slightly different version of the same type, he realized that many of these folks *were* the survivalists who had moved to the "wilderness" in the 1980s. They had integrated back into society, kinda, but hadn't lost their strong opinions about the way the world worked or about the people who disagreed with them.

"You don't think this thing that's visiting your kitchen is a killer, do you?" Retsler asked.

"Naw. It's been coming here since we reopened. It gets mad, but it don't hurt anyone."

"But it causes damage," Retsler said.

"Some," Stanley said. "Don't think we need to waste your time catching it."

"I wasn't thinking about catching it." Retsler tried not to shudder. He'd actually touched some of the supernatural creatures he'd seen on the coast, and he didn't want to touch any of them again. "However, if it is a ghost, we might be able to put it to rest. I've helped with that before."

"I don't think it's a ghost," Stanley said. He looked pointedly at Ron. "I know some of the others think it's one of them poltergeists, but I don't. I can't find nothing about anyone what died in that kitchen."

"What about on the land before the kitchen was built?" Bronly asked, with enough force in her tone to make Retsler realize she had asked this before.

"Naw, nothing," Stanley said. "Not even a worker died while putting this thing up, and considering all the problems the WPA guys had sometimes, and the fact that nobody thought anybody what worked up here was worth much, that's kinda surprising. They had to snowshoe out, you know."

"What?" Retsler asked.

"Freak September blizzard. We're high enough to get that kinda thing once in a blue moon." Stanley cut more pie.

The waitress came by with both burgers. She set them down with a flourish. Retsler's looked fat and juicy and damn near perfect, like burgers he'd had as a kid.

"They ran out of supplies," Stanley said as the waitress walked away, "and no one could get to 'em. So they had to snowshoe out. All of them come back, though. Brought supplies up with a sled. Finished the job."

"Back in the days when men were men and sheep were nervous," Bronly muttered so softly that only Retsler could hear her. He was glad he hadn't taken a bite of burger. He would have choked on it as he stifled his laugh.

"So," he said to Stanley, "no one died here that you know of."

"That's right," Stanley said.

Retsler picked up the burger. Juice dripped along his fingers. He took a bite. The burger was better than he expected, marinated in something before it was placed on that grill.

"What about in the Caves?" Retsler asked. "Anyone die in there that fits the description of this guy—or whatever?"

"Cook's kid or a cook?" Stanley asked.

"Or someone who wanted to be chef, or maybe a tourist?"

"Hell," Stanley said, "lots of people have died in those Caves, more than the Park Service wants us to admit."

"All before the Park Service took over," Bronly said primly. She clearly didn't want Retsler to think something bad could happen in the Caves. Or maybe she was still protecting the area's reputation.

"Most of 'em did die before anyone kept records," Stanley said. "And the ones we know about got written up in the papers. But I figure lots of folks got killed and left wherever. You know, they died deep inside, got stuck or something, couldn't get out, never was heard from again."

"The Caves still haven't all been mapped, even now," Bronly said. "Although I've never heard of anyone finding a skeleton inside one."

"But if there are other creatures living in the Cave . . . ?" Retsler let his voice trail off.

Both Stanley and Bronly looked at him. He immediately regretted the choice of the word "creatures."

"I mean," he said, "you know, cougars, raccoons, rats, anything going in and out that might feast on a carcass. Something like that might mess with the bones as well. You wouldn't find any then."

"Well." Stanley ostentatiously ate the last piece of pie, chewing and talking at the same time. "Things get ate all the time up there. And we do find bones, just not human bones, so far as I know."

Retsler ate some of his burger, thinking.

"So," he said after a moment, "what you're telling me is that we have no idea if someone died in those Caves who had a connection to this hotel or this land, and we have no way of finding out."

"I don't think it's a ghost," Stanley repeated.

"Why not?" Retsler asked.

"Don't act like a ghost," Stanley said.

"A stereotypical ghost," Bronly corrected.

"No," Stanley said. "A ghost. We got 'em all over the hotel. You know, folks die in their rooms or whatever. We got ghosts, we got stories, and this one, it don't repeat actions like ghosts do, and it don't seem stuck in the past like ghosts are. It interacts. That's why I don't think it's harmful. I just think it's young."

Retsler looked at Stanley. "Young? What do you mean young?"

"It acts like a kid. It tosses stuff around that it doesn't like. It gets angry when you tell it no. But it watches, like it's learning."

Retsler set down the last part of his burger. "When you were looking at the Caves this afternoon, when you were talking to me, what did you see?"

"I told you. I didn't see nothing."

"The area looked normal, then," Retsler said.

"I didn't say that neither."

Bronly leaned around Retsler. "If you saw something, Stanley, tell us about it."

"I didn't see nothing," Stanley said with the same emphasis as before.

Retsler frowned. The key to talking with people, he had always thought, was listening. And he hadn't been listening.

"What kind of nothing?" he asked.

"You know," Stanley said. "Like fog. Like a cloud rolled in over the mountain, but just for a minute. Then everything was clear again. It wasn't nothing."

That's right, Retsler thought. *It wasn't nothing. It was something.* But he didn't speak out loud. He didn't want to derail Stanley.

"Where was this fog?" Retsler asked.

"Right near the gate." Stanley gave Bronly a perplexed look. "You know what I mean. We get that kind a thing all the time up here."

"Not in the summer," she said. "Fog's for fall."

"Or spring," Stanley said. "We got lots of ground fog in the spring."

Ground fog. Retsler mulled that over for a moment. Oregon had all kinds of fog that he hadn't encountered since he'd left. Montana didn't have nearly as much fog because it didn't have as much moisture in the atmosphere.

Fog, ground fog, light fog, freezing fog.

Freezing fog.

Something that should have been impossible up here in these temperatures. Like ice cold footprints. Like a childish figure that overturned tables and handed cooking ingredients to a chef.

He went back to ground fog for just a moment. He hadn't seen any in years, but he remembered it clearly. It always looked like it was seeping out of the ground, not forming in the air around the ground. He'd always thought ground fog spooky and Halloweenish, like something out of a Vincent Price movie or out of a Scottish ghost story.

Covering the ground. *Brushing* the ground.

Hiding footprints—his and the ice prints. Covering. Brushing. Hiding.

"Dammit," he said softly.

"What?" Bronly asked.

"Do you have a book of local legends?" Retsler asked.

"Upstairs," Stanley said as if he'd been waiting for Retsler to ask. "Gift shop."

"All right then. I'll go check those books out." But Retsler didn't leave immediately. He had to finish that spectacular hamburger first.

The gift shop was in a room just off the registration desk. The room had beautiful wood walls, so lovely that no one dared hang anything on them except photographs and single t-shirts on hangers. The rest of the merchandise stood on freestanding displays. Snacks, sundries, and local jams covered one display. A large art portfolio filled the area farthest from the window, and the clothing hung on racks in the middle of the room.

It took Retsler a moment to see the books. They were on built-in shelves behind the cash register.

The woman behind the register gave him a friendly smile. "Go ahead," she said in a tone that told him other customers had hesitated to go back there as well.

He did. The store carried some mass-market paperbacks, some used books, and a whole bunch of local color. Books on the Oregon Caves, books on the Park Service, books on Southern Oregon, and books on the great lodges of the Northwest dominated. He saw a few books on the WPA plus a film of the building of the hotel. Then he saw the books that Stanley had mentioned, huddled together like forgotten children on the bottom shelf.

Retsler crouched, then sighed.

Ghosts of the Northwest, Oregon Folklore, Monsters of the Mountains—he'd seen all of these before. He hadn't really looked at them with Marble Village or the Chalet in mind, but he didn't trust the authors of these tomes as far as he could throw them.

But Stanley had recommended them, so maybe there was a kernel of truth in them.

"You're the new police chief?" the woman asked.

Retsler grabbed the *Monsters* book. It was covered with dust.

"We haven't gotten that far yet," he said, knowing it was a lie. He'd already told Bronly he wouldn't take the job, but he didn't feel he should confide in this woman.

"I'll bet you Stanley sent you here, didn't he?" the woman said. "He thinks those books have truths in them."

"You don't?" Retsler opened the *Monster* book. Just like he remembered: hand-drawn images and tiny type. He had tried to read this thing once and hadn't been able to.

"Oh, they have little bits in them," she said, "but nothing like what really goes on up here."

Retsler set the book down, wiped his hands on his pants, and stood. He hadn't expected her to say anything like that. He had expected her to tell him that Stanley was a bit nuts, that he imagined all kinds of things.

"What goes on up here?" Retsler asked, looking at the woman carefully.

She was middle-aged, carrying just enough weight to

make her seem matronly. Her hair was going gray but hadn't gotten there yet. When it did, someone would describe the color as gunmetal gray. Right now, it dulled her red-brown hair. She'd spent too much time in the sun, judging by the faint wrinkles on her skin, and her current tan. But she had spectacular green eyes. She hadn't been a beauty in her day, but she had turned heads.

She said, "You're asking about the child in the kitchens, aren't you?"

"You think it's a child?" Retsler asked.

"I certainly hope so," she said.

She sounded certain, as if an adult would be a bad thing. Retsler frowned. "Why?"

"Because we live on the shadow side," she said.

He leaned against the counter. "That's the second time someone mentioned the shadow side to me, and frankly, I'm confused. There is no shadow side to a mountain. The sun hits all parts eventually. I know there's a shadow side in different seasons—"

"The sun does not hit all parts," she said. "Some sections never see sunlight. They have overhangs or side croppings or there are trenches—"

"All mountains have that," he said.

"Yes," she said a little ominously. "Yes, they do."

He took a deep breath, trying to control the sarcasm that wanted to flow out of him. That sarcasm had almost gotten him in trouble with Bronly, and it was going to get him in trouble here, if he wasn't careful.

He extended his hand. "Dan Retsler."

"MariCate Webber."

They shook, and that gave him a moment to get himself under control. He remembered Denne once saying to him, *Either you accept this stuff or you don't, Dan. You're an evidence guy. How much evidence do you need to realize that strange things exist?*

"So," Retsler said, "what's wrong with the shadow side here?"

"Our shadow side isn't unique," she said. "But that child is."

"You're convinced it's a child."

"Aren't you?"

"I haven't seen it, but others seem to believe it." Then he winced. That "seem to" would have gotten Denne to jump all over him.

MariCate didn't seem to notice. Instead she offered what seemed like a non sequitur. "My grandfather helped build this place."

And suddenly Retsler understood why Stanley had sent him up here. Not to see musty old books, but to talk to MariCate who, like most people in an area routinely flooded by tourists, wouldn't answer direct questions, but might talk to someone she trusted.

"You know they got snowed in," she said.

"Stanley told me they snowshoed out."

"They did, but not to escape or get supplies. That's the cover story."

"What's the real story?" Retsler asked.

She smiled. "It was a rescue."

He didn't follow. "Leaving was a rescue?"

"No, no," she said. "Stanley must've also told you no one

died building this place."

"Yes, he did," Retsler said.

"Which is true. You, as a policeman, probably know that truth hides in the words you choose."

Somewhere in this conversation, he had stopped leaning. He placed his hands on the polished wood countertop.

"People did die then," he said after a moment. "Just not building the place. They died during the blizzard . . . ?"

"No," she said. "They died in the Caves. Where they went for shelter. Most of a family died. The cook, his wife, and his adult son."

"Most?" Retsler's palms felt damp. He removed them from the wood, saw the prints he left, then shoved his hands in his pockets.

"The twelve-year-old daughter, she got out. They rescued her and four other children."

"What were children doing up here?" Retsler asked. "I thought this was a WPA project."

"It was," MariCate said, "but a lot of families, you know, were homeless then. And when the man got work, sometimes the whole family came along. They weren't supposed to, but they camped nearby, on Cave Creek, and probably got sheltered in the buildings the men made for themselves."

"Probably?" Retsler asked. "You don't know?"

"There's a lot I don't know," she said. "My grandfather didn't like talking about this. He was 81 when I divorced and moved up here. He tried to talk me out of it. He didn't want me on this side of the mountain."

"The shadow side," Retsler said.

"You didn't notice, did you, when you drove in that this

is a kind of high valley? Marble Village is actually in a box valley, at 4,000 feet, mind you, but a box valley just the same. Only one real way in. At least there's light there."

"And not here? I seem to see quite a bit of sunlight around this place."

"Around parts of it. But there's never sunlight from the kitchen to the Caves. You didn't notice that, did you?"

He hadn't noticed it. He would check out what she said later. "Why didn't your grandfather want you here?"

"He said it was dangerous. He especially warned me out of those Caves. The access here isn't used at all by the Park Service. It's mapped, but it's blocked inside and out, except for a tributary of the River Styx that they couldn't block without hurting the rest of the Caves."

"Why is it blocked?"

"Oh," she said with that smile. It was impish, and he rather liked it. So far today, he'd found two women his age attractive. Maybe he had been alone too long. "They'll never say why. They'll say it's too dangerous for tourists, which is true, and they'll tell you that there's nothing to see, which isn't, and then they'll tell you that it hasn't been mapped, which is an out-and-out lie."

"They won't tell me," Retsler said, "but you will."

Her smile widened into a grin. "As my grandfather spins in his grave, certainly. The reason is that people die in this part of the Caves, and not normal dying either. They freeze to death, sometimes in a matter of minutes and sometimes over days."

"I thought the Caves were forty-one degrees," Retsler said.

"They are," she said.

"The people just get chilled then," he said.

"If exposure can turn you into a block of ice, then yeah, they just get chilled," she said.

"Block of ice." He wasn't even trending toward sarcasm now, not with that icy footprint. "So you think the child is an ice-ghost? One of the children that died in there while this hotel was being built?"

"Children didn't die in there," she said. "That's what I was telling you. One got out—a girl. She came back to the men huddled in their cabins during the storm. How she found them, well, that's subject to conjecture, because you know how hard it is to find anything in white-out conditions."

He hadn't known that until his sojourn in Montana. The scariest day he'd had as chief there had been during a severe and sudden snowstorm, one that had stranded him beside the highway. Fortunately, he'd pulled off, or his jeep would've been totaled by the idiots trying to drive blind.

He nodded. "Yeah, I know."

"Well, she told them that the cook's family was in there, and a few of the kids, who'd been playing near the River Styx, and asked them to get the family out. The men waited until the snow had eased, thinking the family would be safer in the Caves. By the time they got there, there was a snow barrier, or so it seemed, covering the entrance. Avalanche, they thought, or something. Anyway, as they tried to dig out, they kept hitting rock. They were using their hands and some shovels that broke. They needed more equipment."

"What kind of equipment?" Retsler asked. "They

couldn't use dynamite and there wasn't anything that would have made it up the mountain in a storm, no grader or anything."

"I don't know," she said. "I never asked. My grandfather and his friends snowshoed down with the girl, got help, came back up with supplies. A handful of guys remained. They managed to make a small opening, found the frozen adults, but the children were still missing. So they did a search."

"The adults froze near the entrance then," Retsler said. Of course. That made sense. Nothing supernatural at all. He felt a thread of relief.

"No," she said. "They were nearly a mile into the cave, in a room appropriately called 'The Ice Palace.' My grandfather said after this whole thing, there was talk of digging out that room to see if the stalagmites were actually people, frozen in place, but that idea got scrapped. It haunted my grandfather, though, I tell you."

It couldn't be that easy. It never was. Not here, not in Oregon. Retsler sighed. "And the children?"

"They left on their own, while the men were trying to get the bodies out of the Ice Palace. The kids said they were playing with their friends, and hadn't even known there was a storm, had no idea they'd been there for days, weren't even hungry, and certainly didn't look like they'd been trapped in a cave."

"Denial," Retsler said.

She gave him an appraising look, then shrugged. "They didn't use that word back then, but a lot thought it might be something like that."

"Your grandfather didn't."

"He finished the winter here, and never came back. He kept moving south, away from snow or snow-capped mountain peaks. Died in Los Angeles, in a house where he couldn't see any mountains at all." She was clearly waiting for Retsler to ask a question, and this time, he knew what the question was.

"Why was he afraid of snow?"

"Said there were things in it. He could see them. Creatures. Said Hans Christian Andersen's Snow Queen wasn't a story after all."

"I never read it," Retsler said.

"Think of a winter queen. She had an army made of snowflakes, and commanded the ice. She could steal a man's soul with a single kiss."

"Sounds like a fable to me," Retsler said. "And there are no mountains in Denmark, so Andersen wouldn't have been writing about the shadow side."

"He was writing about snow, and ice, and what some call ice fairies."

"Is that what you think this is?" Retsler added.

"I think the word 'fairy' gets used for all kinds of magical beasts," she said. "But the children lost time, like people do in fairy kingdoms. Washington Irving wrote about that in 'Rip Van Winkle.'"

"Which was a metaphor for the changes that occurred during the Revolutionary War," Retsler said.

Her expression cooled. "I didn't expect a skeptic. They said you knew about these things."

He sighed. "Not snow creatures."

Although snow was water. Frozen water. Ice crystals.

"You said the children were playing with their friends," he said, hoping to get back on track.

She nodded. "That's why my grandfather never let me up here. The children had always talked about their imaginary friends in the Caves. After the incident, he decided those friends were real. He says he saw them."

"Children," Retsler said.

"Yes," she said. "He said they loved coming into the camp kitchen to get warm."

Retsler didn't know if he believed any of it. He didn't know if he disbelieved any of it either. He poked a bit more, discovered that others had died in the Caves, but that the deaths were ruled exposure, which could happen to anyone in prolonged forty-one-degree temperatures.

Plus, he never trusted death analysis from the previous century—at least, not before 1950 or so, when the practice of forensic medicine, like the practice of medicine itself, became more science-based and less reliant on the skill of the practitioner.

By the account that MariCate had given, these men had pulled bodies out of that cave that were "frozen to death," but that phrase got used for everything from exposure to being too cold to actually freezing in a snowbank.

Retsler could imagine what Denne would say. Retsler was using supposition just like everyone else was. Only Retsler's reinforced his own bent to the practical, to the real world, not a willingness to believe in fairies and poltergeists and things that go bump in the night.

Even though he had seen those things, more than once.

He took the proffered hotel room, which was beautiful. It had clearly been redesigned in recent years, with a modern bathroom added, and the most comfortable mattress he'd ever encountered. The hotel had Internet access and more television channels than he had in Montana. Even so, the place still felt rustic. Maybe it was the rough-hewn walls, or the ancient bed frame. Maybe it was the photographs on the walls, black-and-whites of former guides and mountain men and the men who built this place.

Or maybe it was the remoteness. Even with all the connectivity, he still felt far away from civilization. If he closed his eyes, he could imagine himself back an entire century, learning about the real-world magic of the Oregon mountains, the pines, the caves, the breath-taking views.

To Retsler, that kind of beauty had fairy dust sprinkled all over it, and not the kind that made a man lose ten years, but the kind that made him realize there was no other place on Earth like this one.

At a very good dinner in the fancy dining room, the town parents regaled him with stories about Marble Village, true-to-life stories about the town drunk and the occasional domestic and the one real murder the town had had in the past five years.

He'd had a conversation just like this one in Montana before his hire there, and back then, it had sounded like heaven to him. Dealing with everyday problems, with families and bar fights and the occasional true crime.

But this time, he couldn't make himself focus. He had already told Bronly that he wasn't interested in the job, and no matter what kind of stories the town parents told him, he wasn't going to change his mind.

He didn't even change his mind when they offered him nearly double his current salary, plus a house at the edge of town. He had never been in this business for the money. He wasn't about to start now.

No one mentioned the supernatural at all. No one talked about the event in the kitchen or the strange things he'd seen just since he got here, and he didn't blame them.

After talking with MariCate, some of the interest had left him. The others had been right: this wasn't something that a police chief would deal with, even if he did work up here. The vandalism wasn't really vandalism; the intruder was known to everyone.

It was one of those things that people put up with. Had the intruder been an actual person and not something magical, everyone would make excuses, telling Retsler about the kid's bad home life or his poor upbringing or his limited intelligence. No one would ask the chief to intervene, especially since it seemed that no one got hurt.

That was what had cooled him, if "cool" was the right word. So far as he could tell, these creatures hadn't ever killed anyone. In fact, if the story MariCate had told could be believed, the creatures had saved the life of the children during that snowstorm, and got them out untraumatized.

All of the stories were relatively benevolent. There was no evidence that the creatures were what killed the adults; they might have simply died in a colder part of the cave, thinking they were safe. The creature that invaded the kitchen had never harmed a soul, not even when that cook years ago had let the creature choose ingredients for meals. In fact, the meals had to be good because the recipes were still in use.

So, aside from the occasional angry outburst, the kind he'd seen from a variety of humans in a variety of circumstances, the creature seemed somewhat normal.

If such things could be called normal.

After a few bottles of Blackberry Porter from Wild River Brewing (something he couldn't get in Montana and missed, the summertime microbrews from his home state), Retsler planned his drive back to Montana. He decided he wouldn't even go to Whale Rock. He still didn't want to see anyone there, still didn't want to revisit the place.

He was still, despite his momentary lapse, running away from all things unworldly.

And, he told himself, he always would.

Sunlight woke him, which he found ironic since everyone talked about living on the shadow side. Apparently, his east-facing hotel room avoided that shadow altogether.

He supposed he could close the curtains, but they were gauzy and white and wouldn't make a lot of difference. He checked his watch, saw that it wasn't even six yet, which was when the diner opened. He had checked the night before, knowing he would be leaving as early as he could. He could make it back to Montana in one long day, but he preferred to drive sensibly. No reason the chief of police of any town should get caught weaving all over an empty highway due to exhaustion.

Even with a leisurely shower, he got downstairs ten minutes before the diner opened. He found himself wandering outside, to the path. It was dark here, shadowy, the pond itself looking a bit grim and more algae-covered than he remembered.

It was also cold, the kind of cold he loved about the West. Yeah, it would heat up to maybe ninety-five later in the day, but right now, it was fifty and he wasn't wearing a coat.

He looked at the mountain, rising up before him. He couldn't see the peak here because he was too close. The mountain didn't look formidable when you were on it, only as you drove up to it from sea level. Then it seemed impossible to cross.

A chill breeze touched him, the kind he hadn't yet gotten used to in the Montana winters. Some of the locals there called it a prairie breeze because it came from the East, bringing Midwestern or Canadian cold onto the part of Montana that passed for flatland. The weather guys called it an arctic wind, but that suggested gales filled with snow particles. This felt only like the precursor.

And he shouldn't feel it, not in summer. He looked over his shoulder, realized that he was standing near the kitchen door.

He should have been warmer standing here, but he wasn't.

He turned slowly, holding his hands up like a man with a gun trained on him.

The creature stood behind him, just like he had expected from that chill. All of the descriptions were right: childlike, young, maybe male, maybe female. The eyes looked older than a child's ever could, but the slender build reminded Retsler of some paintings he had seen of androgynous figures looming out of the mists.

He didn't know how to talk to it. If he asked it questions, it would probably leave.

So he said, "Beautiful morning, isn't it?"

Its mouth opened, as if it were going to answer him, revealing a slightly pink interior. As he watched, the creature gained a bit of pinkness all over, as if it were trying to mimic his flesh color.

"They think you come down here to get warm," he said. "I don't. I think you come down here for company."

It tilted its head. Its eyes were now blue, the blue of the Montana sky. Its face had no more definition than before, but it seemed to relax a little.

"You like cooking, you like listening to conversation, and you miss your friends. When the Park Service blocked off the interiors of the Caves, did you lose your own people or access to ours?"

It nodded toward him, just once, and his heart leapt. It was answering him.

"I thought so," he said. "Your people, they're not fond of us. The rest of them hide, don't they?"

It raised its shoulders slightly, then let them drop. A small shrug. It had been around humans long enough to learn gestures. He wondered if it could talk. He suspected that it couldn't or it would have spoken before now—not to him, but to the others.

"They call this the shadow side," Retsler said. "You can't travel outside of it, can you? You can't look for your friends anywhere else."

Water dripped off its chin. He didn't know if it was melting in the relative heat or if those were tears.

He didn't know if this thing could cry.

Denne would want him to photograph it. Denne would want him to ask all kinds of procedural questions.

But Retsler wasn't interested in procedure. This creature had done nothing wrong. It was just lonely.

He understood that.

He nodded, glanced at the kitchen door, then back at the creature. "They need to talk to you," he said. "They want to make some changes."

Its head snapped back, its hand came out, and for a moment, Retsler thought it might hit him. He could actually feel the anger coming off the creature.

His heart pounded. He kept his hands up. "They don't want to get rid of the kitchen," he said, keeping his voice calm. "But out here, outside the Caves, our equipment decays. Falls apart."

More water dripped off its chin.

"We repair that damage," he said. "But sometimes we have to replace things. Like the dishes. Remember how we replaced the dishes?"

It watched him. He had no idea how old this thing was, but he would wager it was decades older than he was. And he would wager that it was one of the younger members of its species.

He had no idea if it understood. He hoped it did. Because he finally figured out its anger.

The interior of the Caves had remained the same for hundreds of years. The early deaths might have been caused when humans wandered in, interfered with something important. He would wager that the Ice Palace meant something to this creature's people.

But he didn't know, and obviously, it couldn't tell him. Not easily, anyway.

"Let us make the changes," he said. "Then we'll stay. The kitchen will stay. The path will stay. You can still observe, and maybe even help again."

It wiped a hand along its chin, a very human gesture. Then it closed its fingers around the water it had collected.

When it opened its hand again, it was holding what looked like tiny diamonds. It extended that hand to Retsler.

His heart pounded. He'd learned not to accept magical items from any creature. He'd once lost a friend to centuries-old wine. All of the fairytales cautioned against eating anything offered by the supernatural.

But the creature didn't want him to eat the diamonds, at least so far as Retsler could tell.

He brought his right hand down and extended it, palm up. The creature touched the tips of its fingers to the tips of his, its skin sending an icy shock through him.

Then the creature closed its hand again, and smiled.

The smile was a surprise. The face warmed, and the creature looked almost human.

Retsler smiled back.

The creature nodded, then walked around Retsler, heading down the path toward the Caves.

Retsler watched it until it disappeared around a small corner. The chill slowly left the air. He could feel the warmth of the day wrap itself around him.

No wonder the creature left so early. It would melt faster in the heat of a mountain summer.

His stomach growled. He ate too much up here, and he still wasn't getting full. He glanced at his watch to see how long the interaction took and was startled to see that three hours had gone by.

He had lost time. A few minutes conversation, to him, and he had lost time.

No wonder those children had lost days. He wondered what they had done in the Caves as the snow fell, as their parents died in the Ice Palace.

Then he shook his head slightly. He was intrigued. Dammit. He hadn't been intrigued in years. Frightened, yes. Overwhelmed, most definitely. And then he had run away to a place that hadn't challenged him at all.

He had never been intrigued in his Montana job, although learning the job had occupied him for a while. It had brought him a feeling close to intrigue. But he had never quite achieved it.

He stared at the path down the center of the shadow side, leading to a blocked off part of the Caves. Home, but not home. Water creatures, but no great body of water. A history, but not the history he had grown up with.

A new start, again.

"Dammit," he repeated.

And then he turned, and walked into the kitchen. He didn't run, and he certainly wasn't running away.

In fact, he had some information to give to the chef and the entire staff, maybe to the town parents, and certainly to Stanley and MariCate. He knew how they should treat their visitor, and how to keep that visitor calm.

He also knew he was signing on for a ride. They were, as Bronly had told him, under some kind of assault. But so was Whale Rock. He didn't want to go back there.

But he didn't want to return to Montana either, where he faced domestic quarrels fueled by too much alcohol and an easy access to firearms.

Retsler suspected he would find enough of those up here. It was a rural village after all, despite the obvious wealth backing the hotel. Wealth didn't prevent people from getting angry or drinking too much or losing sight of the things they loved.

Hell, nothing did.

Humans reserved the right to be stupid.

And they deserved the right to change their mind.

THE SCOTTISH PLAY
A WYRD SISTERS STORY
KRISTINE KATHRYN RUSCH

408 Years Ago . . . as I usually picture it from my book-lined office in one of those pseudo-Gothic buildings at Yale. And no, I'm not telling you which one. I'm just sharing the way I think of these things when I'm sitting at my antique desk, littered with books about The Theatre and The Theater, depending on the snob level and the side of the Pond the author lives on.

I am an Elizabethan scholar, among other things, and I know real magic too, and still, this vision comes in mixed clichés.

Just saying I know better, okay?

So . . .

408 Years Ago:

(Or maybe 421 or maybe even 418. I mean, really, how do you know when a man made a deal with the Devil? If, indeed, he did make a deal with the Devil. And not just the

Devil's helpers. Or his handmaidens, as the case may be. Anyway . . .)

These three women are hanging out in their hovel in London. Because for some reason, witches can't afford more than a hovel, even though they have more magic than anyone else, which makes no sense to me and never has. Anyway, they're hanging out and some young playwright with the ear of the Queen shows up, believing they can give him magic powers. I mean, come on. Really?

But it's my imagination, and it's untamable, at least on this. Maybe because the images came into my head so young, before I knew about Elizabethan politics and Guy Fawkes and the Tower of London and beheadings and—

Anyway:

Three women. Witches. Standing around a cauldron. There had to be a cauldron, because Shakespeare describes it later in the Scottish Play and everyone from Bugs Bunny to *The Simpsons* have parodied it. The women circle the cauldron and they give Shakespeare magic powers.

Or they don't give him any powers at all.

I'm betting on *don't*, given what happens later.

He goes away with a sense of magic, the supernatural, and all of its dangers. He writes somewhat subversive plays about kings and abdications and strong women and hidden loves and even though he criticizes the monarchy, still the monarchy lets him perform.

Scholars believe the Scottish Play's witches were added to flatter King James the First, Elizabeth's successor, who wrote a book on demonology, called, of all things

Daemonology. But I know there's more to it than that. I know, because of family lore.

Because I'm descended from those witches.

Because I'm still carrying on their tradition.

I mess with the theater, but only in a good way.

Or so I would like to believe.

Of course, it would be the Scottish Play that tested those beliefs. The Scottish Play, for you Philistines who don't know, is *Macbeth*. It's safer to call the thing the Scottish Play because of the curse.

Everyone knows about the curse, or should. To say the name of the Scottish Play in a theater—any theater (and that includes movie theaters, Philistines)—invokes a centuries-old curse that will destroy someone or someones associated with that theater. Technically, to say the name of the play and *to quote from it outside of rehearsals for the Scottish Play* invokes the curse. But that distinction often seems to get lost in translation.

Theoretically, there are ways to neutralize the curse. They include turning around three times, spitting over your left shoulder, and quoting from one of Shakespeare's "lucky" plays like *Hamlet* or *A Midsummer Night's Dream* ("If we shadows have offended . . ."). Simplistic answers to a simplistic problem, because the problem isn't with the name of the Scottish Play. The problem is with the play itself.

I avoided entanglements with the Scottish Play for years; mostly because I figure anyone stupid enough to a) stage the play and b) call me to fix whatever has gone wrong is beyond help. They have to pretend not to believe in magic, and then call in magic when the curse rears its ugly head. They want that cake. They want to eat it. And usually, they want me to save a multi-million dollar production that should simply be abandoned.

I say no. Then they find someone else. The play's run is plagued with bad luck. The story of the play's production usually appears in articles about the curse of the Scottish Play, and then becomes part of theater lore.

Except this last time.

This last time, I went to London's West End because the idiots in charge hired my mother.

And killed her.

To say my mood was foul as I approached the Lancaster Theatre in the West End really doesn't do justice to just how dark my mood was. If someone were using the over-the-top visuals of horror movies to backlight me, thunder and lightning would trail in my wake.

It was midnight and the moon was almost full, albeit hard to see in the bright lights of the 21st century city. That's the thing about London: It is a modern city. Yeah, sure, it's filled with nooks and crannies of the past butted up against the present, but it's always been that way. That's part of the problem.

The Lancaster Theatre was a case in point. A rebuild on top of a rebuild, the Lancaster first appeared in the West End in the late 18th century, and burned down at least three times. Two of those fires took place after cannons fired on stage in productions of *Henry VIII*. Even the Globe burned after cannon fire from *Henry VIII*, proof of Shakespeare's displeasure with John Fletcher's so-called collaboration.

Despite the pictures I found online, I did not expect the Lancaster that was waiting for me. The online photos made the Lancaster seem like a 1970s monstrosity, all glass and chrome, with too much red in the seats and on the carpet.

Apparently I had missed a remodel, because now the Lancaster looked like a proper British theater of the movie-magic type—a roundish exterior suggesting a 17th century origin, lots of wood (fake I hoped), and solid oak doors that should have kept the riff-raff out.

I was the riff-raff, at least on this night. I didn't go under the marquee, advertising the upcoming opening of *Shakespeare's Macbeth!* (as if someone else had a Macbeth to perform) with Edward Burton, one of the greatest stars of stage and screen, a man who (fortunately) got his start in the Royal Shakespeare Company.

I stopped in front of the posters, staring at Burton's craggy face twisted in confusion and fear as he held a bloody knife. He looked appropriately Macbeth-like. I double-checked the names of the other players, seeing a solid group of Shakespeareans mixed with some up-and-comers. Not even the director was new.

This production should not have had troubles, not in filling the seats nor in behaving properly during rehearsals for the accursed play. The magic here should never have flared, and it definitely shouldn't have caused the death of my mother.

The theater was shut down while Scotland Yard finished its investigation into her death. They believed it an accident; I knew that because they had already released the body to my family—most of whom were angry at me for not going directly to Cornwall for the death rites.

I knew I had time; my aunt Eustacia had to conduct the ceremony, and she was still in Moscow. She had a different theatrical mess on her hands. Had the owners of the Bolshoi Theater called her when the troubles began, the acid attack on the director of the ballet would never have happened. My aunt was caught in an international mystery, which meant she had to keep her head down and her magic quiet—never the best way to work.

Besides, I was afraid she might not be able to do much, with Mother dead.

So far, my mother's death at the Lancaster received little mention. She wasn't an official employee of the theater, and her death had occurred in the lobby. It looked like a heart attack, which is what the authorities concluded it was, and it caused no interruption of the play's already elongated schedule.

I wasn't about to enter by the front door. Even after midnight on a weekday, there were too many people around. The neon displays from Piccadilly Circus lit everything up. Tourists thronged past the shops and pubs, blinking under the glare of lights. It would have felt like Times Square except that Times Square was broad where Piccadilly was close. I always felt not just the press of history here, but the press of pickpockets as well.

The Lancaster was on a side street, and the stage door in a narrow alley around back. Cobblestone of indeterminate age would have made the alley feel old if it weren't for the pubs all around with their moving beer signs and their open doors. Laughter echoed out of them, as did the scents of ale, fried foods, and vomit.

Such things made me nervous when I was thinking of magic. Especially magic that would let me into a theater without the owners' express permission.

Because such magic required speaking the words of one of Shakespeare's plays. Not just one of his plays, mind you. But the Scottish Play.

But in for a penny, in for a pound, as the British say. (And it wasn't until I realized that was a British expression that it made sense; rather like those ancestral witches.)

I went to the door, placed my hand on the knob, and said in the softest tone I could manage, "Open, locks, Whoever knocks!"

The click of the door lock, the snap of a deadbolt, the digital music of a security lock, and the slide of a chain lock followed one after the other.

I pushed the door open, and stepped into the last place my mother was seen alive.

All theaters smell the same. Greasepaint, sweat, shaved wood, and dust. I'm not sure why dust, since most theaters are clean, but the dust remains underneath everything.

I pushed the door closed behind me, letting my eyes adjust. I expected the light. Every theater leaves a light on upstage center, even theaters run by practical people. Most theatrical folk know the light is on to ward off ghosts. A few might acknowledge that the light serves another duty; it makes the backstage clutter easier to see.

But in this theater, the light was wrong. It was both too soft and too bright at the same time.

I realized I was looking at it with both my physical eyes and my metaphysical ones. I closed my eyes, and the light remained the same.

My heart started to pound.

I opened my eyes.

There was more magic in this theater than I had ever seen in a theater before. Usually there are bits and pieces of magic, and they're fun to encounter. A glowing skull, from a particularly magical rendition of *Alas, poor Yorick!* Or a slightly illuminated costume of one of those actors who touches every role with his own special enchantment.

Normally, different kinds of hexes had different colors, lengths, and brightness. A mistaken wish of luck instead of the common and careful "break a leg" should display a small spray of greenish light that remained in the area where the mouth emitted the accidental curse. If the spray touched someone connected with the play, then that person would have had a moment of bad luck. If that person got drenched in the spray, the luck might have been particularly bad.

That moment of bad luck would remain for weeks, maybe months, sometimes years, depending on the power of the person who spoke the curse, whether the curse was intentional, and whether the curse hit the target for whom it was intended.

But I couldn't see little jetties of green or any other color for that matter. Every hex in this theater glowed with a pure white light, the light of sheer power, a light I might not be able to combat.

For the first time, I regretted coming alone. If I succumbed to the magic, no one could pull me out of this place. And that realization led to another: my mother would have come through the stage door. Had she threaded her way through the webbed hexes to the front of the theater?

I folded my right hand and rubbed my first three fingernails against the ridge of my thumb, flicking my fingers forward. My fingers emitted just a tiny bit of magic, a personal magic, one that was almost as old as I was. I had done this before I had any magical control, before I had any memories, before I had language, to summon my mother. She used to laugh at it, and speculate whether or not I made that movement in the womb.

The magic jutted outward, pink and baby fresh, like it always did. It illuminated a trail, twisting and turning through this part of the theater, around the heavy red curtains pulled to the side, and off stage right. My mother had picked her way through the magic to the front of the theater. But the magic had grown so much stronger that most of her path was barred by thin white lines.

To my metaphysical eyes, it looked like a million spiders had worked overtime to create all of the magical lines. They grew thicker and more elaborate on stage, fading off on the sides, and—at least from this vantage—vanishing in the back of the house.

But I didn't trust my eyes—physical or metaphysical. That might have been the mistake Mother made. She had grown cocky in her later years, doing jobs that she should have brought her sisters to. In fact, she should have given up the magic when her oldest sister, Laylee, had died. But neither Mother nor Eustacia had given up their work with the loss of Laylee. In fact, her death seemed to make both of them work even harder.

My sisters and I vowed to quit when one of us died. Mother had laughed when she heard the vow and said it was foolish, that we diminished our powers by remaining sisters instead of growing our own talents.

"See where that got you, Mother?" I whispered, and then gasped at the shoot of pain that ran from my mouth to my heart. My hand flew to my chest, rubbing the ache away.

Mother made me feel like that once. I was ten and I called her a stupid fat-butted hag. Instead of laughing or admonishing me with a single word, she touched my mouth. Pain circled my lips, ran through my tongue, and down my throat all the way to my heart. I fell to my knees, clutching my chest.

You do not curse the magical, Mother had said. *Not in anger, not in jest. Not ever. Do you hear me?*

I had heard her. I never cursed at her again, although I silently resented that, especially in my teenage years. But I never wanted the repeat of pain, and I never experienced it.

Until now.

I tilted my head and stared at the magic lines. Had they found that old memory? Or was the ghost of my mother still here?

I glanced at the light, upstage center like it was supposed to be. It appeared to be on. But was it?

I wasn't certain, and the pain wasn't ebbing. I had to leave.

I backed up, stunned that I had only gone a few feet into the theater. It felt like I had walked half the length of backstage.

My hand found the door. The locks had turned again. They were covered with pinkish magical light. My light, from my spell, one I couldn't repeat or I would be saying the words of the Scottish Play inside a theater, something I never did.

I caressed the pinkish light. "Repeat," I commanded, hoping that would work.

The pink flared and the white lines inched toward it. But the locks all turned at once, and the door eased open. Either the theater wanted shed of me, or it was protecting me by getting me out quickly.

I hurried through the door, and it slammed behind me.

I stood in the alley, stunned to see that the lights of the pubs around me were off. The stench of fried food and ale had faded to a common everyday odor, and the smell of vomit had receded to a near-memory. How long had I been inside?

I did not wear a watch nor did I carry a cell phone—such devices, mechanical and digital, interfered with my magic—so I had no idea of the time.

I looked at the sky, expecting to see some darkness. Instead, the sky was pinkish, and it wasn't from my magic.

Dawn was breaking.

I had lost time, and that was the worst thing of all.

By the time I made it back to the Savoy, the pain in my chest had vanished, leaving only a sharp ache. I was deep-down tired, the kind of bone-aching exhaustion that had nothing to do with jet lag and everything to do with a serious expenditure of energy.

Hotels in the morning were a mixture of bustle and calm. A tour group passed a pile of luggage to the bellman for his storage area. A gaggle of American tourists were making their very loud way to the Thames Foyer in the heart of the hotel. I was surprised the smell of kippers didn't make them leave. Or perhaps that was my personal taste.

I headed toward the wood paneled lift, which always struck me as too rickety for a famous five-star hotel that charged more per night than most Americans made in a month. But I was being picky, partly because my head was starting to hurt now, and I had some decisions to make.

Charles, my on-call butler, scurried toward me, anxious to please. I had forgotten the so-called amenities that the high-end hotels had. I didn't find them amenities at all, and if I had remembered, I would have told the producers who hired me that I needed to stay in an anonymous touristy hotel in the heart of the West End.

I had Charles order me a large continental breakfast with coffee, and let myself into the one-room suite that some hotelier had named after Noel Coward. My grandmother and her sisters told delicious stories about Coward, his wit and his kindness. I had no idea if he would have been kind about the suite. His photographs were everywhere, and they distracted from the view of the Thames.

I passed the living room altogether, and flopped on the bed, reaching for the phone on the bedside table. I punched the code for an outside line, then dialed my sister Viola, the only sister with the right kind of magic that allowed her to carry a phone 24/7.

"Where are you?" she asked without saying hello. She always knew it was me on the other end of the line, even if I called her on a pay phone from a town I hadn't told her I'd be in.

"You know where I'm at," I said.

"That's not what I meant. Aunt Eustacia is about to give up. She says she's going to be here in three days."

I wasn't going to deal with Aunt Eustacia and the Bolshoi, not right now. I had my own theater problems.

"You might want to tell her to hold off," I said.

"And why's that?" Viola asked.

"Because I think the Lancaster killed Mother," I said.

Viola made a dismissive sound that had a magic all its own. "Of course the Lancaster killed Mother. She was alone.

Do you know how hard I've had to work to get Aunt Eustacia to see reason? She can't handle the Bolshoi, not without her sisters. And her sisters—"

"Vi," I said, "it has nothing to do with working alone "

"You would say that," she said. "You're there, in London, on assignment while Rosalind and I are here, waiting to put our mother's spirit to rest."

"You won't be able to do that," I said. "I'm not sure her spirit went with her body."

"Now you're being paranoid," she said.

"No," I said, feeling incredibly tired. "Don't you understand? I'm asking for help."

You must understand the implications of that moment: I had never asked for my sisters' help before. I was one of the only magical dramaturgs in the entire world, and I was in constant demand, even though I only took one or two jobs a year.

My sisters took the remaining jobs, and on the disasters you'd heard of (including that massive superhero musical monstrosity that should never have been allowed in a Broadway theater), my sisters would call *me* for help.

They preferred to work as a threesome, like the women of our family had done all the way back to the dawn of the modern English theater in the 16th century. The industrial revolution actually harmed the threesomes, because it became economical for one sister to travel to a small theater somewhere to solve a small problem. Then there were sister things, the in-fighting sisters always did, especially close sisters, like the women in our family. Going back generations, none of us had been separated by more than a year— three sisters born in three years. There was no real word for that, although my father, ever the naïve man, tried to call us Irish Triplets for a while. My mother hated that.

She also, by the end, hated her sisters. They held her back or so she believed. I personally thought she was like my sister Rosalind, the least talented of the trio. Aunt Eustacia had all of the power, or she did, until Laylee's death. And then it all started to go awry, just like it had for our grandmother when the first of her sisters died.

I figured I had at least six hours of uninterrupted sleep before my sisters arrived. I ate most of the breakfast, then closed my eyes.

I had forgotten Viola's penchant for daring the traffic cameras on the A30 to catch her going double the speed limit. Since Viola's magic let her control technology, she never got caught—and she never hit anything while she was driving. Still, I hated to be in a car with her.

As a result of Viola's singular talent, my sisters arrived at my hotel room in less than four hours. It was almost enough to make one believe that witches really could fly.

I heard Charles the butler arguing with them before one of them spelled the lock and opened the door to my room, claiming all along that I had left a key for them at the desk.

I had fallen asleep in my clothes, spread-eagle on the bed, and I sat up, my hair tangled and my mouth tasting of rancid butter.

"Coffee. Shower. Then conversation," I said as I staggered out into the living room. But of course it didn't work that way. When you grew up with two siblings near your age, you got used to a certain lack of privacy in the bathroom, even an ornate bathroom with a specially designed rain shower.

They shouted questions at me, and I shouted answers, hoping the walls weren't too thin. I wasn't about to get out to tell them everything.

Still, when I emerged and wrapped myself in a ridiculously thick and luxurious towel, my hair dripping on my shoulders and my bare feet sliding on the marble floor, my sisters looked as disconcerted as I had felt in that theater.

The reason? My mention of that pain which ran from my mouth to my heart. I hadn't realized Mother had pulled the same trick on all of them.

Rosalind leaned against the marble counter, her back to the mirror. Her reflection showed up all over the room, reaffirming once again how perfect her dark hair always looked, and how her height accented her trim figure. Her appearance varied depending on needs—she could make herself boyish, even though no one would describe her that way at the moment.

She always made me feel insecure, especially when I was naked and wrapped in a towel, which happened more than I liked.

"Tell me," she said in that cultured Katharine Hepburn voice of hers. "Did that deep pain happen after you conjured her with your childhood fairy dust?"

"After," I said.

"Crap," Viola said. She was sitting on the toilet lid, her

elbows on the back of the toilet. She was the smallest of the three of us, and if I hadn't known she had the brown family mane, I would have thought her the natural blond she pretended to be.

"You do realize, Porty, what this means," Rosalind said. I winced. I hated the nickname as much as I hated my real name. Portia. Gauche American men sometimes conflated me with the car. I could never explain to them that Mother had perpetrated a cruel joke when she named her daughters after three of Shakespeare's most famous women.

"What does this mean, Rosy?" I asked, wishing that my play on her name had more effect.

"Mother's spirit might still be in there," she said.

"Ya think?" I asked.

"That's why Portia brought us here," Viola said to Rosalind. "You really shouldn't stress the obvious."

"Actually," I said, "I brought you here because that theater's a nightmare, and it's dangerous to anyone with even a thread of magic. I know I can't clean all of the warnings and hexes and spells out of it on my own. I'm not sure the three of us can."

"But Mother thought she could," Rosalind said.

"And look where it got her," Viola said. "Perhaps we should call Aunt Eustacia."

"Not yet," I said. "Let's see what we can do first."

What we could do involved computers (Viola), research at museums and libraries (Rosalind), and discussions with the play's producers (me). Viola sat quietly in my suite's living room, happily surrounded by the photographs of Noel Coward, while I sprawled on the bed with the landline, trying to talk the producers out of a joint walk-through in the theater. I wasn't going back inside the Lancaster alone, but I didn't want to go with those folks either.

Finally, I got them to send over an employee with a package of all the materials the theater's unofficial historian had used to put together the "history" of the Lancaster and, more importantly, a key. Charles the butler once again circumvented the room service staff and delivered lunch, promising to order afternoon tea if we were still in the room.

We were. I went over materials, Viola kept making muttery noises, and Rosalind returned, dusty and triumphant, clutching photocopies of ancient records.

"We have troubles," she said, waving the papers at us.

"Toil and tr—?"

"Don't you dare quote the Scottish Play," I snapped at Viola.

"For heavens sake," she said. "We're not in a theater."

"We're surrounded by pictures of Noel Coward," I said. "What if that's enough?"

She rolled her eyes.

"Technically," Rosalind said, picking at the chips, which were all that remained on the plate for my club sandwich, "the Savoy herself could be considered a theater, given all of the performances that occurred here."

"What*ever*," Viola said, not looking up from her computer screen. "So I won't ask if your news is fair or foul."

"*Viola!*" we said in unison. "*Stop!*"

"It's not a direct quote," she said.

This was what irritated me about my youngest sister. She had a terrible penchant for testing the edges of things, including magical rules.

"So what's the problem?" I asked Rosalind, trying to change the subject.

She spread photocopies of very old maps on the table. It took a moment for my eyes to adjust. Still, all I saw were black lines from a badly tended copy machine and images that looked too faint to understand.

"I've seen that before," Viola said, and tapped at the keyboard. An image appeared on her computer screen with a helpful header: *16th Century London.*

Rosalind didn't even look at the computer. She tried not to use technology at all if she could avoid it.

"This map was made sometime in the last two decades of the 16th century," she said, her back to the computer. "See anything?"

"Not really," I muttered.

"No," Viola said.

"Here." Rosalind's finger slapped the center of one of the photocopies. "See it now?"

"No," I said.

Viola tapped at her keyboard and made another humming noise. "That's the site of the Lancaster?"

"*Yes,*" Rosalind said.

"Oh, dear," Viola said.

"Oh, dear, what?" I asked.

Viola raised her head and frowned at me. "It's a house."

"So?"

"You've always insisted on calling it a hovel."

"Oh, no," I said, and sat down. Then I realized what was going on. "You can't know for certain that this was where Shakespeare's witches lived."

"I wouldn't call them 'Shakespeare's witches,'" Rosalind said. "For a so-called scholar, you're incredibly lazy."

"They might've been fairies," Viola said.

"We're not going to get into textual analysis," I snapped. Many modern scholars believed the witches were an addition by Thomas Middleton.

"It doesn't matter," Rosalind said. "The hovel was here."

"Why would they build a theater on top of it?" I asked.

"Let me do a quick search," Viola said. That clicking keyboard was driving me nuts. I glanced at the materials the producers had sent over, and something caught my eye.

A claim, on the original broadsheet for the current performance of the Scottish Play. "Is this true?" I asked Viola, shoving the paper in front of her.

"I'm checking," she said without glancing at it.

"Is what true?" Rosalind asked as she came up behind me. I handed her the broadsheet.

Her skin actually lost all color, and she sat down on a nearby chair. "Oh, my God," she said.

"It's true," Viola said.

We looked at each other. I have no idea how they felt, but my heart pounded so hard that I was sure they could hear it in Westminster Abbey.

"No one's ever performed the Scottish Play in the Lancaster before," Rosalind said. "Not once in three hundred years?"

"Not that I can find," Viola said.

"Obviously the historian looked for it too," I said.

Rosalind rubbed her forehead with her forefingers. "Oh, my God," she said. "We're doomed."

4 08 Years Ago . . . Or maybe 421 or maybe even 418 . . . not that precision matters in this instance . . . familial and theatrical lore state that one William Shakespeare made a deal with three witches. They would share their magic with him, and he would protect them.

Protection was important back then. Witches were persecuted on both sides of the Atlantic. Burned at the stake, stoned, buried alive, drowned, around 60,000 people were executed in the three centuries that witch persecutions infected Europe and her colonies.

Most of those people were innocents—real witches had enough magic to protect themselves (even if they chose not to use it)—but that didn't mean the terror brought on by these persecutions was any less real.

The story goes that Shakespeare wrote The Scottish Play to impress King James I of England (and VI of Scotland) who was one of the prime proponents of smoking out witches. Initially, the play was supposed to be a cautionary tale for the monarch—be careful how you usurp power. Then Guy Fawkes tried to blow up Parliament in the Gun

Powder plot, which would have resulted in the death of hundreds, including the King himself, and Shakespeare decided his timely critique of the King was a bit too seditious.

So he revised the Scottish Play and, some believe (my family believes) added the witch sequences to deflect some of the criticisms.

The witches who had served as Shakespeare's advisors, who taught him the magic that made his words live, grew angry and cursed The Scottish Play, partly to prevent the inadvertent practice of magic the play caused.

Because all those famous lines about boiling and toiling and eyes of newt were actually parts of existing spells. Shakespeare believed if he didn't put the entire spell in there, nothing would get cast, not understanding the nature of magic, the way that a particularly talented actor could call a bit of the craft to himself just by being in character.

What we three faced was a conjunction of magic, a mixing of spells ancient and modern, mixed with superstition, fear, and not a little bit of good old-fashioned revenge, even if it was four hundred years too late.

"No wonder the theater burned down so many times," Viola said. "It had nothing to do with the stupid play *Henry VIII*. The theater got burned down to get rid of the magic."

"You'd think our family would keep records," Rosalind said. "That way we wouldn't have to keep reinventing the wheel, and making it look like Shakespeare's ghost hated that misattributed play."

"It wasn't our family." I was shivering. "If it had been

our family, the magic would have dissipated. We're the ones who originated the curse, after all."

"You mean others tried to get rid of it?" Viola asked.

I nodded. There were other magical dramaturgs over the centuries. Some were even passingly good. But none approached our family in talent or vision.

"That's what Mother was warning against," I said more to myself than to them. "She wasn't upset at me for making a snide comment. She had released the last of her magic at her death to let us know that the curse had come from our lips. Our familial lips. She had solved part of this already."

My heart ached, but this time because Mother died alone, not because of her curse.

"She realized it was too strong for her by herself," Rosalind said.

"It takes three," Viola said staring at me. "Just like it always has."

We snuck back to the theater at midnight. We were making this up on the fly. None of us had ever approached a curse this old, let alone one that had been active worldwide. Nor had we ever tried to disable a curse that had another curse woven into it.

We figured that those lines I saw were the words of the Scottish Play, spoken on stage, spoken backstage, spoken throughout the theater, sent forward like little missiles and wrapping with the existing magic, turning the theater into a thicket of competing curses, one inadequately done.

Until we arrived outside the Lancaster, I didn't even think to ask the producers which version of the Scottish Play they had chosen. Did it include Hecate? In that case, dozens of hands had touched it. Did it leave out the Porter? In that case, it was a modern version without a gateway to the magical realm.

I could have had Viola call the producers, but that would alert them to our presence at the theater. We decided to try this first, and if it failed, then we would try again, with direct knowledge of which version of the play we were attacking.

For good measure, though, Viola left a phone message—a *sticky* voice mail, she called it, which meant one that couldn't be deleted *ever*—for Aunt Eustacia just in case we didn't get out of this. Frankly, we wasted even more time arguing about what Aunt Eustacia would do about this, since her sisters were dead and her son's wife had only recently given birth to his third daughter.

We decided it wasn't our problem—or it wouldn't be. We would be dead, a thought that made all three of us shudder in unison.

Then we got busy.

We decided not to enter through the stage door. The key we had opened the theater lobby, and here was where we found the 1970s reds and silvers. There were fewer webs of magic up here, as we suspected there would be. They were creeping out of the doors leading to the house, but they hadn't arrived.

We all wore black, the closest we could get to traditional witch's attire. Rosalind wore some designer gown that looked like it belonged on this red carpet. Viola had chosen a pseudo Disco revival thing in keeping with the theater's redesign, and I wore the simple black dress I always traveled in. Our only concession to the modern era was black athletic shoes. We wanted to be able to run if we had to.

Viola clutched our great-grandmother's cauldron, which she had thought to bring from Cornwall. The stupid thing was supposed to have been part of Mother's death ritual. The cauldron was smaller than I remembered it, and scarred up with hundreds of years of use.

Rosalind held the proper ingredients for the spell, and I had the spell written down in the correct order, so I wouldn't have to think about it.

Someone had left a light on in the lobby, and it probably wasn't a ghost light, but proper security lighting mandated by a proper security company. We hadn't disabled the security alarm, deciding not to use magic inside the theater until we were ready.

We stopped for just a moment, staring at the bank of doors ahead of us. The box office was covered with a padlocked board that looked like it might discourage even the most determined burglar.

"I would love to set up out here," Rosalind said—and these half measures were why she wasn't as good as Viola and I at dealing with theatrical magic.

"We set up as close to the magic as we can safely get," I said.

"This is close enough," Rosalind said.

"Nope," Viola said. "We have to at least get inside the house. If we do this away from the stage, we negate the powers given us."

She wanted to do a flying spell before we got inside, so that we could fly over the magic to the stage, drop down like the witches of old, set up the cauldron and say our bit.

Flying magic was half-assed and rarely effective. Besides, the story of our three ancestors doing the same thing to the Scottish Play after it premiered was apocryphal. I had looked that much up years ago when I started as a magical dramaturg, and that one thing had led to my degree in Elizabethan history.

"Look," Rosalind said, pointing toward the set of doors leading into the theater proper. Viola and I turned.

A shape rested outside them, curled in a fetal position. I went closer, my sisters following.

It was Mother. Or what remained of Mother. Her spirit, some would say. Her magic, others would say.

"So much for the death ritual," Viola said with the characteristic bitterness she felt toward our mother. "She wouldn't have attended anyway."

"I don't think she would have been able to attend," I said, crouching. Mother's spirit, usually outlined in green, had turned almost completely white. The tendrils of the multiple curses had seeped under the door and nearly enveloped her.

"She's trapped here," Rosalind said.

We looked at each other. We didn't have to speak our single thought: For a moment, we were tempted to leave her and walk away. She would have done so had it been magically expedient.

"Let's try a different door," Viola said, and the moment passed.

She pulled open a door to the right of Mother.

The seats ran downward toward the orchestra pit, the stage illuminated behind it. The ghost light was on, of course, but that wasn't what made this theater so bright.

In the 24 hours since I'd last been here, magical webs had gotten thicker. They coated everything. And now that I stood just on the edge of them, I could see multiple colors of magic.

Rosalind opened her mouth to utter some kind of surprised oath, then clearly changed her mind. She shut her mouth.

"You want us to wade through that?" she asked me.

Even if we could start, I wasn't sure we would get through. I barely made it to the stage the night before, and that was going through a thicket not one-tenth as powerful as this. Now we had five times the distance to cover, and one-hundred times the magic to fight.

I glanced around us. The magic dripped down the walls, coated the doors, and swirled around our feet. It would prevent us from leaving if it could.

"We do it here, I guess," I said, my heart pounding. I'd been a witch all my life, and I'd dealt with some powerful curses, but all of them threatened someone else, never me.

This one could destroy me and my sisters, just like it had destroyed my mother.

"Let's set up," Rosalind said, and, to her credit, did not add, *and do this fast*. Because we all knew if we did it fast, we would do it wrong. We had to pretend we had all the time in the world.

Which we most decidedly did not.

We took the cauldron to the center of the back of the theater, directly across from the ghost light. We deliberately did not set the cauldron near the door that Mother's spirit lurked behind.

We had to fill it with the ingredients Rosalind held. We had to improvise with those, which didn't make me feel the best. Instead of water from the nearest swamp, which Viola took to be the Thames and Rosalind took to be water from the latest rainstorm running down the back alley, I decided we would use local ale, made with local ingredients, made by one of the local pubs. Rosalind found one that had had a series of health complaints and we decided to use that.

That was the easiest ingredient to find. The whole eye-of-newt thing, much tougher. Not even modern New Age shops carried anything like it, and the one true magical store that we knew of had closed nearly a decade earlier.

Plus we couldn't use magic to heat the cauldron. We needed a real fire, which we were loathe to do. Viola bought a gigantic hot plate that ran on batteries of all things, and we hoped it would work.

Modern improvisation meets ancient magic. Fortunately, our family's magic was old enough that we knew these improvisations happened all the time. If we hit on the right formula, we would make it through.

If we did not, then our spirits would be trapped here with Mother's forever, which was my personal version of hell.

We combined everything quickly. As we did so, the

tendrils of white magic climbed up our legs, but the darker tendrils—which some would have called black but which I slowly realized were dark as fresh blood—tried to fight them off.

The family magic recognized us, and was combatting the newer magic. I hoped it would buy us time.

Whatever we had made in that cauldron truly smelled foul. Ale mixed with sewers mixed with the stench of decaying flesh. My eyes watered, and my hands shook.

We circled the cauldron as I recited the original witch's spell from the original version of the Scottish Play. Only part of it appeared in modern reprintings, with certain words changed to take away power. I changed the words back, added the missing ones, and said the spell backwards which was, according to our personal grimoires, the only way to reverse an ancient spell.

By the time I got to the second "boil," and finished the backwards recitation, the magic had reached our hips. It was impossible to walk any longer. Smoke and foul odors rose from the cauldron, but nothing else happened.

Rosalind had opened her mouth to inform me of that, when the air ignited around us.

The white tendrils exploded, the dark tendrils covered them, and my legs felt like they were on fire. My sisters' hair stood straight up, which I would have laughed at in any other circumstance, but this time, I knew it for what it was.

The air had become magic-charged with new and old curses battling each other for supremacy. The cauldron glowed yellow—our combined magical colors—and a spirit rose out of it, waving at us dismissively. The green color near the hands told me all I knew.

Mother's spirit, trying to save us for once.

We didn't need to be told twice. I grabbed the nearest door handle, burning hot against my hand, and yanked the door open. Smoke rose from the spots where the tendrils had been, and a gigantic burn stain covered the carpet where Mother's spirit had curled into its little fetal ball.

We ran across the lobby, and I wished that we had the flight spell now, because we needed to get out. Viola's Disco gown, with its fancy uneven edges was on fire, and the edges of Rosalind's dress had burned off. My feet were bare, and I only noticed that because the carpet felt cool under my toes.

We reached the main doors, shoved them open, and everything ignited around us—air, fire, magic. A deafening explosion followed, and we catapulted into the street without a flight spell at all, rolling along ancient cobblestone, until we came to rest against a parked Mercedes.

We slapped out the fires consuming each other's clothes and realized that we had not been burned. No wonder the ancient witches worked naked. I would remember that for the next time.

If there was a next time.

I vowed there wouldn't be.

Fire trucks, ambulances, police vehicles all sped down the narrow street. I knew they couldn't have arrived that fast based on our explosion. They had come because we hadn't shut off the security alarm and *then* there was an explosion.

I was about to tell my sisters we had to leave when Viola's cell phone rang.

She pulled it out of the pocket of her shredded dress; the screen illuminated with a number none of us recognized.

"Yes?" she asked, her voice trembling.

The voice on the other end was so loud Rosalind and I could hear it too. Or maybe Viola had spelled it so she didn't have to turn on the speaker. Or maybe she had turned on the speaker and I hadn't noticed.

"Confounded device," Aunt Eustacia said. "Girls? That better be you girls. Because there was a major magical occurrence. They just grounded my plane, claiming some kind of electrical impulse, but I know it wasn't me. I'm spent. It was—"

And then the phone cut off.

"Oh, crap," Viola said again. "She's going to be mad."

"Not going to be," Rosalind said. "She *is* mad."

I leaned my head against the car, watching as the Lancaster went up in flames. "We're not done," I said tiredly. "She's right; this spell went everywhere. There will be spot fires throughout the West End."

And there were. Every single theater in the West End had a tiny fire, usually contained to the prop room or an old pile of scripts. In the Gielgud, *Playbills* done for a 2007 version of the Scottish Play went up in flames. At the National, costumes from the 1970s ignited. Fortunately, the resident magical dramaturg at the rebuilt Globe stopped the stage fires as they began, and so did the dramaturg at the Royal Shakespeare Company. But two soundstages at the

BBC went up as well, and something bad happened at Pinewood Studios, although no one would admit what.

We stopped it all. But reports kept coming in, from New York, Tokyo and Berlin, and other theaters around the world. Tiny fires, everywhere, igniting for a moment, and then usually burning out, although several Shakespeare companies lost everything.

The fires did not occur on the same night—the magic traveled at its own pace, as magic did—but they occurred within three days of our little explosion, and when it was done, Viola—tired, disheveled, and looking forever like the Shakespearean *Twelfth Night* character she was named for—said,

"So much for the curse of the Scottish Play."

We looked at her. We were sitting inside the Noel Coward suite at the Savoy, too tired to get up and take showers, even though Charles the butler hinted we should.

"What do you mean?" Rosalind asked.

"That's what went up, you know," Viola said. "The curse."

"You don't believe it," I said.

She narrowed her eyes. "What makes you think that?"

"If you believed it, you wouldn't have called it the Scottish Play," I said.

She grinned at me, then leaned her head back. "I have revised my opinion," she said. "I now believe in caution. Besides, as you reminded me, the Savoy might be classed as a theater."

It was, but I didn't tell her that. Spot fires occurred that night in the famed American Bar and elsewhere in the famous property, all explained away by the typical problems the chefs had when serving cherries jubilee or bartenders had when making flaming drinks.

"Aunt Eustacia's going to be mad that we lost the cauldron," Rosalind said.

"Aunt Eustacia's going to be mad that she missed the death ritual," Viola said. We had all agreed that the events at the Lancaster were the proper death ritual, since that's where Mother's spirit had been trapped.

"Aunt Eustacia is just going to be mad," I said.

I would have too, stuck in some backwater Russian airport while they tried to find a plane that would carry my magical aunt out of the country.

I didn't want to think about it. I didn't want to think about anything—except a shower, and a long winter's nap.

"We do work better together," Viola said.

"Bite me," I said.

She was right, of course; we did work better together. But that didn't change my decision.

I was done with this profession.

Until the next time, anyway.

Disrupt Magic
An Abracadabra Incorporated Story

KRISTINE KATHRYN RUSCH

P ascal liked to surprise thieves. He didn't need to be onsite. He could easily do his work from his basement in his underwear, never ever leaving the apartment, and subsisting on food deliveries and the kindness of his doorman.

But, in truth, his doorman wasn't kind, and Pascal preferred it that way. He also preferred breaking a few heads whenever he worked, which was why he stood on the narrow cobblestone street just off the Rue St. Honoré, back against the ancient white brick wall, one foot pressed against it as he lit a cigarette beneath the Ne Fumez Pas sign.

For as long as he had lived in Paris, which seemed like half his life, he had taken advantage of that Gallic urge to flaunt rules—even though he was only one-quarter French himself. He had come here because he could pass for a native, his French fluent, his accent Parisian, and it was much better after years than it had been when he arrived.

The city had settled in his bones. He noted that whenever he smoked beneath a no-smoking sign, something he might never have done because of his tight-assed American upbringing.

It felt like he had shed all of that in the years he'd lived here. He barely saw the things that shocked American tourists, things that had shocked him during his first summer here, so very long ago.

He shook the match and dropped it to the sidewalk beneath the display window for a high-end men's clothier. The clothes were ridiculous—yellow shorts, striped shirts, and loosely draped scarves. The mannequins looked like boys who were too frail to play rugby, but wanted to. The only thing he had in common with them was the flat cap he had pulled by its brim over his face. His was black, wool, expensive. Theirs were more expensive and probably made of some chic material that didn't keep off the rain.

Not that it mattered: the white mannequins had no faces which was, he had to admit, the way he saw white people much of the time.

He kept his head bent just enough that the CCTV camera across the street would find him as faceless as the mannequins. His clothing was dark—black pants, black boots, a black leather jacket that had seen better days— nothing to distinguish him from half the other men on the streets of Paris this late on a Thursday evening. Anyone who looked out of the expensive apartments above the shops would think he had stopped under the clothing store's awning to wait out the rain.

It was coming down hard now, cold and bitter for April. Whoever sang about April in Paris really hadn't been here much. He'd lit the cigarette as much to keep his hands warm as well as giving himself cover.

He wasn't wearing gloves; delicate spells were impossible with gloves, and the spells he was going to use on this damp, dark night, were the most delicate of all.

He half smiled to himself. Knocking heads and delicate spells. His kind of party.

Movement half a block down caught his eye. A bicycle now leaned against the clean white stone of the no-name hotel, the kind celebrities used, the kind celebrities believed safer than the actual hotels throughout the city, proving, yet again, that celebrities weren't always the brightest creatures in the world.

He took another drag on his cigarette as he scanned the street for someone dressed in all black, moving just underneath the awnings. If he saw that person heading toward La Boutique Secrète, then he would know if the smash and grab he'd intuited from the magic pool was actually happening. It only took a moment to find what he was looking for, a person, barely a shadow themselves, keeping to the darkness, heading toward the closed shop directly across from Pascal.

Then another cyclist turned onto the street to his right, coming in the way tourists sometimes did after they had left the Louvre.

Dark bicycles were hard to see on a good night. The rain hazed the golden light of the famous antique streetlights, and darkened all portions of the city, not just this part.

The thieves probably thought the rain a curse because they got wet, but it was actually a blessing for them. It meant that even if a CCTV camera caught their faces, the camera wouldn't be able to distinguish features without special software.

Rather like those faceless mannequins beside Pascal; the thieves would remain anonymous.

To his left, another movement. The third bicycle had just been placed against the ornate ironwork of the shelter marking the Metro entrance. A final cyclist pedaled onto the street only a few meters from Pascal. He froze for a moment so that the thieves wouldn't see him.

They didn't gather, like he expected them to do. They remained in the shadows, moving beneath the cameras, and keeping their heads turned when the light from window displays would normally have caught their features.

Like him, they were flat caps. Unlike him, they wore turtlenecks, tight yoga pants, and running shoes, which meant their feet had to be getting wet as they stepped in the puddling water.

Pascal's gaze raked their forms, looking for one thing. Then he smiled as he saw it. Gloves.

They all wore thin black gloves.

Not magic users then, just as he suspected.

Brilliant, really. The smash-and-grabs had become the bête noir of the Paris Police Department. They had even hired a specialist in smash and grabs to run La Brigade de Répression du Banditisme, the elite crime unit that specialized in high-end thievery and organized crime.

The past few years, jewel thieves had taken their work to high art, not just in Paris, but in Cannes, the Côte d'Azur, and anywhere else the rich gathered.

Little shops, like La Boutique Secrète, had upgraded their security, but thought themselves safe, since the most famous of the thieves hit the most famous jewelers in the world, those that could suffer the loss of multimillions of Euros and still keep the doors open.

Pascal always found that fascinating too, considering the insurance costs. Someone was losing a lot of money, but aside from the B.R.B. in Paris, the other communities had not focused their resources on recovery. In fact, some had advised the jewelers to consider the jewels lost forever, and to proceed accordingly.

Something he would never advise.

But, then, he wasn't advising the shops. He wasn't working for them. He worked for the conglomerate that had folded so many of these small ancient shops into a kind of cooperative. Protection, they were promised, from the dark and evil changes in the world.

He didn't know if protection extended beyond what he did. All he knew was that magical items had to be safeguarded at all times. And his bosses at Abracadabra Inc. controlled more magical items, through the ancient shops, than any other conglomerate in the world.

The thieves moved with the efficiency of darkness on a stormy afternoon, all heading toward La Boutique Secrète. From a distance, it looked unprepossessing—two small display windows dimly lit. There was nothing to display, not in the middle of the night. All that remained of the daytime visions were the strange necks and collarbones, built for showing off necklaces; the unattached hands, some with wrists, designed to display rings and bracelets; and the empty velvet boxes, tilted slightly upward to show wares that, during the middle of the night anyway, were not there.

To the non-magical, a smash-and-grab would seem foolhardy—a thief would either need brute strength to pry open the various safes and vaults or would need to know passwords and combinations. Many jewelry stores had now invested in smaller versions of the timed vaults that most banks used.

But not La Boutique Secrète.

It had something better.

It had Pascal.

He took one last drag off his cigarette and held the tobacco in his lungs. Then he dropped the cigarette and crushed it beneath the heel of his boot. He slowly released the smoke, reaching up with his nicotine-stained fingers to separate the plume into four tendrils. He wove the tendrils into ropes, sharp as steel and yet bendable.

Then, with the flick of a finger, he sent the first tendril to his right, toward the bike parked the farthest away. He sent the second tendril to his left, to the bike leaning against the Metro entrance. The third tendril went into the alley. And the fourth tendril winged its way to the remaining bike.

Once the tendrils arrived, they would wrap around the spokes, severing them. Then, using some of the energy the tendrils gained from the metal, they would carve their way through the center frame, something that would be impossible to notice until the rider grabbed the handlebars and tried to stand the bike upright or—better—climbed on the bike with the intent of making a quick getaway.

But Pascal didn't watch the tendrils do their work. Instead, he kept his gaze on the four thieves, slowly approaching the windows of La Boutique Secrète.

The thieves did not know he was nearby. He smiled ever so softly to himself, then, using a spell he had refined over decades, he plunged his left hand into the darkness created by his form and the wall of the nearby building. He willed the darkness into a gauze-like solid, then grabbed its edge.

Slowly he pulled all of the darkness toward him, the way that a man would gently pull the blanket off a sleeping lover. The nearby lights grew brighter, but slowly, so slowly that the thieves could not perceive the change.

He pulled the darkness off them entirely, and noted then that two of them were slight females, probably thin enough to wriggle into ancient ductwork or half-open vault doors. One of the men carried a crowbar, and the other had a black bag slung over his shoulder.

They almost looked like a children's cartoon version of French cat burglars, sneaking around at night. But those cartoon burglars always had large personal shadows, and Pascal had stolen these. He held them loosely in his right hand, so that the thieves couldn't feel the pressure from his magic, holding their bodies hostage.

The thieves paused in front of the display window, their faces reflected in the glass. They wore stocking caps pulled low, their turtlenecks folded up to hide their chin and mouths, but their noses were visible as were their eyes.

Their surprised eyes.

Pascal smiled. He loved that moment. The moment when his adversaries not only realized something was wrong, but they also realized that whatever was wrong wasn't normal—at least to their little mundane minds.

The tallest thief looked around, trying to see the source of the increased light, probably revealing his face to every CCTV camera within shouting distance.

Panic had set in.

Within seconds, a decision would be made, with or without consensus. Someone would either run or smash the window. It would all depend on the amount of money the thieves had been promised for a successful completion of the job as well as how willing they were to gamble on the amount of time it would take the police to arrive.

Pascal watched the calculation. If they did not go inside, his work here would be done. He would leave them to their ruined bicycles. But if the thieves decided to smash and grab—

The man raised his crowbar and jammed it into the window with such force that the entire window shattered. Impressive.

Alarm sirens blared across the entire street, making Pascal wince. He hated this moment. In apartments all over the block, locals would pause and wait to see if the alarm turned off. If it did, they would go back to their business. If it did not, they would all start dialing 17, trying to get the police to come and shut the alarm off.

Lights went on across the block, as the alarm continued.

Pascal watched, keeping a loose hand on the thieves' personal shadows, knowing he could control all four people with the flick of a finger. He wanted the thieves to get inside, to find the ebony rings, the blessed silver, and the seemingly misplaced items that had more magic than a dozen mages ever would.

The thieves would have no idea why they were picking up those items, aside from the price they would be paid for doing so. And, Pascal was sure, their benefactor would have told them that they could keep any gold or diamonds or jewelry that they found, provided they got the magical items.

Which, of course, no one would call "magical items."

The team of thieves climbed inside, their pace measured and steady. They had done this before. With his left hand, Pascal removed the darkness from inside the store, illuminating the thieves as they worked their way toward the back.

The magical items would still be in their cases; to the average thief, those items looked worthless. No one needed to put those items in a safe. Even with all the regulations it placed on member stores, Abracadabra Inc. did not require member stores to safeguard their magical items the way that non-magical stores safeguarded their valuables. Abracadabra Inc. didn't want the average person to know that the magical pieces were worth stealing, and placing them in a vault would call attention to them, in just that way.

Pascal half-expected to see the thieves discussing their mission, arguing whether or not they should ignore the magical items and try to get the jewels anyway.

But they didn't. They must have been promised a boat-load of money.

They gathered near one of the display cabinets and one of the women went behind it, to see if she could open it without getting glass everywhere.

They had to feel the clock ticking, the gamble growing. Police weren't that far away from anything in the Eighth Arrondissement—too much money here, too many wealthy people.

Time to take matters into his own hands.

Pascal tugged on the shadows, and all four thieves looked up as if someone had yanked on their clothing. Which, in essence, he had.

They all looked frightened, peering around to see what had happened. Then he saw them consulting with each other—*Did you feel that? Did something happen?*—before returning to the job ahead of them.

He tugged again, but this time, as he did so, the magic wavered.

He felt it like a gale-force wind rippling down the street. The magic—delicate and frail—tore like a house in a hurricane. He was dragged away from the building before he realized he had to sever his remaining connection to the magic.

The light faded, the darkness returned, and the shadows probably slapped to their owners. But he couldn't see clearly enough to know if the thieves had a reaction to the return of their shadows or not.

The disruption continued, and Pascal had to shut off all of his magical awareness.

The thieves had no magic; they couldn't feel the wind at all. So that had come from elsewhere.

Which he couldn't think about, not yet, because if he did, he would fail at this job. Failing at this job would cost him other jobs in the future, and he liked his work.

He sprinted across the dark street, the misty rain instantly soaking his face and his hands. The chill had returned. He had thought it gone, because he had been focused on the magic, but that had simply been a distraction.

The alarm seemed softer in the rain and the darkness or maybe he still felt the effects of that magical wind. As he leapt up the curb, he looked at the nearby CCTV camera on purpose.

Now that he was going in, he wanted a record on official security that he was a Good Samaritan, not one of the thieves.

He climbed over the broken display window, not as easily as the thieves had because he was that much bigger. He knocked some of the headless necks onto the floor, catching the attention of at least one of the thieves.

She saw him, squealed, and pointed. The man with the crowbar turned, wielding it like a bat.

Pascal caught the bar, and used its forward energy to yank the thief toward him. Then Pascal wrenched the bar away from the thief, and, in the same movement, slammed him against the far wall beside the door. The thief hit with a sick thud, but Pascal wasn't watching any longer. He didn't need to.

Anyone who hit that hard might not be unconscious,

but he would need a moment to recover. The breath would have left his body.

Pascal took a step toward the remaining thieves.

"You'd better run," he said in guttural French, making it sound like he was from Marseilles rather than Paris. "Or you will wish you had."

The woman who had pointed at him had frozen, but the other woman scrambled away. She wouldn't make it far with her bicycle disabled. She probably wasn't even thinking about dodging the CCTV cameras.

The other man ran toward Pascal, bent just enough to catch him in a sports grab around the waist. But Pascal sidestepped, then stuck out his foot, so that the man tripped and fell face forward into the glass from the window.

Pascal put his boot on the man's back, pressing hard. But Pascal didn't look away from the woman.

"I told you to run," he said in that same rough French.

This time, she listened, vaulting over the counter, and running toward the door. Pascal did not remind her that her team had failed to unlock it. Instead, he watched her scramble over her unconscious partner's legs, grab the door-knob, and pull, only to realize that she was still trapped.

She climbed onto the display, then tumbled out onto the street just as police sirens pulled closer.

In a moment, the entire area would be overrun with police.

Pascal picked up the man he'd been standing on, and flung him out of the window. Then Pascal climbed out after him. The man lay, stunned, on the sidewalk, blood dripping out of a dozen cuts on his face.

"I would consider retiring," Pascal said in the same tone. Then he stepped over the man, and crossed the street, heading back to the window he had started at, in case someone wanted to track his progress on CCTV.

He almost used his magic to whisk himself back to his apartment, but he didn't want the spell to fail. He could still feel the wisps of the wind.

He waited a moment as the police arrived, first one car in front of La Boutique Secrète, then another, and finally a third. So unlike the outskirts of Paris where the police did not show up, even when called. Only when someone determined that a manhunt was necessary.

The police did not know yet that Pascal had been involved. They wouldn't figure that out for several minutes. He glanced down the street, saw one of the women holding the seat of her bicycle as the bicycle lay in pieces on the sidewalk.

He smiled ever so faintly.

At least that had worked.

Then he put his head down, and walked toward L'Église de la Madeleine as if he had intended to go there all along.

He didn't hurry to the church, although he wanted to. He was walking in the direction the wind had come from, and he was doing so deliberately. But he couldn't track it without magic, and he wouldn't be able to use his magic until he shook off that wind.

If he had his powers, he would capture a piece of the wind like he had captured the darkness. But he didn't want to test, not right now. Someone who could disrupt magic like that might know the next level of spell, the kind that could light it, and its user, aflame. He wasn't going to volunteer for that test.

Instead, he pulled out his phone and pressed the number he'd been given.

"Non-magical," he said in English when someone answered on the other end. "Thwarted, but the shop is a mess. Someone needs to safeguard it. Oh, and magic in the area is disrupted, so do it onsite."

"You've left?" The voice was gender-neutral, the accent ever-so-slightly British.

"Couldn't stick around without answering questions. The police will be there for some time. The B.R.B. will show up because of the smash and grab. It will be a large investigation. I'd hurry."

Then he hung up. Pascal walked quickly, seeing no one in the darkness. The lights were brighter when he reached the Place de la Concorde. Tourists always photographed the Egyptian obelisk, but he generally tried to avoid the fountains, the traffic circle, and the entire area.

It still stank of the executions performed three hundred years ago. The magic here, ancient magic, had been warped by blood.

There was almost no traffic. At this time of night, Paris —unlike New York—slept. He felt like the only man in the city, although he knew he was not.

He ignored the Concord Carousel, the gigantic Ferris wheel beloved by tourists, shut down for the night, and continued toward the Seine. He could smell the river now, and its magic as well. He needed it, more than he wanted to admit to himself.

He took the steps halfway down to the Quai des Tuileries, but stopped five steps down. There, away from the tourist boats docked nearby, he could just barely see the dark waters of the Seine. He hefted the phone he still held in his right hand, then nodded to himself. He still had a good arm, even without the magic.

He tossed the phone in the water, destroying it completely. He rarely did that. He usually placed the phone beside a trash can, so that someone less fortunate could still use the minutes.

But tonight seemed different, with the magical attack and the strange wind. He didn't want to be traced—not even the way that the non-magical could do it.

Then he took the remaining stairs down to the Quai, hopping over the small security gate, and onto the little road that ran closest to the river.

The streetlights seemed brighter here. The glow around the lights themselves looked like a halo. Several bateau were docked to his right, so close he could climb on them if he wanted to set off another alarm. The boats seemed sad and quiet as they waited for the morning tourists to take their rides and think they'd experienced Paris.

Maybe they had, but not the Paris he knew.

The Paris Pascal knew had back alleys and dark edges. The Paris he knew smelled faintly of piss beneath the Pont de la Concorde.

The Paris he knew had a magic deeper and older than the magic of love promoted by the advertising executives.

And that old, deep magic could be found in the oldest parts of the city. That was why ancient Christians built

L'Église Saint-Germain-des-Prés, the oldest church in the city, not too far from here, why Notre Dame overlooked the water, why the churches in this part of the city were all so justly famous, set up as a warning to all the non-believers by believers who did not understand the powers hidden in the land itself.

He glanced back at the bridge, stately and solid, silent because there was no traffic this late. He could actually hear the water lapping against the boats.

Pascal let out a small sigh. He had not been followed.

Now he had to determine how he had been found.

If he had.

His skin still tingled from that wind, but that might have been the magical disruption unsettling him. He was drenched from the mist, which should have washed some of the disruption off of him. Maybe not all of it, though.

He had to be careful.

So he stood with his back to the brown stone wall facing the river, and then put out his left hand, palm up. He would do a small spell, an illuminate, the first one that children learned. No one would note the magic because it was so common even the non-magical could occasionally pull it off with the right tutoring.

He was strangely nervous, strange for him because he almost never got nervous doing magic. Spells were as easy as breathing, and, he supposed, this feeling was the feeling a person got when he couldn't draw breath easily. There was a vague edge of panic to it, an unsettling edge of not-right.

He made himself exhale, then inhale. He needed to be

centered to perform the spell—any spell, really. Even, *especially*, one of the easiest spells ever created.

When he believed himself calm, he focused on the center of his palm. He didn't want a large light. Something that mimicked the flare of a match, the glow of a dimmed phone screen.

He concentrated, and light appeared, tinged orange because he had been thinking of fire.

He let out another breath, relieved, then angry that he was feeling relieved. He didn't want to feel relieved because that meant he had been worried.

But he had been.

His magic hadn't been disrupted like that since his training, decades ago.

The skin tingling had faded as well, but just an edge of it remained. Rather than worry about that now, he welcomed it, because he needed to perform a delicate spell to harness it.

He closed his fingers over his palm, dousing the illumination he had created. Then he lifted his forefinger and traced his right wrist, thinking only of the tingle, isolating it.

He rolled the tingle around in his fingertips, making it into a small hard ball. Then he gripped it between his thumb and forefinger, holding it tightly. He brought it up to eye level.

The ball was clear, like the wind, with only a hint of white around its edges. The white was an illusion, created by his own magic to give the ball shape.

He then used the ball to create a small thread, a thread that contained an element of that wind. He added the white to the element, letting it run backwards toward La Boutique

Secrète. That little maneuver was a risk, just in case someone magical was monitoring the boutique, but he had to try it.

He wanted to find the source of that magic.

The thread retraced his steps, floating up to the Place de la Concorde, all the way back to L'Église de la Madeleine, and beyond. He let a tiny part of his consciousness travel with it, along with a small portion of his vision, so that he could see where he was going. The white grew near the church where the bit of tingle magic intersected with the actual wind.

He had to grab the wind, the way he had grabbed the edge of the darkness, and hold as if he were trying to get blown across the city. Even though the wind had dissipated, its energy remained, restless and untamed.

His breath caught, and his heart started to pound. Untrained magic, loose and wild. He hadn't seen anything like that in a city as old as Paris. Here, untrained magic was dangerous. It could link up with all the remnants of magic, and the remnants of historical evil, and create something powerful and out of control.

He paused all of the magic, holding it still the way a digital playback could be stalled. He considered his options, heart still pounding hard.

He was just an enforcer and a glorified security guard for Abracadabra Inc. He didn't like going into an office or running a shop. He hated training others. He liked standing on street corners, observing from the darkness, and busting heads.

He didn't like involving anyone in his work.

But he did get accused of being reckless, and sometimes

those accusations were accurate. And this wind, this disruption, could be a huge problem.

Either he left the wind to the experts at Abracadabra Inc., or he worked it himself. Because if he called them in to help him now, he would lose his temper within the hour. They would quiz him, work against him, and doubt that he even experienced the disruption.

Perhaps your own magic failed, and you're simply covering?

He could imagine someone asking that question in a supercilious British accent, using a damn quizzing glass and looking down their pointed nose at him.

He corralled his imagination. He had to concentrate on what was, rather than on what could be. What could be sometimes came from his own insecurities. He had taken the job with Abracadabra Inc. when he had been in the most trouble, when he couldn't go back to the States and he couldn't see his way out of a hole he had created for himself with the local police in Nice. They thought he had been dealing drugs; he couldn't very well tell them that he had been trading in tiny love potions for too much money.

Caught, hooked, and saved. Then, later, unwilling to give up the work with Abracadabra Inc. Part of him felt he owed them.

But he didn't owe them this. He wasn't sure what he would find at the tail end of that wind. Or rather, *who* he would find. He didn't want to co-opt someone else into this work, not without proper vetting.

Which gave him an answer, of sorts.

He would go after the creator of that magical disruption.

387

Others might find that reckless, but he thought it was the most prudent course for the moment.

He took a deep breath and unpaused the magic, letting it ripple and flow. With that extra vision, he followed the magic, rippling with it, riding it as if it were waves on an ocean.

As with waves on an ocean, he couldn't let them swamp him. He couldn't go too deep or he would drown, destroyed by magic that somehow flooded his own.

Bits of other magic intersected with the wind. He had to investigate ever so slightly.

The bulk of the magic intersecting with the wind came from La Boutique Secrète. The official Abracadabra lockdown team had arrived. They were handling the police, vying for jurisdiction. The B.R.B. wanted this case, believing the smash and grab important, and Abracadabra was trying to finesse them away, without using magic.

And the magical artifacts glowed just under his consciousness, locked up and protected now by spells so sophisticated, it would take him hours to break through.

He wrenched his consciousness away from La Boutique Secrète, away from his colleagues doing their job, away from the tension that always existed between the magical and the non-magical, and surfed the wave backwards, tracing it over the Rue St. Honoré, past the protected Louvre (so many magical items there), and over the Seine.

The magic grew stronger above the water, feeding on the ancient power below. He could walk to the magic now, directly, having gone a half circle. But he still couldn't see the source.

And he wasn't sure he wanted to tap it from this side of the Seine. The magic had come from the Left Bank.

Which shouldn't have surprised him.

Still, he was already too close to the magic to entirely let go. He had already dipped into the Seine's magic. He could feel it shuddering through him, threatening his own power. He set the small tingle magic through the wave as a last-ditch protection, before he could do anything else, and to his surprise, the thread stopped.

It formed its own circle, cutting open the darkness and revealing a conference room in a cheap American-style hotel not far from the Sorbonne. Young mages sat in the center of the floor while others watched. Some took notes.

A thin female figure, dressed in all black, sat cross-legged near a corner, magic bounding and rebounding off the walls, the thumbs and forefingers of each hand pressed together, creating the disruption wave.

Dozens of people had gathered around her, watching as if they could see the disruption in real time.

His breath caught and destroyed the vision at the same time.

She had been advertising her services. They were bidding on her magic.

A chill fell over him which had nothing to do with the mist and the night's cold. Such bidding was illegal in all organized magical communities. It went so easily awry.

And somehow this woman had known about the proposed heist at La Boutique Secrète. Somehow, she had known Pascal would be there—or someone would be there —to thwart it with magic.

And then she had used that moment to send the wind.

Or had she been aiming at something else? Because her widespread disruption spell would have caught any magic user in the path of that wind unawares.

He was making an elementary mistake of investigation, assuming that the attack on him had been the focus of this wave, but perhaps it hadn't. A wave like that, monitored, would have illuminated every single spell it disrupted. It would have revealed dark corners, opened magical doors for just a moment, and shown where each bit of magic lurked along the wave's path.

His chill deepened. But he straightened his shoulders, and then smiled a little to himself.

The way the spell was used showed the mage's lack of training. Yes, it had been a powerful spell, one that would reveal all the magic along its path, but the powerful spell had also called attention to itself.

He couldn't be the only one who had noticed.

She was working some kind of bidding war, showing off her powers, not considering what the consequences *outside* of that little room would be.

He couldn't be the only one tracing her.

He could leave her to all of them, but he wasn't built that way. She would be in danger. Or everyone else would be, if she had done the spell to expose the magical.

He worked alone, which meant he would probably be one of the first to find her. Most of the other lone wolves in the city would approach her cautiously or wait for others to destroy her.

He had too much curiosity for that. And besides, he might want to recruit her.

She clearly needed money.

He would see how averse she was to work.

P ascal walked to the hotel.

He had enough magic to transport himself there, but he rarely did such spells, even on good days. He didn't like the surprise. He liked to see what was happening in a neighborhood before he entered it.

Besides, the fabric of magic was unstable in that area, thanks to the woman's disruption wave. He didn't want to use any more magic than he had to—for anything.

The walk was quiet, and gave him time to reflect. The mist, falling around him, seemed lighter. He walked to the Pont Saint-Michel avoiding the wave's path.

Still, he stopped in the center of the bridge and looked up and down the Seine. The lights of the city glowed, hazy and strange, in all the water. The Eiffel Tower looked like a badly made child's toy, the water in the atmosphere making the tower's outline seem wobbly and unstable.

He briefly opened a magical eye as well, to see if anyone else was traveling in the same direction, or had sent retaliatory magic to the Left Bank, but so far, he saw nothing.

Perhaps the others did not care about the magical disruption. It had been brief, and faint, and most might not have been using magic at that time of night at all. Perhaps, the worst disruption had fallen on him.

Perhaps the disrupt spell was unnoticeable to everyone except those who were actually mid-spell, as he had been.

Which made the wave even more insidious.

Which also explained why, after such a large disruption, he stood on the bridge alone.

No one joined him by the time he reached the outskirts of the hotel. It took up half of a block. Some American hotelier had bought out several smaller hotels, left their facades, and remade the interior as much as French law would allow.

The mishmash made Pascal uncomfortable, which was why he tried not to come here. It had the worst of both countries—an American bland functionality trying to marry itself with the impossibility of French historical regulation.

Tiny elevators, big bathrooms, bad food, and three conference rooms, which had necessitated destroying entire floors of the old hotels to make way for all that space.

He had come here on Abracadabra duty once, and he had hoped he would never come here again.

He sighed, then put his hand on the handle of the front door, testing it. As he expected, the door was unlocked, following the American custom. He stepped inside, caught the scent of lilacs near the door, part of a floral bouquet so large that it blocked the view of the front desk.

He stepped around the table with the display, saw the empty breakfast room to his right, and was about to use his magical vision to scan for trails throughout the hotel, when his skin tingled again.

This time, he shut down the new spell, but reactivated the spell that had shown him the disruption wave. Another wave was flowing through the floors above, crashing down like a foot breaking through wood.

He stepped to one side, waited, and when the wave hit the ground floor, he grabbed the wave's edge, and tugged. He used a capture spell and a weaving spell at the same time —delicate magic, but strong—and wound the wave into a gigantic ball.

It looked, in his magical vision, like a comet, complete with tail. As the tail thinned, he yanked on the ball. He added power to the yank, so that whoever was guiding the spell would reach him instantly, as if he were standing near her, and pulled her toward him by the front of her shirt.

She crashed through the floors, bouncing off the joists, but not doing any real-world damage. He caught her as she came through the ceiling, then pulled her close, just like he had in his imagination.

Her eyes were black, lined with some kind of mascara, and her skin was pale. Her hair had been dyed a black so dark that he knew it never occurred in nature. The tips of her hair were purple, and she wore purple lipstick.

If she was thirty years old, she hid it well. The only way he knew she wasn't fifteen was because of the power of her magic. Magic like that didn't develop in anyone, no matter how gifted, until they were older than twenty.

"Hello." He spoke in English, following a hunch "I think you lost something."

Then he shoved the ball against her, and made it dissolve so that she reabsorbed the magic. Or rather, the disruption. Because a disruptive magic of that size would block her powers for a long time. Days, if she was lucky. Years, if she was not.

He let go of her and she tumbled to the floor, her skin even paler.

"Who are you?" she asked in English. And, as he suspected, she had an American accent.

"I'm one of the people you messed with tonight," he said. "I don't take kindly to it."

Footsteps resounded on the stairs, thumping down. The people who had been bidding on her services were coming. He waved a hand, transporting the non-magical to De Gaulle airport. The magical could stay, not because he wanted a fight, but because he wanted them to learn something.

A dozen skinny people, all wearing black, all looking to be in their thirties except one bald man with a bad comb-over and a gut that made it look like he had swallowed the disruption ball, came halfway down the last flight of stairs before stopping.

The girl huddled on the floor, clutching her own stomach.

"What did you do to me?" she asked, her voice quavering.

"You don't know?" Pascal asked. "I thought you were a magical expert. You're selling your services, right?"

She pushed herself off the floor, standing, legs shaking. She had to be in a lot of pain.

He admired the toughness, in spite of himself.

"It's not like that," she said.

"Enlighten me," he said.

"Don't talk to him," the bald guy said. "He's not one of us."

Pascal reached a hand in the air and made a zip-it movement, sealing the man's mouth shut.

Then Pascal glanced at the others. "You can listen." he said. "I might even let some of you talk, should you become relevant. But right now, this conversation is between me and—"

He looked at her, expecting a name. Testing her, really, because if she gave him her real name, she would give him even more power.

"Diva," she said.

He smiled in spite of himself. *Brava, Diva,* he thought, but did not say. *Brava.*

"This conversation is between me and Diva." He was speaking to the others, watching them out of the corner of his eye, as he continued to look at her. "You were going to enlighten me."

She glanced at the man on the stairs. He was struggling to open his mouth, which Pascal found amusing. That man thought he had magic, but he had never had training, or he would know how to beat such a simple spell.

Anyone who had interned with a mage learned how to open a zipped mouth. Pascal was tempted to reinforce the spell, make the man live with his closed mouth for days rather than the spell's usual hours.

"He's not going to help you," Pascal said. "You can tell me what you're doing, or I will use extraordinary measures to figure it out for myself."

He loved that phrase *extraordinary measures.* No one

knew what it meant—including him—but it sounded threatening. Extremely threatening, which was exactly what he wanted.

"You ever hear of Anonymous?" she asked. "Wikileaks?"

He wasn't going to dignify that with an answer. The words were in the air, but he didn't care about them. The cyber world had very little to do with him. He didn't care about traditional governments either. They had never been very accepting of people who looked like him, and they simply didn't believe that people with his powers existed.

"We're going to hack all of the traditional magic systems," she said. "We're going to disrupt the magical traditions, just like the new technology has disrupted all of the old ways of doing things in the real world."

Pascal couldn't help himself. He smiled.

"To do such a thing," he said, "would require more magic and control, not less."

"I have control," she snapped.

"Oh?" he asked. "Show me."

She reached backwards with one hand, groping until she found a chair. She sank into it, apparently realizing that she couldn't do her magic and stand at the same time.

"I'll help, Deevs," one of the women on the stairs said.

Without looking at her, Pascal lifted his hand, and made the same zipping movement he had made for the bald guy.

"Hey!" one of the young men said. "You can't do that!"

Pascal zipped that young man's mouth shut too, then turned to the group on the stairs. Pascal decided to freak them out.

He grabbed the darkness created by the poor light in

that part of the room, and pulled it toward him. He wrapped his lower body in the darkness as if he were wrapping a blanket around himself.

Then he looked at them, their eyes wide in the bright light. Cobwebs glinted around them, showing just how shoddy the cleaning service was in this hotel.

"Anyone else?" Pascal asked. "Because, as I said, this conversation is between me and Diva."

He waited, knowing that young Diva was using the moments he had given her to try to reassemble her powers.

He also knew it wouldn't work.

No one else spoke. The three whom he had silenced were pawing at their mouths, trying to pry them open.

He turned back to Diva. She gripped the wooden arm rests, sitting up very straight.

"You broke my magic," she said, surprising him. "You fix it."

"I did not," he said. "*You* broke your magic."

She frowned. "That's not possible."

"And that belief of yours is why your small attempts to disrupt magical systems that have been in place for thousands of years will fail. Because you do not know what is and is not possible."

Pascal swept a hand toward the group on the stairs.

"You allow yourself to be swayed by someone who cannot defeat the most basic of spells. You think that because you are the best mage in a room full of amateurs that you can destroy a system so old that we cannot document its beginnings. You don't look like a delusional fool, Miss Diva. But you are verging on it."

His speech, rather than cowing her, made her raise her chin. He could feel the pain of her movements. She was a powerful mage—or would be with the right training. That spell he had forced her to absorb had disrupted her entire system.

He was probably going to have to do some repair work before she actually sustained physical damage.

"So train us," she said.

"And why would I do that?" he asked.

"Because we have a just cause."

He laughed. He couldn't help himself. He had stopped believing in just causes long ago. They always started out idealistic and then turned into something warped and evil.

True believers never adjusted for reality.

But he had learned that over time and many mistakes. He was not going to tell her that either, because it was a lesson she needed to learn for herself.

"If you promise me you will stop sending wild magic into the streets of Paris, I will leave you," he said.

"Wild magic," she repeated.

He nodded, just once. "It is dangerous," he said. "Magic here is old. Some is good, some is not, and much has no affiliation at all. It is simply looking for an outlet. If you send wild magic too many times into the oldest parts of the city, you will lose yourself."

"My *soul*," she said, with such sarcasm that he actually felt it. "I don't believe in souls."

"I didn't say your soul," he said. "I said *yourself*. Everything you hold dear. Including that idealism."

"Like you did?" she asked.

She was good. She saw things too clearly for one that young. She had trained the part of her gift that allowed her to see past human surfaces, probably so that she could manipulate the people around her.

"You are lucky," Pascal said, "that I'm the one who got here first. Others whom you disrupted will not be as kind as I'm being."

"You're not being kind," she said.

He leaned forward, and touched her shoulder, pulling the bulk of the disruption spell from her. He held it on his palm, a ball the size of a basketball.

The rest of the spell was still part of her, but it wouldn't harm her physical body any more.

He tucked the ball under his arm, the way a basketball player would hold a basketball.

"I will keep this," Pascal said, "and if I sense you releasing wild magic again, I shall send this back to you. It will work its way through your system and it could destroy your magic, because you don't have the training to prevent it from doing so."

Her eyes flashed. "You are arrogant."

Pascal gave her a half-smile. "I'm not the one who believed I don't need training. I spent more than a decade as an apprentice, learning my craft."

"And now you are a slave for Abracadabra Inc.," she said.

He let the word *slave* reverberate through him. He imagined himself taking that magic ball, throwing it at her, and enhancing it as he did so, so that it wouldn't just disrupt her magic, it would disrupt anything magical about her, from her smile to her mind.

He *loathed* that word, and she probably knew it.

That thought calmed him.

She was watching him closely. He had no idea how much she had seen in his eyes. He was usually good at keeping such things off his surface. But she was good at seeing through surfaces.

"I work for Abracadabra Inc.," he said gently. "And if you do not understand the difference between working for pay and being a slave, then you are not as intelligent as you seem to be."

He hefted the ball, spun it on his finger, then put the ball under his arm again.

"If you end up believing you are too good to become an apprentice, too good for training, I would suggest that you hold your next conference somewhere that does not have a deep magical history like the ones you'd find here in Europe. Perhaps an ice floe, or a cruise ship would work, although you do need to be careful of water magic. No, scratch that advice. Because there is no place without wild magic, and you will be tapping into all of the wrong things."

He headed toward the door.

"And you are comfortable finding and protecting magical items for the biggest magical conglomerate on the planet?" she asked.

He knew she was trying to mess with him, to pay him back for hurting her.

"You do realize that they are consolidating their magic, don't you?" she asked. "You aren't afraid of that much power in so few hands?"

His face was reflected in the glass beside the door. His gaze met hers from the reflection.

Finally, she told him why she had avoided the formal training, what she was really doing, and how she felt about the world she found herself in.

"If you want to disrupt magic," he said, "truly disrupt it, then you must learn how it works first. You're decades away from that."

"So help me," she said.

He smiled. "I don't know you," he said, and let himself out of the hotel.

The mist had ceased, but a fog had settled. The air was wet and white, the streetlights now reflecting the fog rather than creating halos. He walked back to the Seine.

He should have been thinking of a place to store her magic, because he couldn't bring it with him. That would be too dangerous.

Instead, her words caught him, held him.

Abracadabra Inc. was consolidating magic. He tried not to think of it, tried, instead, to think about the upside, the way that it kept the old traditions alive, the way that it nurtured the old shops.

But he disliked others accumulating this much power.

And the tenor of the entire world had changed. The world he had come to know at the end of the previous century hadn't really been gentle, but it had been a lot more accommodating than the world was now.

Cruelty had risen to the fore. It had become chic to insult people who looked different than the white elite, different than those mannequins he had stood next to by La

Boutique Secrète. The world had become more dangerous in all of its places, not just in pockets.

Sometimes Pascal thought that better: at least the ugly was on view, so it could be slaughtered.

But what if Diva was right? What if not all of the ugly could be viewed? What if that consolidated magical power found its way into some hands he trusted, hands he would not recognize as ugly until much too late?

Then he let out a small sigh.

Pascal was not an important man. He did not have an important mission. He had deliberately avoided those.

And Diva had gotten a sense of him. She had seen the lost places he buried, the mistrust he had for *anyone* in power, not just the people of Abracadabra Inc.

She had used it against him.

And on this night, at least, it had failed.

He had succeeded. He had corralled wild magic, preventing something even darker from seeping out of the earth, reviving the ugliness of the past.

She would have done it accidentally.

Of course, if she was right, someone at Abracadabra might do it on purpose.

Right now, Pascal had to trust that Abracadabra would not do that. He had to trust that they had the same goals he did.

Because if he did not, then he had worked these last few years in vain.

He sighed again and headed toward the nearest bridge, wishing he had another job to perform. Because he felt like breaking heads. He felt like disrupting lives.

He felt like surprising those who least expected it.

Instead, he would place the magic somewhere safe, and head home, to his basement, and wait until he was summoned again.

Although he would keep an eye on this Diva, on this entire troupe. And he wouldn't tell Abracadabra Inc. about them.

Not yet.

Because the troupe was—and would remain—his own little secret.

So that he had an element of surprise, if he needed it.

If someone he knew got out of line.

If someone he worked for violated his trust.

If the world got even darker than it already was.

DEAN WESLEY SMITH
SECTION

THE PARK, THE YARD, AND OTHER COLD PLACES

A BRYANT STREET STORY

DEAN WESLEY SMITH

Bobbie Liebert killed his wife, Stephanie, on the afternoon of April 6th in the spare bedroom, second one down the hall, of their three-bedroom ranch house on Bryant Street.

He told her he was painting the room because she had always complained that the robin's egg light blue wasn't the best color for her sewing room. So he promised to paint it and three years went by before one Friday evening he finally moved all of her stuff out into the other bedroom, which had become her reading room, covered the shag carpet with a large painting tarp, made sure she had approved the color, and then killed her in that room, on the painting tarp.

He used a hammer to the back of the head and managed to keep the bleeding on the tarp.

He no longer loved her and she clearly no longer loved him. And just killing her seemed so much easier than divorce and still having her around in the same city.

His plan was simple. Kill her and bury her in the park down the street.

Bobbie was a short man at five-three and identified with being short. His suits were always perfect and he had three of them in his closet, all identical brown. He owned five different ties that went with the suits, one for each day of the week.

He ate the same Frosted Flakes every morning for breakfast, the same peanut butter and honey and lunchmeat sandwich every lunch, and often brought home dinner from a Chinese restaurant or Kentucky Fried Chicken depending on the day of the week.

He carefully planned everything every day. Including killing Stephanie.

Stephanie hadn't worked a day since they got married. She did a lot of sewing and also said she hoped to be a writer, but had a lot of reading to do first.

The first couple of years of the marriage, Bobbie didn't mind at all. His job as a manager of a major grocery store paid them enough money to live in the nice house on Bryant Street. Buy food and clothes and put some away.

And they only needed one car, so they lived within their means just fine.

But five years into the marriage, when he suggested she go to school to learn how to write, she didn't speak with him for months.

Actually it had been a relief because she talked all the time about nothing and Bobbie loved his quiet more than anything.

Everything about the marriage just got worse.

She was asleep when he went to bed and still asleep when he got up and left for work. And when they were together over dinners, all she did was talk and nag and talk, usually about nothing.

And Bobbie was a problem solver, so he solved his Stephanie problem and just killed her.

Very, very simple. Now he just had to bury her.

He pulled his SUV into the garage, made sure the garage door was down, and after wrapping Stephanie up in the tarp, he dragged her to the car and lifted her into the back. Thankfully, she had stayed as light as when they had first got married. She was taller than he was, but very skinny.

He went back into the house, cleaned up his hammer as best he could and hung it back in the garage. Then he moved the furniture back into her sewing room. He didn't bother to paint over the robin's egg blue. He kind of liked the color, actually.

Then, around one in the morning, with a shovel in the back seat and Stephanie all the way in the back, wrapped up, he drove down Bryant Street to the neighborhood park called The Bryant Street Park.

It was about five square blocks and took up the center of the subdivision. It had a few tennis courts, a playground for the kids, and a lot of grass and old oak trees. Park benches and picnic tables were scattered in different locations under the trees.

Bryant Street ran along the west side and Stephanie had always commented how beautiful the place was. Every single time they drove by, didn't matter the season.

But heaven forbid they should ever stop. Take a walk. Enjoy the beauty.

"Later," she would always say. After a few years he had stopped suggesting it.

Seems like now was later. At least for her.

He pulled off the road near a group of tall old oak trees just getting their spring leaves. Houses across the street from the park were dark.

He took the shovel and a fresh painter's tarp and walked back into the park, looking for a place to silently dig a grave for Stephanie that was dark enough that he wouldn't be heard or seen.

She had never wanted to stop here, but if he had his way, she would soon exist here a long time.

He found a perfect place about ten paces beyond a big oak, far enough away to not be troubled by the roots.

He carefully cut out a rectangle from the sod, putting it on one side of the tarp in the exact way he had taken it out. He wanted to return it in a way that it wouldn't be seen.

Then, as quietly as he could, he started digging in the soft, moist soil. He was used to work, lifting boxes and such at the store, and he knew this would be work, so he went slowly, letting the hole get deeper and each shovel-full of dirt carefully piled on the tarp.

It was going fine until about two feet down he ran into a painter's tarp.

And when he got down and felt around in the hole, it quickly became apparent that there was already a body buried there.

And it had a pretty nasty odor to it.

So he quickly filled back in the hole and then put the sod back. He had been tempted to leave the hole open, but he knew his prints might be all over the tarp he had put the dirt on.

He folded up his dirt tarp and went looking for another location.

One spot looked perfect, about twenty paces from a picnic table and beside a row of bushes.

So once again he laid the tarp down, carefully removed the grass sod, and started digging. Again, down about three feet this time, there was a body, this one of a woman in house dress, no tarp covering her. And she had been dead for some time.

Bobbie just couldn't believe his luck.

Was there a body under every perfect spot in this entire park?

So once again he filled back in the hole, put the sod back in place, folded up his tarp and headed for the car. He was going to need to get Stephanie into their big freezer in the garage so she didn't start smelling and himself cleaned up and to bed. The sun would be coming up in an hour.

He got everything cleaned up and Stephanie in the freezer that they never used and hadn't used even though Stephanie had thought it would be a great thing to have.

He woke up the next morning at around 11 am, Saturday, with the sounds of a neighbor's mower.

And no sounds of Stephanie snoring.

He turned on some light jazz, something that Stephanie

would have never allowed, had a wonderfully quiet break-fast, then went out and looked into the freezer.

"Morning, dear," he said to the curled up corpse still wrapped in a painting tarp.

He took stock of how much room was in the freezer, then headed to his own store to check in on how the Saturday crew was doing and to buy some meat.

"Stocking up my freezer," he told his assistant manager, then got all the meat home and covered Stephanie's body. It looked like a very well-stocked freezer when he was done. No sign of anything in a painting tarp under the meat.

He thought about just leaving her there, then decided he really felt he needed to bury her.

So Sunday afternoon, after another wonderful night's sleep, he headed out into his own backyard where the previous owners used to have a garden and started to work on it. He would never actually plant a garden. Didn't interest him, but he needed to have his neighbors think he was going to.

He got down about four feet when he found another body. This one of a woman about Stephanie's age, wrapped in a tarp almost identical to the one he had her frozen in.

The buried woman had been buried long enough that most of the smell was gone, so he opened the tarp just a little and looked at her. She had been beautiful, he could tell that much.

He closed the tarp back up and quickly replaced the dirt, making sure that it looked like he was about to plant a garden in the freshly moved soil by the time he was done. Right down to digging rows and everything.

Then he headed back inside, stored the shovel in the garage and got cleaned up and decided to go out and get KFC and a bag of chips to eat later watching television.

Stephanie would never let him do that.

When he got back, the sun was starting to go down. He just stood on his driveway and looked up and down the street of mostly identical ranch homes, all well-kept.

How many killers like him lived on this street? Clearly more than one. He had killed Stephanie, but not the others. It seemed like such a nice street, on the surface.

And if he found two bodies in the park, how many others were buried there?

And in the back yards of all the homes.

Bryant Street was no doubt a very strange place.

He went inside and put the chips and chicken on the counter and went into Stephanie's sewing room. It was no longer her sewing room, now. He could do with the room as he wanted.

And if anyone asked, which no one would, she had moved back East where her family had been from, but were now all dead.

He got a handcart out of the garage and loaded up her sewing desk and took it to the garage. He put the clean side up of the painting tarp on the top of the freezer and then put the sewing machine desk up on the freezer.

Then he stacked her chair on top of the freezer and a couple boxes of her clothes from the closet so for the first time he would have room for his own clothes.

And over the next few weeks, he had so much stuff

stacked in and around the freezer, the big white thing was almost impossible to see.

He had buried Stephanie, just not in the ground, but in her own stuff.

He had tried to bury her in the ground. He really had.

But on Bryant Street, there just wasn't enough room.

You Forgive The Night's Scream
A Poker Boy Story

DEAN WESLEY SMITH

ONE

I woke with the sound of a woman's scream echoing in my head.

High-pitched.

Full of terror.

I sat bolt upright in bed.

My heart pounded like it wanted to get out of my chest and run for the closet and every Poker Boy superpower sense I had was amped up to full power.

Beside me, my girlfriend and sidekick, Patty Ledgerwood, aka Front Desk Girl, lay sleeping soundly, her wonderful long brown hair like a shadow over her pillow in the dim light coming from cracks around the side of the drapes.

Outside, the city of Las Vegas never slept and certainly never turned off its lights. The strip was only a few blocks from Patty's apartment building and my invisible office floated just to the west of her apartment and directly over the MGM Grand Hotel and Casino complex.

I held my breath, waiting for another scream, trying to listen over the pounding of my heart.

Nothing.

A little noise from a truck on the street below Patty's apartment. Then a couple quick beeps as it backed up.

Nothing else.

Yet every danger Poker Boy sense I had was shouting, making me want to get out of there.

That scream had been close, as if it was inside this very apartment. Yet Patty was still sound asleep.

Something was very wrong.

Very wrong.

I've had bad dreams before, but when that scream let go, I have no memory of actually being in a dream.

The scream was real. Outside of my possible dream.

At least real in one fashion or another.

I gently touched Patty's shoulder.

She stirred and rolled to look up at me. "What—"

I put my finger to my lips and shook my head. Then I eased out of bed. I was wearing sweatpants and nothing else. I slipped on my thin brown slippers.

Patty came awake at once, saying nothing and moving silently out of the other side of the bed, slipping on her white bathrobe over her nightgown and her slippers as well.

I stood near the door to the bedroom that led out into the living room, listening for any noise coming from either the living room or kitchen area.

416

Silently, Patty came over and touched my arm, using her powers to calm me down some. The pounding of my racing heart subsided and I mouthed the word, "Thanks." One of her superpowers was the ability to keep people calm and focused. I loved it in stressful situations when we worked together. We had discovered that as a team we were far stronger together than apart.

Plus, I was head-over-my-slippers in love with her.

She pointed to her ear and shook her head, meaning she was hearing nothing.

I wasn't either, so silently I went out into the living room.

And as I walked ten steps, the temperature of the room dropped a good thirty degrees until suddenly I could see my breath in the dim light.

Patty grabbed my arm and pulled me back into the bedroom, a panicked look on her face.

I'm glad she did. I would need a lot more clothes to go back into that living room.

"Out of time," she whispered and I did, slipping us between instants of time. It felt like I stopped time when I did that, but in reality, time never stopped. I just moved me and Patty inside an instant of time.

Normally, in a busy casino or outside, I could tell instantly when I did that, but in the silent and dark apartment, nothing seemed to change.

"You know what caused that chill?" I asked, shivering as I tried to warm up a little. All my senses were still screaming that there was danger close by and the memory of that scream seemed to echo in my mind.

I moved over and grabbed a sweatshirt that said "The Golden Nugget Poker Room" and pulled it over my head, easing the chill some.

"Did you hear something?" Patty asked.

I nodded. "A woman's scream. That's what woke me up."

"Oh, no," she said.

Even in the dim light I could tell her face went white.

I glanced up at the ceiling. "Stan. Help!"

Patty nodded and a moment later Stan appeared.

The God of Poker had on what he always seemed to have on. Tan slacks, button down sweater, and loafers. In all the years I had worked for him, I had seldom caught him out of that outfit, day or night.

"Wow," he said, instantly spinning around, looking for the danger. I could feel him strengthen the time bubble and put a shield around us, which helped my screaming warning senses some.

"What is causing that?" he asked.

I shrugged, since I honestly had no idea.

"He heard a scream," Patty said. "In his sleep."

"Oh, shit!" Stan said and instantly vanished, leaving the shield and the stronger time bubble.

I looked at Patty who clearly wasn't in the mood for any of my one-line jokes, so I wisely said nothing. Not a skill I often had, but at the moment with every warning sense I had still going off, it seemed prudent.

Besides, the way they were acting was starting to scare me to death.

The longest five seconds later, Laverne, Lady Luck

herself, appeared in our bedroom with Stan and Ben beside her.

Lady Luck didn't have on her normal power business suit, but instead wore a pair of jeans and an old sweatshirt. She looked downright normal for one of the most powerful beings in all the universe.

Ben was a god in the book world that was a member of our team. He looked like a little old librarian and had a perfect memory of everything he had ever read and the history of all the gods.

Lady Luck instantly strengthened the shields around us even more and the sense of warning and fear again decreased but didn't vanish by any means.

"Who heard the scream?" Lady Luck asked.

I sort of half raised my hand.

"Damn it," she said.

Now when Lady Luck swears, you know things can't be good. And I wasn't sure if I wanted to know just how bad things actually were, since all the bad seemed to be focused at me.

TWO

Patty held onto my arm, keeping me as calm as her superpower could manage. But I was feeling anything but calm.

"So what's out there in that cold?" I asked.

"A banshee," Lady Luck said.

Ben nodded, confirming what Lady Luck said but not adding to it.

I almost said that I thought those were myths, but then realized who I was and who was standing around me. I just hadn't been in this superhero business long enough to know what was a myth and what actually had some reality attached to it.

"So tell me exactly what you are worried about," I said.

"The banshee is a fairy that is known to mourn the coming loss of a life," Ben said.

"By screaming?" I asked. "More like it would scare a person to death."

"By screaming," Stan said, nodding. "And the person who hears them is supposed to be the one who will die very shortly. It's both a warning and a sad cry that the person is dying."

Well, I had to admit, I didn't much like the sound of that.

I took a deep breath and could feel Patty's calming influence flow through me. Honestly, over the last few years, I had faced death and the end of the world a few times. And a lot of really tough players in no-limit poker games. So if some being was giving me a warning, I needed to thank her and just flat ask her what was going to happen.

And when.

Never hurt to know when a fella was going to die, I figured.

Seemed so simple. I'm sure there were a dozen reasons it was a stupid idea, but my friends around me just seemed determined to stand next to me when I died and do nothing, so I needed to do something.

And my terrified mind couldn't come up with one other idea. I knew death could follow me anywhere, since I had met two gods of death so far, and sort of liked them both, honestly. So running was out of the question.

I moved over to the closet and pulled out my heaviest Oregon coat. Since I was originally from Oregon and my home casino was in the mountains of Oregon, I at least had a few heavy coats, one of which I had brought to Vegas and stashed in Patty's apartment because at times I had been damned cold here as well.

"What are you doing?" Patty asked, again taking my arm as I came back to her zipping up my parka.

"Going out to talk with the banshee," I said, giving her a quick kiss and heading for the door into the dark living room.

"Not a great idea," Lady Luck said.

I stopped and looked at her. "Has a banshee killed anyone?"

"No, she just warns people," Lady Luck said, her voice sounding sad and tired.

"Then it seems I'll be fine. When was the last time anyone just talked with the banshee?"

Ben shook his head. "There are no records of anyone doing such a thing."

"Five hundred years," Lady Luck said softly.

Ben glanced at her and said nothing. He knew something he wasn't saying.

"Well, if this kills me," I said, doing my best to screw up

every ounce of courage I had, "someone tell the next person to not try it."

"I'm coming with you," Patty said.

"No, I heard the scream, I'm the one the banshee is trying to warn."

I glanced at Lady Luck and nodded. I almost said, "Wish me luck" and then stopped as I realized how stupid that really would have sounded to Lady Luck.

Her expression didn't change from extreme seriousness combined with sadness, something I had never seen on her face.

"While I'm gone," I said, standing near the door of the living room, "someone might want to check with Death, see if I really am on a list at the moment. We did save his ass and help his daughter."

Lady Luck nodded. "I'll do it," she said, and vanished.

I took a deep breath and turned and went into the living room.

The intense cold slapped me and I staggered, but managed to move forward.

"My name is Poker Boy," I said to the cold air, my breath freezing in front of my face. "I heard your scream and came to see if I could help."

Being brash seemed to be the most logical thing I could do.

And that's what people who rescue other people do, after all, go toward the sound of a scream.

"Thank you," a soft female voice said from the other side of the couch.

"Can you stand a little light?" I asked.

"It is not a problem," the voice said.

An instant later the table light beside the couch clicked on. A beautiful and mostly nude small woman sat on the couch under the light. Her skin was a light blue and she had two fragile-looking silver wings tucked behind her.

Her beautiful, long, silver hair cascaded around her and covered most of the important parts.

But there was no two ways about it, she was stunning.

I moved over to a large chair facing her across a frost-covered coffee table and sat down, my hands in my pockets of the heavy ski parka. Somewhere between the door and the chair I had lost touch with my feet, since they were only in thin slippers and I was sure they were already frozen.

"So I assume you were calling me for help?" I asked, doing my best to not push any power toward her for fear she might think I was trying to meddle.

"I was," she said, nodding, moving her silver hair around in such a fashion that any good strip club would hire her in a moment.

"Not warning me like you normally do."

"No, calling you for help," she said.

Relief flooded through me but did nothing to warm me up. You would think it would have.

"I have been stuck in this frigid-state for almost five hundred years now," she said, her voice taking on a little more power. "I have done my job as instructed for five hundred years."

I nodded, a little worried about what was coming next.

"I would like you to help me become free of this punishment."

Oh, great, she's asking the newest member of all the superheroes in God's world for help with something that happened five hundred years ago, as if I should know what that was.

"Why do you think I can help with this?" I asked.

"I have watched you and your team save many, many lives," she said. "I hope you can now save mine."

I nodded. "We can try. But can I bring a few members of my team in here to help me?"

"You can," she said, nodding.

Being afraid to stand on my frozen feet, I shouted to the door. "Patty, Stan, Ben, could you join us?"

She nodded, making her hair dance around the important parts of her body. "I am honored you are willing to try to help me."

Stan had bundled all three of them up in parkas and gloves and they came in slowly like an expedition to the South Pole lost in Patty's apartment. No dog sleds, luckily.

Patty came over and sat on the arm of the chair beside me, calming me some with a touch. Stan and Ben both nodded to the banshee and remained standing.

She nodded back.

I turned back to the banshee and said, "We are ready. Could you tell us what caused this punishment five hundred years ago?"

"It is not punishment for a crime," she said. "It is punishment for love. I loved the wrong woman."

Well, I was as liberal as the next person, but honestly, that answer surprised me, right down to my frozen feet.

THREE

I needed to get this going before I froze completely to the chair. "May I ask first who put this punishment on you?"

I glanced over at Ben who was shaking his head from side-to-side. "You don't want to know," he said softly.

"I did," Lady Luck said, entering the room right after Ben said that.

She did not have a ski parka on and seemed oblivious to the intense cold.

If I got many more surprises like that, the blood actually might reach my feet again.

Patty squeezed my arm to keep me calm.

"How are you, Laverne?" the banshee asked, smiling.

"I am well," Lady Luck said, moving to the end of the couch and sitting down and facing the banshee. "You are as beautiful as ever."

The banshee nodded her head thank you, again doing wonderful and alluring things with her hair over her perfect blue body.

Who knew a blue body could be perfect?

Then the banshee said something that got me even more confused, which in this frozen state, was going some.

"Thank you for saving my life."

Laverne smiled and nodded. "I am sorry that it had to be in this fashion. It was what your husband would accept as a punishment short of death."

"I have survived," the banshee said. "Loving you was worth it. Is my husband still angry at me?"

"He is not," Lady Luck said. "He is retired, his daughter has taken over his month of duties as Death just last year, and he spends most of his time surfing in Hawaii with his new wife."

I just about choked. This banshee had been married to Death himself. And she had been in love with Lady Luck. Wow, I really needed to spend time with Ben and learn about some of the history of the Gods.

"Then is it possible to return me to the normal world?" the banshee asked.

"I just spoke with your ex-husband," Lady Luck said. "Poker Boy and his team helped his daughter make the transition last year, and I told him that Poker Boy was trying to help you now after five hundred years of punishment."

"Thank you," the banshee said. "He never knew you were the one?"

"He knew," Laverne said. "Right from the start. And he knew it broke my heart, as well as yours, to do what I did. That's why he allowed the punishment."

"I have been wailing over death and broken hearts now for five hundred years," the banshee said. "And with every one I mourned the loss of your love."

"You never lost it," Laverne said.

Once again my toes felt warmer from the shock of that statement.

"You are married, have four grown daughters?" the banshee asked, staring at Laverne in clear surprise.

"My husband and I have," Laverne said, smiling, "shall we say, an open arrangement."

I just about said, "More information than I needed." But

my teeth were chattering too much, luckily, to get that stupid joke out.

Laverne stood and with a "thank you" into the air, more than likely to the banshee's former husband, she waved her hand.

Intense heat filled the room and the banshee sat there, smiling, soaking it all in.

And then finally, after a few seconds, it was over.

I did feel warmer, but not much.

Water was dripping all around Patty's apartment from the melting frost and I could feel the temperature on my face returning to normal, although it would not surprise me to have frostbite on my nose.

The banshee now was no longer blue, but a tanned golden brown all over. And I do mean all over. And her hair was now just as long but a rich brown. And her wings shimmered in a rainbow of colors.

Laverne reached out her hand to the banshee and then said, "Jayne, welcome back."

Jayne took her hand and stood, smiling, her long hair doing little to cover some pretty amazing assets.

"It's a pleasure to be back."

Then Jayne turned to me and said, "Thank you, Poker Boy, and your entire team, for being willing to take a chance on talking to me."

I just nodded, not trusting myself to say anything sane

"We have some catching up to do," Laverne said, smiling.

"Now that's something I've been looking forward to for five hundred years."

Then, like two teenage girls, they both giggled, and vanished.

Lady Luck giggling was unsettling, to say the least.

Stan shook his head and said, "See you tomorrow."

Then he and Ben vanished.

Patty stood and shivered, water dripping off her coat from the melting frost.

"Would you do me a favor," I asked as she offered to help me out of my chair.

"Anything, my frozen love."

"Would you start a warm shower running? I'm just going to teleport out of these clothes and into the shower from here. I don't think my feet will carry me."

She laughed. "I'll be there, naked, standing under the hot water, ready to catch you."

And she did.

And I got real warm, real quick. I'll leave it at that.

THE ROAD BACK
A DOC HILL STORY

DEAN WESLEY SMITH

When you are short-stacked in poker,
and in life, the road back
to being in contention
often has a very sudden end.

ONE

"**D**o we have any idea where he might be?" I asked Annie over my shoulder.

She had crouched down behind my chair at the no-limit ring game I had joined a few hours before at the Bellagio. I was almost a thousand up and had been enjoying the game as a warm-up for a series of poker tournaments coming later in the week to the Bellagio.

I seldom played regular ring games anymore, only tournaments. But at times it felt right to just sit and play for a time. This hot September afternoon was one of those times to relax in the air-conditioned poker room and drink iced tea and win a little money in the process.

"Not a clue," she said. "Dad's got all the information."

Annie had her long brown hair pulled back and the white blouse and dark slacks she wore accented her perfect body. She was the best-looking *former* Las Vegas detective I had ever met, with brown eyes that could stare through to your soul. Actually, she was one of the best-looking women I had ever met, and also one of most deadly poker players in the modern game.

In the year we had been together, she had taken down a dozen tournaments and won two World Series of Poker bracelets for two different events.

Now she wanted my help to find some guy her dad thought was missing. Actually, her dad, Detective Bayard Lott, also a former Las Vegas police detective, wanted her help and she was asking if I would help out as well.

"You want me to deal you in, Doc?" the dealer asked.

"No, thanks, Al," I said, pushing back from the table as Annie stood and stepped back. I flipped him a twenty-five dollar chip and he tapped it and nodded thanks before slipping it into his tip slot.

I turned and nodded to Ben, the brush in charge of the room at the moment, who was headed my way from the poker room desk.

"Cash you out?" he asked.

I flipped him a twenty-five dollar chip as well and said, "Thanks. Just add it to the account."

I had had a running account at the Bellagio for almost ten years now. Made it easier than hauling racks of chips to the cage all the time. And after the two tips, I had five hundred in starting money in my stack and another eight hundred and fifty in winnings.

My chip vanished into Ben's pocket and he worked to rack the rest as I turned and headed with Annie out of the poker room and into the noise and bells of customers filling the slots.

"Dinner?" I asked, realizing I was starting to get hungry as we turned toward the front of the casino.

"Dad's meeting us in the Café Bellagio," she said.

I laughed, taking her hand. "You were pretty sure I was going to help you, huh?"

"Not really," she said, smiling at me as we wound our way through the people toward the restaurant. "I would have gotten the information from Dad and told you later if you were really interested in staying in the game."

"It was enough warm-up," I said. "More than enough, actually."

"Lucky for those guys at the table," she said, laughing. "You warm-up much more and they would have been broke."

"That's the point, isn't it?" I asked.

She agreed and then waved at her father sitting at a semi-private four-person table off to one side of the café where it looked out over the pool. The smell of hamburgers and steaks drifted from the direction of the kitchen and my stomach rumbled. I really was hungrier than I had realized.

I liked her dad a great deal. He looked pretty sharp for his sixty-three years with short-cut white hair, broad shoulders, and only a hint of a gut around his stomach. He had a wicked sense of humor and his laugh could start an entire room laughing with him.

He and a bunch of his retired detective friends played poker every week in the basement of his house and worked to solve cold cases for the Las Vegas Police Department on the side. They called themselves the Cold Poker Gang. Annie and I helped them when we could.

But from what Annie said, this didn't sound like a cold case. More like a missing person problem. And in Vegas, there were always a lot of those.

For all sorts of reasons.

TWO

I was into my rib steak and onion rings, Annie was picking at her hamburger, and her dad was about halfway done with his French Dip before Annie finally broached the subject.

"So who is missing and why are you involved, Dad?"

"Steve Benson Junior," he said between bites.

Both Annie and I glanced at him.

Finally Annie asked exactly what I was thinking. "The son of Chief of Police Steven Benson?"

"One and the same," her dad said. "Chief Benson called me, asked if I would look into it for him."

"He thinks his son is in trouble?" I asked.

Annie's dad shook his head. "Not that kind of trouble. He's a good kid, graduate student at UNLV focusing on Nevada history. But his dad this morning went to meet him for breakfast and Steve didn't show up. Steve's best friend hasn't seen him either."

"And his dad's worried?" Annie asked.

"I would be too," her father said, smiling at her. "Steve is like you in that he calls when he has to cancel something."

"He have a car?" I asked.

"Red Jeep SUV," he said. "About a year old. It's missing as well."

"So he went somewhere and hasn't returned yet," Annie said. "More than likely he's fine."

Her dad nodded. "That's what the Chief thinks as well, but he's still worried. Steve's cell isn't picking up. I think that's really why the Chief called me. He doesn't want this out yet, so he's just calling in personal favors at the moment."

I sat back munching on a crisp onion ring, thinking. My little voice was telling me that something was wrong with this kid. I didn't know him and I didn't know his father, but this felt wrong for some reason I couldn't put my finger on.

However, when at a poker table, I had learned to trust that little voice when it told me something was wrong with a play another player made. And in life I had also learned to trust that voice. And right now the very same voice was telling me we needed to move on this and fast.

I finished the onion ring and leaned forward toward Annie's dad. "Could you call the Chief and ask him if Steve is back yet? And if not, could we go look at his apartment?"

Detective Lott slid the key across the table at me, smiling. "Steve wasn't back five minutes before you two showed up, and I got this key from the Chief before coming over here."

I just shook my head and grinned as Annie patted her father's arm, smiling. It was no wonder the guy had been such a great detective in his day. He was a half step ahead of everything.

THREE

Steve's apartment near the university seemed far neater than I would have expected a grad student's apartment to be. And it was clear with only a quick look that there was nothing at all out of place.

Nothing.

The apartment had one bedroom with a living room with only a couch and chair and a large desk in it. A small, clean dining room table with four chairs sat near the open kitchen. There was a bathroom off the bedroom.

There was no sign at all of any woman's touch in here. Everything was standard apartment except the large computer on a L-shaped desk on the left side of the living room and large wall of books on the right side, mostly text-books that at a glance I was glad I never would have to read. My college days were a long ways behind me now.

However, one full shelf was full of books on various aspects of Nevada history that looked very interesting, from the gold rush towns to railroad history to the founding of Las Vegas.

All of them in perfect order by author.

Annie was looking through Steve's desk. There were a couple of books open on the desk on Nevada place names and another on lost mines of Nevada.

"Can you access that computer?" I asked Annie. "See what he was researching before he left?"

"If it's not password protected," she said, sitting down in the chair and moving the wireless keyboard closer toward her.

Her father came out of the bathroom shaking his head. "This kid is the cleanest kid I have ever seen. Nothing out of place, no sign that anyone else but him even visited here. Not even a hair on his comb."

"He folds his socks and underwear," I said. "His bed is made, even though he slept in it recently. And he washed his breakfast dishes before he left, more than likely yesterday morning, since the dishes are completely dry as is the dish towel."

Annie brought the computer up and then shook her head. "Protected."

"He's going to have a password book," I said. "Upper drawer on the left."

She opened the drawer and pulled out a small notebook, shaking her head. "How did you know that?"

"Someone like Steve is completely predictable. Every move, every detail. It's how his mind works. He has no choice."

"Easy pickings on a poker table," Annie said.

"He'd never sit down at one," I said. "He wouldn't be able to handle the uncertainty that comes naturally with the game."

"Obsessive-compulsive?" Annie's dad asked.

"Borderline," Annie said, nodding. "It goes toward hoarding or being neat freaks."

"We know which way Steve goes," I said.

As Annie worked on the computer and bringing up the history, I went back into the small apartment bedroom. Steve had his shoes lined up perfectly along the bottom of his closet, from dress shoes through tennis shoes to boots. There was an empty spot between a pair of tennis shoes and a heavy pair of boots. That's where he would put his hiking boots.

His shirts were lined up hanging in his closet and there was a clear opening where a light casual shirt had clearly hung. More than likely brown from the patterns of the colors.

I went into the bathroom and opened the medicine chest. There was an empty spot where a tube of suntan lotion would have sat right between a small jar of Vaseline and a tube of blister cream.

I closed the cabinet and turned went back into the living room with the desk and books. "He's gone into the desert. More than likely yesterday morning. My guess is he was planning on returning before dark last night and something happened."

Annie's dad looked around at the apartment. "I can see why the Chief was worried, now."

"Got it," Annie said, moving back through the history of what Steve had last looked at on his computer.

The very last thing was a map of an area of the Nevada desert to the north and west of Las Vegas along Highway 95.

"Skeleton Mountains," Annie said, hitting a button to print up the map just as I was sure Steve had done.

One of the books open on the desk referred to the area as well, and I picked it up as Annie kept going back through the history on the computer.

Seems the Skeleton Mountains were a group of rocky peaks sticking up out of the desert about ten miles to the west of the highway. The article said that no one knew exactly how it got its name. From what I could tell in the book, the rocky peaks had just always been named that.

And they weren't that big, with the largest being not more than six or seven hundred feet off the desert. Compared to the mountains I spent the summer in every year in central Idaho, guiding rafts on the River of No Return, these Skeleton Mountains were nothing more than large piles of rocks.

"He was researching some old patented mining claims in those mountains," Annie said, again hitting the print button. "All of them are long dormant and never produced anything of real value."

"So we know where he went," Annie's father said, nodding.

"Get a search team set up from the Chief," I said to him as Annie printed a second copy of the map of the small group of mountains.

"Where are you going?" Annie's dad asked, as he pulled out his phone.

"Fleet's in town and he loves testing out his new helicopter," I said, and Annie laughed. "He'll get us up there and we'll see what we can see from the air, see if we can spot his car before you and the Chief get there."

I was on the phone to my best friend and business partner, Fleet, and Annie's father was talking with the Chief of Police as we headed out into the hot early evening air and Annie pulled the door to the apartment closed behind us.

FOUR

Fleet lived in Boise with his family. Annie and I had a house there as well, but unlike Fleet, we were seldom in Boise. Fleet had a wonderful wife and two kids there, but at the moment they were all here, letting the kids have one last vacation before school started up again.

Fleet had decided that our company needed a helicopter to go along with our own private jet. It seemed that over the years, his investments of my poker winnings had made us, as he said, stupidly rich. We gave millions away to charity every year and spent what we wanted and somehow just managed to get richer.

Fleet was that good with business and investments.

My father's death a year ago had just added more millions than I wanted to think about into the picture.

When Fleet bought the jet helicopter for the company, he had decided he wanted to fly it, much to his wife's horror. And in the last year he had become a very good pilot.

On the phone I told him what was going on and he almost beat us to the airport, even though we had a shorter distance to go. Any excuse to take out the helicopter was a great idea as far as he was concerned.

Within forty minutes after leaving Steve's apartment, we were airborne and headed for the Skeleton Mountains, the loud drone of the chopper a constant noise around us.

"So what do you think we're going to find?" Fleet asked through the communications links we all wore.

Annie was in the co-pilot chair because she had taken a few lessons with the chopper last year. I was behind them, strapped in tight. I wasn't afraid of flying, but I had to admit having my friend from childhood doing the flying didn't instill great confidence, even though he had a lot of hours in the air already.

"Besides rocks and snakes?" Annie asked.

She moved slightly so I could see the wink she gave me.

I smiled. Fleet was deathly afraid of snakes. Any kind and size of snake, actually. And everyone knew it.

"Not funny," he said.

"If we have to land, you can stay in the chopper," I said. "There will be snakes."

Fleet shook his head. "You two sure know how to kill a good flight."

Less than fifteen minutes after leaving the Las Vegas airport, the mountains sort of rose from the rolling desert floor in front of us. They were sure nothing to look at. Mostly rocks and scattered open areas covered in scrub brush. I hadn't been kidding Fleet. Those rocks would be infested with snakes, since it was clear the area got little or no attention by humans at all.

"Come in from Highway 95," I said to Fleet. "See if you can spot a road into those mountains."

Fleet nodded and slowed until Annie pointed ahead.

A bare excuse of a dirt road left the highway and wound toward the mountains.

Fleet banked over it and followed the road, moving slowly as we all studied the area.

There was no place to hide below us at all. Just open desert and scrub.

Up ahead the road started to wind up a small canyon and then seemed to break out into an open flat area before going back into another canyon and deeper into the piles of rocks laughingly called mountains.

Nothing but huge rocks and scrub brush.

"On the right," Annie said, pointing.

It took me a moment, but finally I saw what she was pointing at. A glint of the sun reflected off some metal. At closer look I could see hints of a red car hidden beside a rock and covered with scrub brush. Someone had spent a lot of time in the task of hiding the car and had the car off the road so it couldn't be seen by anyone driving in.

"Someone really wanted that hidden," Fleet said, shaking his head.

My stomach was twisting like my rib steak was suddenly not agreeing with me.

"Same speed," I said to Fleet. "Just keep going straight and off into the desert on the other side of the mountains."

"Like we're on Fleet's tour of the desert," he said and did as he was told.

Annie had her cell phone to her ear as all of us watched

the ground below. To the right of our flight path I could see a trail going up to what looked to be an old mine entrance. There was no sign of anyone there, but that meant nothing.

Then, near where the dirt road came out the other side of another rock canyon and started across the desert, I spotted an old pickup truck parked under a rock outcropping. It was brown and clearly dusty and blended in perfectly with the rocks.

"Truck on the right," I said as we went past and out into the desert just as if we were a sightseeing chopper doing nothing unusual.

"Get us away from these rocks and turn back toward Vegas until we are completely out of sight," I said to Fleet.

"Looks like the kid found some real problems he didn't expect in there," Fleet said.

"Dad," Annie said into her cell. "We found Steve's car, but looks like he's in trouble with someone living in an old mine in the Skeleton Mountains."

She waited for a second. "They hid his car," she said. "Spent a lot of time doing so, actually."

Again a pause as her father said something on the other side of the conversation that I couldn't hear.

"There is," Annie said. "A brown pickup, dirty, also hidden. We've moved away from the mountains to not spook anyone in there."

Then she gave a description of the truck to her father.

This one-sided conversation was driving me crazy. I had a hunch that the longer we delayed, the less chance Steve was going to make it. He had clearly walked into something ugly.

You don't go to that much trouble to hide a person's car if you ever plan on letting them leave.

She nodded for a long minute, then she glanced at me, her brown eyes big. Then she said, simply, "Shit."

Then she hung up.

Fleet had the chopper flying low over the desert and had turned back for Vegas. We were out of both hearing and sight of the mountains.

"Dad and the Chief and a bunch of Vegas police and the State Police are all coming hard and silent from all directions. They are going to button up all ways in and out of that group of mountains."

"What did he say?" Fleet asked just before I could.

"A brown truck matching the description of the one back there has been connected to a string of disappearances. Maybe up to a dozen women going back years."

Now the steak in my stomach was really twisting around. Steve really had stumbled into something far, far bigger than he could handle.

"Take us back up to where the road into the mountains hits Highway 95," I said to Fleet. "Drop us off there and then make a wide circle out and around the rocks to the other side and out of sight and watch the road on that side. We don't want this guy getting away before the police get here."

Fleet nodded and two minutes later had us on the ground next to the highway. Then he lifted off and swung back to Vegas, climbing and moving fast.

I had tossed in an older twenty-two Remington saddle rifle from my car in case we needed to take out a couple of snakes and Annie had brought along her revolver. We had both grabbed bottles of water.

The air around us was hot, and there were very few cars passing by on the highway. The sun was low on the horizon, but not low enough to cut off the heat. It would be dark in less than two hours.

As Fleet vanished and the sound of the chopper faded off, Annie pulled out her phone to call her dad.

She told him what we had done and then asked how far out they were. As she listened to the answer, she shook her head.

"They are still a good fifteen minutes out," she told me. "And it will be thirty minutes or longer before they can have the entire place locked down from all sides."

I glanced at the half mile of road between us and the first edge of the rocks they called Skeleton Mountains. I wasn't sure that Steve had that long. If the guy had a police scanner, he would know the police were on the way.

I glanced at Annie and she could read my mind. She nodded and then said to her dad. "We're going in on foot. Warn everyone we're in there. And don't put that on the scanner."

Then before her father could object, she clicked off the phone and tucked it in her pants pocket.

"Up for a jog?" I asked.

"Why not?" she said, smiling as she made sure the clip in her gun was in place and ready. "Seems like a perfect evening for some exercise."

I knew there was a reason I loved this woman.

FIVE

It took us less than five minutes to run the length of the dirt road to the edge of the first rock canyon. It was a tough and hot run since we both had to keep looking ahead and also down at our feet to watch ruts and rocks that could twist an ankle.

We slowed as we entered the shadows of the canyon and walked, both of us drinking from our water bottles.

The rocks towered a good hundred feet over the road that ran up a wash. Annie watched the left side, I watched the right.

And I had been right about snakes. A couple nasty Speckled Rattlesnakes lay on rocks. As we approached, they slipped down into the brush. Both of them were large, far larger than I had seen in some time, actually.

In Idaho, as a guide on the summer rafting trips on the River of No Return, I warned people away from climbing the rocks near the river. The rattlers there were much smaller, but could still ruin a good rafting trip if you cornered them or got too close.

The road came out of the rocks and opened up through an open area a quarter mile across before ducking back into the rocks on the other side. Steve's Jeep was hidden to the right about a hundred yards into that canyon ahead.

We stopped, still in the shadows and both took another long drink. Then we left the bottles beside the road. I had a hunch we were going to need our hands free from here on out.

I glanced at my watch. Eight minutes had passed since we left the highway.

"You ready?" I asked?

She nodded.

Running low, bent over, we headed out into the sun and across the open area. I kept expecting to hear a shot or something, but we made it quickly to the shade of the other canyon, both of us panting.

From there we slowed to a walk, Annie again watching the right walls of rock while I watched the left.

As we got even with where Steve's Jeep was hidden, Annie pointed it out. No one would have ever seen it simply driving this dirt path up this narrow canyon between all the rocks.

We kept moving up the road and within a minute we were at the place where the path left the road through some scrub and up a narrow cut in the rocks toward what looked to be an open mine.

"Got any ideas?" Annie asked as we stopped in the shadows and studied the path.

"Nothing," I said. "Trying to climb these snake-infested rocks to get up there another way would be suicidal."

"Going up that trail won't be very healthy, either," Annie said, studying the trail up to the mine opening a hundred feet above us. "It would be like shooting ducks in a pond for anyone above."

We both stood there, with not an idea in the world between us. The heat of the day had really baked the rocks around us and even though we were in the shade, everything was just radiating heat. I would have bet the temperature was a good hundred and twenty and there wasn't a breath of wind. Sweat dried so fast it left my skin feeling coated in dust and salt.

Annie took out her cell phone, then shook her head and put it back.

Then an idea hit me. "Car alarm."

Annie glanced at me, puzzled and listening. There was no sound at all out here in the desert in these rocks.

"Steve's car," I said. "I'm going to go back and see if I can set off that car alarm. If the guy up there doesn't know anyone is on the way to look for him, he's going to come out thinking a snake set it off or something."

"Good idea," she said.

"Don't let him get back in that cave or Steve is dead."

She nodded and glanced around for a place to hide. I started back down the road and behind me she whispered, "Watch out for snakes."

"You too," I whispered back.

Actually, snakes were my biggest concern with this entire plan. With brush all over that Jeep, there could be a dozen rattlers in there already, both in the car, in the engine, and under it. The car formed a perfect snake cave and I wasn't looking forward at all to wading in there.

I spotted a long piece of brush in the ditch beside the road and grabbed it. It was a good six feet long and sturdy. A rattler needed to get within four feet to strike, maybe more if they were big ones like we had seen coming in.

I glanced at my watch as I neared the Jeep's hiding place beside the road. Annie's dad and the State Police would be almost into position. If this guy ran, and Annie couldn't stop him, they would.

I just hoped Steve would still be alive if the guy did run.

I took a deep breath of the warm afternoon air and started off the road toward the red Jeep buried in the brush. Then, before I had taken two steps, I heard Annie's clear voice ring out through the rocks.

"Stop! Police. Let him go and put your hands up!"

Then two shots filled the air.

Running low and silently, I headed back up the road, not allowing myself to think about Annie getting hurt.

As I neared a corner in the road that would allow me to see the road ahead and the area where the trail left the road to the mine, I slowed.

Annie somehow had gone up the trail a dozen steps and then climbed into some rocks. Somehow she had managed to stay hidden as the guy holding Steve had come down the trail to the road. He must have had a scanner and finally clued to the fact that they were coming for him.

She now had him basically pinned on the road using Steve as a shield.

Steve looked tired and scared out of his wits in his tan slacks, hiking boots, and tan shirt. The guy holding him was short, about five-four, and wore jeans and a light green T-shirt that was stained by sweat. His face looked like it had a five-day growth of beard and his dark hair looked like it hadn't seen a comb in days.

He had a large pistol pressed against Steve's temple and was holding it as if he knew what to do with it.

Annie saw me and nodded.

"Police!" I shouted. "You are surrounded!"

The guy spun in my direction, trying to drag Steve with him, but Steve tripped. The guy's gun left the side of Steve's head as he fought to get his hostage back into position. In doing so he gave Annie a clear shot.

And she took it.

The guy spun from the impact and smacked back into the rocks and brush in the shallow ditch beside the dirt road. His gun flew away from him to the left.

Steve spun the other way, tumbling to the ground in the middle of the road.

I came in fast and Annie was almost faster down the trail, both of us watching for any movement in the guy. Annie had gotten him in the right shoulder. He had been holding his gun in his right hand. It didn't look like the wound would be fatal. There was blood, but not enough to cause him any danger.

A huge rattlesnake came out of the brush under him and struck at the guy's left arm. Clearly the snake wasn't happy about some guy landing on him.

The kidnapper moaned and jerked away.

All I could do was laugh.

"That's going to make his recovery a little longer," Annie said, laughing and shaking her head as she turned to help Steve to his feet.

"You all right?" she asked the son of the Las Vegas Chief of Police.

Steve nodded and didn't say anything. He was clearly in shock.

"You dad will be here shortly," Annie said, patting

Steve's shoulder. "Is there anyone else up there in that mine?"

Steve shook his head. "No one alive."

Then he dropped to the road and buried his head in his hands and just sobbed. The guy in the ditch moaned and the large rattler slithered off down the ditch, clearly not happy, as I glanced at Annie.

She looked up at the mine entrance and shook her head.

I had a slight desire to see what was in there, but my better judgment quickly got control.

Some things were better just left unseen.

SIX

I had managed to go up the dirt road a short distance and get a clear enough phone signal to get word out that it was clear.

Then I called Fleet and told him it was clear and to meet us back at the intersection on Highway 95. But I told him that it might be awhile. He might have to transport Steve to the hospital with his dad before he could take us. We had some paperwork to fill out and a story to tell before we would be released, of that I had no doubt.

By the time I got back to Annie, I could hear two Las Vegas Police cars powering up the road.

They slid to a stop just short of us in a cloud of dust and Annie's dad and Steven's dad both piled out.

"You two all right?" Annie's dad asked.

"Had to put a bullet in his shoulder," she said, pointing to the guy in the ditch.

"And then a snake helped keep him down as well," I added, smiling.

Annie's father just shook his head and studied the moaning man for a moment before turning back to us.

The Chief helped his son to his feet and eased him back toward the patrol car as a number of State Police officers arrived on the scene sending up even more clouds of dust into the hot evening air.

As we watched, two Nevada State Police officers carefully worked to extract the guy from the ditch and made sure he didn't have any other guns on him. Then they flipped him over on his face in the dirt and handcuffed him in the middle of the road, not seeming to care at all that he had been shot and snake bitten.

I moved over to the tall State Police officer who seemed to be in charge and pointed up the trail. "From what the Chief's son said, that cave up there isn't pretty. More than likely a major crime scene."

The guy nodded. "Which one of you put the bullet in this guy?"

"I did," Annie said, coming up and handing him her gun. "Retired Detective Annie Lott."

"Thank you, Detective," the officer said, handing the gun to one officer to put away. He didn't seem to care at all about the rifle in my hand.

Then he motioned for two other officers to follow him up the hill.

Annie's dad, Annie, and I moved into a deep area of shade and stood watching as the three State Police officers went into the cave while another stood near the prisoner in the road.

A short minute later one came out, moved to the edge of the mine entrance, and threw up.

"That can't be good," I said.

Both Annie and her father just shook their heads. In their days I was sure they had seen things I flat didn't want to know about.

A few minutes later the other two came out and came back down the trail, a haunted look in all of their eyes.

The Chief climbed out of the patrol car where he had been sitting with his son.

"Your son is going to need counseling help after what he saw up there," the officer said. "He's going to have a long road back to normal."

"That bad?" the Chief asked.

"Worse," the officer said. "This is going to solve a lot of missing persons' cases. More than either of us care to think about."

I had never seen a police officer look so haunted in his eyes. He also was going to have some trouble dealing with whatever horrors were in that old mine.

Then the State Police officer walked over to the guy lying handcuffed face-down in the dirt and kicked him square in the side of the stomach.

After that, the officer turned and walked away down the road past the patrol cars, leaving the desert silence and heat closing in around all of us.

At that moment I was so glad I had resisted the slight temptation to go up to the mine opening.

The Chief glanced over at us, a look of relief in his eyes. Then he said simply, "Thanks."

"You are more than welcome," Annie said as her father put his arm around her.

"Just take care of Steve," I said.

The Chief nodded and went back to the car to sit with his son.

As the door to the patrol car closed, I turned to Annie's father. "Think all the good feelings will cut down some on the paperwork for us?"

Both Annie and her father laughed, as did the state cop standing near the prisoner on the ground.

"Not a chance," Annie's father said between laughs.

Annie stepped over and kissed me. "You always were a dreamer."

THE REMARKABLE WAY SHE DIED

A COLD POKER GANG STORY

DEAN WESLEY SMITH

Retired Las Vegas Detective Debra Pickett had seen a lot of death over her decades-long career. And now that she was a member of the Cold Poker Gang task force with the mission to solve cold cases, she saw even more.

But how Connie Dipkin had died was maybe the strangest of them all.

She had died standing up, alone, in the middle of a side-walk. She had no marks on her body, no wounds, nothing medical or poisonous that anyone could find.

And she had remained standing in the middle of that sidewalk, completely dead, for almost three hours before someone actually noticed something was wrong with her.

That alone shouldn't have been possible, but yet it had happened. There was even surveillance film of her from the moment she died, completely alone, until the police arrived three hours later.

One moment Connie was walking along seemingly just fine. Then she slowed and just stopped.

The day had been a nice, calm spring day in 2010, no winds, not too hot either.

The medical examiner had labeled Connie's death as unexplained, thus it was investigated. Since nothing was ever found to push it toward natural causes or murder, the case went cold.

And now Pickett was holding the thin summary file in her hand while sipping her morning coffee and waiting for Retired Detective Ben "Sarge" Carson to get out of the shower and get dressed.

Around her, the morning Las Vegas sun filled their large condo with bright light. It was late October and the weather was about as perfect as it got here in the valley.

Their three cats, Pete, Ree, and Nose, had finished their morning routine of chasing each other through the place, followed by bathing, which was now followed by naps in the sun.

This morning Ree, a large orange tabby, had taken over one of the brown armchairs, while Nose, a black-and-white tuxedo, occupied one end of the tan cloth couch and Pete, another large orange tabby, the other end.

Pickett loved those three cats and couldn't imagine this large place without them. They gave it life and energy.

At the moment it was nap energy, but still energy.

And massive cuteness.

Their condo had been decorated in shades of wood and tan and browns, sort of like the desert, only richer. And the kitchen she stood in was state-of-the-art modern, with white granite counters and a fridge that was larger than anything Pickett had seen before. Sarge had once said that a small family could live in the stupid thing. Pickett had not disagreed.

But what she loved more than anything else about their penthouse condo was the natural light that flooded the entire main room and kitchen. Even though they were on the top of one of downtown Las Vegas's largest buildings, it felt like the outside was being invited in, but without all the heat and wind.

Behind her Sarge came from the master bedroom area, his thick silver and gray hair still damp. He had on a light-green dress shirt with rolled up sleeves and jeans. He had his badge on his belt and his gun in his holster under his arm.

She wore her normal as well, this time a tan silk blouse and jeans. She carried her gun and badge the same way Sarge did.

Every morning she was struck by how handsome he was with his deep hazel eyes and square jaw. She couldn't believe he had fallen in love with her and how lucky she was to find him this late in life.

They had only been together for a year now, but it felt like she had always known him.

And even though she was a lot shorter than he was at five-four, people said they made a great couple. More than likely it was because they were both always smiling and laughing and joking.

She handed him a cup of coffee and he took a sip, then glanced at the Connie Dipkin file.

"Any idea on that one?" he asked.

Pickett just shook her head. "Never seen a dead person remain standing before."

Sarge laughed. "That's a new one on me as well. Seen a couple vics propped up, one against a jukebox like in the song, but never standing on a sidewalk right out in the open."

"I was at one funeral," Pickett said, "where they stood the deceased near a pool table with a pool cue in his hand."

"Now that's weird," Sarge said.

"It actually felt sort of right for the guy who had died. Creepy, but right."

"To each his own," Sarge said, shaking his head.

"I'm not sure this was murder," Pickett said, pointing to the file on the counter.

Sarge took another sip of his coffee and nodded to that. "Let's hope Robin and her magic computers can come up with something, because I got nothin'."

"I'm still stuck on the woman dying standing up," Pickett said.

Retired Detective Robin Sprague was Pickett's best friend and when they had been active detectives, they had been partners. Now the three of them worked together on cold cases for the task force. Pickett and Sarge did the legwork while Robin did all the computer work.

Together they had solved a lot of cases in just a year working together. Sometimes Pickett and Sarge found the leads, other times Robin did with her computer. They had balanced well.

Sarge finished his coffee and they both put on light jackets to cover their badges and guns, then headed out for the five-block walk to breakfast at the Golden Nugget Buffet.

Pickett loved the morning walk and the routine of it. They ate at the Golden Nugget Buffet every morning and Pickett never got tired of the food because when she wanted, she just changed it up and ate something different. And she never had to do dishes. Or cook. Good food, someone to wait on her, no dishes to wash. To her, that was retirement heaven.

Robin was already there and eating, completely absorbed in reading something on her computer.

While Pickett was thin and short, Robin was solid and square, like a swimmer. She wasn't overweight in the slightest, just solid. She had always been that way.

Sarge and Pickett got their breakfast from the buffet and went back to sit with Robin. The three of them had the same table every morning, away from the tourists on the other side of the room near a massive wall of windows looking out over the hotel pool.

The room was decorated in oak tones, lots of plants, and brass everywhere. It actually worked as a décor and felt comfortable. And the staff knew the three of them and saved their table every morning and also made sure to not sit anyone close to them. Sarge had asked for that favor and made sure he tipped generously to keep the favor alive.

They talked about cats through most of breakfast until Robin smiled and said, "I know what killed Connie Dipkin."

Sarge laughed and Pickett just shook her head. That was so like Robin to do something like that.

"Connie was injected with a very rare drug out of Australia that causes slow paralysis of the muscles. The drug shut off her breathing and stopped her heart."

Robin got out a picture of Connie standing on the sidewalk, dead.

"Three reasons she stayed standing," Robin said. "One, there was no wind to knock her down and other people on the sidewalk never touched her. Two, the drug froze her muscles just long enough for rigor to start to set in as the drug cleared. Three, her large shopping bags served as balances."

Pickett stared at the picture. Connie was holding a shopping bag in each hand. And the two bags were wide and low, close to the sidewalk.

"I'll be go to hell," Sarge said. "Strangest thing I have ever seen."

"So how come no one spotted the poison in her system?" Pickett asked.

"Because by the time they found her it was gone," Robin said. "If she had fallen over and died, the tests would have spotted the poison. But since she died standing and remained standing until rigor started to take over, the poison was no longer detectable with surface tests."

"So we have no toxicology proof of this?" Sarge said.

"Oh, we do, I'm sure," Robin said. "If a test is done looking only for the specific poison, residual amounts will still be there. They just didn't do that test."

"And it can still be done?"

"Without a problem," Robin said.

"Well, that's darned fast progress," Sarge said. "Great work there. I thought this would be a no-movement case."

"So did I," Pickett said.

Robin smiled. "I got more. Once I came up with the poison, I learned how long it takes to kill a person and freeze them up. Exactly ten minutes."

"So you backtracked Connie's movements?" Pickett asked, smiling.

Robin always had a way of being ahead of puzzles like this one, one of the many things Pickett loved about her.

Robin nodded. "Take a look at this. The detectives on the case originally had pulled all surveillance footage since from what she was carrying they knew exactly what stores she had been in."

Robin started an image of Connie just leaving a women's clothing store, her two bags balanced, one in each hand.

A man in his thirties, dark brown hair, glasses, bumped into her, excused himself, and went on into the store.

"Exactly ten minutes from the moment she stopped on the sidewalk," Robin said.

"And tell me you know who that man is?" Sarge asked a half second before Pickett could ask the same thing.

"His name is Preston Barker. It seems Connie's husband Jake had a secret. He was gay and meeting Preston on the side."

"And Connie had all the money, right?" Pickett asked

"All of it," Robin said, nodding. "And Preston was working as a pharmacist, so he would know rare poisons like this one."

"Did the detectives at the time interview him?" Pickett asked.

"They didn't know he existed," Robin said. "Jake was deep, deep, deep in the closet. But Preston and Jake are now married and living happily on Connie's money."

"Not for much longer," Sarge said.

Pickett could only agree to that with a smile.

"We have enough evidence to actually get an arrest on this?" Pickett asked.

"The tests will find the traces of the drug that killed her and its time to take effect. I am sure there is evidence of him ordering the poison somewhere, and that film will cinch the deal," Robin said.

"Got a hunch good old Jake will roll on Preston, no pun intended, when faced with first-degree murder charges."

Pickett was certain he was right.

She looked at Robin, then at Sarge. "I think Robin should make the call on this one since she did all the work."

"Hey, I sat here and ate breakfast," Sarge said, smiling. "I should get credit for that at least."

Robin laughed. "Pickett, give him credit, would you?"

"Later tonight he'll get what's coming to him."

"Do I get extra credit?" Sarge asked, smiling.

"Only if you are a very, very good detective," Pickett said, laughing at the man she loved.

Robin waved her hand in the air. "More information than I needed."

Robin grabbed her phone to set up an appointment with one of the active detectives who could take this case and make sure all the details were in place for an arrest.

"In celebration of Robin solving this one," Pickett said to Sarge, "I'm going for desert."

"Let me guess... bread pudding?" Sarge asked, smiling.

"Damn you are a good detective," Pickett said. "That might be even more extra credit tonight."

Pickett leaned over and kissed Sarge and he kissed her back.

"Would you two get a room," Robin said, shaking her head.

"No," Pickett said, standing and pulling Sarge to his feet. "But we will get some bread pudding."

"I'm going to need the energy," Sarge said.

All Robin did was groan and that made Pickett laugh all the way across the dining room.

DEAD WOMAN WALKING
A SKY TATE STORY
DEAN WESLEY SMITH

ONE

She sat tucked in the back corner of the small restaurant, not really hiding against the yellow-colored walls or protected by the too-loud oldies music. She had her brown hair tied up on the top of her head and secured by barrettes of polished, handmade wood. Her tank top barely hid her sports bra and her sandals tapped a nervous energy on the brown tile floor under the table.

I could tell the fricking instant I walked through the large glass front door of Benny's Diner that out of the twenty others in the place, she was my client and I was in trouble. She had the look of the almost-dead about her and I doubted I would be able to save her. And I was the best superhero detective there was. If I couldn't save her, no one could.

I walked up to her and stuck out my hand. "Sky Tate. Best Woman Detective In the Business. I understand you are looking for me."

As with most new clients, she looked at me like I had lost a bolt.

I didn't wear what most young women in Las Vegas wore. I always had on the standard private detective trench coat, gray and slightly wrinkled, a gray felt fedora, and gray slacks with loafers. A white blouse peeked out from under the trench coat.

In the hot summer months of Las Vegas, I knew what I looked like and flat didn't care. I liked how I looked. And weirdly enough, the trench coat kept me cooler at times.

And sometimes hid that I was a woman, which played as an advantage when I wanted it to. I also kept my long brown hair tied up like a kidnapped prisoner and hidden under the fedora.

My face was long and very thin and my nose looked more like a beak than a nose with the tip turned down. Gave me the appearance I was looking down my nose disdainfully at a person I was talking with, and sometimes I actually was.

Not sometimes. Most times.

Screw it. All the time.

She tentatively reached out and took my hand and I instantly knew what the problem was and why she was almost dead. Her cheating bastard of a husband, whom she had left two years ago, was stalking her. And she had no doubt that at any moment he would kill her. The guy liked his guns.

I had no doubt he would do it either. She was almost

dead. Just the smell of it damn near covered the greasy hamburger smell coming from the kitchen.

Yeah, I got all that through her handshake. One of my many superpowers.

"Melissa Harding," she said, nodding.

I sat down and faced her across the table, looking into her brown eyes. She was terrified. And clearly feeling lost.

"So tell me about your ex and why he wants to kill you?"

She jerked back and stared at me, her eyes wide.

I tried to smile, but my smiles usually came across as smirks and I was sure that was what happened this time.

"I'm a detective," I said. "I know things."

That was my line I gave people and for some reason they just nodded to that. Most people thought all detectives had superpowers, but in reality most didn't. I don't think there were more than a few hundred of us around the entire country and maybe a few thousand more around the world. We are a small area of the superpower world, where every business and craft and hobby has superheroes.

And that's not counting all the damn gods of things. There were a shitload of gods, more than I could ever keep track of, that was for sure. I reported to Matt, one of the gods of detectives. He was a squirrelly guy, real short, with a pretend mustache. I have no idea who he reported to. More than likely Lady Luck herself. Never met her, actually afraid to, honestly.

And most things didn't scare me. In fact, damn near nothing but Lady Luck herself scared me.

So for the next fifteen minutes I heard about Melissa's bastard of an ex-husband, Ed. She had left him after she caught him cheating and settled in court that she wanted really nothing from him. She had the good job, the good car, and friends. He was a loser who couldn't hold a job and still drove a Rambler station wagon. I didn't know there was a Rambler left on the roads. That was the only thing she said that actually surprised me.

Seems after good-for-nothing Ed lost his last job, he blamed Melissa. Standard for losers.

And started demanding money from her. Also standard.

And threatened her. He was three-for-three in the cliché world.

Melissa had done all the right things, including getting an injunction against him to keep him away.

The last straw was when she had had him arrested for violating the injunction. He was getting out tomorrow and I had no doubt that in twelve hours, after Ed drank his courage, Melissa would be dead. Ed would then go back to jail for a very long time, but that would do dear old Melissa no good at all.

Melissa could do two things to solve this problem. Run and start a new life. She would always be looking over her shoulder, but it was an option. Many, many very smart women and men did exactly that to get away from abusive spouses.

Or the other option was to take out Ed before he could get to her. I was fairly certain that was why she had hired me. Now, I didn't kill people, but I could be a fine witness to the fact that it was self-defense.

"So what do you want from me exactly?" I asked Melissa

when she finally stopped talking and dried the last of her tears.

"Can you help me?"

"Help you find a new place to live and a new name or help you stop Ed tomorrow night when he comes calling drunk to kill you for sticking him in prison?"

"The second one," she said.

"I can do that," I said. "My retainer is five hundred dollars up front and I'll bill you for the rest."

I didn't want to tell her that I got the money up front just in case Ed turned out to be a little smarter than I had figured him for. Getting promised money out of an estate was always a pain. And even superheroes had to eat and pay mortgage payments. Although, I must admit, it had been decades and decades since I had actually needed money. In my almost two hundred years of doing this job as a superhero, only the first few years had I actually worked because I needed the cash.

Now I just charged clients because they wouldn't appreciate my work if I didn't.

She paid me with five folded one-hundred-dollar bills she had tucked to one side of her purse. She had been warned what I would cost. Made it simpler.

I nodded and tucked the money into a pocket of the trench coat, then stood.

"I will be at your house tomorrow evening around five," I said. "Don't worry, we'll get this stopped."

Before she could say anything, I turned and headed out the door, my trench coat flapping like a cape behind me as I walked. I liked that cape aspect. After all, I was a superhero.

. . .

TWO

Even though I hadn't told Melissa I would, I kept on eye on Ed just about every moment of the day He stayed on cliché, getting out and heading to his favorite bar where he proceeded to get more and more drunk and more and more angry.

Right on schedule. I could have set my watch by this jerk.

His next stop after the bar was to his ratty-ass apartment to get a gun. Just to be sure that nothing bad happened to my client, I had gone into his place the night before and made sure that none of his guns would actually fire. He would be too drunk to tell.

I had also planted a few cameras around so I sat in my wonderful Cadillac with the air conditioner going and watched on my laptop as he took one of his handguns, loaded a clip into it and pulled a shell into the chamber.

Then he stuck it down the front of his pants. Damn if I had known he was going to do that, I would have made the trigger misfire and shoot off his obviously tiny dick. Damn, that would have been fun to watch. I missed an opportunity there, that was for sure.

As he headed out of his apartment, I checked my watch. Quarter to five. Right smack on time.

I pulled out my cell phone and called a superhero friend I had on the Las Vegas police force.

"Got a drunk with a gun headed to kill an ex-wife," I said. "Could use a little help."

Then I gave my friend Melissa's address and the make of Ed's car.

"There's still a Rambler on the road?" my friend asked.

"Station wagon," I said.

"No shit," my friend said and hung up laughing.

I pulled out ahead of good old Ed in his Rambler station wagon. And made it to Melissa's house just as two cop cars with lights flashing pulled up just behind Ed's Rambler.

I went up to the house and knocked and Melissa let me in.

I am convinced Ed thought I was a guy making a move on his ex-wife, whom he still thought of as his property.

At least that was what I hoped he would think.

He came out of the car, gun drawn, drunk and angry as could be expected from such a lowlife.

I shoved Melissa inside and on the ground behind her couch as the police shouted for Ed to stop and put the gun down.

I looked back through the open front door as Ed turned at the four cops like he was an actor under the bright light of the streetlight. No doubt the cops had their body and dashboard cams running.

Ed, always the rocket scientist, raised his gun and aimed it at them and tried to fire. More than likely in his pea-brain, he thought he was in the Wild West and was defending his ranch.

There were two clear clicks in the night air before the four cops opened fire and Ed went right to the ground.

Problem solved.

Case solved.

I turned and helped Melissa to her feet. Her face was completely white and her entire body was shaking.

"What happened?" Melissa asked as I walked her slowly to the door.

"Ed tried to kill some cops," I said. "It didn't turn out well for him."

At that point one of the cops reached Ed and kicked the gun away slightly out of Ed's reach. Then another cop touched Ed's throat for a pulse.

From what I could tell, that would find negative results since there was a pretty good-sized hole in Ed's forehead.

"Is he dead?" Melissa asked.

"Dead as any cliché gets," I said.

I took off my trench coat and fedora and put them over the back of a nearby chair, then let my hair down.

Then I moved over beside her and she just leaned against me. We stood there in the front door watching the police go through their routines, leaving dear old dead Ed right there on the front lawn.

Then Melissa put her arm around me and gave me a slight hug, looking up at me with those puppy-dog brown eyes of hers.

"Thank you."

I gave her a nod and a slight hug back.

I didn't mind at all. Once you took the almost-dead smell and look away, Melissa was a nice-looking woman. And I was not only a superhero detective, I was pretty good at comforting good-looking women in times of need.

IT'S MY PARTY
A BRYANT STREET STORY

DEAN WESLEY SMITH

Julie Reinhart stepped back from the decorated living room of her three-bedroom home on Bryant Street and studied what she had just completed. Along the blinds over the front window looking out at the sunny day and the green lawns beyond, she had hung streamers of bright blue and orange and green. And numbers of balloons, mostly red and orange and yellow, hung from the blinds.

On the mantel of the stone fireplace, she had a huge sign that said "Happy Birthday" in hand-drawn and colorful letters. And she had balloons everywhere of all colors, tied with colorful ribbons and hanging from the bookshelves on both sides of the couch.

It had taken her all morning to blow up all those balloons, but it had been worth it, since they really gave the room a festive feel.

She had "Happy Birthday" colored napkins scattered on

the coffee tables and end tables giving the entire room the final blast of celebration colors.

"Perfect," she said to herself and then turned back to the similarly decorated dining room. She had hung a big hand-lettered sign on the sliding door out to the backyard. The sign read, "Happy 30th!!!"

She had outdone herself this year, she knew it without a doubt. But her wonderful husband, Frank, deserved the best and he was going to love this, with all his friends showing up to help him celebrate. A guy didn't turn thirty that often, after all.

She checked the fridge to make sure there were enough beer and other beverages, and enough extra ice, to last. There was.

And the cupboards were stuffed with chips and pretzels and other snacks, including cans of peanuts. She didn't need to get those out until people started showing up.

She headed down the hallway to their master bedroom where she changed into her party dress and made sure her long brown hair was combed and tied back like Frank liked it.

Then she glanced at her watch. Ten minutes until five. The guests should start arriving at any point now and Frank would be here at five thirty, just as he was every night.

She went back out into the kitchen, looked around at everything once more and then smiled. She had done well

The house looked like a party.

She sat down at the kitchen table, feeling tired. Surprisingly tired. And empty.

She put her head down on her arm and closed her eyes. Maybe she could just rest until the first guest knocked.

Two hours later she awoke with a start. She had been drooling slightly on her arm and it was asleep and tingling.

She glanced around at all the decorations, then glanced at her watch. Seven in the evening and it was nearing dusk outside.

She nodded to herself and turned on the lights in the dining room and a couple of the lamps in the living room. Then with the end of a safety pin, she popped all the balloons along the front window, took off the colorful decorations and pulled the blinds closed.

In thirty minutes she had all the decorations down and in garbage bags and her living room and dining room back to their normal pristine condition.

She stored the two signs in the garage next to her new Lexus. She would put them in the attic above the garage tomorrow.

She put the bags of decorations in the garbage. Then she went back inside and moved the bags of chips and beer into the pantry. Then she changed out of her party dress into her kick-around-the-house sweatpants and light sweatshirt, and made herself a tuna salad to go along with a glass of red wine.

She sat at the dining table eating slowly and savoring the wine.

Then at five minutes until eight, she raised the glass into the air and said simply, "It would have been a great party, Frank. Always love you."

Then as she was cleaning up her dishes from dinner, the

door from the garage opened and the love of her life, Cynthia Davis, came in.

Cynthia was dressed in her office clothes, her long blond hair pulled back, and a black briefcase that matched her black jacket and slacks was in her hand.

Cynthia came up behind Julie at the sink and hugged her from behind. Then as Cynthia moved to put her brief- case on the dining room table, she asked, "How was the party?"

"Just like every year," Julie said as she finished up putting her dishes in the dishwasher. "It would have been a great party."

"You think it is still helping?" Cynthia asked, leaning against the table and looking at Julie with a worried expression.

"I honestly don't know if it's helping like it did twenty years ago," Julie said. "But it's not hurting either. And gives me a few hours to remember Frank each year on his birth- day. I honestly don't think much about him the rest of the year anymore. Kind of sad, actually."

Cynthia nodded. "I just worry that it keeps that horrible night fresh as well."

Julie shook her head. "I don't think about what actually happened that night. I don't even dream about getting that call anymore from the police and seeing the pictures of the accident. That part is all tucked away in the past. Staging the party just helps me remember how much I cared about him."

"And that is valuable," Cynthia said. "And I miss him as well."

"How did your remembrance go?" Julie asked.

"I rented the same room we used that afternoon, like always," Cynthia said. "After twenty years it is getting a little run down."

"I bet," Julie said.

"I ordered two glasses of champagne just as Frank and I did that afternoon, and just took my clothes off and stretched out on the bed to remember him. I fell asleep just as I do every year, now."

"Yeah, I fell asleep at the table again," Julie said. "Does it still help you?"

"More of what you said. It helps me remember him once a year. Like you, I don't think about him otherwise. And yes, that is sad."

"Too bad he didn't make it to the party," Cynthia said. "It would have been so much fun to see his face after everyone left and you and I were in the bedroom together, naked."

Julie laughed. "Yeah, that would have been a birthday to remember. He just had no idea how good that birthday party was going to be."

"So do we still do this every year to mourn him or celebrate him bringing us together without even knowing he was doing that?"

Julie just smiled and went over to Cynthia and hugged her. "I think it's a little mourning of a man we both loved, but lately it has become a celebration of you and me in my mind."

"Mine too," Cynthia said. "So you think the guests would all be gone by now from the party?"

"I do," Julie said, smiling.

"So let's go get naked together in that big bed and show Frank what he missed by hitting that truck on his way from me to you."

"Think he can see us?" Julie asked, laughing as they headed down the hall.

"Oh, I really hope so," Cynthia said, also laughing.

"If he can see us, it will serve him right," Julie said, "for him having an affair with the love of my life."

"Yeah, that will teach him," Cynthia said. "At least for his next life."

"You think?" Julie asked.

Cynthia pretended to consider the question, then laughed and shook her head. "Frank? Not a chance."

"So true," Julie said as she watched Cynthia get undressed. "But that night, you got to admit, it would have been a hell of a party."

"And it will be tonight," Cynthia said, "if you ever get out of those clothes."

LOST CANYON
A THUNDER MOUNTAIN STORY
DEAN WESLEY SMITH

ONE

Randall Martin, just Martin to his friends, eased his gray mare Susie forward slowly with a pat on her neck, keeping her calm and not hurrying over the rocky creek bed. It was late enough in the summer that no real water was flowing, but clearly from the looks of the canyon walls around him, the water in here would be another matter in the spring. It looked like it would be fast and deep and fill the entire passage.

Now the water was nothing more than puddles that trickled from one to the other.

He knew that ahead of him was a steep-walled canyon that had a nice-looking meadow, a beautiful twisting stream, and a small waterfall over the rock cliffs on the high side. It was called Lost Canyon on the satellite maps, but he could find nothing in history that gave the canyon that name.

It seemed like every little nook and cranny in these central Idaho Mountains had a name that was documented in one way or another to some event or reason or another.

But for Lost Canyon, he could find no reason for the name, other than it was hidden from the main Monumental Creek drainage behind him, and seemingly impossible to find. He had known exactly where it was and he had trouble finding it earlier.

No record of who found it originally and who gave it the name Lost Canyon.

Back in 2023 he had even flown a drone over the canyon. It was there. It existed, but now he was going to step foot in it in 1903.

His focus over the last numbers of years as a researcher was to visit all the "lost" places in Idaho, both in the past and in the present. Luckily, he could do that because he could spend time in the past thanks to the Historical Institute.

And he had done just that, researching the reasons why, say, Lost Meadow was named that because of a lost packer in 1923 getting lost in the heavy tall grass of the meadow. Or five Lost Creeks had the name because at one point or another they dove underground and vanished.

There were twelve official "Lost" places in Idaho and he had visited them all in first the past and then in his present in 2023. He had written about them all, giving perspective and color from the past and the present and the history of each place.

Except for Lost Canyon. That was last on his list and now in July of 1903 he was about to find it. Then he had to find out who named it and why before he could visit it in his present and finish up his book.

In 1903, about two miles up Monumental Creek, the boom mining town of Roosevelt was in full growth and active and alive. The town and most of this region would die in six years, covered by water backed up behind a huge mudslide. That's why he had left this one to the last in his research because the history of this entire area was rich. And that would be a great addition to his book *The Lost Places of Idaho*.

In essence, this entire area of Idaho was a lost place, almost forgotten in time.

He didn't expect to sell many copies, but the book would be a great addition to libraries, gift shops, and historical centers around the West. Especially with the pictures he had been managing to get.

Even though now the sun was almost directly overhead, Martin got little light in this narrow canyon leading up to Lost Canyon. In a couple places he wondered if he could even turn Susie around, it was so narrow.

The canyon actually smelled of mold and a lot of moss grew on the rock walls, something that you didn't often see at this altitude in the Idaho Mountains. No plants grew at all, more than likely scrubbed away every year by the fast and angry water of the snowmelt.

Finally, as it got steeper, he dismounted and picked his way forward, leading Susie slowly over the rocks until finally he could see that the narrow canyon widened out into bright sunlight.

Five minutes later, as Martin and Susie reached the top,

it was like coming from a dark hallway directly into the bright sunlight of an intense green yard.

"Wow," was all he could think to say.

TWO

Martin climbed back into the saddle and moved forward through the deep grass slowly. It was already starting to turn brown and by the first snowfall in late September, it would be completely brown.

Rock walls towered over the valley on all sides, and the only thing left of the waterfall at the head of the valley was a slight mist that broke into rainbows. It had maybe enough flow to fill a pan for boiling, but even that would take a minute.

The massive mountains of Central Idaho towered over the valley, making it feel more like the bottom of a bowl instead of an actual valley. The entire valley itself was maybe a football field wide and three fields long. Big enough to be comfortable, but small enough to easily explore.

So the place was even more beautiful than he had imagined and the slight breeze coming down off those high peaks kept the grass moving and the middle-of-the-day air cooler.

He decided to stay to the right and just work his way around the valley, looking for any sign that anyone else had been here before him. There had to be a reason this was called "Lost Canyon." That meant about this time in history someone else had found it and named it and the name stuck.

More than likely someone managed to find this place,

got in here, then tried to tell someone else how to get in here and they couldn't find it, so they called it "Lost Canyon."

Martin, for the book, just needed to find out who.

He was all the way up the right side when a tied-up horse grazing on grass surprised him. It was behind a slight rise and well-hidden from anyone coming in the valley. In fact, if he hadn't been going along the cliffs on the right, he never would have seen it.

He immediately pulled out his saddle rifle and silently levered a shell into the chamber, then he slid it back into is sling.

"Hello!" he shouted, his voice echoing off the walls. "Just exploring."

A woman's voice came back strong. "Take that shell back out of the chamber on your rifle and I might believe you."

He glanced around, but couldn't see her hiding place or her camp. So he raised his hands in surrender, then pulled out his rifle and opened the lever and took out the shell and put it in his pocket, then put the gun back in the sling.

He heard a woman's laugh. "You know, Mr. Randall Martin, that is not how a person from this time period would have done that."

He was so shocked he jerked backwards and Susie protested.

At that moment, a stunningly beautiful woman came out from behind a boulder, put her pistol away in her holster, and walked toward him through the knee-high grass, smiling.

She looked to be about his height at five-ten, had long brown hair pulled back and tied under a wide-brimmed hat.

She had on women-of-means riding pants and blouse and jacket, but since she knew him, clearly she was another traveler.

But one he didn't recognize and he knew, without a doubt, if he had met her before, in any time period, he would have remembered.

He dismounted and turned to greet her.

"Patricia Freed," she said, "traveler from 2024. Nice to meet you, finally."

"2023." That was all he could think to say as she reached out to shake his hand and he was drawn into her deep green eyes.

"I know," she said, clearly not wanting to let go of his hand any more than he wanted her to let go. "Everyone calls me Freed. I hate Patricia."

"Martin," he said, smiling. "Not real fond of Randall."

Finally she let go of his hand and he felt disappointed.

"It's your book about lost places in Idaho that led me to find this valley," she said. "Great book, by the way. And wow did you describe this place well."

"Haven't finished it yet," he said.

She laughed. "You will and it will be great."

"Thank you," he said, wanting to ask her if he had solved the riddle about who named the place, but not really wanting to know at the same time.

She smiled. "I was hoping this summer in 1903 would be the time you visited this place. That way I would get a chance to meet you."

He was very flattered that she wanted to meet him. "How long have you been camped here?" he asked.

"About a week," she said, indicating that he should put Susie on the line with her horse. "Bring your saddlebag and I'll show you my camp and then what kept me here for a week and more than likely longer."

As he got Susie taken care of, Freed told him about her passion of writing about the details of women traveling and camping in the Old West. She had already done books about women-of-means traveling and was working on poorer women and how they managed.

"How many years have you been traveling into the past?" he asked.

"2024 time, less than five months," she said, "but actual living time, about a thousand years, maybe a little more."

"Wow, you got me by about five hundred years," he said. Then shook his head, realizing what he was saying.

She just laughed. "Sounds very weird from my old college professor days."

"Yeah, mine too," he said.

THREE

After he got Susie settled in, he carried his saddlebag and supply bag around a boulder, following Freed to where she had a really nice camp set up.

She had cut back any grass out of the flat area and had a small fire ring with a small fire going, plus a tent pitched to one side of the fire. The site was far enough away from the cliff to avoid any random rock fall, yet behind the boulders to give her a protected view of the entire valley and the entrance.

"Nice," he said. "Natural campsite. Find any evidence that someone had been here before you?"

"Nothing out here," she said. "But that's what I want to show you. You bring a flashlight with you?"

"Two of them disguised as pencils," he said. "And a modern disguised lantern that will toss out a lot of light if turned up."

"Good," she said. "Grab the lantern and the flashlight and let's go."

He did as she said and then followed her toward the waterfall.

The air cooled near the small falls, but not by much. This time of the summer there just wasn't a lot of water flowing.

She went behind a boulder that a lot of the time the water hit and then ducked into a cave there.

He clicked on the lantern after ten paces or so and then the cave turned to the right and his light illuminated a horror show.

Five human skeletons bundled up in as many clothes as they seemed to be able to wear sat against the back of the cave. Three to one side just were slumped over, the two in the center of the cave had bullet holes in the skulls and their guns were either in their laps or beside them.

Skeletons of two horses were off to the left and looked like they had been butchered for meat at one time.

Martin felt like he wanted to be sick. The smell was of a moldy old house and the air was colder than outside. He took a deep breath and steadied his nerves. He'd seen a lot of dead people before in his travels. Just not a scene like this.

Freed took the lantern from Martin and sat it in the middle of the small cave on what looked to have been a fire pit. Then she went over to the three on the far right.

"I am betting these three died first," she said. "More than likely just froze to death, or having a fire in here killed them from smoke or lack of oxygen when the snowfall outside covered the entrance."

She pointed to the two in the middle. "Killed themselves when they realized there was no hope. More than likely right about the time those three died."

Martin made himself look closer. He couldn't tell the time period exactly from their clothing, but clearly they had been in here for a good ten years, at least. There were not a lot of miners in this area until just three years ago, so this group was ahead of its time for some reason.

He looked over a Freed. "1890s?"

She nodded. "Early. Two of these on the right are women, although you can't tell with that many clothes stacked on them, some of them men's clothes to try to keep them warmer, more than likely. So a party with two women and three men."

"Might have been larger when they started and lost a few along the way," Martin said. "There should be records of a group this big vanishing."

Freed nodded. "And if we can pinpoint through research when they vanished, we can come back at that time and stop them. Clearly they got surprised by a snowstorm in the early fall and couldn't get out down that entrance."

Martin nodded. "That would save them in an unlimited number of timelines, that's for sure. I can have Director Parks have the computers in the future calculate the impact of us rescuing that many people, make sure we don't screw something up royally."

Freed nodded. "Really good idea."

Freed and Martin studied the bodies and the entire scene for a few more minutes, then headed back out into the evening sun.

Martin had never been so glad to be back out in the open in his memory.

FOUR

Martin pitched his tent and Freed made them some outstanding coffee, the best he had tasted back in the past. She admitted she always brought a bag of premium coffee with her from the future that usually lasted for six months of any trip into the past.

He thanked her and said he was honored to be able to share her coffee. And he was.

They got the fire going a little more and enough wood to last through the night, then they rolled over a few rocks to sit on. By this time the valley was in almost darkness, even though the sun was still shining on the top peaks of the mountains, slowly turning them pink.

Martin set up his lantern so it felt like almost daylight around the camp and the lantern also kept back any night bugs.

Then Martin made dinner with trout that he had caught earlier in the day before coming up into the valley. He added in a couple of baked potatoes that he had brought back with him on this trip.

It turned out to be a wonderful dinner, and he loved talking with Freed. They seemed to match in so many ways. And more importantly, she laughed easily.

In fairly quick order over one dinner, he felt like he had known her for years. And attracted to her didn't begin to describe how he was feeling.

So at one point he asked her, "You married?"

"Nope," she said. "Came close a few times before the Institute, but could just never pull the trigger."

"So you've been traveling alone all thousand plus of those years?"

"Nope," she said. "Traveled for about eight hundred years with my best friend, Susan Depoe. She and I were both shown the caverns and invited into traveling in other time-lines at the same time. Her specialty and the books she writes are about marriage at the turn of the nineteenth century. She dove into the romance of the marriages and the horror of them at the same time."

"What happened?" Martin asked.

"She met a guy in Kansas City and fell in love and stayed there with him," Freed said.

"A non-traveler?" Martin asked. He had been attracted to women who were non-travelers at times, but just not enough to do anything about it.

Freed nodded. "I went back to the Institute early and she stayed with him. Of course, we both got back at the same time, touching the same box, even though she had lived with him and died of old age at the age of eighty-seven."

"She turned around and went back to do it again, didn't she?" Marin asked.

Freed again nodded. "I had a book to write and wanted to stay in 2023 and write in my condo, so she went back ten minutes later to a different timeline and met him again and married him again and again lived to eighty-seven."

"Wow," Martin said, trying to imagine that.

"She told me that while I was still getting changed in the locker room. Said she was going back again and not to worry about her."

"How long?" Martin asked.

"It's been two months in 2023 time," Freed said, "and as far as I know she is still looping like that. She has more than likely lived so many hundreds of centuries now with that man, she wouldn't even remember me. I know after a week I didn't hear from her when she returned."

"I'm so sorry," Martin said. "Not easy to lose a friend like that."

"I've lived and traveled on my own now for three hundred years and her memory is fading with me as well. So how about you? Married?"

"Was once," Martin said, "back when I was teaching in Oregon. But got into the Institute to do research and wife at the time had no desire to move to Boise. She just loved Eugene. Marriage was over anyway, for the most part. So we got a divorce and off I went to research for a year in Boise and then got introduced to the caverns."

"Been traveling alone the entire time?" Freed asked.

"So far," Martin said. "I've been out now over five hundred years and I'm starting to forget what my ex-wife even looked like, even though for her only a few months have passed. I'm betting she's wondering why I haven't called. We tried to stay friends."

"So what are we going to do about those poor folks, exactly?" Freed asked, pointing in the direction of the cave.

"I like your idea about trying to rescue them," Martin said. "So we figure that out first. When exactly do you return from this trip?"

"March nineteenth, 2024," Freed said. "Two in the afternoon if I remember right."

"Fantastic," Martin said. "I get back from this the last of August 2023. So I go back and spend a few months finishing this book and getting it out so you can read it so that you come back here now and we can meet."

"Good idea," she said, laughing. "Yes, please finish the book."

"I have to clear up some personal stuff in our present time as well that I have been meaning to do, then the research on these poor folks with the Institute big computers, and I'll meet you when you get back in the big cavern. I'll have sandwiches waiting at the bar. We'll be on the same schedule at that point."

"You'd do that?" she asked.

"Just seven months," he said, shrugging. "Going to take a while to finish the book and then a while to research who those five are in there and see if it is even possible for us to rescue them. So no problem for me at all. More than likely I would spend that time out of traveling timelines anyway.

Besides, if I get the lost book done, I have to come up with another project to research and get some basics on that done."

"And if we can or can't rescue them," Freed asked, smiling at him. "You up for doing some traveling together? I would sure love it."

"I would love that as well," Martin said, smiling back.

"You know," she said. "At times we would have to travel as a married couple. Customs, you know."

"Easier," Martin said, nodding.

"So before I pretend to be your wife," she said, looking serious, "I need to know how you are in bed."

"Been a few hundred years," he said. "But don't think I've lost the memory of how to do that. How about you?"

"Three hundred and ten years and five months," she said. "But who's counting? So I have a hunch we need to do some testing to see what we have or haven't forgotten."

"Research," he said, smiling.

"We're both good at research," she said, then laughed.

He took her hand and helped her to her feet and into his arms.

And for two people who claimed they could barely remember what to do, they did just fine and barely made it to her tent.

The first time. After all, they had a lot of years of research to catch up on.

A Golden Dream
A Jukebox Story
DEAN WESLEY SMITH

She came through the heavy front door of the old hotel with a face as young as yesterday. And for just a moment the stale piss smell of the thick air, the stained and faded linoleum floors, the peeling paint on the smoke-yellowed walls were forgotten by the three of us in the front foyer.

For just a moment we forgot our long, dull days of old men's boredom, moving like zombies from our rooms to the sitting room with the television, to the front stoop, back to the sitting room, then back to our rooms, punctuated only by a silent lunch and an even more silent dinner in the small kitchen.

Mitchel, Hank and me. When she came through that door, we forgot we were three corpses too damn old to just lie down and be done with it. We forgot we were the last residents of The Golden Dream Hotel for men. We even forgot it was Christmas Eve.

A year ago, crusty Jamison bought the old hotel from a development agency. We all had an understanding that the four of us would be able to live in the hotel until we all died. Jamison died the next month at the age of sixty-eight, giving me the hotel in his will. Now all the three of us did was sit around and wonder who would be next. But no one talked about it. Since I am the youngest at sixty-six, I figured I would have the longest to wait. Since I owned the place that sort of made sense.

And now, as she stood there on this cold winter evening, her short, perfect-skinned nose wrinkling at the smell of old age, even the thought of dying was forgotten.

She blinked in the dim light and then focused on the old black and white television flickering in the corner. I could see she had bright, large eyes, thick eyebrows, and a full mouth. The kind of mouth I remembered that Alice had back what seemed like a million years ago. Alice was my first love, my first sexual partner, my first real girlfriend. We never married and I always wondered why.

The young women brushed a long, slender hand against her nose, then straightened her shoulders as if she were going to face a firing squad. She stepped toward the three of us. Her high heels clicked on the linoleum floor and I wondered when that floor had last felt the steps of a woman.

"Excuse me," she said. Her clear, soft voice seemed to fill the old hotel with life. She stopped and glanced around, as if startled by the sound of her own words. "I'm . . . I am looking for a Mister Fred Thorpe."

I thought I was going to swallow my teeth. She was looking for me, as if I actually existed to someone outside of these walls besides the social security department. "That's me," I said, sort of waving a hand in her direction. My voice sounded really odd following hers.

She seemed relieved and took another step toward me. "Would it be possible for us to talk?"

I shrugged and pointed to the vacant chair that had been Jamison's.

She shook her head. "In private, if you don't mind."

Again, I shrugged and without looking at the others pushed myself up from my chair in the most dignified manner I had managed in years. I nodded toward the hall that led past the old front desk cage. "We can talk back in the kitchen."

She said fine and I shuffled ahead of her distinct and firm footsteps down the hall and into the kitchen.

After we were both settled at the old wood table, she took a deep breath. She started out saying that I wasn't going to believe her.

She was right.

I didn't.

The old Wurlitzer jukebox sat like a king at the end of the oak bar in the Garden Lounge. Radley Stout, the owner of the Garden, polished the old jukebox every week and the chrome and glass sparkled as if the machine had a life and energy of its own. Above the jukebox was a polished wood and glass case that held four drinking glasses with the old Garden Lounge logo and a name etched on each. *Carl, Dave, Jess,* and *Fred.*

Except for Christmas Eve, the jukebox was always unplugged and the glass case always locked.

The Garden Lounge was a local, quiet bar. It had old-styled booths, a hundred regular customers and enough atmosphere in plants and low lighting that everyone felt safe when they came in. Radley Stout had owned the bar for eleven years and for ten Christmas Eves he had plugged in the jukebox. Tonight was to be the eleventh and he hoped it would be something special.

T he kitchen smelled of the hot-dogs we had had for lunch and the dirty pan and plates were still in the sink. I couldn't remember if it had been my turn to do dishes or Hank's. It was Christmas Eve. What did it matter?

"My name is Sandy Reeves," the good-looking young woman said to me across the kitchen table. "I am a private investigator and I was hired to find you by a Mr. Radley Stout."

I laughed and leaned toward the woman who looked like she might be barely old enough to be out of high school. "Right. So what is the gimmick? What are you selling?"

She didn't seem bothered by my rude question at all. Calmly, she reached into her large purse and pulled out a small, black pistol. With a thump she placed it on the table between us. "I have a permit for that," she said, smiling slightly.

All I could do was stare at the black gun while she pulled her wallet out of her purse, flipped it open, and slid it across the table at me. Then she scooped the gun back into her purse.

Open in front of me was her driver's license and her private investigator's license from the state. I glanced at her birth date. She was twenty-six. At lot younger than any child Alice and I might have had. I nodded and slid her wallet back at her. "So what does this Mr. Stout want from me?"

She sort of shrugged. "Actually, I am not exactly sure. He owns a place called the Garden Lounge, down on Main. He said he just wanted to buy you a Christmas Eve drink."

"That's all?" I shook my head. "He hired a private investigator to find me to buy me a drink?"

She nodded, almost looking embarrassed. "I am just supposed to take you down to the Garden Lounge. And Mr. Stout gave me strict instructions to not force you in any way. He knows nothing about how you are living or even that you are alive. So are you interested in having a drink?"

I glanced at her and then around at the old kitchen and the dishes in the sink. It was Christmas Eve and I had absolutely nothing better to do. "What the hell," I said. "I've always believed that you never look a gift horse in the mouth."

"True," she said. "You just never know when a miracle might happen."

I stared at her, but she only smiled, not explaining at all. Slowly I pushed myself back from the table and stood. "I could use a drink tonight."

She nodded. "So could I."

Jukeboxes, by their very nature, are time machines. Not only do they look as if they belong in another decade, but by playing songs they sometimes take the listeners back to the memories associated with those songs.

The jukebox in the Garden Lounge did a little more than that. It physically took the listener back to their memory from a song. And the listener could be there, inside the listener's younger body, until the song finished.

The listener could also change events that occurred during the time the song was playing. And by changing those events, change the future. That was what made the jukebox so dangerous. That was also the reason the jukebox was never plugged in. When new customers in the Garden asked about the jukebox, Radley Stout just told them it was broken.

Radley Stout, the owner and only bartender of the Garden Lounge, originally saved the old jukebox from the bankruptcy court a good hour before the bank locked up his first bar. For the year he had tried to run the bar the jukebox had sat in the back hall, covered with a blanket and a good inch of dust and grime. It had been just part of the old furniture and things that came with the bar. Almost as a lark he took the jukebox to his garage, hiding it from the bank, figuring that he would fix it up some day.

That day came another year later on a Saturday. He was thinking about buying a second bar and giving the bar business another try. The old jukebox would make a great item to have in the new place if he could get the jukebox to work.

When he opened the jukebox up, he found a lot of sealed boxes and weird looking electronics that seemed far beyond anything needed or standard in an old Wurlitzer jukebox. He studied the insides for a few hours without figuring any of it out. Finally he just dusted everything off, fixed the electrical cord that looked as if someone had ripped it from the back, and plugged the jukebox in.

The jukebox blinked a few times, the colored lights came on, and nothing blew up.

So Radley went in search of a record to play on it. Luck would have it that the only forty-five record Radley owned was an old song he and Jenny had bought. It was *their* song and it reminded him of the night he wanted to ask Jenny to marry him, but hadn't. The next day she went back to college and eventually met another man.

He dug the old record out of his scrapbook, cleaned it off, put it on A-1, and punched the buttons. With the first note the world shifted, his garage disappeared, and he suddenly found himself sitting in his first car with Jenny beside him.

The air of the warm summer evening smelled of mowed grass and Jenny's perfume. Jenny had on her blue shorts and a white blouse. Her light brown hair was pulled back and off her face. She was nodding in time with the beat of the song.

And smiling. Night after night for years Radley had remembered, and would remember, that smile.

The seat was hot and sticky under him and his hands seemed to be glued to the steering wheel. The song, *their* song, was on the radio and he stared at the radio for a moment before turning to stare at Jenny. He could not believe this. He could remember all of his older memories and his younger ones, too. He knew exactly that he wanted to ask her to marry him and exactly what his future held because he hadn't.

The thought of that future scared him even more than asking her to marry him.

He sat there, not saying a word, staring at Jenny and her smile until the song ended and he found himself back in his garage. He took a deep shuddering breath and then barely made it to the back door before he threw up.

The next day, after a long night of no sleep, he finally got up the courage to play the record again.

And again he did nothing but sit next to Jenny and stare.

He never played their song again, even though it remained for eleven years as A-1 on the jukebox.

Except on Christmas Eve. On Christmas Eve, the only night he plugged in the jukebox for his friends, he takes that special record off and places it in the safe.

Sandy Reeves, Miss. Private Eye with the Big Black Gun, held the front door of the Garden Lounge open for me to shuffle through. I had passed by the Garden a hundred times and always thought about stopping. Never had. It had just not been the right time. I never expected Christmas Eve to be that right time.

The place smelled of smoke and green plants and I immediately felt at home. Much more than at the hotel. Empty tables cluttered the center of the room and booths filled both side walls. Christmas candles were lit on every table. An old-looking polished-wood bar filled the wall opposite the front door and three men sat on stools near the bar's center with their backs to the door. They were the only three customers. A medium-sized man in a white apron was standing behind the bar and when I came through the door he looked up and said, "Holy shit."

The three men at the bar turned around as if pulled by the same string and the bartender put a glass on the bar and headed around the end to meet me.

He dodged around a few tables with ease and we met in the middle of the bar. He grabbed my hand and shook it as if we were old friends seeing each other again after many years.

I studied his face as he stared at mine. He looked to be in his early fifties, with thinning gray and brown hair. His eyes were green and his smile seemed to fill his entire face. After what seemed like a long moment he took a breath and sort of shook himself. "I'm sorry. I'm Radley Stout. I own this place. And I'm really glad you came."

All I could do was shrug. "Not as if I had much else to do," I said. "And you did offer a free drink."

He just laughed and patted me on the back. "Come on up to the bar. I have a few friends I want you to meet."

I took the stool on the left of the three men and the lady P.I. took the open stool to their right. Radley Stout went around behind the bar as he did the introductions. Dave was the closest to me. He was an airline pilot and his daughter was the private investigator who had found me. Next to him was a big guy named Carl who did construction and beside him was a convict-looking man by the name of Billy. I nodded at them without really noting what any of them looked like, then turned to Radley Stout.

"All right," I said. "Why bring me here?"

Again, Stout laughed. "As you said, to have a Christmas drink. Give me a moment and I will explain." He rummaged in the drawer under the cash register and came up with a key. Then he went to the end of the bar and unlocked a glass case that was mounted on the wall over an old jukebox.

Everyone at the bar watched in silence as he pulled out three of the four glasses that were in there and walked back to the sink in front of us. He rinsed out one of the glasses and held it up for me to see.

It was a crystal-type glass, with the Garden Lounge logo etched near the center and the name Fred over the logo.

"So you needed a Fred to join the toast this year. That it?"

Stout shook his head, sat the glass down on the mat above the ice and started to rinse out the other glasses. "No, actually that glass was yours eleven years ago."

No one else said a word. They either watched Stout wash the glasses, or they stared down into their own drink, as if slightly uneasy about something.

I had never seen that glass before and had never met Stout before or been in this bar before. This gift horse was starting to look like a bust, just as most of them had in my life. I laughed for a short moment and then said, "Not highly likely."

"That's true," Dave said from beside me. "It isn't highly likely. But I think it's true."

I turned to Dave. He was a clean-cut sort, with short hair

and wrinkles on his forehead that cut lines across his tanned skin. "Were you there when I supposedly owned that glass?" I pointed in the direction of Stout and the glass. He had just finished washing out a glass that had the name Dave over the logo.

"In a manner of speaking," Dave said. "I was. But I too do not remember the first time. However, I do remember the second."

I just stared at him for a moment before shaking my head and pushing myself back off my stool. Free drink or not, this was just a little too much. "I knew this entire thing was crazy, but you folks are all a bunch of loonies."

Stout put the third glass on the rubber mat. It had the name Carl etched on it. "Fred. Please just hold on for a moment. I just want to buy you a drink and tell you a story. I know you won't believe me, but what can it hurt? It's Christmas Eve."

Sandy looked down the bar at me and sort of smiled. "I told you that you wouldn't believe this."

I stopped with one hand still holding onto the back of the bar stool and looked down the line of faces staring at me. It seemed clear that everyone wanted me to stay and everyone was taking this craziness very, very seriously. I took a deep breath and let it out in a noisy sigh.

Sandy laughed. "You said never look a gift horse in the mouth. So stop looking."

At that I laughed. "All right. One drink and then Miss Private Investigator there can take me back."

"And a story, too," Stout said. "Don't forget."

I nodded and climbed back up on the stool. "A story too. As long as you don't want me to buy anything."

Stout nodded and smiled. "I promise. Now what would you like to drink?"

I ordered a vodka tonic and for the next half hour the conversation was light and fun. I could feel the heaviness and gloom of the Golden Dream Hotel lifting from my shoulders as everyone laughed and talked and sipped their drinks. There seemed to be a friendship among these people that I had not felt before. A closeness that went far beyond customers in a bar.

I ended up asking for a second drink and Stout refilled my special glass. As he placed it on the napkin in front of me, he said, "I think it's time for the story."

Everyone nodded as Stout went back to stand in front of the well where he was sipping on a glass of eggnog. He leaned against the back bar and raised his glass. "First, a toast. To friends again united."

I drank to the toast not knowing what he was talking about. I assumed the united friend he was talking about was me, but since I had never met the man before, that was going to be some story.

"I had the Garden for just over a year," Stout said. "And I had some really good, regular customers. But four of those customers had become my good friends. Dave. Carl. You, Fred. And Jess." With each name Stout tipped his drink in the person's direction. With the last name he tipped it in the direction of the glass case that still held one glass over the jukebox. I assumed the name on that glass was Jess.

"Fred," Stout said, "you see that jukebox there?" I

nodded as he went on. "Everyone here except you knows just how special that jukebox is. This is the part of the story that you will not believe no matter how hard or well I explain it, so just think of this part as fiction. All right?"

Again, I just nodded, so he went on. "That jukebox can take a person back to a memory. Not just in your mind, but in real flesh and blood. It's a sort of time machine."

"Fiction is right," I said and Stout just held up his hand.

"I discovered how the jukebox worked by accident before I ever opened the Garden. Ten years ago on Christmas Eve I decided I would give my four friends a chance to go back into their pasts. A special Christmas present from me. At that time you were divorced from a woman by the name of Alice and you had two kids."

Suddenly the bar felt very warm. He was assuming that I had been a regular in here for almost a year and once been married to Alice. But I knew that wasn't true. I must have had too much to drink with just two drinks, since it felt as if the room was spinning. How could he know about Alice? And he was saying that I had married her and divorced her after having two kids.

Stout was watching me and after I looked up at him he went on. "You had been divorced from Alice for ten years and you hated her. Completely and totally hated her. It was a standing joke among the five of us. You also had a daughter by the name of Jenny."

"So what happened to her in this crazy world of yours?" I asked. My voice had more anger in it than I could remember.

Stout just shrugged. "I assume she was never born.

When you left here through the jukebox, you said the song reminded you of the night you and Alice first made love. The night you conceived Jenny which forced you two to get married out of high school."

Again the room felt too warm. The night Alice and I first made love was the night her parents were gone to a Christmas party. Right before going over to her house I had gone to the drugstore to buy some rubbers. I remember almost chickening out and then the next thing I knew I had a pack of them in my hand and was heading out of the store. Alice and I always used one every time we made love. She met another guy a year later and left me because she said I was never going to ask her to marry her. She was right. I never did.

"You all right?" Stout asked. I glanced up. He had moved down the bar and was standing in front of me. Everyone was looking at me. I tried to laugh, but it sounded sort of weak, even to me. "You did your research real well. Sandy there must be a really good investigator."

"She's good all right," Stout said and Sandy held up her glass in a thank-you gesture. "But she didn't find any of this information out. I knew about Alice and your divorce because you told us over and over for almost a year."

"So how come I didn't live any of this?"

Stout just sighed. "Because you lived a different life after you changed whatever it was you changed that evening. The only reason I remember you is because I was touching the jukebox when the song ended. For some reason that allows me to remember the old time-line. I remember you being in here, but no one else does." He pointed at the glass in front of me. "I was holding onto the glass, too, when you didn't come back."

"Didn't come back? What do you mean I didn't come back?" Again I was trying to keep the anger out of my voice. But all of this was making me mad. And damn tired.

"You changed something while you were back there. And whatever you changed did not lead you to the Garden again in your new life. At least not until now. If you had not changed anything, you would have come back when the song ended."

Dave was nodding beside me. "That happens every year to me. This year I plan to go back and watch Sandy being born. It will be a Christmas present to myself. Trust me, I will be very careful to not change anything."

I looked at Dave for a moment and then shook my head. "So why bring me back here now? Assuming that all this is true, which I find not likely, why now?"

Now it was Stout's turn to look slightly embarrassed. "I guess I just wanted the old group back together again on Christmas Eve. Selfish, I guess."

"Looks like you didn't pull it off," I said. "What about that other glass? Didn't your P.I. there find the guy?"

Stout took a sip of his eggnog and then looked up at me. I could see the pain in his eyes and the sadness that coated his face. The silence in the bar seemed to fill the room with a thick, heavy feel. "Sandy found him all right," Stout said. "He changed something, also, when he went back that Christmas Eve ten years ago. In the new world he created he was killed by a drunk driver. We found him up in Memorial Cemetery."

I shook my head in disbelief and looked down at my name in the old glass. "So what did I do in the previous life? Be a lawyer or something?"

Stout took a deep breath and then laughed. "Not hardly. You worked for the city. I think you had something to do with streets or something like that."

It was my turn to laugh. "I did that in this life, too. Fancy that. So how come, if that machine can change someone's past, you just don't go back and stop that guy from getting killed?"

Stout shook his head. "I am actually glad it doesn't work that way. Way too much responsibility. No, you can only go back to your own memories. You can't change other people's memories. Or their lives."

Dave stood. "Tell you what, Stout. Plug in that jukebox and I will go watch my daughter being born. That might just give old Fred here a new outlook on life."

Stout shrugged and walked down the length of the bar to the jukebox. Dave downed the last of his drink and joined him.

"You got the record I brought on there?" Dave asked as Stout reached around behind the jukebox and plugged it in. The colored lights flickered for a moment and then held steady. It was a beautiful old Wurlitzer, with the chrome arch, red, green and blue colored lights, and bright red buttons. Inside I could see the disk full of forty-five records all waiting to be played.

"Just punch up old B-4," Stout said and handed Dave a quarter.

Everyone at the bar had swung around on their stools

and were watching intently. I felt uneasy and nervous, even though I knew the only thing that would happen was that the song would start playing and that would be that.

Dave dropped the quarter into the slot, punched the two buttons and then stood back as the machine clicked and whirred. Inside I could see a record being picked up and placed on the turntable.

Stout saluted Dave.

"Don't go changing anything, Dad," Sandy said. "I want to be here when you get back."

Dave laughed. "Don't worry. Just going to watch."

The jukebox clicked and the song started. I recognized it immediately. An old Rick Nelson song called, "It's Up To You." That song reminded me of . . .

The bar shifted and was gone. For a quick instant I felt dizzy and then everything went black.

And then came back to a bright white spotlight. Right in my eyes.

"God damn it!" Stout shouted as the song started. Sandy, Billy, and Carl had all been looking at Dave and Stout. But as one they turned to look at the bar stool where a moment before Fred had been sitting.

"Oh, no," big Carl said.

Sandy just shook her head. "Every year we do this and every year something weird happens."

Stout moved down the bar and put his hand on Fred's bar stool, as if that would help bring him back. "Damn it! I forgot to ask him if he had a memory with that song. What the hell was I thinking?"

"Don't worry about it, Stout." Sandy said. "He'll be back."

Stout picked up Fred's glass and looked at the name. "He didn't come back last time he left here through the jukebox." Stout reached over and picked up Dave's glass. Then he headed back for the jukebox. "I want everyone holding onto the jukebox when the song ends. If he doesn't come back this time, I want someone besides me remembering him."

Sandy laughed. "Boy, won't Dad be in for a surprise when he gets back."

When a spotlight hits you square in the eyes, your first instinct is to raise your arm to cover your face. And that is what I did. Only my arm hit the steering wheel of my '57 Chevy.

"What . . . ?" I said out loud as I glanced around like a frightened dear caught in a hunter's sights.

The car's engine and lights were off and the windows were rolled up tight. Rick Nelson belted out the song on the radio. Sweat trickled down the side of my face and down my bare chest. The temperature inside the car must have been that of a steam bath and the spotlight was coming through the fogged-up front window.

"Oh, no!" A young woman's voice said from beside me and I turned to look at her. That was when the memories flooded in like light poring through an open door between a dark room and a lit one.

Marcy was struggling to get her bra back on. We had dated for two years after Alice left me. She worked at the department store downtown in the men's section and wanted me to be her husband more than almost anything. That fact had suited me just fine because it made parking with her a lot of fun. She ended up marrying a guy from the appliance section of the store and had three kids last I heard.

Tonight was our first anniversary of going out and we were parked on the canal bank behind the orchard to the south of town. It was the only night we ever got caught parking by the police.

"This can't be," I said. I looked completely around the car. It was my '57 Chevy all right. The one I wrecked in 1969 while driving drunk on New Year's Eve. A moment ago I was sitting in the Garden Lounge with a bunch of people who I thought were nuts and now I was back here parking with Marcy.

I held onto the steering wheel with sweaty hands. I could still freshly remember getting here and what Marcy and I had been doing just a few short moments ago. I remembered taking her bra off and almost putting my hand up her skirt. In fact I was still aroused from all of it and I hadn't had anything but a piss-erection in years back at the old Golden Dream Hotel.

I had said I never looked a gift horse in the mouth. The Private Investigator's words now echoed back through my mind: *You just never know when a miracle might happen.*

So this was what she was talking about.

Marcy smacked my arm. "Hurry! Get your shirt on."

Outside I heard the car door close and a vague shape through the fogged window started toward the door. I had a clear memory that we had gotten dressed before the cop got to the window and he let us go with a strict warning to be moving along. We had laughed about it for days.

Stout had warned David not to change anything when he punched up the song. And he said that the reason I didn't end up back at the Garden was because I changed something when I did this music/time-travel thing the last time. If what Stout had been saying back there at the Garden was true, and it looked like it was, I had better do some fast dressing. Real fast.

Marcy was already buttoning her blouse as I turned around and grabbed my shirt off the back seat where my younger self had tossed it a short time before. I had it on and buttoned, in what seemed like impossible speed to my sixty-two-year-old brain, just as the cop tapped on the window

Marcy straightened her hair as I rolled down the window and looked into the cop's flashlight. "Wow, that's bright."

I remembered that was the exact same thing I had said when I didn't have sixty years of memories to draw upon.

The cop shined his light on me, then on Marcy.

She smiled at him.

I turned and smiled at him.

Then Ricky Nelson stopped singing.

And I was back on my bar stool at the Garden Lounge.

Stout, Sandy, Carl, and Billy stood around the jukebox, touching it.

Dave stood in front of the jukebox staring at them.

"Wow," was all I could say.

All four cheered and Stout held up my empty glass as if in a toast.

It felt really good to be back.

I had another drink as I told them about my adventure with Marcy, getting caught parking, and who she was to me and my life now. I explained that my two years with Marcy had mostly been trying to forget about being in love with Alice. It was a fun time, but nothing really important, or life altering.

After I got done telling my story and Dave told his about how great it was to watch his daughter being born, Sandy went back through the jukebox to visit her senior prom. She came back smiling and laughing and told us all about it, right down to where she and her girlfriends spiked the punch to get the guys drunk. I remembered in my time that the guys were the ones who put booze in the punch. Things do change.

Carl went back to visit his mother and when he came back he didn't say much and no one really pushed him.

It shocked me both times when they just sort of popped out of existence and then back again when the song ended. And before each song Stout asked me if I had any memories associated with the song.

Stout and Billy both declined to play a song, so when Carl returned and dropped back onto his bar stool, Stout moved down the bar and stood in front of me. "Usually," he said, "we only go back once, but since your first trip was an accident, are you interested in giving it another try this year?"

His question surprised me, for some reason. "Give me just a second to think about it." I slid my glass toward him. "How about a refill?"

He nodded and moved down the bar with my glass as I thought about Alice. She had turned out to be the one woman, over all the years, that I truly loved. Now Stout was giving me a chance to go see her again. And maybe tell her how I really felt. Maybe keep her from leaving me.

He was offering me another gift. And this was a very special gift.

I turned on my stool and looked out over the empty Garden Lounge. This evening had been one of the nicest, and wildest, I had spent in more years than I cared to remember. I enjoyed the people and I enjoyed the place. Why leave it at the moment?

Besides, if Stout was right, Alice and I ended up in a really ugly divorce that I hated enough to change once. Maybe I was just cut out in this life to live alone, as I had done. Maybe on this gift, this year, it was better to look the old horse in the mouth.

Stout sat the glass on the napkin and I turned around to face him again. "Thanks for the offer," I said. "But I think I will pass this year. One was enough. Maybe next year if you want me back."

Stout broke into a huge smile. "Every year. You are always welcome."

He moved down the bar and unplugged the jukebox. "That's it for another year," he said.

We all toasted the jukebox and then we spent the next hour laughing and talking about anything and everything, including what Stout could remember of my previous life, including how really unhappy I had been with Alice.

At a little after midnight on Christmas morning Sandy dropped me off in front of the Golden Dream Hotel for Men.

I almost bounded up the front stairs, feeling younger and more alive than I had in years. I'm not sure why a few drinks and a trip into my own past would make me feel that way. But it did. And for the moment that was all that mattered.

I unlocked the front door and went into the front foyer. The place was dark, the only light the one over the old front desk cage. Hank and Mitchell were long asleep. In fact, this was the latest I had stayed up in years. I looked around at the deep shadows and the worn furniture. It was as if I was seeing it for the first time. Seeing the age and the stagnation. Nothing had changed in this room for as long as I had lived here.

I patted the back of Hank's chair and a small cloud of dust rose in the dim light. Maybe it was time to bring some life back here.

I wandered over to the open area beside the cage and looked up at the high ceiling. Twenty feet, maybe. More than enough room for a Christmas tree. Tomorrow the three of us would stop down at the Garden to have a Christmas drink with Stout. He had promised he would fix us his special eggnog. And then we would go buy a Christmas tree for the hotel. It was time we started a few traditions of our own. The guys would piss and moan, but they would enjoy it.

And then maybe the following week I might find an old jukebox. A real one that only gave you memories instead of trips. You didn't always have to go into the past to change the present. As I discovered tonight, with a very special gift from the strangest gift horse I had ever met, sometimes you can do it right now.

A LAWYER'S HOLIDAY
A GHOST OF A CHANCE STORY

DEAN WESLEY SMITH

ONE

Gail Kelly watched as her partner Dan Carson, aka The Sunset Kid, scanned through his morning news on an iPad sitting on the kitchen table. She was still learning to make her touch firm enough to control a computer or even move something on a table. Every day she felt she got closer. Dan had told her that things took time to learn. After all, she had only been dead five months.

Five months ago she had been a successful prosecuting attorney on the Oregon Coast. Then a truck coming over the center line and into her BMW convertible had ended that phase and started her ghost phase.

Just as with every morning, Dan looked like he had come right out of court and had just taken off his tie. He had also been a lawyer before dying and had perfectly styled brown hair and large brown eyes. His dark suit was made of silk, as

514

clearly was his shirt, and he had on expensive shoes. He was, by far, the most handsome man Gail had ever seen.

She was dressed in what made her feel comfortable. Dark dress slacks, comfortable matching shoes with short heels, a silk blouse and silk bra under it.

She and Dan made a perfect power couple, but so far they were just partners even though she was flat out in lust with him.

She watched him work at the computer for a moment longer, then turned to stare out the large windows. Outside her wonderful penthouse apartment, the Portland, Oregon skies were gray. The fall had been beautiful, but now heading into November the season was changing, the air getting a bite to it, and the leaves on the trees turning stunning shades of orange, red, and brown.

She actually loved the fall and winter in Oregon. This was going to be her first winter as a ghost, so she didn't know what to expect, exactly.

Dan, when he had been alive, had been a lawyer in private practice and had spent a lot of time helping out in poor areas and giving free legal advice at a clinic in the northeast side of Portland.

He had died seven years ago in a boating accident on the Willamette River. As he had freely told her, he had had one too many tequila sunsets and when his friend who had been driving their ski boat made a sharp turn, Dan had fallen out and hit his head on the side of the boat.

He said he sat on the bank for an hour watching them search for his body after trying to wave them down before he realized he was a ghost. No one had been there the moment he died as he and three other ghost agents had been for her. It wasn't until an hour later that someone from the Ghost of a Chance agency showed up and tried to start explaining things.

As Dan said, they didn't get off well together right from the start.

Gail, on the other hand, had been met the moment she died in the car wreck by Dan and then trained. Where Dan had learned most things himself about being a ghost agent, Gail couldn't imagine doing that.

So, now as a ghost for the last seven years, Dan had tried to help those that seemed to need some help. When Gail asked him his record, he shrugged. "Some are beyond help."

The condo they were in was owned by a corporation that Dan had started. He had done that by going inside the body of a live lawyer and getting the lawyer to do the work, then clearing out any memory of what that lawyer had done.

And not leaving any record of the lawyer on the documents either.

Dan was an expert in computers and legal issues involving computers and how to leave no trail. Gail had a hunch she hadn't seen the level of his expertise yet.

Dan had hired a "record firm" to be the address of record for the corporation, again just going inside a person in the firm to set it up.

Money to buy this condo and others had come easily from a few scams that he had busted. He drained the accounts of the bad guys and made sure that the money could never be traced out of the country and then back into his corporation. He used the money to buy land and places like this condo he had given her. Often the land and build-ings he bought he lowered the rent for social services, trying to help them out.

Gail had been stunned over and over the last few months at how Dan, who had come off brash and pushy at first, spent most of his days trying to figure out ways to help others.

After her training, they had taken to meeting every morning in her place to plan the day. So far, they both had managed to hold the physical part of the relationship at bay, but she wanted to change that and change that soon. Who knew a ghost could get so horny?

Being a ghost and being able to be inside a live person had been one of the more stunning things Gail had learned. At first she hated it, but as her training had gone on, she got good at directing a live person and sometimes helping them.

And, of course, the live person never knew Gail was there.

"So how about we tackle something larger today?" Dan said, staring at the iPad. "Now that there are two of us, we might be able to."

"What are you thinking?" she asked, moving over and putting her hand on his shoulder and leaning down to see the screen better. She loved touching Dan and she loved when Dan touched her as well.

She pushed the thought aside about taking him into the bedroom and focused on the computer screen in front of her.

"Out in Gresham there's an investment firm that is starting to get complaints," Dan said, pointing to an article.

"Got a hunch they might be thinking of covering their tracks here shortly if we don't do something to help out the police."

Gail smiled. "White collar crime. That's my favorite type."

He laughed. "Me too.

"Let's go see what we can see," she said, looking at the address of the main office. "You want me to jump us there or you want to do it?"

"I don't think you need the practice, but what the hell, go ahead," Dan said.

She took his hand and a moment later they were standing to one side of a fairly busy office on the main floor of the three-story building. The office was bright and had large windows along one wall. Doors into smaller offices lined the far wall and one sidewall. Twenty desks with cubical walls around them filled the space, all with a person at the desk behind a computer, talking with someone on the phone over a headset.

They all looked relaxed and busy.

The place didn't feel like it had just had a negative article written about it. It felt like an active business on just a normal day.

"Did I get us to the right spot?" Gail asked, glancing around as two people walked by, laughing at some conversation.

Dan just shook his head. "This is not at all what I was expecting. Not at all."

TWO

Dan felt stunned at the big office in front of them. This place should be a stress-filled office with workers huddled whispering and panicked looks on manager's faces. That article this morning in the paper had been damaging to say the least and would be fatal to a business playing a scam as this one clearly was.

But nothing seemed to be wrong here. Maybe the article had just been a revenge piece from someone who had lost money here. But it hadn't felt that way. It had been done by a major reporter for the paper and clearly had the backing of the editors of the paper.

In his years as a live attorney, or his years as a ghost agent, Dan had seen the pattern of a scam investment company numbers of times once the rock they had been hiding under was lifted. They fled like bugs afraid of the light.

No one in this room was fleeing or even seeming to be worried about their job or the company they worked for.

"This is off," he said to Gail.

"Way, way off," Gail said, nodding.

Over the last five months, Dan had come to really respect Gail's opinions. She was smart, more than likely smarter than he was about many things. And she was the best-looking woman he had ever met. They were just settling into working together, but what he really wanted was for them to take the partnership to a relationship.

And soon. Real soon.

Across the room was a guy in an expensive gray suit without a tie smiling at some other manager type.

"I'm going to see what he is thinking," Dan said, pointing to the expensive suit.

Gail nodded. "I'll see what the brunette here at this first desk is worried about."

Dan jumped over beside the guy in the suit and merged inside of him, making sure to be very careful that the guy didn't know Dan had joined him in any fashion. Most people didn't notice when a ghost was riding along in their minds, but a few, a very few, could sense something different.

Dan didn't need to worry about this guy. His mind was mostly a blank slate. His entire focus was to sell the many forms of securities this company was selling. And he really, really believed that this company was helping people.

Dan stayed inside the guy's mind. It felt as off as the entire office felt. Almost as if Dan was inside an empty gym. Most people's minds were full of a thousand thoughts, all jumbled.

In this guy, all that was gone.

Slowly, digging back into the guy's past, working through memories of his wife and kids, Dan finally found what he feared.

This guy had been run through a therapy brain-washing system of some sort. It had been quick and complete, of that there was no doubt.

Dan eased out of the guy and jumped back to where Gail had gone inside the brunette sitting in front of one of the desks.

After a moment Gail appeared, looking shocked.

And angry.

In the few short months, Dan had never seen Gail angry

and he had a hunch she would be a power to get out of the way of when she did get angry.

"The poor thing was brainwashed," Gail said. "So much so that she left her boyfriend of three years, moved in with two other women working here, and all they talk about is how fantastic this work is."

"So was the boss," Dan said.

"We have to figure out how far this spreads," Gail said.

Dan agreed completely. They quickly split up the building. She would take the rest of the main floor, going into random people to see what was going on with them, and he would go to the second floor and check that. They would meet near the elevator on the second floor and both check out the top floor at the same time, where they expected the bosses to be.

Thirty minutes later they stood in front of the president of the company's office. He had been as brainwashed as everyone else in the entire building.

That fact had shocked Dan more than he wanted to admit.

The big evil of this place didn't work here.

"So now what do we do?" Gail asked, shaking her head. Dan could see anger was clearly still there.

Dan was angry as well, but it was covered by a feeling of sadness for the almost two hundred people in this building.

Dan looked at Gail. "We need lunch, then we need a lot more research on this company."

"How about we do a little research before lunch," Gail said. "How about we go visit that reporter who wrote the article this morning, see what he has already dug up?"

Dan smiled. "Really, really good idea."

This time he took her hand, something he loved doing, and jumped them both to the reporter's office on the second floor of the newspaper.

THREE

Gail was barely controlling the anger she felt at how all those people were being controlled. And being used to hurt other people.

Whoever was behind this was the scum of the earth. And in Gail's training, Jewel had shown Gail a few tricks to make the really ugly people suffer. Gail just hoped she remembered a few of those when she met the person or people who were behind this.

The reporter was a solid man, about forty, with a beer gut. He wore jeans and a plain tee-shirt and a Cubs baseball cap that more than likely covered a bald spot.

His office was a messy control and when they arrived, he was sitting behind his computer, typing.

They both nodded to each other and went inside him together, still holding hands.

The guy's name was Ryan and he was a bubbling mass of anger. The article he was working on was about the company they had just visited, about how much money the company scam had taken for worthless property and investments. All from innocent investors who bought into the sales line.

The guy had really done his research. The company in

Oregon was nothing more than a shell company. All the money came in and vanished into overseas accounts. And his article had done nothing at all to dent their business and that was why he was angry.

He wanted to take them down and hard and fast.

Gail agreed with that completely.

His focus on the new article he was writing was the investors, warning them away, trying to convince them to sell their investments and try to get some of their money back.

Ryan had no real hope anyone would get any money back. In fact, his research had uncovered this kind of operation in five other states and knew, without a doubt, this one was within one week of shutting down. That was the pattern.

But in one week a lot of people could and would still be hurt.

And Ryan flat didn't understand why even the president of the company was just giving him the company line, even though there was a chance the guy would end up in prison.

Gail knew. Everyone, including the president of the Oregon company, had been brainwashed in such an effective manner as to be frightening. Every person in that building totally believed to their core they were doing good for people and their money.

Gail and Dan stepped out of the reporter's body and then Dan jumped them to a wonderful deli-style restaurant in the Pearl District. They grabbed a few ghost sandwiches a couple customers had ordered and then jumped back to her condo to eat at the table, since the weather was too cold to eat out on the deli's outside space.

She got them some plates and both a bottle of water. Then they ate in silence for a few minutes, both thinking. She liked that about being with Dan. He had no problem with silence.

Finally, she looked at him and asked the question she didn't know the answer to.

"Think we can clear their minds?"

Dan nodded. "One at a time," he said, "but we can do it."

"How?" she asked.

"We go into their minds and simply wipe out the few hours of brainwashing sessions. We erase it."

Gail was shocked. "We can erase someone's memories? Jewel never said a word about being able to do that."

Dan nodded, looking slightly pained. "I learned how to do it with a rape survivor who couldn't stop wanting to kill herself. The memories she had were so vivid, it was as if she was living them again and again every day. I finally went in and not only dulled the memories, but erased most of them. It gave the poor kid a chance to find a way to recover."

Gail nodded, not wanting to imagine how hard that must have been for Dan to do.

"So you can show me how?" she asked.

Dan nodded. "But I am suggesting we erase not only the memories of the brainwashing, but the memories of the months working for the company. The longest is about five months."

"That would leave a big hole in all their lives," Gail said, stunned that he suggested that.

Dan nodded. "Better that then those poor people living

with the guilt of what they did to others. Suicide would be a choice a number of them would make with that kind of guilt."

She nodded. Damn, he was right. It would be better to have a person just sort of wake up and learn about what they had been doing from others than remember it and regret it deeply.

They finished their sandwiches, talking over the plan of how to cover the entire building. They were both worried about how bosses would react, how workers would react, and how the people they hadn't gotten to yet would deal with others suddenly stopping. There were over two hundred people in that building and there just was no way to clear them all quickly.

And Gail had no doubt they couldn't do it before five when everyone went home.

Finally, Gail said simply, "We can't do this alone. We need help."

Dan nodded, clearly agreeing.

Gail sort of looked up at the ceiling, focusing on the two that had trained her, and said, "Jewel? Tommy? We need your help."

She and Dan had gotten into a case too big for them to deal with in the first few months of their partnership. Didn't that just figure?

FOUR

D an really had come to like and admire Jewel and Tommy during Gail's training. And the four of them had had a lot of fun meals together over the months as well.

Jewel and Tommy appeared in just moments after Gail asked for them. Both of them were wearing their normal jeans and dress shirts and running shoes. Tommy kept his dark brown hair cut short and Jewel had her hair pulled back as she seemed to always do.

They had both been ghost agents for less time than Dan had been, but they had quickly proven to the powers running everything that they were the best at what they did. Dan had learned some things from them as well during Gail's training.

"Problems?" Jewel asked.

Dan indicated that Gail explain what they had found. And what they needed help doing.

When she was done, Jewel looked at Dan. "You can cut out that much memory permanently from a person?"

"I can," Dan said. "I can show you how. Some of these people will be dealing with doctors and such trying to regain their memory of the months, but they never will."

"We figure that would be better than the guilt they will experience," Gail said. "This financial scam has hurt thousands, will take many families entire savings. I would have trouble living with a memory of doing that to anyone."

Jewel and Tommy both nodded.

"No sign of who is in charge?" Tommy asked.

"Going to be spending a lot of time on digging out that worm," Dan said, "once we stop this and stop more people from getting hurt. But the reporter who dug all this up knows that the money is vanishing into overseas accounts. He just can't confirm that yet."

"So the key right now is stopping this," Jewel said. "Lay out your plan for us."

"We clear the brainwashing of the officers and board members and upper management, but leave the memories," Gail said. "They will be able to help prosecutors and also, more than likely, end up in jail."

Dan nodded. "The rest of them we go in and just cut out everything that happened from the moment they were put under control of whoever is doing this to the present."

Jewel and Tommy nodded.

"I have one question," Tommy said. "You ever hear of anyone being able to do this kind of mind control at this level?"

"Besides one of us when we are inside someone," Jewel said. "No."

"But we will be researching that after we get this done," Tommy said. "So anything from any of these people that we can get today as to how this was done will help."

Dan nodded, but doubted they would find anything. Of the people he had been in their minds, the brainwashing had happened seemingly instantly as they sat in front of a computer screen answering a few basic questions.

Something on that screen had got to them, implanted this belief about this scam company being the greatest. More than likely the people really behind this scam weren't even in this country.

They certainly weren't in that building.

Eventually, they would be found, but that wasn't going

to be today. Today they had to stop this cancer right here in Portland.

"Be careful around that moment of brainwashing," Gail said. "We don't want any of us getting hit with it."

Dan nodded to that and until one in the afternoon, when employees would be returning from lunch, they planned their attack on the two-hundred-plus people in the three-story building.

FIVE

Gail felt terrified at what they were about to do.

All four of them jumped to a back room on the lower floor of the building and all four of them went into one poor man's head.

He was a mail-room guy fresh out of an MBA degree who had only been working for the company for a month. His goal was to work his way up in this fantastic company and maybe someday own stock in it as well.

Dan quickly, using this guy as an example, showed Gail and Jewel and Tommy how he removed a section of the man's memory.

Gail was surprised at how simple it was. Dan simply put a clear mental box around the memory and then just shrunk the space inside the box until the box was nothing more than a dot.

Instantly the guy seemed confused as to where he was at and what he had been doing.

Dan gave him some calming thoughts and told him to just go home.

Then Jewel and Tommy and Dan and Gail left the guy's mind as the poor MBA grad left.

"We're going to have to plant some memories," Jewel said, "in people as to where they parked their car, where they live if they moved while working here, things like that."

"And calming thoughts," Gail said. "I want to try to keep these people calm because it's going to feel like they are just waking up."

All three of them nodded to her suggestion. That would take them all more time, but it would be worth it for the people they were saving.

"So here we go," Dan said. "Let's get the officers first. Just clear the brainwashing in the same way. A mental box around the time they were at that computer, squeeze it down to nothing."

Gail took a deep breath and a moment later they were walking into the plush offices on the third floor.

It took the four of them about thirty minutes to clear the brainwashing from the officers and then erase the memories of the support staff working upstairs. Gail dealt with two women who had been with the company since the start. She calmed them as much as she could and gave them the suggestion to just get their coat and things and leave.

Then Gail and Dan and Jewel and Tommy went to the second floor.

They started with the managers first, then worked their way through each room. In one hour they had that floor cleared.

The ground floor was looking a little slightly frightened as everyone upstairs seemed to be going out the front door, looking confused.

Again the four of them started with the managers of the room and by four in the afternoon, the building seemed empty.

Gail had so many people's memories and thoughts in her head, she felt a little confused herself. But a few deep breaths and things seemed to sort out some.

The four of them had done it before five.

They spent the next thirty minutes making sure they hadn't missed anyone. By that point, Gail felt a lot better. The only people left in the building were the officers of the company upstairs, huddling together, talking about what they should do.

One man was just sitting in his office crying.

Gail hated to see that and pointed the guy out to Dan who went into the crying man and a moment later the guy stopped, stood, squared his shoulders, and went to talk with the other officers.

"I just gave the guy a backbone is all," Dan said, smiling at Gail as he appeared next to her.

"I'm going to go tell the reporter to check the building now," Dan said. "Maybe contact the officers. You guys up for dinner?"

"I'm sort of missing the buffet dinner at the Golden Nugget in Vegas," Gail said. That was the restaurant that the four of them had eaten in the most during her months of training.

And today, this had felt like a lot more training.

"Wonderful idea," Dan said, smiling at her. "I'll meet you all there."

He vanished.

"Great by us," Jewel said.

Jewel and Tommy smiled and vanished.

Gail stopped and looked around the now empty main room full of desks and computers. The four of them had saved a lot of people a lot of grief and lost money this afternoon.

They had shut down a scam. As a prosecuting attorney, that had always felt good to her.

She had been dead now for five months. And as each day went by, she felt more and more useful.

And that felt wonderful.

She nodded to the empty room and jumped to join her friends and the man she was head-over-heels in lust with.

Maybe after a good dinner in Las Vegas, she and Dan could come back to her apartment, have a few drinks, watch a movie, and then end up in her big bed in celebration of a job well done.

She would like that. Far more than she wanted to think about before dinner.

Not Easy To Kill The Light Next Door

A Bryant Street Story

DEAN WESLEY SMITH

Cayden Cavanaugh was done.

Fed up.

Last straw.

Over his limit.

And every other damn cliché a person could think of.

The light had to go.

And he would make it go. That stupid white light towering over Bob and Stephie's garage had cost him sleep, his job, his wife, and most of his money. In a few days it would cost him this house.

The light would pay.

And it would pay tonight.

He should have done this long ago.

Cayden sat at the table in his once beautiful and modern suburban kitchen. His former wife Hanna had insisted on the best white granite counters, the most expensive light-blue glass-tile backsplash, and top range steel appliances when they built this dream home. He had loved every bit of it.

Now he could only see those things by the light mounted above the garage next door. He had no money to pay the power bill and the power had been turned off three days ago.

But Cayden could see enough from the light next door to load the pistol he had bought two days before.

Tonight the light would pay.

The sink was full of unwashed dishes and they smelled like rotten fish, but Cayden no longer cared. Hanna was long gone and he would be soon. He couldn't hold off the bank any longer. They were taking the dream home, taking everything, and all because of that stupid light.

And even leaving the house, moving to another city, another country, he knew he would never escape that light. He had to finish this once and for all right now, tonight.

Things had been fine just a short year before.

Then at one summer neighborhood barbeque Bob had told him he was putting in a security light on his garage, on a pole sticking up from the garage peak. Bob said it would cost a bunch, but it would make his house safer and also the entire area.

Cayden had thought it a wonderful idea.

How stupid had he been?

So three weeks later, when the light first clicked on as the sun set, Cayden was stunned at how bright it was. So bright that it seemed to fill every room in Cayden and Hanna's house with a dull white light that washed out all the colors they had so carefully picked.

He and Hanna took to closing the blinds at night, but for Cayden the light still seemed to fill everything. It felt like a disease eating away at something that had once been beautiful.

Hanna said she didn't much notice the light with the blinds pulled, but Cayden hated it with a passion. As far as he was concerned, the light was ruining everything they had built.

A month later they put up those room-darkening blinds for their bedroom and the rooms on the side of the house facing Bob and Stephie's home. At that point Cayden was having trouble sleeping and getting more and more angry at the slightest things.

But most especially at all the light and how it washed everything out.

The darkening shades didn't seem to help, even though Hanna said the room was pitch black.

It wasn't pitch black.

The light was there.

Cayden could see it.

He could feel it.

It kept him awake.

He knew it attacked the walls of his home like a tiny army never letting up. It was always right outside the window, right against the walls, flooding the roof, trying to get in at the slightest mistake on his part.

He wasn't sure why Hanna couldn't see the gray in how the light out there was so strong it took even total blackness and robbed it of power.

Two months after the light first came on, Cayden went

to Bob and asked him to take it down. Cayden said he would even pay for the cost of the light.

Bob said it made him and Stephie feel safer, so he refused.

A month later Cayden and Bob got into a fight over the light and Cayden slugged Bob. Actually, it seems that he did more than just slug him, although Cayden didn't remember most of it he was so angry. Turns out he put Bob in the hospital and Bob pressed charges.

Cayden spent two nights in jail and still had his case pending for trial.

Then Cayden found himself yelling more and more at Hanna and finally three months ago she left to go live with her parents. She begged him to get professional help.

He knew he was fine.

It was all the light's fault.

The light was eating at him.

At work, about the time Hanna left, Cayden noticed the light had followed him to work, that it was washing out all the colors in his office. He started working with the lights off and the blinds pulled to try to block out the light, but it still got in.

He got angrier and angrier.

The light had now infected everything.

A week later he lost his job.

His boss told him to get help.

Cayden knew he was fine. He didn't know why everyone kept telling him to get help, that he wasn't his old self. He knew he would be fine as soon as he got rid of the light.

Tonight he would do just that.

Finally.

Cayden looked around at the dark kitchen, a room that had many good memories. He was going to miss this home as much as he missed Hanna.

Then he made sure the gun was loaded and stood. It was time to face the devil.

Once he had won, maybe he and Hanna could start over, plan a new life in a new home, away from the light.

Maybe get some color back in their lives.

Holding the now loaded pistol in his right hand, he went out the back door into the yard that seemed so bright it could be daylight. The gun felt extra heavy, far heavier than it had felt in the store when he bought it.

That evil light above Bob and Stephie's garage seemed to flood his entire yard, washing out the wonderful shades of darkness with a pale, white world of blandness.

His barbeque no longer looked black, but a light gray. The green grass looked almost pink. The dark, oak-stained fence seemed like it had been painted dull white.

The light was so powerful it leached all the color out of everything, just as it had leached away his life.

He turned toward the fence to get closer to the light and then realized it felt like he was walking upstream against rushing water.

The light knew what he was planning and wanted to stop him.

He would not stop.

He had to win this fight.

He leaned into the light, focusing on the sidewalk in

front of him with every step, the gun in his hand getting heavier and heavier.

Now it felt like he was in a strong wind that seemed to get stronger and stronger with each step.

And the light got brighter, if that was possible.

He finally stopped and planted both feet firmly. Then he looked up at the light.

It blinded him like looking into the sun.

The pain was intense, filling his entire head.

He wanted to scream in agony, but somehow he managed to raise the pistol and fire at the white light above him.

The sound was so loud it shocked him. It echoed over the neighborhood and a dog barked.

He staggered back, the pain in his head worse.

The light still blinded him.

He couldn't let it win that easily.

He fired at it again.

And then again.

He heard glass shattering, but the light was still as bright, if not brighter.

He fired over and over until finally the gun clicked empty and he dropped it.

He then sat down, his back to the light, shaking.

The light had won.

Everything around him was still washed out of all color and his eyes burnt from looking into the brightness.

The pain in his head radiated out like someone was poking sharp sticks into his eyes.

He finally just lay down, staring upward into the white light. He was in too much pain and too tired to move.

The light had won.

He was not sure how long it was until the police arrived and led him to the police car.

He could barely see any of it because of the bright light and the stabbing pain in his head.

By the time he reached the station he could only see white, with wonderful blackness around the edges.

A short time later he found himself in the hospital with a police guard. A young-sounding doctor was trying to shine a light into his eyes.

But Cayden couldn't see the light.

Or the doctor for that matter.

The blackness had slowly crept in from the sides of his vision until finally, thankfully, everything was black.

Everything.

The light was gone.

He had finally killed it.

He could finally sleep.

The next thing he heard was Hanna talking with a doctor. They were talking about him and an operation it seemed he had had.

Around him machines beeped and there were sounds of others talking out in the hallway.

The intense pain in his head was gone, replaced by a dull ache, and everything was blissfully black.

It felt wonderful to hear Hanna's voice again. Calming, not at all like the last time he had talked with her. He couldn't remember now why he had been so angry.

"We got the tumor completely," the doctor told Hanna. "But we don't think his vision will ever return I'm afraid. Just too much damage."

Cayden wanted to smile, to shout for joy, but instead he just lay there, not moving.

Blackness was fine by him.

The blackness was a victory.

He had fought the light and he had won and that was all that mattered.

He never wanted to see light again.

In blackness maybe he could live again.

Hear From Kris & Dean

Want More From Kris and Dean?

For Kristine Kathryn Rusch's newsletter
go to kriswrites.com.

For Dean Wesley Smith's newsletter
go to deanwesleysmith.com.

Get the latest news and releases from all of WMG's authors
and lines, including Kristine Grayson, Kris Nelscott,
Pulphouse Magazine, and so much more...

To sign up, **go to wmgbooks.com.**

About the Author
DEAN WESLEY SMITH

Considered one of the most prolific writers working in modern fiction, *New York Times* and *USA Today* bestselling writer, Dean Wesley Smith published over two hundred novels and over seven hundred books in forty years, and hundreds and hundreds of short stories. He has over thirty million copies of his books in print.

At the moment he produces novels in four major series, including the time travel **Thunder Mountain** novels set in the old west, the galaxy-spanning **Seeders Universe** series, the cold case mystery series, **Cold Poker Gang** series, and the superhero series staring **Poker Boy.**

During his career, Dean also wrote a couple dozen *Star Trek* novels, the only two original *Men in Black* novels, Spider-Man and X-Men novels, plus novels set in gaming and television worlds. Writing with his wife Kristine Kathryn Rusch under the name Kathryn Wesley, they wrote the novel for the NBC miniseries **The Tenth Kingdom** and other books for *Hallmark Hall of Fame* movies.

He wrote novels under dozens of pen names in the worlds of comic books and movies, including novelizations of almost a dozen films, from *X-Men* to *The Final Fantasy* to *Steel* to *Rundown*.

Dean also worked as a fiction editor off and on, starting at Pulphouse Publishing, then at *VB Tech Journal*, then Pocket Books, and now at WMG Publishing where he and Kristine Kathryn Rusch serve as executive editors for the acclaimed *Fiction River* anthology series. He took over the editorship of the acclaimed *Pulphouse Magazine* in 2018.

For more information about Dean's books and ongoing projects, please visit his website at www.deanwesley smith.com

facebook.com/deanwsmith3

patreon.com/deanwesleysmith

bookbub.com/authors/dean-wesley-smith

ABOUT THE AUTHOR
KRISTINE KATHRYN RUSCH

Kristine Kathryn Rusch has sold more than 35 million books. Generally, she uses her real name (Rusch) for most of her writing. Under that name, she publishes bestselling science fiction and fantasy, award-winning mysteries, acclaimed mainstream fiction, controversial nonfiction, and the occasional romance. Her novels have made bestseller lists around the world and her short fiction has appeared in eighteen best of the year collections. She has won more than twenty-five awards for her fiction, including the Hugo, *Le Prix Imaginales*, the *Asimov's* Readers Choice award, and the *Ellery Queen Mystery Magazine* Readers Choice Award.

Publications from *The Chicago Tribune* to *Booklist* have included her Kris Nelscott mystery novels in their top-ten-best mystery novels of the year. The Nelscott books have received nominations for almost every award in the mystery field, including the best novel Edgar Award, and the Shamus Award.

She writes goofy romance novels as award-winner Kristine Grayson.

She also edits. Beginning with work at the innovative publishing company, Pulphouse, followed by her award-winning tenure at *The Magazine of Fantasy & Science Fiction*, she took fifteen years off before returning to editing with the original anthology series *Fiction River,* published by WMG Publishing. She acts as series editor with her husband, writer Dean Wesley Smith, and edits at least two anthologies in the series per year on her own.

To find out more about her work, go to her website, kriswrites.com

facebook.com/kristinekathrynruschwriter
patreon.com/kristinekathrynrusch
bookbub.com/authors/kristine-kathryn-rusch

The Make 100 Kickstarter Series

Dean Wesley Smith's Make 100 Challenge

The First Thirty-Three

The Second Thirty-Three

The Final Thirty-Four

Colliding Worlds

A Science Fiction Short Story Series

by Kristine Kathryn Rusch and Dean Wesley Smith

Volumes 1-6

Crimes Collide

A Mystery Short Story Series

by Kristine Kathryn Rusch and Dean Wesley Smith

Volumes 1-5

Fantasies Collide

A Fantasy Short Story Series

by Kristine Kathryn Rusch and Dean Wesley Smith

Volumes 1-5

Hearts Collide

A Strange Romance Short Story Series

by Kristine Kathryn Rusch and Dean Wesley Smith

Volumes 1-5

ALSO BY DEAN WESLEY SMITH

THE POKER BOY UNIVERSE

POKER BOY

The Slots of Saturn: A Poker Boy Novel

They're Back: A Poker Boy Short Novel

Luck Be Ladies: A Poker Boy Collection

Playing a Hunch: A Poker Boy Collection

A Poker Boy Christmas: A Poker Boy Collection

GHOST OF A CHANCE

The Poker Chip: A Ghost of a Chance Novel

The Christmas Gift: A Ghost of a Chance Novel

The Free Meal: A Ghost of a Chance Novel

The Cop Car: A Ghost of a Chance Novella

The Deep Sunset: A Ghost of a Chance Novel

MARBLE GRANT

The First Year: A Marble Grant Novel

Time for Cool Madness: Six Crazy Marble Grant Stories

Also By KRISTINE KATHRYN RUSCH

THE FEY SERIES

The Original books of The Fey

The Sacrifice: Book One of the Fey

The Changeling: Book Two of the Fey

The Rival: Book Three of the Fey

The Resistance: Book Four of the Fey

Victory: Book Five of the Fey

The Black Throne

The Black Queen: Book One of the Black Throne

The Black King: Book Two of the Black Throne

The Qavnerian Protectorate

The Reflection on Mount Vitaki: Prequel to the Qavnerian
Protectorate

The Kirilli Matter: The First Book of the Qavnerian Protectorate

Barkson's Journey: The Second Book of the Qavnerian
Protectorate

Incident at Serebro Academy: The Third Book of the Qavnerian Protectorate

Unexpected Hero: The Fourth Book of the Qavnerian Protectorate

(Coming 2025)

MORE FROM THE FEY

Destiny: A Story of The Fey

Lessons From The Writing of The Fey

THE RETRIEVAL ARTIST SERIES

The Disappeared

Extremes

Consequences

Buried Deep

Paloma

Recovery Man

The Recovery Man's Bargain

Duplicate Effort

The Possession of Paavo Deshin

Anniversary Day

Blowback

A Murder of Clones

Search & Recovery

The Peyti Crisis

Vigilantes

Starbase Human

Masterminds

The Impossibles

The Retrieval Artist

THE DIVING SERIES

Diving into the Wreck: A Diving Novel

City of Ruins: A Diving Novel

Becalmed: A Diving Universe Novella

The Application of Hope: A Diving Universe Novella

Boneyards: A Diving Novel

Skirmishes: A Diving Novel

The Runabout: A Diving Novel

The Falls: A Diving Universe Novel

Searching for the Fleet: A Diving Novel

The Spires of Denon: A Diving Universe Novella

The Renegat: A Diving Universe Novel

Escaping Amnthra: A Diving Universe Novella

The Court-Martial of the Renegat Renegades

Thieves: A Diving Novel

Squishy's Teams: A Diving Universe Novel

The Chase: A Diving Novel

Maelstrom: A Diving Universe Novella

Writing as Kris Nelscott

THE SMOKEY DALTON SERIES

A Dangerous Road

Smoke-Filled Rooms

Thin Walls

Stone Cribs

War at Home

Days of Rage

Street Justice

AND

Protectors

Writing as Kristine Grayson

The Charming Trilogy, Vol. 1

The Charming Trilogy, Vol. 2

The Fates Trilogy

The Daughters of Zeus Trilogy

www.ingramcontent.com/pod-product-compliance
Lightning Source LLC
Chambersburg PA
CBHW010725100726
47899CB00009B/2925